THE FALL OF MAGIC

BOOK ONE OF THE MASTER'S CORE

PHOENIX ROKNI

The Fall of Magic
Book One of The Master's Core

Copyright © 2024 by Phoenix Rokni

First published in Tulsa, OK, USA by Phoenix Rokni.

Library of Congress Control Number: 2024920959
Hardback ISBN: 979-8-9916377-1-8
Paperback ISBN: 979-8-9916377-0-1
eBook ISBN: 979-8-9916377-2-5

Book Cover by Jeff Brown
Edited by Dana Alsamsam

First Edition
10 9 8 7 6 5 4 3 2 1

To contact the author or learn more about his works visit www.themasterscore.com

TABLE OF CONTENTS

Prologue..1

Chapter 1: A Knight of the Phoenix 7
Chapter 2: Ode of the Twin Flames 21
Chapter 3: No Task Too Small......................................35
Chapter 4: Legacy Lost..47
Chapter 5: Tower of the Sage......................................63
Chapter 6: By the Storm...77
Chapter 7: Chosen Knights 89
Chapter 8: The Aelethrien Road 103
Chapter 9: The Hidden Coast 117
Chapter 10: The Saena Tree.......................................129
Chapter 11: Nearing Twilight.....................................141
Chapter 12: The Dark Prince 159
Chapter 13: The Starlight Inn 171
Chapter 14: A Noble Sacrifice 183
Chapter 15: The Enigma Elixir....................................201
Chapter 16: Haven of Darkness....................................219
Chapter 17: Humbled Hearts.......................................233
Chapter 18: Promise to the Peri..................................243
Chapter 19: End of a Bloodline...................................253
Chapter 20: The Fall of Magic....................................269

Epilogue...279
About the Author 285

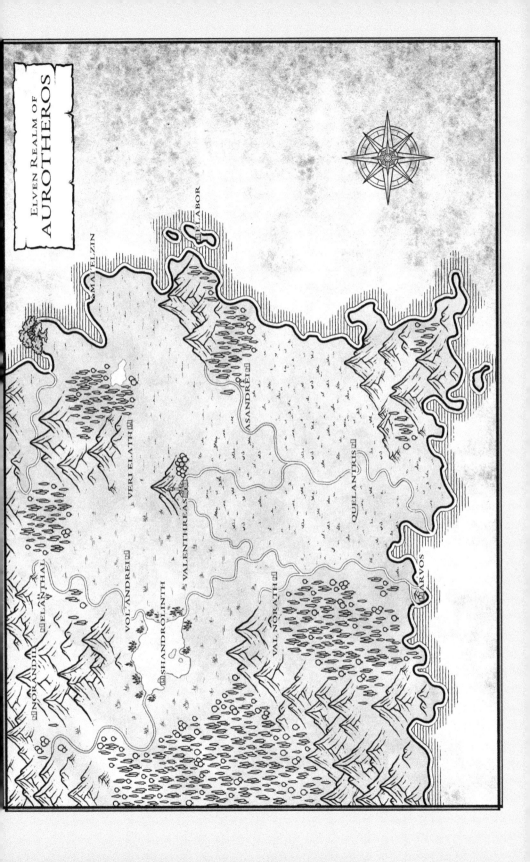

ELVEN REALM OF
AUROTHEROS

MATELIZIN

ELABOR

ASANDREI

VERI ELATH

QUELANTRIS

VALENTHREAS

VOL ANDREI

SHANDROLINTH

VAL NORATH

NORANDIL

ELÂNTHAL

ARVOS

PROLOGUE

The shattered spire crumbled down over the ruined Aurodite stronghold of Illonel, now bathed in bright flames that illuminated the night. The enemy was overwhelming in their presence, having flooded past all of the stronghold's defenses.

At the center of the stronghold, the temple, from which the illuminated spire once rose, there was an unsuspected secret within its foundation. This secret could almost be seen by the enemy through a thin, horizontal embrasure at the base of the temple's foundation wall.

Peering through the space were two bright blue eyes belonging to Anaryen Valenvon. Anaryen was the understudy of Archmagus Etrius Evenon, who had just been murdered by the dark prince moments ago.

The darkness and the cold felt overbearing in the presence of the enemy. It was alarming for any rational person to consider how dark it was on that night. For under the moons, the world would usually be illuminated in beautiful, faint auras and ambient, glowing colors. Neither moon seemed visible under the gloomveil's presence here where all things hidden seemed to be revealed by the flames burning around them.

Anaryen moved quickly to pull her hood over her head, covering her blonde hair. As she exhaled, her breath could be seen so brightly one might wonder if frost was forming on the air itself. As she continued to peer out, she moved to further cover her mouth, eliminating her breath from sight.

Alongside Anaryen were two of the other Aurodites who had been commanded to aid her in her escape from Illonel. These two faithful companions, Molvalan Molandro and Elenfia Ven Louten, had accom-

1

panied Anaryen through the hidden passages leading out of the central spire only moments before the archmagus had been murdered. The three Aurodites would soon find themselves to be the only magi to survive the onslaught now coming to a bloody end.

Their escape seemed hopeless. "Quickly, you must cover your faces, even the cold can give us away now," Anaryen said in a faint whisper.

"Yes, my lady, but we've got to keep moving," Elenfia said as she swept her cloak over her head and mouth, covering most of the freckles on her face. "We've got to reach the hidden coast by morning; it's vital we get the avolans stationed there to fly warnings out. I'd only rely on their winged people to see that our messages make it there in time."

"Wait, Elenfia, our lady is wise to observe," Molvalan said, having just shrouded himself in his dark blue cloak. "They swept past us so fast, and it would be prudent to understand why this has happened. We may be able to uncover more of their plans and share them with the knights at Valenthreas." Molvalan was right in his sentiment, for he knew the hallowed city of the elves should be made aware of such atrocity; it was the center of the world since the beginning of all things.

"Quiet you two, let's watch them before we leave for the hidden coast," Anaryen said, now staring with great focus out of the narrow, stone embrasure in front of them.

Standing proudly in the courtyard, the dark prince, Drazius Khorvek, watched as his soldiers slaughtered the last of the magi, who were desperately fighting to defend what was left of their desecrated stronghold. His frosted breath burst from the opening of his black ohrinite plate helmet, which was locked as securely as the rest of the plate armor covering his body. Beneath the prince's plate armor was scale mail armor that could be seen covering his arms and legs. He wore a long, dark red cape that draped down from underneath his large pauldrons, which resembled the terrifying Dahaka that had fallen in the great war. The pauldrons were shaped to form the black dragon's head with its notable red eyes, a glowing inlaid ruby for each eye. The metal dragon's skull was resting firmly on each of the prince's shoulders.

The black metal polearm he carried was crafted to elicit terror in those who saw it. It was akin to a long spear but the blade was nearly as long as a short sword. At the base of the large spear point were two additional arched blades which extended from either side of the socket, curving down toward the black steel shaft. Just as the blades reached the shaft, they veered back outward before their tips came to an end. The large shaft looked like dragon scales except where black leather had been bound and fitted in the middle for a handle. Where the shaft ended was a dragon's claw grasping at two golden gems in its clutch. The large polearm was also equipped with a dark red banner hanging from the base of the polearm's socket.

With his massive weapon in hand, Drazius took aim and launched it at the last visible Aurodite who was trying to escape. The polearm impaled the young magi through the back, pinning him onto the scorched outer stone wall of the fortress. With ominous, subtle laughter, Drazius walked over to the wall and pulled his weapon out of the student's body. As the magi's lifeless corpse fell to the ground, Drazius kneeled down and wiped his victim's blood off of his cherished weapon, using the young magi's own robes.

As Anaryen watched, tears began to swell up in her eyes and a single tear rolled down her cheek. She was not alone in the bleak silence of the moment. Molvalan shook his head in utter disbelief, while Elenfia felt herself sinking back into the dark passage where they remained hidden.

Elenfia reached out and took Anaryen's hand and the two looked at each other, sharing in their moment of grief.

"Monster," Anaryen whispered softly as she closed her eyes, hiding the horrifying scene she had witnessed before her. In fear, she looked back to see two men now standing in front of the embrasure of the wall.

The men were looking away from the three hidden Aurodites, awaiting their prince. Drazius was walking back toward them, every step delivering a horrifying clank from his heavy armor. The sound of the metal could easily be perceived by others as the shrieks of the souls from those he'd murdered.

Drazius looked up to see that his two commanders, Holcurt Harkhon and Griles Grentin, had returned to report back to him after clearing their assigned sectors of the stronghold. The prince removed his helmet, revealing his dark, piercing eyes as he wiped the magi's blood from his chin and combed his armored fingers through his dark brown hair.

The prince's face shifted quickly to a grimace. "Holcurt, Griles, your status."

"The outer wall and towers are purged of the Aurodites, my liege," Holcurt said, bowing his head in fear of Drazius and his bloodlust.

"Yes, our troops have purged the magi quarters; they're all dead, my prince. There's not a student, professor, or battlemage left alive," Griles boasted.

"My troops," Drazius said, correcting him.

"Yes, my prince, your troops," Griles said as he bowed, now even lower.

The prince looked over Griles, who was now nearly on his knees as if begging for forgiveness. Drazius enjoyed seeing Griles bow before him, wearing his own matching ohrinite plate and mail armor with the royal crest of the prince's family engraved on the chest plate. The crest was that of the royal house of Khorvek, one of the great human kingdoms which had long reigned in the lands of Elandrokh, north of Illonel.

Every soldier who marched in the prince's army had the same style of ohrinite armor and a brand on their neck showing their allegiance and dedication to the dark master, Ohrimah. The scar with a branding mark, visible on the soldiers, including the one on Prince Drazius, was the same, but it was not the prince's royal crest. On every visible neck was a brand of two circles next to one another, with a single larger circle centered above them.

Anaryen gasped and steeled herself, softly speaking a single word: "Merdah." The brand on their necks was unmistakable—a symbol of dedication to the dark master, Merdah, the fallen god originally known as Ohrimah, who sought to break the world during the War of Strife and Sorrow. Once in harmony with the other Masters and the Twin Flames, he had long since sought the destruction of the world alongside his counterpart, Master Anieva.

Anaryen now knew some aspect of the prince's purpose. Not only had Drazius turned away from the light of the gods to follow the dark master but he had also mustered up an army and set out on his own dark crusade in Ohrimah's name. The fact that his soldier's carried this mark meant that they too had taken a vow to the dark god; it was sure that anyone who carried such a mark had chosen to forsake the gods and sought to destroy what they had created for the people of the world.

"Oh yes, grave indeed, my lady," Molvalan whispered.

"It's on every one of their necks, they all have the mark," Elenfia whispered, staring in disbelief.

Anaryen was speechless, lost in contemplation. She knew Drazius from when they were children, and it was unfathomable to her that he was the person now before her, committing these unthinkable acts of horror. She knew it was impossible that he could rally so many to serve his purpose and that of the dark master unless his father, King Nailor Khorvek, was gone. Her thoughts were interrupted by the voice of Drazius.

Prince Khorvek signaled for Griles to stand back up. "Gather the bodies and pile them in front of the center; you will burn every last magi that was here. I want everything left in ashes, not a clue left that can indicate our purpose. We have a great deal to do in preparation for the assault on Valenthreas. Lord Grindam's instructions were quite specific."

Both Commander Holcurt and Commander Griles bowed their heads, eager to obey their prince.

Drazius smiled, and his grin was utterly terrifying to the two commanders. "Any safe haven or stronghold that can aid the elves must be destroyed. We will do this before we lay waste to their city's defenses."

The commanders both scurried away and began to rally the branded soldiers to head out the gates of the desolated stronghold. Prince Drazius mounted his steed and took another glance at the crumbling spire. With a devious grin, he placed his helmet back on his head and exited out of the once great gate of Illonel.

Illonel had been the magi headquarters and central academy for all the new Aurodites who trained to learn the way of the elements. It was a beacon of light for all the magi and all life that gazed upon its brilliant illumination. Its spire had risen high from the temple and up toward the heavens, but now it had been brought down in total ruin. Once a symbol of their dedication to the Masters and the Twin Flames, it became nothing more than burning rubble in the wake of Drazius and his branded soldiers.

As the prince and his troops moved further away from Illonel, the light of the two moons once again illuminated the land, having been, just moments earlier, unnaturally darkened by the enemy's presence. The light of the moon Valos once again imbued the flora and fauna to radiate their diverse, ambient colors, revealing the absolute beauty of the world under the light of the two moons.

This beauty once again shone through the embrasure, almost as if signaling to Anaryen and her companions. "Very well, you two, I've seen enough," Anaryen said. She now had all the information she needed to aid the elves and warn them of what was to come.

"Lord Grindam? Do you think the dark orc is really alive, my lady?" Elenfia said. "How's that even possible?"

"There are a number of ways that he could have lived so long, but none of them are natural," Molvalan said. He had moved to point his hand in the direction of the corridor ahead of them, beckoning the two to move on.

"Molvalan is right, Elenfia, we must make our way forward for this dark tunnel is long, and the quicker we get there, the quicker the avolans can fly to Valenthreas."

"Yes, my lady," Elenfia said as she accepted Molvalan's guidance— she trusted her unwaveringly.

"As you command, my lady," Molvalan said. "Please, this way."

Anaryen and her fellow Aurodites moved on from the horrifying scene they had witnessed and made haste through the long, deep passage that would take them safely to the hidden coast far to the south in the elven realm of Aurotheros. There they could send word to the great elven city and warn the stewards and their allied Knights of the Phoenix. Soon they could meet and decide on a plan in the hopes of protecting the elves from a horrifying fate, similar to the one they had just escaped.

As Anaryen continued further through the corridor, she couldn't rid herself of what she had witnessed. Even more unsettling, she couldn't shake the fact that her instincts and attunement with nature were warning her that something much worse was soon to come.

CHAPTER 1

A KNIGHT OF THE PHOENIX

Lying on his back, covered in blood, Volir looked up at the great Dahaka, which was preparing to devour him. As he scanned the battlefield with mottled vision, he saw a staggering swarm of the drothkin killing many of the elven citizens of Valenthreas. These horrifying and grotesque creatures were feeding on the dead around him and impaling his fellow elves with their bloodstained weapons.

Volir felt the jolting pain in his body from the great Dahaka's claws, which had grazed him moments before he fell down in defeat. As he lay bleeding out in his most hopeless state, he struggled to focus through the pain and saw the Dahaka closing in, its massive dragon jaws opening wide. The Dahaka reached him and bit down into his flesh. As he felt the crunching of his bones, and his blood splash upon his face, Volir gasped his last breath and woke up.

Lying in the darkness of his room, Volir struggled for air, faltering to breathe through the realization that what he had just witnessed was only a horrible dream. He sat up in his bed, taking a deep breath before feeling his two small cats tugging on his shirt. They had desperately been trying to wake him from the nightmares that once again invaded his sleep.

To his left was Angor, the small black and white cat with light green eyes and a white nose. The cat sat up, looking at Volir, appearing relieved to see him awake after the frightening sight of him thrashing and wincing through his nightmares.

To Volir's right side was Siam, a slimmer cat who was light-whitened grey with dark grey on his ears and face. Siam's eyes were a very light blue with a grey tone that almost matched the lighter color of the rest of his coat. Volir giggled as he watched Siam looking at him, his head tilted to the side, trying to make sense of what he had witnessed. Siam's uncontrollable purring began, soothing Volir all the more.

The nightmare may not have been real, but it was one of the many unfortunate events that occurred in his youth over five hundred years ago during the War of Strife and Sorrow. It was how Volir often imagined his parents' final moments; such was the fate of many of the elven defenders of the great city of Valenthreas—the city he lived in and wished to leave.

Escaping the great elven city was something he thought about often, and this morning was no different. As he saw his two companions gazing at him, Volir sat up and uttered in his deep, sleepy voice, "All right you two." He heard a further purr of agreement from Siam in response.

Volir sat up with his legs off the bed and planted his feet on the floor. As he wiped his foggy eyes and the cold sweat from his brow, he gazed sleepily around his empty room. He was proud of its sparse simplicity. He never kept much in his quarters, and most of his possessions were meant to provide comfort and play for Angor and Siam. He kept few keepsakes or mementos, as he had a tendency to avoid collecting items that bound him to places or people.

He could feel both of his cats pouncing around on his lap and on one another as they played. Siam often lost when the two cats challenged each other for dominance. He was the more innocent of the two, while Angor was a bit of an instigator, making sure Siam knew who was the strongest.

It wasn't long before Siam retreated to Volir's lap as he had just been defeated by Angor. "I always admire your spirit," Volir said as he picked Siam up and placed him on the floor.

Both of his cats were comforting to him; their relationship was something he no longer had with any other being. The last time he remembered feeling that way was with his parents before they were killed during the great war.

In joyful laughter, Volir spread out his arms, allowing his loose black sleeves to drape over them. When he stood up out of bed, his black pants dropped down over his legs, hovering above the wooden floor of his room. He was taller than most elves and was quite muscular and toned. Many of his fellow knights were in similarly good shape, but Volir always stood a bit taller and had an aura of strength and command about him, even though he was generally silent and spoke little.

Volir stretched out his arms revealing the warm olive complexion of his skin. His long black hair was tucked behind his pointed ears before it fell blanketing down toward the center of his back. His short, neat beard was also black, and he had a sharp jawline to match his strong almond eyes and prominent angled eyebrows. As he exhaled, he could see the faint glow of his breath.

As it happened, only thirty days were left before the end of the year, when the two moons, Ailos and Valos, would align in a convergence that would give birth to another of the great auvinots. The auvinots were the sacred creatures born from the very magic of nature itself every five hundred years when the moons align perfectly in the night sky. This had only occurred twenty times since the time of the first people, who lived when the gods walked among them. While this upcoming event excited many of the people on the planet, for Volir, it only served as a painful reminder of his past.

Now that he was out of bed, Volir's two cats jumped down onto the floor by his feet. They often followed him around when they weren't tucked away in one of the pouches on his belt. Volir made his way to the fireplace and grabbed a piece of wood. As he tossed it into the fireplace, he waved his hand across the chopped log and spoke the words "Cinde En Dokh." The log immediately burst into flames under the kettle hanging there, providing some warmth to the chilled room.

As his cats began playing on the floor, Volir walked to the cabinets and gathered several black tea leaves. The spicy aroma wafted across his nostrils welcoming him to start brewing it. He enjoyed the scent of the leaves before closing the lid of the shiny tin and returning to the fireplace where he tossed the leaves into the kettle, added water, and poured the remaining water into the bowl on the floor for the cats.

Several moments had passed as Volir attended to his morning ritual of cleaning and refreshing himself before starting his day. He heard the kettle whistling and scampered over wearing only his underwear to pull the kettle away from the fire before setting it on the table. He grabbed his old slate mug and poured the hot tea into it before turning to his cats with a serious look. "No poking your head in my tea today," he said. Both of the cats just looked up at him as if deciding how to react to the authority in his voice.

Volir hastily pulled on his pants and shirt, which hugged his skin snugly. They were made from the twin quills of phoenixes and they were incredibly cool and light, yet they provided absolute protection against flames. They were so durable that not even an aurosteel blade could slice through them, although they could be punctured only by a powerful thrust.

He fastened the buckles on the leather straps of his cinder steel tassets, breastplate, and pauldrons. His armor was quite light compared to many other types of armor, a gift of the master craftsman at the cinder forge of the city. He pulled up and fastened his plate boots and plated leather gloves. To finish his ensemble, he donned a twin quill cloak which he fastened to his breastplate using the golden suns on either side, each representing one of the suns which warmed their world with daylight. He pulled his cloak over his eyes as usual, for he was leery of others gazing upon him. His cloak was special in that it held an enchantment to help conceal his true appearance from others.

Volir noticed it was silent in the room and found that both Angor and Siam had jumped up onto the table, sniffing his tea. He walked over and sat down before picking up his mug and taking a large drink from it. Then he looked at both of them. "I thought I told you two to keep off the table," he said as they both began purring and laid down on the table to watch him finish his tea.

By the time the log had burned out in the fireplace, the suns were shining bright, visible through the windows on either side of his room. "Angor…Siam, it's time to go," Volir said. The two cats hopped down and drank water before jumping up his legs into the two pouches he had connected to his belt on either side of his hips. They loved to travel with him everywhere he went. He had found Angor outside his door almost fifteen years ago. Five years later, he saw Siam hiding in the corner of an alley under a box, afraid of everything around him. Volir never wanted pets, but he found himself obligated to them, unable to let them go after he first took them in.

Volir stepped outside, where he was greeted by a crisp, cool breeze. The knight quarters were spread throughout different parts of the city of Valenthreas, but Volir's quarters were located in the southeast area of the city, close to the outer wall. He preferred this location as it kept him away from most people, and it was much quieter than many other parts of the city.

As he closed the door behind him, a deep scratch in the shape of the number one could be seen just above the steel door knob around the center of the dark wooden door. "Strange, I wonder when that got there," he said. His focus was soon interrupted by the faint hint of honeysuckle which he caught on the air.

Volir made his way toward the center of the city, where the order hall of the Knights of the Phoenix was located. The further he walked from his front door, the more he blended in with the different folk of the city, to become another unknown figure in the crowd.

The morning suns were rising high into the sky by the time Volir arrived at the order of the knights. He entered the large gateway and passed by several corridors and meeting rooms on either side of him as he continued beyond the main entrance. Most of the buildings in Valenthreas were made of white stone, and the order's hall was no different. On either side of him as he entered the courtyard, there were stone stairs that led up to the top levels towering out around the massive sanctum. Ahead of him, Volir could see a group of his fellow knights gathering in preparation for dawn drills, led by the leader of the Knights of the Phoenix, Valothas Ear'thol.

Every knight, whether a new recruit or a veteran patrolling the city and surrounding lands, reported for dawn drills. All of the knights followed a strict code of preparation for any threat posed upon their realm, and the dawn always brought preparedness for those members of the order. As Volir approached the rest of the knights, he motioned to his two companions to post in their usual places where they could watch him train. In typical form, the two small cats leaped out of his pouches and climbed a wooden post to his right. There, they jumped up to the banister running along it until they reached the ledge, where they found a place to perch themselves and watch. Across the upper ledge were phoenixes that were oathbound companions to several of the knights who had earned their devotion.

It had been nearly ten thousand years since the first phoenix, Ai'ner, was born during the first convergence of the moons. Since Ai'ner's first rebirth, there had been an unknown number of phoenixes born from its ashes. Many of the phoenixes choose only the greatest knights to bind themselves to. The Knights of the Phoenix were formed by the elves, and it was the eldest phoenixes who gifted much of themselves to aid in the creation of the first cinder swords, twin quill cloaks, and cinder-forged armor. Each phoenix dedicated to the order shared a vital bond with the knights, both in name and with their very being. For a Knight of the Phoenix, it was their greatest achievement to be chosen by a phoenix who could aid them, strengthening their abilities and persevering with them through the ages, allowing them to become the strongest knights of their order.

This achievement was one of Volir's greatest desires, and he had been diligently striving to achieve it for many years. Above him on the railing, he saw his cats take their place next to Ol'nar, the phoenix companion of none other than Elder Knight Valothas. Ol'nar was one of the oldest known phoenixes, and its feathers appeared as blackened amber surrounded by an amber aura, radiating from it as if it was ready to burst into flames. Being near a phoenix caused most elves to feel both calm and focused. Their presence was a welcomed gift to every knight of the order, even if they didn't have a companion phoenix of their own.

Angor and Siam often tried to play with the phoenixes. Some would let the cats chase them around and fan sparks on the ground so the cats would have something to chase. Ol'nar would frequently scare them away with a quick flap of its wing, which would burst into flame. Spotting a winged flash of flame in his periphery, Volir saw that today was no different. Trying not to laugh at them, Volir looked back at the group of knights who noticed him and stared for a moment as he moved to join them.

Looking sternly at the knights, Valothas stood tall with an inquisitive stare. He quickly raised his right arm and pounded a closed fist onto the left side of his chest, letting out the bursting crash of his plate gauntlets. "Knights, converge," he shouted. His armor was much like Volir's, but it was clearly more ornate, with features such as radiant amber jewels, gold-laced mail, and a cinder sword crafted from the very cinders of his phoenix, Ol'nar. As he stood steadfast, he was nearly as tall as Volir and a fair bit broader across the shoulders. He had lightly bronzed skin, light grey eyes, and long white flowing hair down to the center of his back. His face was marked with battle scars, which could be seen in his goatee and through parts of his bushy eyebrows. Aside from his white hair, he appeared as young as the day he reached adulthood.

Valothas was one of the oldest living elves and few of his age had survived the great war. While elves could live endlessly, it was still possible for them to be killed and his scars served as a reminder of this to those he led. Valothas had become the leader of the Knights of the Phoenix when their former leader, Vorthelos Va'Threas, was killed by the Dahaka in the War of Strife and Sorrow.

Volir watched the elder knight pace across the front of their formation and recognized his commanding presence with respect for the heroic deeds he had displayed in the great war. Although knights of all ages were quick to move at the command of Valothas, Volir was known for being a bit more reserved in doing so.

Volir positioned himself in the formation of knights, finding his assigned place in the front and center. However, Volir did not like being at the front, as he often found himself the focus of attention from Valothas. Although Volir wished to be chosen by a phoenix with hopes of gaining a duty station far away from Valenthreas, it always seemed that Valothas had plans to transform him into a leader who could one day take command of the knights.

Volir remembered that it was during the Ifrit invasions when he and many of the Knights of the Phoenix repelled the invaders back into the dark realm. It was because of his ability to rally his fellow knights that Valothas took notice and became excited by his potential; the others seemed eager to follow him. At that time, Volir only sought to end the threat, but still he felt the elder knight's gaze begin to focus more intently upon him. That focus was now something Volir tried to avoid. He had only one desire, to blend in with the others.

His own insecurity around leading was something he fought to hide beneath his hood day after day. He remembered how his father had been so committed to lead others and how it came to a devastating end. Even after all the years that had passed, he could remember the pain of his parents' loss and denied himself of what it would mean to follow in their footsteps. As Volir stood attentively, he hoped that on this day, he would escape any focused attention from the elder knight.

Valothas walked across the front of the formation, slowly reviewing each knight's armor and cloaks for cleanliness. Volir noticed that Valothas had a smile of pride which was quickly interrupted by Valothas's stern command. "Volir, Salenval, Nahul, Kaylos, and Syvon over to this wall," he said as he motioned to one side. "Leavesa, Vael, Drelion, Kaervo, and Arvasiel move over to this wall," he said as he motioned to the other. "The rest of you form a circle around your exemplars."

As the rest of the knights of the order formed a circle by the outer wall surrounding the two groups, Valothas pulled the Knights of the Phoenix banner from the stone post on the floor beside him and raised it over his head. As he held it high, the pointed gold cap at the top sparkled under the light of the suns and caught the attention of Volir who felt further challenged by the light.

"Volir and Leavesa, you will lead your knights to either defend or capture this banner. Your teams have until I tell you to stop, so work quickly and strategically. We don't have all morning, and I won't waste the light of the Twin Flames."

Valothas threw the flag toward Leavesa's group and pierced it into the ground behind her. As this occurred, Leavesa Solendrei peeled back the hood on her cloak to reveal the flowing waves of her shiny auburn hair. Although quite petite, she was known for surprising people with her skilled fire magic in combat. She gazed over at Volir with her bright blue eyes and smiled in an attempt to raise a response from him. Then, in that fleeting moment, she turned back to her group of knights as they made their preparations.

Volir remained unwavering in Leavesa's attempt at provocation. He often wondered why she was so keen on attempting to influence him and whether it was rivalry, attraction, or a challenge out of camaraderie— he could never quite understand her intentions. While he was truly the strongest knight of the order, it never seemed to bode well for him when matched up against Leavesa during dawn drills.

Volir turned to his group of knights, but when it became clear that they already knew what to expect of him, he abandoned the thought of taking their suggestions. He saw the uncertain looks upon their faces and remembered how many times they had looked at him that way before. The looks almost immediately caused him to shut himself away; to him, it seemed easier to do that than to open himself up to the possibility of being responsible for others. In truth, he would rather have the looks of uncertainty upon their faces as opposed to seeing hope and trust in their eyes.

Finding himself uncomfortable under their gazes, he muttered his instructions: "Nahul, Kaylos, and Syvon, ignite your solar shields at the front, forming a wall. Hold steady as we press forward. When we are close enough, Salenval and I will circle around the sides to put pressure on them. Don't drop your solar shields until we move to flank them. Once we do so, push ahead and put pressure on them."

The knights nodded in agreement, but their expressions were those of disappointment, as if they predicted what was to come. This only made Volir all the more focused on how he could end the drill as fast as possible. He also thought that maybe if he just failed it then Valothas would stop pushing him so hard into leadership roles in the first place.

Volir looked ahead to see that Leavesa and her knights had formed a circle around the flag, where she stood in the center, prepared for the assault. Ready to take the flag from her, he signaled to his knights, and they made their move. Nahul, Kaylos, and Syvon all ignited their solar shields. They spoke the words of magic, "Sola En Dokh," as if their three voices were one. In perfect harmony, their radiating shields of pure light formed around their left hands, extending in perfect circles between their fists and shoulders. Moving closer together, the shields unified into a wall of light.

As they pressed forward, Volir and Salenval prepared themselves and withdrew their cinder swords over their heads from the scabbards under their cloaks. Edging closer, Volir ignited his cinder sword, bathing it in flame, and steadied himself. The thick smoky scent of the engulfed sword bathed him. "Engage," he shouted.

With quick precision, both he and Salenval darted out from behind each side of their group that had begun moving forward. As the two approached the barrier, Leavesa raised her flame shield over her head which connected to her companion's flame wall, further surrounding her and the knights defending the flag. The radiance of what had become a flame dome distorted the view of all those behind it with its brightness.

Volir now focused on taking down the barrier and began hammering it with one arching strike after another, with amazing force from his cinder sword. Bursts of flame exploded off the barrier like solar flares from a sun. Salenval began doing the same as the rest of the knights charged forward, attempting to weaken the barrier protecting the banner. Volir's entire group unleashed strike after strike from their weapons, filling the air with an acrid odor as the fiery explosions continued.

While fissures seemed to be forming upon the dome, Volir could hear Valothas chuckling as he and the other knights of the order looked on at the spectacle before them. Leavesa's group had already begun reinforcing the dome with their own magic which was sure to repair any damage being done. The flame barrier was as beautiful as gazing upon the suns in the sky and it quickly inspired cheers from some of the new recruits of the order.

Volir suddenly forgot about the knights at his command and was trying everything he could on his own to break the barrier. For him, success was now everything. He wanted to end the laughter of Valothas and the others by showing everyone his power. He briefly noticed that Salenval and the others had begun looking to him for guidance on what to do next, realizing it was impossible to break the barrier protecting the banner while Leavesa's team reinforced its strength from behind.

Volir took multiple steps backward and then rushed forward leaping up as high as he could and mustering all of his strength. The flames upon his cinder sword swelled, and as he brought his sword down onto Leavesa's group, the bright barrier surrounding them exploded sending all of his knights and hers to the ground. As the rumbling sound of the explosion cleared his ears, he heard the collective sounds of awe mixed with gasps coming from the knights of his order and he thought to claim victory.

As he was just about to step forward to grab the banner, he heard the sound of Valothas's voice ring out. "That's enough, the exercise is over. You have failed, Volir! Return to your sides and extinguish your flames, all of you," Valothas said.

The knights walked back to where they were standing previously, but Volir was still breathing heavily by the flag as Valothas began walking toward him. Expecting a lecture, Volir started to walk away until he heard Valothas, who stopped him sternly. "Stand fast, Volir," he said as he walked toward the flag and withdrew it from the ground. "As you all can see, it takes cooperation and group cohesion to accomplish some objectives. Sometimes, no matter how powerful one is, they must rely on their fellow knights to overcome obstacles and tasks. Never forget the importance of working together."

"I was about to collect the banner," Volir said, but he was quickly cut off.

"Silence, Volir. We'll speak privately about this in just a moment," Valothas said, looking to him for obedience. "It's not enough to expect that we can accomplish a goal alone. We must all be capable of working as one, unified under the same purpose, no matter what the goal. It's especially important for us when we're expected to lead; our responsibility is to our duty. Speaking of duty, may you be off to your own. Knights in training, report to your command knight. That is all," he said as he motioned for Volir to follow him and began walking toward the back end of the sanctum where the elder knights' chambers were located.

As Volir entered the sanctum following his commander, he looked back toward his two cats and signaled for them, making a clicking sound with his mouth. Angor and Siam both hopped down from the railing and raced to catch up to him, running up his legs and purring as they made themselves comfortable in his pouches.

Valothas stopped at the doorway of the sanctum and turned around with a serious look, like that of a father about to give a talk to a son. "I know your desire for many years has been to be chosen by a phoenix so you can get out of the city. I have never been able to make sense of why you've served as a knight for so long yet seek to leave this place where you are duty bound, but as long as that remains your goal, you will find yourself continuing to fail. The ability to lead and commit oneself to selfless service is but one of the many virtues you would need to adhere to before your own personal goals might even be possible. The noble tenets are absolute in the way of ascension, as well as rising within our order. You know this to be true."

"Yes, Valothas," Volir said, his head hanging low in solemn contemplation.

Valothas looked at him with care and what appeared to be the empathic concern of a parent. "If a phoenix is ever to choose you, then you must be willing to lead others. I hope one day you might be capable of leading the Knights of the Phoenix. While you may not wish it for yourself, it's known to me that the quality is there within you, and it lies hand in hand with your own strength and potential that remains unrealized. I wish for nothing more than to see you prosper and abandon this solitary path you've been on since coming to join the order."

"I understand," Volir said. The truth was, he rarely had faith in anything outside of himself—the primary reason why he avoided leadership. As such, he would nearly always attempt to accomplish tasks alone, and while he was more than capable of doing so, it often came at the cost of accomplishing goals as a team. Trusting in others was nearly impossible for Volir, and the idea of leaving himself open in such a way was unfathomable to him.

Despite his undeniable power and capability in wielding the light and the flame as weapons, he was often seen as selfish by others. He had no friends or close relationships, even though many had tried to befriend him.

Valothas could see that Volir was not taking the opportunity to talk so he cleared his throat and brought his attention back to the task at hand. "Alright then, no need to keep on with this; I know you understand. Now, I would ask you to head to the alchemy shop here in the city," he said as he handed Volir a roll of parchment. "Everything is written down, just get these items from Deklain and bring them back here. There is a demonstration later for some of the new knights, and preparations are necessary."

Volir looked up to respond reluctantly, "Isn't there something more useful for me to do than running errands?"

"There is no task too small or large for any one person. Duty is not measured by the importance of the task but by the dedication of one's spirit to stay the course."

"Yes, Valothas." Volir took the parchment in hand and turned to head out of the doorway.

"Good, see you soon enough," Valothas said.

As Volir walked back through the courtyard of the order, he found himself drifting through his own frustrating thoughts, weighing the use of his time and everything the elder knight had said about being chosen by a phoenix. As he walked, he saw one of the knights with a phoenix perched on his pauldron, whispering something to several other knights. When Volir looked in their direction, they laughed, and he felt sure they were talking about him.

He imagined how they were probably laughing because he failed his team or because he knocked everyone down and made such a mess of the drill that was meant to be a showcase of teamwork. Worst of all, he imagined how they probably laughed because they thought that was the reason he had not been chosen by a phoenix after all of his time in the order. He hated feeling that maybe they were right. Even with those intrusive thoughts, he knew being chosen was much bigger than that.

Continuing out through the large gates, he heard Angor and Siam meow, and he knew that they were hungry. He decided he would take them home on the way to the alchemy shop and clean up a bit himself while there. Volir pressed on into the city crowds in the light of late morning.

As he continued to fade into the city, he found his thoughts drifting away from his duty and toward the time he chose to become a Knight of the Phoenix. He reminded himself of his oath to the order and the people of the city whom he served. He remembered why he chose to become a knight—he'd lost everything that the evil minions of the dark master took away from him. Most importantly, he remembered why he couldn't make the mistake his father had, a mistake he promised himself he would never repeat.

CHAPTER 2

ODE OF THE TWIN FLAMES

Volir stepped up to the door of his living quarters, and for a moment, paused in reflection before opening it. The thought of what the elder knight had said was haunting him. Feeling the impatient movement of his cats near his belt line, he opened the door, stepping into the dim light of his home as the cats hopped out. He opened the cool provision cabinet, pulling out some scraps of baked chicken from the previous night, and tossed them into the bowl on the floor.

At the sight of the food, both of the cats charged toward the bowl, fighting to shove their heads in. After a moment, they politely made room for each other and shared in the enjoyment of the food now sating their hunger. Volir walked over to the foot of his bed where the conjuration bowl was located. Above it on the wall was a beautifully crafted aurosteel mirror that seemed to illuminate the corner wall.

Standing in front of the mirror, Volir removed his hood to expose his bright gold glowing eyes; he was aware of their light which radiated like two suns. Some could still describe what it was like looking into the eyes of an Auron elf, and they often said it was like seeing a part of the Twin Flames there before you. There were none who had eyes like his anymore, and they were a large part of the reason he chose to hide them under his cloak. He was the last Auron elf—the last on the entire planet with eyes like this—and so, he hid them from everyone. The longer he looked at his eyes, the more he resented having them at all.

In an attempt to purge his mind of his memories, he closed his eyes in a solemn moment of silence. Feeling calmer and more peaceful, he opened his eyes to be met again by those two radiating rings of fire. The longer he stared at them, the closer they seemed to get until they appeared as two overlapping suns. Volir felt himself take in a deep gasp of air as a furious storm of images began racing through his waking mind, a vision commanding his attention as if to bear witness to an event.

In what seemed like an instant, he felt a release and stumbled backward. He closed his eyes and shook his head, attempting to release the imagery from his mind. Volir's vision was desperately clear, and he recounted what he had seen. He saw the people of Valenthreas fleeing a destructive force bearing down on the city. He had seen city defenders dying in destructive bombardments coming from outside the city walls. He saw the overbearing presence of a dark and ominous shadow in the smoke of the ruined city, glaring at him with piercing black eyes. He couldn't make out what it meant but as the moment passed, he felt that a looming presence remained in his very room.

What Volir really couldn't understand was if the visions were warnings being sent to him or foresight which he had been gifted with. Very few among the races of the world had the power of foresight and most of those rare souls were among the elves. It was said that when someone had the power of visions it was a gift from the gods. He had only a few visions such as this over the course of his life and they always preceded an important event to come. They showed him a glimpse of the future and also some of the different possible outcomes. The visions had started after the loss of his parents. Pondering this reality, he knew he needed to leave this city one day. It seemed to only keep him haunted by the past. For now, he had to carry out the tasks of picking up the items Valothas had requested of him.

As he looked down at his two friends, who were pleasantly enjoying their food, he wondered if the moment he just experienced had even taken place at all. The cats were completely uninterrupted by what he had seen, and he thought it was just as well. He only wished peace and happiness for his two pets and with this in mind, he finished cleaning up and pulled his hood back over his eyes. As he headed toward the door, he could hear the sounds of the cats' mouths smacking as they ate, and with a smile he uttered, "I'll be back, boys." He walked out, closing the door behind him.

Volir had begun making his way back through the crowded city streets on route to Deklain Deynan's alchemy shop. It was on the opposite side of the southernmost part of the city. Few humans were allowed to establish a permanent residence within the city of Valenthreas, which many of them carried animosity about, though plenty still visited.

Volir passed by the Sleepy Gryphon, which was the greatest inn of the city. It was always lively and cheerful, and he would enjoy a sparked or frosted brew there from time to time. As he passed by the door, he slowed to a pause as he could hear the famous odist Mina, who was singing her famous Ode to the Twin Flames.

Twin Flames, our beloved,
Your love ignites our hearts,
Bringing life, hope, and beauty,
To nourish every part.

You embody heaven's truth,
Cleansing darkness from our world,
Guiding us to the warm hearth of home,
Where your blessings ease souls unfurled.

Radiant with love, truth, and mercy,
You offer the light of our beginning,
Showing us the way to ascend,
Forever praised, our world spinning.

Twin Flames, our beloved,
Your flames burn bright and true,
We honor your eternal dance,
In all we say, think, and do.

Mina's songs were legendary in the elven realm, and her fame had traveled to all corners of the world since she began writing her odes over the last several hundred years. Her song wasn't the only thing Volir had heard as he stood outside of the inn. He overheard gossip between two of the tavern's patrons who were sitting at an open window by the door which seemed to be projecting their voices right at him.

Volir listened in as the man and woman continued back and forth. "You know that old sage just sits up there in his tower, you know, Avestan. Don't you find that strange? He lives in that tower on the mountain just watching everything going on down here," the woman said.

"You know they say he only talks to the stewards and never leaves that place. If you ask me, I'd say he's up to no good," the man said.

Volir's attention on the two was interrupted as the door to the inn opened, revealing some of the patrons who were walking out the door laughing together, reveling in their enjoyment of Mina and her songs. As Volir watched them pass in front of him, walking away, he heard one of them mention the human prince, Drazius Khorvek. Out of sheer curiosity, Volir began to follow them, wondering what they would say.

The man on the left straightened himself out and uttered the first comment. "The king was a good man and always treated all the folk well when I was there. He never treated us like we were low," he said.

"Do you think the prince will raise an army and try going after anyone else? I don't know about you but I won't be going up north anytime soon," the other man said.

"I don't know what he's planning now, but I'm betting that Prince Khorvek has been infected by the fade. There's no other reason to kill his father the way he did, none of them phoenix knights, magi, or even the stewards seem to be worrying about it," the man responded.

Volir had already heard this story and knew it was true. Volir was disgusted by the news and wondered how the prince could walk up to his father and murder him on his own throne after returning from his travels abroad on a mission of peace. What was even more puzzling was how the people of his father's kingdom would follow the prince after knowing what he had done to their beloved king.

It was only in the past day that word had come to the Knights of the Phoenix from their Aurodite allies delivering the sad news. It had caused the knights order to become hypervigilant as they carried out their duty's concerned by what they worried may soon come. The same could be said for the rest of the elves who had been privileged with the information.

While not all the elves had yet become aware of this news, Volir was sure that many of them would react similarly upon hearing the dire tale. It was the elves who were paragons to the world and as such they guided and looked over the other races, especially in the ways of the gods. Such news would only cause the elves to seek a prepared state of protection and assistance to those they shared the planet with as they had many times in the past when the dark master brought calamity to the people. To Volir, the story of the dark prince was only more added evidence to what he feared was true about the state of the world.

Volir felt the desire to confide in someone about his sense of the world and what he had been feeling. He had always been very intuitive, and his pulse on the ebb and flow of nature and the dynamics between people was always one of his greatest strengths. It helped him both in combat and in his own mastery of the Essa, which allowed him to use magic from within, without spoken spells. Although right now, he felt his mastery would not comfort him with his thoughts of this perceived shift. He thought of all the times he deflected engaging in conversations with others, keeping them from knowing much about him or his past. He knew safeguarding himself and his past only came at the cost of developing friendships or having those he could confide in or trust. This was another moment in which he felt alone, left with his thoughts once more.

Volir continued walking through the streets, contemplating the rumors he had heard about the sage of Avestan. The patrons at the tavern had claimed that the he never left his tower, nor did he speak with Valothas or the knights of his order. Volir knew better and wondered if this sage, who advised the stewards of Valenthreas, knew anything about the changing state of the world. What secrets did he possess, and how well could he discern hidden truths?

As Volir walked, he overheard more people gossiping about Prince Khorvek. Some people found it hard to believe, as the prince's family had a noble lineage dating back to the first humans. Others viewed those who spread such rumors as fearmongers, disturbing the peace of the city.

As he neared the humans ahead of him gossiping, Volir heard an argument between the two.

"Prince Drazius has gone dark, he has," the man said.

"I won't believe that nonsense. You're a fool to think that the house of Khorvek of all houses would fall in such a way. He wouldn't do that; I'll never believe it," the next man said.

Their argument was cut short by the town crier's announcement at the central street leading through the city. The crier blew into the horn with its high and low pitches sounding out loud at once, catching the attention of everyone along the street for as far as the eye could see. He called out to the people, requesting their attention as he began to announce the important news from the stewards of the elven city. "Please everyone, your attention, there is an important decree from the stewards," the crier shouted as he cleared his throat to read from the stretched parchment in his hands.

Dear citizens of Valenthreas,

It is with great sorrow that we must inform you of the tragic news concerning the kingdom of Khalandro and their beloved king, Nailor Khorvek. We have received reports that the king was murdered by his own son, Prince Drazius Khorvek. We currently have no knowledge of the state of the kingdom or what has transpired since the murder of their venerable king.

In light of these events, we urge caution for all those who choose to travel outside the borders of this city. As we are unable to guarantee the safety of those in the open territory of Aurotheros, it is advised that those who must travel take necessary precautions.

Until we are able to understand whether or not the kingdom of Khalandro poses a threat to our realm or the surrounding realms, we ask that all citizens remain vigilant and cautious. May the light guide you all.

Your loyal stewards of Valenthreas.

The city crier continued shouting, "The stewards' decree will be posted here and on every city board. Please share this information with everyone you know and be safe beyond the borders of Valenthreas." He hammered the decree onto the city notice board which sent a tapping sound down the streets surrounding the southern square where everyone had now gathered.

Volir had continued forward throughout the crier's announcement and was very aware of the citizens who appeared to be consoling one another and gossiping. It was much the same as the rumors he'd overheard just moments before, only now everyone was settling in to accept the reality of the news which had just been formally shared.

This now left Volir to wonder about the sage of Avestan, and he expected this announcement would only fan the flames of the citizens' gossip. Volir expected that many of the citizens would want to know what the sage knew and how he would be advising the stewards. Some might say that as a human advisor he shouldn't be trusted. More extreme cases might even speculate that he was in on it.

It wouldn't be the first time that the elves of Valenthreas became paranoid about protecting their sacred city. Even with these wild rumors, there were plenty of others who believed the sage was a venerable man who spent countless hours day after day scrying the truth behind events which took place across the world, all in a tireless effort to keep the people safe from the evils that would threaten all life.

As he walked further away from the central square, Volir's thoughts were interrupted by a shadow that was cast on the road ahead of him. As he looked up into the sky, attempting to make out what passed in front of the light of the suns, he was left bewildered. He couldn't seem to make out what cast the shadow, even while straining to see with the clarity of his Auron eyes. With little concern for the moment, he continued forward, making his way to the alchemy shop.

Volir stood in front of an arched door with its large reinforced wooden sign that read "Deynan's Herbs." Embedded in the white wooden door were gems of every color. The window in the door was arched and very clear, as if the glass was made of fine, polished crystal. On either side of the door were two matching, arched windows inlaid on the white stone wall of the shop. The top of each arched window was embedded with green emeralds.

As Volir entered the shop, he was greeted by the hearty aroma of herbs. He saw an upset man shouting demands at the shopkeeper behind the front counter, who wore a white apron equipped with various pouches containing his wares. Below the apron were fine green pants with black, buckled boots and a white, tailored shirt with several buttons open on its chest. He had a neatly groomed, thick, black beard with streaks of white, and his hair was combed back to match it. His eyes were dark brown, blanketed by his thick eyebrows, and he had a large pipe in his mouth from which smoke rose, certainly the same pipe herb he sold in the shop. This man was Deklain Deynan, and he was well known to Volir. Deklain was one of the many generations in his family who continued to serve the city as an herbalist and alchemist of Valenthreas. In fact, he was in one of the most distinguished human families living among the elves of the city.

Less than one percent of the city's population was made up of human residents, with even less of the other races residing within the city walls. Those who had been approved to live there were often envied by their counterparts. Deklain had experienced his fair share of prejudice by the humans who visited the city and would come by his shop; today seemed to be no exception.

The customer in front of him had both hands planted palm-down on the counter as he leaned in and shouted. "Those honey vines I bought yesterday were all bad! I demand new ones as compensation."

"Well, sir, did you bring me back the bad honey vines? How can I accommodate your request if you didn't bring back what you had bought yesterday?" Deklain said, crossing his arms over his chest.

"I don't have them anymore; my kids ate them all," the customer said, raising his hands.

"Well, then, I'm afraid you'll just have to buy new honey vines if you want more of them. The return policy is quite clear," Deklain said.

"I want my money back or you can just give me new honey vines. If you don't, then I will tell every other human who visits this city that you take advantage of your own kind," the man said, now becoming noticeably red in the face.

"Sir, visitor or not, I remember your purchase yesterday, and the vines were fresh, crisp, and unwilted. My family has run this shop for hundreds of years, and we'll be here for as long as a Deynan remains living in this city. You can ask any customer who has come through here and they'll tell you the same; our reputation will remain untarnished."

"I won't be forgetting this if I ever do return to this ridiculous place. You've lived here so long you act just like one of them in this righteous city looking down on us, treating us as lesser," the man said as he turned away to walk out of the shop.

Just as Volir continued to walk forward, the man looked up at him with his plump red face and scowled, squinting his eyes in an attempt to see under Volir's hood. Volir looked down as the man passed by him and exited the shop, before noticing another man on the right side of the shop who he witnessed stuffing alchemy tools into his pocket. The thief had been using the dispute as an opportunity to try and steal some supplies that would have otherwise cost a hefty amount of coin. Seeing this, Volir cleared his throat and spoke in a stern tone, standing tall. "A thief in the city of Valenthreas and in Deklain's family shop—how would you like this moment to end?"

"Uh…I'm sorry. If I put everything back, can I leave without you elves imprisoning me?" the thief said, appearing to shake under Volir's gaze.

"We elves wouldn't imprison you, but we never forget those we meet who make such choices in Valenthreas. You are known to me now. May our next encounter be on better terms, or your welcome to this city will be revoked."

"Yes, sir, I'm sorry. I won't do it again," the thief said as he piled the stolen items on the counter in front of Deklain.

"If I catch you in my shop again, I'll call the city guard to have you removed," Deklain shouted. "We'll have none of that here. You get going now."

"Yes, sir, I really am sorry, sir," the thief said as he walked carefully out of the door, thoroughly embarrassed and afraid after his run in with a Knight of the Phoenix.

Volir walked toward Deklain at the counter, who was now beginning to laugh, dropping his arms open toward Volir in a greeting. "Welcome back, Volir," he said. "It's always good to see you in that flashy hood you love to wear. I'm in your debt. If you hadn't been here and caught that thief, he would have made off with some of the most expensive merchandise. What can I get you today? Everything for your knights is free, but if there is anything I can add special for you today, then please, tell me."

"Nothing for me, but I did bring a list of supplies that Valothas has asked me to acquire for some exercises later," Volir said as he handed Deklain the parchment.

Taking the list, Deklain opened it. "Ah, yes, I see. So, he would like three bundles of phoenix flower, two bundles of twin leaf, and two bundles of volenweed. I expect you have the solvents and other ingredients for the cinder sword oil that I assume he will make with this? How about a ball of string for those two little companions of yours?"

"We have all the other needed ingredients. Valothas is quite accurate with these sorts of things," Volir said.

"How about that string for your little buddies," Deklain asked.

"If you can spare it, I'd be glad to accept it, those two really enjoy playing with it when I have time to toss it around."

"Consider it done. Now just a moment, I'll head into the back and gather these herbs for you."

"Thank you," Volir said as he began to look around Deklain's well-organized shop. He always did admire how neat and clean Deklain kept his family's shop. He enjoyed entering the shop because the mixed aroma from all of the herbs that hung at the different displays around the shop relaxed him. Across both walls on either side of the shop hung all manner of herbs from across the world. The displays were even organized by region from which the herbs were collected. Each row held a blend of scents unique to the realm where they were gathered. The row where most of the northern herbs were setup smelled very fresh and airy while the herbs from the south were musky and spicy.

Whether someone needed winter leaves from the dangerous frozen north or saffron from the Olynthian Plains, it never surprised Volir as to how much care was put into the presentation of the shop displays. Everything was presented in pristine fashion, from bottled rose water, gold mint, moon leaf, one blade, and even the simple but sweet treat, honey vines. Some of the more dangerous items such as ohrin bloom or ohrivain also could be found in the shop. Sometimes lovers would visit the shop to acquire fresh sun lilies, often presented between lovers as a symbol of eternal devotion.

Deklain emerged from the back of his shop carrying three bundles of herbs, which he placed into an elven preserving bottle to keep them fresh for an extended period. Elves were known to store items in these containers, with some items remaining fresh for up to ten years or more. With a tap on the lid, Deklain slid the bottle across the wooden counter with pride. "There you go," he said. He reached under the counter to retrieve the ball of string which he placed next to the bottle.

"Thank you, Deklain," Volir said as he slowly raised his closed fist over his breastplate and nodded.

"You're welcome my old friend," Deklain replied as he sent him a parting smile. "You take care now, until I see you next."

Volir picked up the ball of string and the bottle, placing them in a hide bag bound to the left side of his belt, hidden under his twin quill cloak. As he exited the shop, he caught the fragrance of fresh pipe herb from a jar on display by the window. Looking up into the sky, he saw the suns were high above now, bathing him and the city in their light.

Thinking of his two companions, he decided to return home to gather them so that they could accompany him back to the knights' order hall. There was still time before he was expected to return, and he wasn't usually without Angor and Siam by his side in some manner or another.

As Volir turned to walk back to his quarters, an unsettling wave washed over him. While his Auron senses were different from the other elves, he found it challenging to identify the cause. Then again, he really wasn't very happy to be running errands in the first place. He always desired patrols in the wilds and visiting locales of the realm over the monotony of errands that not even the new recruits were expected to perform. As he felt himself growing frustrated, Volir knew that he would feel welcomed by his two furry companions' greetings as he walked through the door.

The walk back home seemed to have gone by much quicker than the walk on the way to Deklain's shop. Arriving at his door, he could hear his two pets inside playing. As he peered in through the glass window, he could see them rolling around on the floor and pouncing on one another. It was a pleasant sight to see these two happy, and through his solitude, the cats always seemed to be enough companionship to sate any sense of loneliness or heartache. As Volir opened the door and startled them, the two jumped away from one another which caused Volir to laugh. As he entered his home, both cats walked by his legs, rubbing up against them. Volir made a loud clicking noise from his mouth, and the two quickly ran up his legs and into the pouches on his belt.

For a moment, Volir just stood there in the silence of his room, doing absolutely nothing. As he looked down into each of his pouches, he couldn't help speaking out loud to his two friends. "As much as I love being here with you two, I have to get out of here. Maybe I can find us some remote watchtower by the sea or over by those mountains on the border of the Mosslands," he said. As he felt them purring in his pouches, he smiled, turned around to the door, and left.

Walking through the city, he had slipped from one memory to the next, until he found himself standing in front of the order hall of the Knights of the Phoenix once again. The walls of the order rose up from around the inner sanctum, the top of the walls reaching up toward the suns. As glorious as the knights' order was, it was but a small fraction of the size of the central spire of Valenthreas, now visible as he looked just up to his left.

The massive spire had a very wide base, and the further it reached toward the sky, the narrower it became. Along the way up, additional towers rose from its base, housing many of the highborn elves who had lived there since the spire was originally constructed. At that time, this massive structure was the whole of Valenthreas. Only over thousands of years did the city expand and grow into the size it was today.

Volir turned back to the gates of his order and made his return to the central sanctum. As he entered, he could see several knights in the courtyard ahead of him training. Some of the phoenixes had left with their fellow knights while others flew around above the order hall engulfed in their brilliant flames, leaving their streaking trails through the sky above. Walking into the courtyard, Volir could only think of his desire to be free of this place. One day he would leave, and he was never more ready for that moment than he was today.

CHAPTER 3

NO TASK TOO SMALL

Volir stepped up to the doorway of Valothas's chambers and noticed that the elder knight was engrossed in thought as he reviewed an important letter bearing its freshly opened seal. Valothas was so focused on the contents that he didn't even notice Volir standing outside his door. Although Volir didn't always appreciate the attention he received from Valothas, he cared for the knight deeply and saw him as someone important to him. However, he would never reveal these feelings to Valothas, as to do so was no longer in his nature.

Volir had come to the Knights of the Phoenix not long after the War of Strife and Sorrow. When he requested to join the order, it was Valothas who was eager to welcome him in and reinforce him with a sense that he had found a place to call his own. Where Volir once showed his appreciation to Valothas, he had since become hardened by the passage of time and apathetic outside of his duty as a knight. As such, it had been many years since Volir truly revealed his emotions around others and when he did nowadays it was almost always by accident.

Seeing that Valothas wouldn't notice him unless he made his presence known, Volir raised his hand and knocked twice on the dark wood frame of the door. Valothas was startled by the sound and quickly closed the letter, clearing his throat as he greeted Volir. "You're back; I take it you obtained all the requested items," Valothas said.

"Of course."

Valothas pointed to the seat before him. "Please have a seat."

As Volir settled into the chair, he could feel Angor and Siam stirring but it seemed they were still asleep. Ol'nar, Valothas's phoenix companion, flew into the room and perched on a tall stand beside the desk. Valothas greeted the phoenix warmly, while Ol'nar turned its attention to Volir with a steady gaze.

Volir's curiosity got the best of him. "What's so important in that letter on the desk?"

"Nothing much, just some correspondence with the stewards about things happening in the human realms. I assume you heard one of the criers' decrees while you were gone."

"I did."

"Although there have been no attacks yet, they're concerned that one may take place soon. I suspect something bigger is at play, the council will meet soon to discuss it further."

"What do you think might be driving these events," Volir asked. For him, this news only confirmed his own suspicions regarding the attack.

"I suspect...something has changed the prince, and we both know what kind of evil brings about such change. A prince who loved his father dearly leaves and returns only to commit such an unspeakable act..." Valothas trailed off.

Both of them sat for a moment in silent contemplation, working out what they imagined to be at play.

After a moment, Valothas continued. "The servants of the dark master have remained hidden from us for many years, although we kill the dark creatures roaming the land, the daevos and many of the dark incarnates have not been seen since the great war. From time to time, we hear of the el'ani tempting poor souls to the darkness. Other times, the i'nei or maie are found linked to stories of terror shared by victims who have a weakened spirit. In those instances, we can't be sure. The Dragonstrike Woods outside the city remain a mystery, but I don't believe any of these facts are at the heart of the prince's horrific acts."

"Something does seem out of balance and it has for some time now," Volir said.

"I think so too, and Grindam has not been reported anywhere since the great war, but his influence is unmistakable."

"You think he or the dark master could be responsible?"

"I do and they both enjoy possessing those souls who are lost, they always use strife and sorrow as tools. Strife, most of all, is the tool of the dark master. If Prince Drazius was already having dark thoughts and fed them enough then he could have strayed too far from the virtues. Only then could it be possible for the dark master to have a partial hold on his ability to make decisions. Drazius would feel intoxicated by his success, and the fade would grow within him—a dark desire to kill his own father and feel nothing but seeking resolution to his strife. Which we know–"

"Will only cause him to give in to the will of Merdah; his purpose will only be guided by one thing," Volir finished.

"Exactly—a puppet with a purpose. All he'll think of is completing whatever he believes will end the strife he carries within," Valothas said as he stood up, his arms now crossed over his chest. "This is the only thing that makes sense; we saw something similar happen to many of the vorelans in the great war."

"Yes, far too many vorelans lost their way," Volir said. Matching his mentor, he stood up and took the jar out of his hide bag, setting it on the desk. "Here are the supplies you requested."

Valothas held up his hand. "You hold onto those. I would like you to head down to our apothecary lab and create the radiant potions and cinder oil for today's training showcase. We have several of the newest recruits who have not yet seen how we use these tools to effectively strengthen our spells."

Volir let out a heavy sigh. "Another task for me? I don't see any of the other seasoned knights being asked to run errands or craft basic potions and oils. Why don't you have some of the knight trainees do this and send me out to patrol instead?"

"Because I have chosen you to do it; now you may choose to further stray from the path of your knighthood or you can accept this duty assigned to you, which will it be?"

"I'll go to the lab and do as you require of me."

"Good, be sure to report back before the day's final formation. I would like you to help me."

"It will be done," Volir said as he took the jar and placed it back into his hide bag. He turned around, taking a final glance at Ol'nar, who continued to stare at him with piercing eyes, before proceeding out the door and across the empty courtyard.

Before he reached the order's gateway, he arrived at his destination. There, just on the right was the lab. He entered and could see the apothecary was empty, the solitude of the laboratory quite inviting. He signaled to the sleeping cats in his pouches, but they were both quite content to remain asleep, leaving him to begin working on the potions and oil.

Around the alchemy laboratory were flasks and bottles of all shapes and sizes. Under each neatly aligned table were the tools needed to craft potions and elixirs of every variety. Volir walked through the aisle lined by rows of tables to cross the room. He removed the herbs from the preserving jar and unwrapped them from their individual packaging. He placed the herbs into the corresponding preserving jars, holding back a small amount to make the potions and oils for the day's exercise.

He took a seat at one of the tables and got to work using the alchemical equipment to prepare the radiant distilled water needed for the potions. At the same time, he crushed up the different herbs with a mortar and pestle before he used the vials available to mix them. It wasn't long before he had created the radiant potions and cinder oils, never even waking the two companions asleep in his pouches.

From behind him, Volir could hear the knights walking past the door, making their way to gather in the courtyard. Many of them had been passing by the alchemy lab while he was hard at work. He could also feel that his cats were waking up from their cozy naps in his pouches. As such, they both peeked their tiny heads out and began purring. Sensing this, Volir looked down at each of them with a greeting. "Hello, my friends; I take it you've slept well."

Both cats responded with purring which told him they were very pleased. "Alright then, let's get to it," he said as he rubbed them both across the sides of their faces.

Volir hastened out of the apothecary and headed toward the gathering of knights. As he passed them, he noticed their gaze fixed on him. He sometimes caught these kinds of looks and wondered if it was because

Valothas always used him as an example in lessons or because he had been a knight for so long and had not yet been chosen by a phoenix. Upon entering Valothas's chamber, he once again caught Ol'nar's inquisitive eyes. Volir could see that Valothas was getting ready to leave, and it was quite time, too, for the knights awaited him outside.

"Volir, always arriving at the anticipated moment," Valothas said.

"So it seems; here are the potions and oils," Volir replied, placing the glowing amber potions and clear oil on the desk.

"Well done. Now let's get to the demonstration," Valothas said, motioning to the doorway.

"As you command," Volir said. Still aware of Ol'nar's gaze, Volir turned and exited the leader's chamber and walked to his usual place in the knights' formation. As he did so, Volir commanded his two cats to find their place above the courtyard. Angor and Siam leaped out of the comfy pouches and ran up the stairs to find their places for the second time that day.

As Valothas walked out in front of the knights, he raised his right arm, pounding his fist onto his chest with a clash of metal resounding from his breastplate. "Knights, converge," he commanded.

Valothas began pacing back and forth across the front of the formation. As he did, his phoenix, Ol'nar, flew down and landed on his right pauldron. "Knights, there are several of you who haven't yet experienced the use of cinder oil or radiant potions. Yes, you likely know of them and what we use them for, but knowing and experiencing their benefits are quite different things altogether. When cinder oil is applied to our swords, it increases the power of their flames alone by tenfold. Respectively, when a knight drinks a radiant potion prior to casting their solar shields, they are capable of strengthening and enlarging the size of the shields in several different ways. First, the shield's strength can be increased between ten to twenty times. Second, if the shield is enlarged to twice its normal size, the strength of the shield usually remains the same, but it gains a much greater range of protection. If multiple knights create a solar shield wall, their shields can unify much like our display this morning. However, the size of the shield unified remains the same, but with greater strength and cohesion."

As Valothas continued to walk across the formation's front, he stopped and gazed upon the knights once more. "Very well, knights. Leavesa, Volir, Tarothas, Syvon, and Vael, in our first round, you will attempt to take down my shield. Douse your blades with cinder oil and prepare yourselves. Knights, form a circle around the outside of the courtyard," he said.

Valothas smiled at Volir and his fellow knights. "You five, gather a formation across from me. Prepare yourselves," Valothas said as he pulled out his radiant potion and drank it until it was completely empty. Ol'nar flew away from Valothas up into the air above him. Valothas tucked away one vial of cinder oil into his belt pouch and threw the bag of potions and oils at Volir. As he did so, he uttered one word, which he expected only Volir would hear. "Lead."

Volir, having heard this, was not welcoming of the command. Still, he distributed the oils and potions to Leavesa and the other knights. "Potions and oil, let's try and catch him by surprise. I don't want to let him show us up again," he said.

Leavesa nodded without confidence. "What's the plan?" she questioned as she passed out the potions to the others.

"I'm going to force him to turn his shield to me and put pressure on him. He can't cover two sides at once. When you find the opening, disarm him," Volir said.

"We'll see it done, but you know he's not going to let us win that easily," Leavesa said.

"I know," Volir said. "We'll have to move fast but we can do it. Let's prepare ourselves."

As Volir saw agreement from the knights, they all began to apply the cinder oil to their swords and ignited them using their fire magic. The flames burned brighter than usual and created a bright white color akin to peering into the suns.

"Knights, take down my shield," Valothas shouted as he raised his left fist to reveal a glowing light that grew outward from his hand and across his forearm to his shoulder. His glowing solar shield disk glowed quite bright before them and behind it he was obscured. He did not draw his sword yet, much to the surprise of the new knight recruits who were watching with all their being focused on the elder knight.

Volir pointed his flaming sword at Valothas. "With me," he shouted as he began charging toward the leader of their order. Leavesa and the rest of the knights followed along and charged toward Valothas. Volir, now nearing the elder knight, slid close to the ground past Valothas who he believed would soon be surprised by the others. Volir came to a stop behind Valothas as the knights closed in from the other side. He then swung his blade at a distance, sending blistering arches of flame spiraling toward Valothas.

The elder knight made the quick adjustment, turning toward Volir in order to protect himself from the blasts of fire. As Valothas absorbed and deflected the flame blasts, Volir moved to place more pressure upon Valothas's shield and charged toward him, delivering one devastating blow after another. From around him, Volir could hear the new knight recruits begin to cheer as the time to strike came for Leavesa and the rest of the knights. As Valothas looked toward the knights approaching, he pushed Volir back with his solar shield and turned toward the others.

Volir looked up to see Valothas turn toward the knights and pull his sword out, clashing it onto his empowered shield, which caused a blinding flash, disorienting the knights as they approached him.

Volir sought out the fastest way to stop Valothas and leapt into the air above the leader bringing down his sword with all his might, taking full advantage of the distraction the knights had provided for him. As his sword met the solar shield of the elder knight, a flash of flames burst forth, knocking Valothas to the ground and leaving Volir standing above him, his sword pointed down at the fallen leader.

The knights surrounding the scene began to cheer; Leavesa, Tarothas, and Syvon joined in while Vael smiled smugly. Valothas let out a chuckle as Volir raised out his hand to offer aid off the ground. As the elder knight accepted his hand and rose up, he muttered, "Well done, Volir." He turned his attention back to the surrounding knights in observance before addressing them.

"That's right, knights. Even with your solar shields supported by alchemical means, it is still possible to be overwhelmed by the unexpected.

Even the greatest leaders can fall to the might of another. Your fellow knights showed you one way to exploit my weakness but was it the best way? One could critique that it might have been wiser for Volir to sacrifice himself instead of his fellow knights to achieve the same victory. Unfortunately, that was not the display you stood witness to today." Valothas had a hint of laughter in his voice as he dusted himself off and centered himself within the knight's circle.

Many of the new recruits were applauding the elder knight for his wisdom while others were celebrating that Volir and his team had succeeded in disarming Valothas. He continued, "Now gather up, and prepare yourselves for my attack, defend yourselves and show everyone the strength of your defenses unified." Valothas walked to the center of the courtyard where he coated his cinder sword in oil, igniting it in a brilliant flame.

Volir stood stoic, unaffected by the words of Valothas. The knights around him seemed impressed by how quickly he'd used his powerful attack to disarm the elder knight. Volir could sense the affirmations of his fellow knights as he adjusted his hood, preparing for the next task at hand. He walked back toward the knights assigned to him, who were now back on their feet and looking at him, their expressions questioning.

As Volir gathered with the knights, he pulled out the radiant potion and drank the entire vial. His fellow knights did the same and with the knights now prepared, Volir gave his command. "This time, we'll focus on bolstering our shields and deflecting any of his attacks. Keep your footing, and I will call for a change in position if needed," he said. The knights only nodded their heads, though their confidence in his plan seemed to wane.

"Incoming," Valothas shouted as he began to sling balls of fire from his sword toward the knights in a relentless barrage. Each hurling flame exploded upon the knights' shields, which had immediately gone up and began merging together.

The knights continued to withstand the flames, but before they could consider their next move, and after enduring so many of Valothas's fire barrages, the knight leader surprised them with an unexpected display of strength. Cutting through the very flames he had been unleashing at them, Valothas launched himself into the air with his cinder sword raised over his head, ready to strike. None of the knights seemed concerned as they all stood united with their shields, as Volir had instructed. Even with his cinder sword imbued with the increased magic from the cinder oil, it was inconceivable to Volir that his sword strike would make a difference to them in their defensive state.

As Valothas brought his arching sword swing from over his head and down upon them, his phoenix flew down from the sky, meeting his sword as it made contact with their unified shield. What happened next was a brilliant display from the leader of their order, who, in an explosion of light, destroyed the knights' shield, knocking them to the ground once more.

The knights, bewildered, picked themselves back up, and in admiration, both Tarothas and Vael cheered for their leader and his display. Volir stood up, unfaltering in his stoic expression, and said nothing, while several of the knights watching looked toward him with a disapproving expression.

"Well, I knew he'd have a surprise for us," Leavesa said.

Volir sighed as Valothas stepped toward him and the others, motioning for the rest of the knights to come closer as he stood before them. "Gather around everyone, closer...yes, good. You've seen today how well the radiant potions and cinder oil can aid you in battle, but you also saw how important coordination is and what can happen when you lead without considering all the possibilities. Even the best and strongest among us can lose sight of the other possibilities in battle with all that unfolds before us so quickly," he said, snapping his finger. "Just like that, everything can change. It's your duty to be among those who don't lose sight of the different possibilities and maintain a watchful eye for all things which are unexpected by others. With that as your lesson, those of you on duty tonight, report for your assignments. Until dawn. Have a good evening."

After the demonstration, some of the knights gathered to chat, while others were off to their duty. Some of the new recruits approached the elder knight with questions about the skills they had seen on display. Leavesa looked to Volir for any reaction, but once again, he remained unmoved. As she turned to walk away with several of the others, Volir reflected on how many of these displays could be eliminated if he were to be chosen by a phoenix himself. Those with phoenixes never were selected to perform in front of the others.

Volir also truly believed that if he had not had these other knights with him during the combat scenario, he would have been more focused on his goal and better capable of succeeding. Valothas spoke of sacrifice, but to Volir, the lesson's only result was a bruised ego—a shameful reminder as to the cost of showboating for some new recruits.

Volir's frustrated thoughts were soon interrupted by the sound of flapping wings overhead. There above him was one of the avolan messengers, who appeared quite exhausted, almost collapsing as his legs met the ground. Avolans were similar to humans but they held many features akin to the birds of prey across the world. Their fingers were like falcon talons, as were their toes. Their wings spread out wide from their spine, the only part of their body where large, tough feathers were present. Their smooth flat down feathers flowed flat across their bodies and across their faces. The down sprouted from behind their beaked mouths and across their faces, leading into the hair upon their heads.

Avolans were the only avian race of people and held dominion over much of the sky, often aiding others across the world in delivering news throughout the lands with great haste. As such, many of the avolans served as messengers between different regions and even several kingdoms within the various realms of the world. They were known for being capable of traveling great distances unmatched by most other methods. What often would take land dwellers days to travel would only take an avolan a single day.

The avolan who brought news today was known to Volir as the messenger Feycir, who often traveled between several of the Aurodite academies and strongholds of the northern regions to many of the eastern coastal areas of the continent. Feycir was an elder avolan with gray and white feathers, a white beak, yellow eyes, and dark gray claws on both his hands and feet. He was a frequent visitor to the city of Valenthreas and had been dedicated to his carrier routes for many years.

As Volir could see that the avolan was having trouble standing, he darted over to aid him. "Feycir, are you alright?" Volir asked.

"I'm so tired, I came as fast as I could," Feycir said, still breathing heavily.

"Feycir, what news do you bring, old friend?" Valothas asked as he too moved to aid the avolan, extending his arm to help hold him up.

Feycir accepted both Valothas and Volir's aid. "Thank you, both; I bring grave news. I have flown all day from the hidden coast where three surviving Aurodite magi arrived early this morning. They traveled from Illonel, and they arrived through some old hidden tunnels. Their leader commanded that I only deliver the news to you, Valothas," he said as he struggled to catch his breath.

"Yes, please relay the message, old friend," Valothas said as he beckoned another knight. "Eyvris, quickly bring water for our friend."

"Thank you, Valothas. The Aurodite leader arrived from Illonel this morning. She brings urgent news about Prince Drazius Khorvek. I'm afraid only she and two other Aurodite magi survived. They said they witnessed Prince Khorvek slaughter the other Aurodites. They overheard the prince's plans through a hidden place below the spire as the stronghold fell. She sent me to tell you that the prince has a plan to siege Valenthreas and requests the knights meet her at the hidden coast," Feycir said taking the water brought to him by the knights.

"She? The archmagus is the leader of the Aurodites of Illonel. Who's this magi that sends word?" Valothas asked.

"She's Lady Anaryen Valenvon of the kingdom of Valaryen in Eden Throvon. The lady was at Illonel when it fell and was urged to escape by the archmagus," Feycir said.

"This is very troubling news. Thank you Feycir, rest until you are strong again. I'm sure we'll need your aid again soon. Until then, I'll share this news with the stewards. We must aid the lady," Valothas said.

Volir guided Feycir to a stone bench against the wall next to the stairs. There he could see Valothas walking up to the second level of the order's walls toward the overview. Volir walked up following him, curious about what plans the elder knight would make to aid the lady and the Aurodites who accompanied her.

As Volir followed Valothas, his two cats joined him and leapt up his leg into their pouches. Walking up to the top of the stairs, he continued until he was on the top level looking out over the city to the west where he could see the suns lowering closer toward the horizon. This could be one of the last suns setting over a calm day—the last hint of peace for some time. He could sense something different in the light, overwhelming him in a way he couldn't make sense of.

After several minutes, Volir walked over to the eastern side of the wall, which stretched above the knight's order hall. Valothas was looking off toward the direction of the hidden coast, across the easternmost side of the realm.

He stepped up next to Valothas, overly curious about what he might have planned. "Valothas, I'd be happy to go look for this prince. I could seek him out, locate where he is. Maybe then we could learn more about the army he leads and—"

"You should focus on the instructions you are given and honor your responsibilities instead of investing energy in your own self-interest," Valothas said.

Volir paused for a moment, almost feeling scolded, a feeling he knew only from his father. "I know I frustrate you, but I can sense something is shifting, I can't just stand by knowing this prince is marching upon our city. I could go tonight," he said.

"Wait until morning; for now, you will honor my command. There is much to be done, and this is bigger than you or I yet know, Volir."

"Very well, Valothas."

"Good, now you should get some rest. Something tells me by dawn, every one of us will need it," Valothas said as he began walking away.

Volir was frustrated, but he had too much respect for the elder knight to disobey his command. He knew that whatever was coming, Valothas would need him one way or another. As he stood there above the city, high upon the outer wall of the knight's order, he turned his gaze away from the east and up toward the north. At the base of the mountain, the tower of Avestan rose high, as if watching over the city. He wondered again about the rumors of the sage: was he up there now? Did he know of the darkness taking seed at this very moment?

CHAPTER 4

LEGACY LOST

Drazius Khorvek slowed his horse, guiding it toward the top of the last cliff of the mountains through which he and his soldiers had been traveling. As he gazed down toward the flowing river below, he could see the bridge that served as the gateway into the elven realm of Aurotheros. Welcoming to all who wished to enter their realm, the elves served to help guide and protect the other races of Auro, directing the way of ascendency and honoring the gods—something the prince had come to despise.

At the prince's side, Griles rode sitting straight upon his black horse, taking his helmet off to reveal his thick white hair, combed back and tucked behind his ears. He had scars on his long, weathered face, and pale blue eyes with thin, straight eyebrows. As he watched below, his face was contorted by the strong grimace he wore. The twisted expression forced his eyes to bulge under the pressure of his brow as he snarled in silence like a rabid dog. He hated the elves in the watchtower at the bridge down below and was eagerly gripping his sword as he readied himself for the opportunity to slay them.

Griles was well known for being prejudiced toward the elves and despised elves with a fierceness that most of the soldiers couldn't appreciate until now. With Drazius's dark crusade at hand many of the soldiers in the prince's army developed the same type of prejudice and hatred of the elves, a far cry from the type of adoration and reverence most humans had long held toward them.

To the prince's other side, riding a mottled horse, was Holcurt, who had bushy, red eyebrows and a red, shaggy beard to match. He had green bloodshot eyes and rode heavy on his horse, which seemed to be strained by the weight upon its back. He was a large man, and while much of his size was from being quite muscular, it was also because of his weight; he was known for his frequent overindulgence in food, drink, and women. Many often remarked it wouldn't be battle that would lead to his death but the wrong night with the wrong woman at a tavern.

As his two commanders closed in by his sides, Drazius pointed down below with his polearm. "Look there, Griles, the first of many elves you'll watch die."

"Yes, my prince, I'm ready. Just give me the order, and it's done," Griles said as he clenched his weapon tighter, eager to lead the charge.

"As dedicated as you are, these elves will not die by your hand or by our men tonight," Drazius said.

"Then who will kill them, my prince? I don't understand," Griles asked, sounding heartbroken.

"The drothkin," Drazius said. He made sure to observe both Griles and Holcurt carefully, curious how they would respond.

"Drothkin," Griles and Holcurt spoke together, seeming puzzled by this statement.

"You heard me," Drazius said. Then he said something neither of the commanders would have expected to hear from his mouth. "Five thousand drothkin should be here soon. When they arrive, they will follow my commands, and with their numbers, we will have nearly nine thousand troops to roll over whatever we choose."

"But how can you command the drothkin?" Griles asked. "Only Grindam led those soulless creatures; no human has ever led the drothkin. I don't see how you could be capable of such a thing."

"You sound as if you doubt me Griles," Drazius said. "I'll control them the same way I control the gloomveil that shrouds us here. Through the will of my master, I control more than you can understand," Drazius replied. The prince's eyes dimmed to a misty dark blackness that seemed to terrify Griles, nearly causing him to fall off his horse.

"Of course, my prince, sorry," Griles said, petrified at the sight of Drazius, whose rage seemed to be secured by the darkness around him.

At that moment, the army of drothkin could be seen down below at the base of the mountain where the prince and his army remained perched. At the head of the drothkin army was an unknown alpha— the perfect example of what a drothkin was meant to be. It had every look about it, an ideal example fashioned in the way of its maker. In fact, it was much larger than any of the other drothkin it led as it fiercely charged ahead of the others on all fours before slowing abruptly and rising to stand upon its back two legs. As it did so, it towered far over the other drothkin and howled fiercely in its mangled wolfen tone signifying its authority and instruction to stop. The alpha would very soon tower over the soldiers in the prince's army even; it looked up toward them, bearing its large dripping fangs as it hissed.

The drothkin were created long ago as an act of defiance toward the Twin Flames through the empyreal flames of Ohrimah and Anieva. The two Masters used some of the wulvor creatures as a template to birth some of the monstrosities that now roamed the world. The wulvor were made by Masters Vorlah and Thaesa, to serve as guardians of the sacred Aeth'Quelinth Forest which stretched far beyond the western borders of the elven realm. The drothkin were a far cry from the wulvor creatures which could communicate with the people of the planet. The aspects of kindness and protection which the wulvor embodied were stripped away and replaced by the cold reptilian nature of predators without a care for life, a mockery set to insult the Twin Flames.

The drothkin had evolved over time to have scales instead of fur and hair across the majority of their bodies. They bore sharp horns, venomous saliva, and much larger ears than their wolf-like counterparts, the wulvor. They also had chitinous armored regions on their chest and back, parts of their legs and arms, and their tail was barbed with a venomous tip. Worst of all, they devoured those they killed in battle.

There were no further words from Griles or Holcurt, who watched as the dark prince nodded down toward the drothkin alpha, somehow communicating with it and guiding its instructions to the others in the bestial army. The drothkin let out a horrific screeching roar, leading their army toward the bridge before entering the tower where the elves within were sure to be consumed after their demise.

Drazius was pleased at the display and, with the overwhelming numbers he now had at his command, issued his orders leading his army's descent down the mountain. "I hope the drothkin enjoy what little feast they will get from the elves down below," he said. "We will move down to meet them—come now."

"Yes, my liege," Holcurt said.

"Any who could aid the city of Valenthreas must be destroyed, and I'm sure the drothkin would enjoy any hefty feast they can get. Illonel was nothing compared to what the elves have coming to them. Move now, for night is soon to come," Drazius said.

Evening had only just begun and the city of Valenthreas was starting to glow in the beauty of nightfall. The city's buildings were illuminated with light, as were the outskirts that stretched seamlessly into the land surrounding it. Between the light of the moons, the ambient light glowing from the plants, and the reflecting shine off the white walls of the city, it certainly lived up to its name as the city of light. Volir was almost home, and running close by were his two small companions, intent on accompanying him tonight. The two felines enjoyed being outside at night, finding it to be the perfect playground.

Upon arriving at the door of his quarters, Volir waited as Angor and Siam walked through the door. As he entered, he looked down to see that Siam had a small piece of rolled-up parchment in his mouth that he was carrying like a toy. After shutting the door, he lit the candle on the wall next to him and moved to light the rest throughout his room. He could see Siam looking up at him from the center of the room where he was now sitting. Volir hastily threw a piece of wood into the fireplace and used a quick spell, lighting it on fire. As he walked over to Siam, the cat dropped the piece of paper and ran off to play with Angor. Volir sat down in the chair at his table and began reading the note.

The world is in flux and I know you sense it too. It's time we have a meeting that's been long overdue. Your mask must be shed, and you'll need to face your truth. I have information that you may want to know about your parents. If you wish to learn what that is then meet me at the Sleepy Gryphon at nightfall. Choose a table and I'll find you.

Volir looked down at Siam bewildered. "Now, who gave this to you, my little friend? How is it I didn't notice you were carrying this?" His cat looked up at him and responded with a purr. Volir laughed in response to his expression but nothing could distract him from how alarmed he felt now. It was near impossible that someone knew who he was; he'd worked so hard to conceal it. He knew he never slipped up once since he had joined the Knights of the Phoenix. There was no way he could think of that anyone would know his true identity; if even one person knew his name, then all the years invested as a knight of his order would be in vain. Not only was he confused and frustrated by this letter, but what was worse was how vulnerable and exposed he felt as a result. He knew he would have to meet with this mysterious messenger and seek an answer to the cryptic message.

As Volir sat stunned, he thought to play with Angor and Siam using the ball of string he received as a gift from Deklain earlier that day. He had less than an hour before he would meet the mystery being at the Sleepy Gryphon, and he knew he would need to be cautious. He had no way of knowing who the message was from or what their motives might be.

At the peak of nightfall, Volir arrived outside the Sleepy Gryphon, having left both of his small companions back in his quarters. He wore his twin quill cloak but had changed into plain clothes, now only wearing a long red shirt with black pants and his usual belt. He had on reinforced leather boots that made up the perfect ensemble for the cool of that night.

Inside the inn, Volir could hear the beautiful music of the odist Mina, who had returned for the night, singing her songs by the bar. As Volir entered the tavern, he was hardly noticed by anyone and carefully made his way to the back and center of the tavern. He passed the bar while breathing in the fragrant scent of the different drinks on his way to the back corner to the far right.

Volir sat down at the furthest table from the bar, where he could observe patrons who were laughing and drinking, while others were playing the favored card game known as embri. Being away from most of the patrons seemed like the best decision, for he had no idea what to expect from the person he'd be meeting. It wasn't long after Volir had taken a seat before the human barmaid arrived to serve him.

"What'll it be, darlin'?"

"A frosted brew, thank you," Volir said. He kept his head down low as he placed a gold coin down on the table and slid it toward her with a nod. "The rest is for you."

"Oh, thank you…and so generous. I'll be right back with that brew, darlin'."

As the barmaid walked away, Volir glanced from under his hood. He saw there was nothing out of the ordinary. Many of the patrons were familiar faces who visited the Sleepy Gryphon on any of the nights he had been there. The usual city guards were there, relaxing after their shifts, and he even saw a couple of knights from his order talking with some of the new recruits. The tavern wasn't like many of those one would see across the elven lands or in the other realms. Everything here was pristine, tidy, and clean. Volir had only glanced off toward the bar for a moment before hearing a noise at his table. As he looked back, there sitting in front of him on the opposite chair was a nayran.

Volir was quite surprised by this, as most of the nayran race stayed in their woods or schools and rarely were seen in such busy places. As the beastial children of the wood, nayrans were found anywhere a large forest rose and it was rare to not find their people settled there in some capacity. Being beastly themselves, the nayrans held a close bond with all creatures of the world, aside from those created by the dark master.

As this nayran sat in the chair, he was no taller than a human child of five or six years. He was wearing green and brown scholar's clothes, with leather gloves and boots. He had dark brown hair and his furry, floppy ears were tucked under his green hood. He had a nose like a cat, with small fangs that could be seen protruding only slightly from his mouth. His eyes were orange, but as Volir looked over his face and head, he could see that this nayran had no horns or antlers visible.

"A nayran? You seem to be missing something important for one of your kind," Volir said, pointing toward the top of the nayran's head.

"Ay, well, they're not missing, I file my antlers. It makes it easier to wear all sorts of clothes this way. I'm called Kayris. I bring warm tidings from Armatay of Avestan."

"The sage? What of his message?" Volir asked.

"Ay, oh yes, well…I've been instructed to tell you where to meet later tonight in two hours' time. En, if you'd like answers, then you'll need to come with me to Avestan. The sage assures me your questions will be answered then. En, I have transportation to get us there quite fast, so yes, two hours, and we meet at the center of the Vaelothi Gardens. There at the big tree before the doorway of the spire, yes."

"What is a nayran doing serving the sage of the tower?"

"Ay, I don't serve him, we serve together, and most proudly I do. So…tonight then?"

As Volir was about to respond, he looked up across the tavern to see two knights from his order looking toward him with a confused expression on their faces. When Volir looked back to where the nayran was sitting, it seemed that he had just vanished. As the patrons at the front of the tavern began laughing, Volir realized it appeared he was sitting in the corner talking to himself, one more reason for people to gossip about him.

"A frosted brew as requested, darlin'," the barmaid said, catching Volir by surprise.

"Thank you. Did you, by chance, happen to see a nayran sitting across from me in this chair?"

"A nayran, darlin'? Well, I wasn't watching the whole time, but no, I saw only you."

"Never mind then, thank you," Volir said, now eyeing the cold perspiring drink before him.

As he sat there enjoying the frosted brew, he settled into the state of shock he was experiencing. All this gossip floating around the city about the sage and now he was contacting Volir directly. While he was curious about what the sage had to say to him, he was also growing concerned that he may know the truth about him, too. His eagerness to learn what the sage knew grew exponentially by the second. The cryptic message about knowing who he really was couldn't be ignored, and deep down, he wondered if there was more—he could learn of his parents' death. For there was a great deal of mystery surrounding the final moments when they met their demise. He was unsure whether he wanted to know the answers but before he could give it more thought, Volir heard Mina begin singing her song, The Lights of Va'Threas.

The lights of Va'Threas
How we love you always
Your brilliance and glory
Though sacrifice was your way
Never forgotten, our dear teachers
Forever honored and mourned

Va'Threas, Va'Threas, you guide our souls
Va'Threas, Va'Threas, with the light you hold
The Dahaka came, blotting out both the suns
With devotion and duty, you kept our world safe

The lights of Va'Threas
How we love you always
Your legacy and compassion
Brought an end to dark days
Never forgotten, our dear teachers
Forever honored and mourned

Va'Threas, Guiding Light
Your brilliance shines forever bright
Your sacrifice, noble and true
Teachers and guardians, we honor you

Va'Threas, Va'Threas, your light guides our souls
Through dark days and trials, your strength consoles
When the Dahaka came, both flames blotted out
Your devotion and duty kept our world from doubt

The legacy of Va'Threas
Endures with compassion and grace
Your teachings and wisdom
Bring light to the darkest place

Never forgotten, always revered
You are the guardians we hold dear
Va'Threas, Guiding Light
Your brilliance shines forever bright.

The song was a solemn one upon Volir's ears, and as he finished his drink, he knew he had less than two hours before he was going to meet with the sage. Unsure of when he would be back home that night, he thought it best to bring his two companions with him. To him, the nayran seemed harmless enough, and the sage was a revered advisor of the stewards of Valenthreas. Despite the rumors about the sage, Volir had never believed them to be true. It was mostly the gossip of the city's visitors who would speak ill of the sage, questioning his intentions toward the people of the city with some suggesting he was there to deceive the elves, harboring dark intentions.

With many of the recent events in the human realms, the rumors seemed to be magnified. The people questioned whether or not the sage was there in service of or to undermine what the Twin Flames had left the elves to protect. For the elves who resided in the great spire of Valenthreas, there was little question about the trustworthiness of the sage; Volir shared the same belief that the sage was there with good purpose.

Volir also knew that the sage had come into the service of the stewards around the same time he himself had come to the city to serve the realm as a knight.

The time would soon come for Volir to meet with the nayran and travel to see the sage. As he stood up and walked through the tavern, he felt odd, as if he was being watched, but he knew it was probably just because of the song. Mina's music always had an impact on him after all, and as he exited the tavern, he quickly put the thoughts out of his mind.

Volir had wasted no time returning to his quarters to retrieve his small friends. As he stepped out of his quarters, he inspected Angor and Siam who were now nestled in the pouches on his belt. The two small cats had just finished their evening meal and were content to travel with him once more. Their trust and devotion to Volir was unwavering; they were always happy to go wherever he went, and so their next adventure together was at hand.

Walking through the city streets in the evening was enchanting, and as Volir turned his head toward the center of the city, he gazed at the titanic spire and its connecting towers that rose high into the sky. The spire of Valenthreas, along with the gardens below, were renowned as one of the great wonders of the world. Vines with glowing flowers hung from various parts of the spire, reacting to the magical energy that bathed the land at night under the light of the blue moon, Valos.

Approaching the center of the city, Volir saw the great Morlin Twins high up in the atmosphere. These twin birds, made of pure ethereal energy, were born during the convergence of the two moons only centuries after the Twin Flames left the world. Unlike other creatures born during a convergence, the Morlin Twins had no offspring and were some of the earliest auvinots to come into being. They traversed the highest reaches of the world, bound between the stars and the sky, and were so large they covered the majority of the visible night sky directly above the city. Their songs, which could be felt, though unheard on the ground, produced a calming effect that brought a great sense of peace and joy to those lucky enough to be in their presence.

Passing by the order hall, Volir entered the Vaelothi Gardens that opened up ahead of him. The gardens spread directly around the great spire and its towers. The center ring, as it was often referred to, was just ahead of him, and beyond that were the large gateway doors leading into the elven spire, a place Volir had not visited in so very long.

The garden stretched out around him, pulsing under the lights in the night sky. While Ailos shone in a warm gold, it was the crystalline moon, Valos, that radiated the magical light that nearly all plants, trees, and many creatures responded to. The realm now glowed in ambient colors, revealing the wonder of the unseen world and the magic infused into the planet. Valos itself was a beacon of high magical energy, formed by the gods to bathe the planet in the Essa, reminding all to cherish and love the world, its life, and its people.

As Volir walked toward the central part of the outer garden ring, he saw one of the largest trees in the city standing between him and the spire. The tree was quite tall, and its branches stretched out far and wide, forming a brilliant canopy of glowing arches, which spread outward from the tree into the garden on either side. As he walked underneath the great tree, a glowing, blue, humming sprite came flying by, and for a moment, it hovered in front of him as if to inspect him. It didn't linger long and ended up buzzing away just as Angor took a swipe at it from inside of Volir's pouch, leaving only a trail of blue and gold star dust behind. Volir looked down and started laughing before being interrupted by a voice calling out to him.

"Ay, so the knight does laugh after all," Kayris said as he looked down toward Volir and his pets from atop one of the branches of the large tree.

"I have my moments," Volir replied, snapping to his more guarded demeanor. "So how do you intend for us to reach Avestan so quickly?"

"Ay, and an enchanting evening it is, eh? Valos does show us just how beautiful our world is. En, I will have that fun surprise for you soon. Eh, knight Volir."

Kayris scampered down the trunk of the tree and walked several steps toward Volir, who was eyeing the nayran suspiciously until Kayris laughed and returned a curious look. "Ay, I see you hid those eyes of yours even from the likes of me down below. En, I must say you do a good job of it…Who are these cute little creatures?" The nayran began to run up to pet the cats whose heads were both sticking out of Volir's pouches.

"Not too close," Volir said as he took a step back instinctively to guard his two cats.

The nayran's curious and joyful expression quickly turned to that of bewilderment as he paused. "Ay, I meant no offense, forgive me. En, I only wished to greet them and know them better. Surely, you understand as a nayran this is our way."

Kayris was right, and Volir knew it. Nayrans were never known to hurt animals for it was their greatest purpose to bond with nature and the creatures of the world. "Ay, it has been long since I have come across precious ones such as your two friends here. It would bring me such joy if I could say hello to them. With your blessing, of course," Kayris said.

Volir hadn't even given consideration to the nayran as he was so quick to protect his two pets, quick to forget about the nayran traditions of greeting animals as they greeted their own. "Very well, if they will come to you, then you may greet them," Volir said.

"Ay, thank you," Kayris said as he kneeled down before the two animals and greeted them. "Ayo, you are seen young ones, I am Kayris." He lowered his head in a bow close to the ground.

Both Angor and Siam hopped out of Volir's pouches and ran down his legs. As they did so, they both meowed and chattered as they approached the nayran, who was now extending both his hands with the palms facing down to greet them. Both Angor and Siam walked forward, and both rubbed against each of Kayris's arms; Angor even placed his paw on top of one of Kayris's hands.

"Ay, hello Siam, hello Angor. It's so good to know you both. They're both so kind; they care for you very much, you know," Kayris said as he continued to pet both of the cats who were now purring louder and rubbing against him.

Volir looked down unsure of what to say, his mouth revealing his surprise.

"Ay, don't be so shocked, animals know the good ones when they meet them. That's why they care so deeply for you. En, you've been very good to them; they tell me very good things about you. It warms my heart," he said as he stood up looking toward the still knight.

The cats had finished with their introductions and ran back up Volir's legs to find their place in his pouches. Volir could feel them purring and knew they must have really liked Kayris or they wouldn't have behaved in such a way. They were both quite picky about letting others aside from him touch them.

"So, with that out of the way, the sage," Volir said.

"Ay, oh yes."

"I'd like to hear what this sage has to tell me, I'm ready when you are, Kayris."

"Ay, as you are," Kayris said as he placed his thumb and first finger into his mouth and blew out a melody that was more than just a whistle.

Within no time at all, a large volgriff in the colors of amber and brown began gliding down from over the top of the large tree they had been standing underneath. Close behind it was another, which was a bit fluffier around its mane and was black with red highlights at the tips of its fur. Volir was fixated on it.

"Ay, I thought you might like this one; you're free to hop on him when you're ready. En, I favor the other one myself," Kayris said as he climbed up the first volgriff which had just landed.

The volgriffs were much like hippogriffs in that they had large wings, and the majority of their body was structured like a horse. Where they differed was that the volgriff had a head like a horse and wolf, with the front legs also much like a wolf and including the same dangerous claws. The wolf-like coat around their heads extended down over the volgriff's chest. Their tails had large, long feathers similar to phoenixes, and they had many smaller feathers running along their backs, becoming fuller the closer they were to the tail.

While appearing quite ferocious, most volgriffs were very friendly when they became comfortable with others and often have great relationships with anyone who befriend them. Volgriffs reproduce, but like many of the other auvinots, it was rare to find them around a city for they mostly spent their time around mountains or more solitary locations.

As the second Volgriff landed, Volir stepped forward and greeted it with a few strokes upon its mane and whispered, "You are a beauty; hello, friend." As he pulled himself up, he looked to the nayran who had managed his way up the other volgriff with ease.

Volir looked to Kayris who was all smiles. "Ay, yah," he shouted. In an instant, his volgriff began running at a quick speed and flapped its wings gracefully, lifting it and its nayran rider fast into the air. They passed through the large tree branches above and high into the sky, moving quickly out of sight.

A covert smile opened up on Volir's face as he looked toward his pouches. "You two, stay in there and hold on. Yah!"

As his volgriff began running and flapping its wings, Volir was impressed by how fast the auvinot flew up through the large tree branches and high into the sky over the city. The volgriff was marvelous to him—a quick, elated burst of laughter broke through his lips and he looked around at the world below with wide eyes, his hardened demeanor completely broken. As he held onto the red and black mane of the creature, he felt privileged to be riding it.

Volir rose high over the city and was nearly as high as the rising towers and spire of central Valenthreas. As he flew behind Kayris toward the solitary mountain ahead, he took a look down to the dark woods below where the Dahaka had fallen long ago. Over the fallen dragon had grown the dark Dragonstrike Woods. Volir could see where the dragon's claws had torn away at the terrain outside of the city walls and created three great waterfalls that now ran into the river below, reaching toward the border of the dark wood.

Redirecting his attention ahead of him, Volir could see he was fast approaching the high rising tower of Avestan which was halfway up the solitary mountain, Aelinrith. Moving fast to the northeast, he was in awe at the sight of the world glowing under him, illuminated by the light the gods entrusted them with. He felt the Morlin Twins' song, and for a moment, he was completely content high above the world beyond the city and his duty as a knight.

Kayris was already lowering as he flew toward the base of the tower of Avestan. Volir followed along, regaining his focus in preparation for the meeting with the sage—the reason he'd traveled here on this cool evening. Volir dived downward, now with his body close to the volgriff, and felt a sharp pain on his right forearm as he approached the landing where Kayris was now dismounting.

Volir landed and dismounted the Volgriff, which was quick to begin behaving playfully next to the other of its kind. The two seemed to be a pair, a male and a female, content in the service of Avestan.

"Ay, one of your friends made a mess of your arm," Kayris said, pointing to Volir's right arm. "En, I see there's blood."

Volir looked down at his arm to see scratch marks. It appeared that Siam had reached out of the pouch, and tried to hold onto Volir's arm during the descent through the sky, leaving some pretty deep scratches on his arm. "Eh, I think that will certainly leave a mark," he said as he smiled to Siam, who didn't seem to realize he had injured Volir at all.

Volir pulled a cloth from out of his belt and wrapped it around the wound on his arm. As he tied it off, he looked up to see Kayris by the door of the tower. The round tower was massive and made of white stone. As Volir walked up to the door, Kayris opened it and welcomed him inside by pointing through the doorway. Above the doorway on the keystone of the archway was an engraved symbol representing the gods.

Volir entered and made his way down a hall, leading to a large chamber as Kayris closed the door and looked up to him. "Ay, I have served with the sage for many years. Whatever secrets you hold are already known to him. En, it would serve you well to trust your instincts, be open to him. Don't let the scars from your past guide you here like they have out there. The sage knows we're here; he'll be right down."

As Kayris led Volir ahead through the hallway, he knew there was truth and wisdom in what the nayran had to say. The sage likely already knew the truth, and there was no use in hiding it here. Still, there was one thing above all else that he hoped to learn—what did the sage know about his parents' death?

CHAPTER 5

TOWER OF THE SAGE

As Volir took his first steps into the great chamber of Avestan, he felt small within its walls. He looked up at the high, vaulted ceiling with its dark, arching wood beams which held a large chandelier at their center. Most of it was unlit save for several candles which did carry a small flame but hardly put off any light. Across from him was a great fireplace that had gone cold, leaving only embers to release little warmth. Several large wooden chairs were placed before the fireplace, along with a table which held a small candle upon it to light the seating area. On the right side of the chamber, a stone staircase appeared to circle around the tower within the outer wall, leading to the upper levels. On the left side, the wall was almost completely covered in bookcases, which were packed full of books.

Volir walked toward the bookcases and browsed over several different books that caught his attention. Among the books were *Chronicle I of the First Age, The Teachings of the Twin Flames, Ascendency and The Virtues*, and *The War of Strife and Sorrow*.

As Volir continued walking around the great chamber, he paused at the sound of Kayris clearing his throat to speak. "Ay, many of the notable mysteries of the world can be researched in this very room. En, I would even say it is close in knowledge to the library of Valenthreas."

As Volir was listening to Kayris, he looked across the chamber toward the opposite side of the room and saw an aura of white light slowly making its way to the bottom of the staircase. As Volir continued to watch the light, Kayris became silent and lowered his head in respect. Both Volir and Kayris gazed at the stairs to find the light slowly dimming until the sage became visible. As he stepped off the final stair, the light that had been somewhere up the stairs only a moment earlier was gone, and now only the wise man stood before them.

The sage stood tall wearing a dark grey robe with a pointed toppled hat of the same color. He appeared to be human, yet he was the same height as Volir and emanated a youthful energy despite his aged appearance. Under his toppled hat flowed long, light grey hair that appeared wavy and ran down just below his shoulders. His eyes were pale blue, and his eyebrows were thick and bushy, darker grey than the rest of his hair. He had a long, flowing beard that stretched down just below his chest with braids hanging down from the top of his beard and from in front of his ears. He wore a dark yellow sash embroidered with symbols depicting the Twin Flames and the eight Masters around his waist. Around his neck hung a pendant depicting two suns overlapping, and on his hand, he wore a ring with a symbol of a singular golden flame.

"Greetings, Volir. I am Armatay, the keeper of Avestan, and I am honored that you accepted my invitation," he said, smiling warmly.

Volir was just about to speak when Armatay spoke again.

"That is what you have called yourself for the past five hundred years. But now that you know my name, perhaps you will allow me to call you by that which you were given, Lord Aurotos Va'Threas, the Last Light of Auro."

"So, you do know...I accept your welcome, Armatay," Aurotos said, dropping the cloak from over his head to reveal his two golden eyes, which glowed bright in the dimly lit chamber. "How is it that you came to know my identity? You must know how cautious I've been to guard my true self from others."

"Oh yes, you have been very cautious..." Armatay continued as he glanced down into Aurotos's pouches, where both cats' heads were sticking out, intently staring toward him. With childlike laughter, the sage pointed to the cats and inquired, "Who might these two precious creatures be?"

"This is Angor and this is Siam," Aurotos said as he motioned to each cat, who seemed mesmerized by the sage and focused on him in a way Aurotos had never seen before.

Armatay laughed at the cats and then glanced over at Kayris. "Thank you, Kayris, for guiding Aurotos to Avestan. I am ever grateful for your help. Now go, enjoy some time to yourself, my young friend; I would like to speak with Lord Aurotos in private."

"Ay, Armatay. I will rekindle the fire and be right here if you need me," Kayris said, lowering his head cheerfully. Then he bowed even lower toward Aurotos as he excused himself to attend to the fire.

"Aurotos, would you follow me to the top of the tower? There is something I wish for you to see, and there is much for us to discuss." Armatay extended his arm from under his large grey cape and pointed toward the stairs.

Aurotos looked at the sage and nodded. "Yes, I want to hear why I'm here; I don't expect it was just because you knew my identity. Lead the way, Armatay," he said, catching the rich aroma of pipe herb upon the sage whom he moved closer to.

"It's quite a risk to conceal your identity for so long under the nose of your fellow knights and people of this city. One might wonder if a part of you wished to be found. Of course, it would be a shock for your people to learn that the son of Vorthelos and Eilendrei is still alive."

"The elven realm has prospered well under the stewards. Ethlain and Evolin have honored my parents and done their duty well; the realm is in no need of an Auron king."

"Is it not? Your parents were born of the Twin Flames and you exist as a guide for all life across Auro. Your decision to turn away from the throne after losing them changes nothing. It is not only the elven people who need you, but the world. The light of creation burns within you, and I can see their light in your eyes looking back at me now."

Aurotos looked down at the winding steps they were walking upon and remained silent as they continued toward the top of the tower. As the clacking of his feet continued, he wondered what more the sage could know. After a moment of silence, he asked the thing he had been wondering the most. "You said you had information about my parents; what more is there to know?"

"Yes, they were among those who passed in the Dahaka's great onslaught, but you also remember that all manner of evil had been led to attack the city by the dark orc himself."

"Grindam, the foul servant of Merdah, but it was Merdah's partner Anieva who created that beast."

"Indeed. You also remember that the elven lands were targeted, along with many of the sacred places of the world that lay between the frozen north and your homeland."

"I do, but what are you getting at?"

"Aurotos, the dark master wished to destroy everything that gave the world hope. Anything that could serve to remind the people of the Twin Flames was to be destroyed. The singular example of the gods wasn't the city."

"You mean to say that it wasn't Valenthreas he wished to destroy, it was my parents?"

"Yes, Ohrimah wished for the people of Valenthreas and the world to serve him. Your parents were the first two created in the light and by the light of the Twin Flames. They were of the gods, and he could not allow them to reign. They were the primary target in the great war, and when the Dahaka attacked the city, Grindam drew them out. He was there to see the Dahaka deliver them to their deaths."

Aurotos was unsettled by this information about how his parents had died. He knew they died defending the city, and that his parents had been pronounced dead, but to hear that they were the ultimate target of the dark master was very troubling. He understood this meant that the plans of the dark orc had ultimately succeeded. In the time since the great war, it was always believed that the great sacrifice of his parents and many of those who fought to defend the realm had been the reason the city was still standing.

To the misfortune of Grindam, when the Dahaka fell, it landed on much of the enemy army, crushing them under it as it lay dying out-side the city of Valenthreas. The dark orc was never seen again and was believed to have died when the Dahaka fell. Most of the enemy army that remained alive were soon vanquished thereafter by the defenders of the city and their allies. Though Aurotos was struck with grief losing his parents, many believed they fell with the Dahaka, for it was in the moment of the Dahaka's defeat that they were last seen.

What little semblance of solace Aurotos had about the past had become more shaken than ever after hearing what the sage had to share. "If my parents were targeted then why not me? Why leave me alive if they truly wished to end the Auron reign for good?"

"That is the question of questions. I believe it has to do with Ohrimah's original nature. You remember he once embodied good purpose before he was known as the Lord of Strife. His good purpose may have guided him to spare you as you were not yet on the throne. Further, I think he may have hoped keeping you alive would serve him better in some other way. Your mysterious absence may have helped aid his grand scheme somehow. I suspect there are a great many in your kingdom who would like to know how you were able to vanish so mysteriously while under the protection of the Solguard."

"That was the day after the memorial service was held for my parents. I went to the sanctuary to rest my mind and pray to the Twin Flames to help me in my grief. It was one of the last times I prayed. Anyway, I asked for privacy and when they left me at the altar, I used a hidden passage there that only my parents and I knew of. They created it when they built the temple long before the spire was finished. As to where that is and where it led me, I'll keep that secret to myself."

"Very well, my lord, I can understand the need to keep something such as that so secret. Heh, truth be told, I would have advised you to keep it to yourself," Armatay said as he smiled contently.

Aurotos wondered about how Armatay could know so much. Perhaps this was exactly why the stewards trusted him. Nothing about his secrecy in knowing hidden truths seemed nefarious nor did Aurotos's own instincts about him raise any alarm. "How did you come by these details about my parents?" Aurotos asked.

"Well, I was there," Armatay said with a solemn, hesitant smile upon his face.

"I don't remember you as an advisor or warrior from those days. I'm curious how you're nearly my height, considerably taller than any human I have ever met. Even if you were one of the eldest humans, most don't live beyond five hundred years, and when they reach the age of their greatest elders, they appear far older than you."

"A keen observation, Lord Aurotos. No, you would not have known me then. I was a witness to the events, just not in the way you might expect. You are quite the observer yourself, still, I am afraid I have some secrets of my own to keep for a while longer. Please do not worry yourself with that. I am no danger to you, and your secrets are safe here, my lord."

Aurotos had passed several chambers on his way up and finally reached the top of the tower. As he stepped onto the final step beside the sage, he investigated the large dome in the top of the tower. Aurotos was surprised to see an expansive painting outlining the story of the beginning of all things. He saw two lights in the cosmos symbolizing the Twin Flames, from which sprang the eight Masters who became the gods governing the course of creation and the various aspects of the virtues. The painting continued around the outer edges of the dome, showing the Masters helping the Twin Flames in physical form on the face of Auro as they brought to life every creature that then roamed the planet's landscape. It showed the creation of the races and then the Twin Flames departing the world leaving its people to the care of the Auron and the elves. It showed Vorthelos and Eilendrei ruling over Valenthreas as guides for the other races where they reigned to maintain order. The painting circled around as the end led back to the two suns set in the cosmos, where the painting seemed to begin.

Aurotos was fascinated by the painting and found it curious that it was in the tower. Such paintings with this level of reverence were nearly always on display in places of worship. Such a scene wouldn't normally be found hidden away in a solitary place. The entire chamber was surrounded by windows, allowing the sage to view all the land around him as far as the eye could see, except for the northwestern side, where the windows were blocked by the singular mountain it was perched on. The chamber had a fire pit in the center and seating around it. It was this seating area that the sage was now waving him to.

"Please sit with me by the fire," Armatay said.

"Very well," Aurotos replied, clearly lost in contemplation about what he had just learned.

As Aurotos sat with Armatay, he found himself troubled by the knowledge that the dark orc had been the one to deliver death to his parents in their final moments. He was haunted by the memory of their final conversation—they urged him to remain under the watchful protection of the city Solguard deep in the heart of the central spire of Valenthreas. He remembered the final hug and kiss from his mother, and his father's arm stretched around him with a smile telling him to remain there until they returned. The moment of their return never came, and it haunted him ever since. His parents were both skilled warriors who thought they were defending the city, but the reality he now knew was that the great war was about seeing to their murder. While many saw the war as a success, Aurotos now realized it meant that the goals of Ohrimah and Grindam had ultimately succeeded.

"The truth about your parents changes things. I know this, yet there is more that I wish to share with you," Armatay said. The sage sat forward in his large, padded, wooden armchair and waved his hands over several cinder stones in the pit before them. In an instant, the stones ignited, illuminating the great chamber, and warming the pair as they sat in the silence of the sanctuary.

"The painting is remarkable," Aurotos said looking once more toward the dome above.

"Thank you, I enjoyed the time I spent on it, although I no longer remember how long it took for me to complete it. I find it has served as a happy reminder of the order of things.

"You completed this yourself?"

"Well, yes, I did. Is it such a surprise that I might choose do so?"

"No...it's just such a marvelous painting. I don't think most would expect to find such a masterpiece hidden away in Avestan."

"I suppose there are rumors about me hiding away, whispering secrets to the stewards, never being among those who are the most curious about me," Armatay said with a wry smile.

"Perhaps...you spoke of the order of things," Aurotos said.

"Order of the past and of the future, the events that have aligned us to this very moment today," Armatay replied.

"To this very moment," Aurotos said.

"It has long been known to my kind that only the Last Light of Auro could help see to the end of Ohrimah and the darkness that will soon befall this world. You must be sensing that things have changed, and it is only you who can help me reveal that change. The dark master has plotted against the moments now before us, pulling the strings of his puppets from within his gloomy realm."

"So, I'm here to help fulfill some prophecy? I know of the stories about the gods, but I think if they wanted, they could end all the suffering in this world right now," Aurotos said. He stood up and walked toward the windows overlooking the city of Valenthreas. Then he peered down below to the Dragonstrike Woods and clenched his fists. "Where were the Twin Flames when my parents died? Their own children. Where were they when countless people were murdered when the darkness came? Where were they to rid the world of the evils that the dark master created? They could have stopped him before he began down his dark path, they could if…"

Armatay stood up and walked slowly toward Aurotos, speaking from his peace. "The Twin Flames are not a fable. They are as real as the world they created, and as true as the radiance in your eyes. You are the last one to carry their light, and you can no longer choose to be dead or lost as many believe you are," Armatay said letting out a long sigh as he joined Aurotos in his gaze toward the dark woods.

"My only wish is to be rid of this place, but until I'm chosen by a phoenix, that's unlikely. I'm dedicated to my order and I've served too long to throw my progress away. I don't accept that I'm bound by those chains of fate, all because of the light in my eyes and what that is supposed to mean."

"You seek to get away, yet you chose to serve the very order your father founded to protect these lands and the people of Auro."

"In a way, it was more about knowing my father and being closer to what my parents cared so much about. I didn't do it because I wished to take his place. Wanting to better understand my father isn't the same thing as a desire for his crown. I never wanted the throne. I could never rule as my parents did. No one could take their place or accomplish what it should mean to rule as they did. No one could replace them, least of all me."

"Well, that certainly is an interesting way of seeing the situation."

"Interesting in what way?"

"Well, I find it interesting because your father believed that leading his people as a king was a way of serving them. He led the knights in service of the people and it gave him great humility. He cared deeply for every soul he encountered, and this was at the core of his purpose, as it was for your mother. For them, to rule was to serve, much like your service as a knight."

"You speak as if you knew them, yet I have never seen your face before, Armatay."

"Yes, I knew them in my own way. I understand how that may be confusing, considering we have only met today."

"You remind me too much of Valothas."

"Oh yes, the elder knight of your order. He is quite the warrior, and he was a good friend to your parents."

"Yes, he was," Aurotos said as he let out a frustrated sigh and looked at Armatay, who only had a peaceful smile to share in return. Aurotos had wondered many times whether Valothas had ever caught on to his true identity, though he never gave Aurotos any indication that he knew. Even with his enchanted hood, Aurotos found himself wondering from time to time if it could truly be enough to disguise him under the watchful eyes of someone who he had known for so many years before. Aurotos felt himself straying deep into thought and was sure it had to do with the sage's presence. He couldn't explain why he felt so mindful around the sage, but he sensed that there was more to him than just some wise old man in a tower. Although it was curious to him, he was still frustrated in being reminded so directly about who he was. It made him feel too exposed, something he had worked hard to rid himself of for so long.

Armatay directed his attention to the top of the central spire at the center of Valenthreas. "By now, I'm sure you've heard about Prince Drazius Khorvek, who destroyed the Aurodite stronghold of Illonel," he said.

"Yes, such horrible news."

"Aurotos, I urge you to join me, we could seek out the prince's plans. Together we could work to protect your people against whatever scheme Drazius is hatching. If you truly wish understanding of your parents, then helping me to uncover what is causing these changes in the world is the way. Tomorrow, I fear it may be too late."

The offer was tempting, and for a moment he considered it, thinking back on how he had wanted to pursue the dark prince earlier that day after Valothas received the news about Illonel. "I'm afraid I can't leave the knighthood; I swore an oath. Whatever this prince has planned, the knights will be needed and that is where I believe I will be most useful," he said.

"You have a greater responsibility. I could speak with the elder knight and request your aid in a way that would not jeopardize your role as a knight. The world is changing, and it will inevitably be up to those of us who understand what is happening to keep the people safe. This task is not one I would wish to take on alone. The prince has goals which I am sure are not his own agenda, and I think I would have a much better chance of discovering them with you by my side."

"This belief you hold about me isn't my responsibility. The elves are in the safe hands of the Thri'nethil stewards. If I had a phoenix, I would have already left this city and the people to carry on as it will."

"Very well, Aurotos, I will not press the issue further. You know as well as I do that you cannot hide from yourself forever," Armatay said as he looked to the sky, noticing that rain had started falling and clouds now began to darken the sky further.

Aurotos also noticed the thunder that began high into the clouds above the elven realm. As rain began to fall, the landscape seemed to dim, and the moonlight was now blotted out by the dark clouds high in the night sky. As Aurotos looked down toward the city, he realized it had gotten late; he thought about the news Valothas had received. Realizing how important the morning would be, he expected Valothas would probably send knights, and he hoped now more than ever that he might be able to help by going with them.

"Oh, Aurotos, I had one other thing I wished to share with you this evening," Armatay said as he walked back toward his large armchair. As he reached the chair, he kneeled down and pulled out a large item from behind it. It was long, wrapped in cloth and bound, as if concealing what was hidden underneath for quite some time.

Aurotos began walking toward the sage and pointed at the object curiously. "What's bound beneath those wrappings?"

Armatay released the bindings and opened it to reveal a regal long-sword. "This is Ai'ethe, The Radiant Blade," he said. This was the sword of your father. It was the first cinder sword ever made, and it was created from the remnants of the first phoenix. When it was forged, it was imbued with the light of Valos in the early days, long before your knights' swords were crafted in a cinder forge." Armatay then extended his hand, passing the sword to Aurotos. "This sword is much more powerful than the one you carry. It holds within it powers very few have witnessed and it is unmatched by the weapons of darkness. If you are to see its power for yourself you must learn to wield it."

Aurotos reached out to accept the sword. As he took it, he felt it connect to him. "This was my father's sword." With the ancient blade lying across his hands, he felt the hardened black leather scabbard bound by a glowing aurosteel chape and locket. The locket of the scabbard had a bright golden gem on each side of it. The grip of the sword was wrapped in the same hardened, black leather, which somehow seemed almost new. The pommel appeared to be made of the same shiny aurosteel and was shaped like the star representing the noble tenets. There was a bright red ruby set into a perfectly round casing of aurosteel. The guard was straight across, with gems on either end set in the metal, and the center where the blade met the guard and grip appeared to be a large circle with an even cross, which bound a large round golden gem within it.

As Aurotos pulled the sword from the scabbard, he heard it sing of the dawn. This sword did not appear at all like his own cinder sword or any others he had ever seen. It appeared as if it was polished aurosteel, but there was an essence of gold and amber wishing to break through its surface and burst into flame. As he turned the blade, it not only reflected the fire's light but gathered it and sent it back outward, illuminating all it was near—it was made to fend off darkness. The sword was a masterpiece, and as he held it, he could see his own eyes glow across the surface of it. Even his two companions seemed to be curious about it as they took quick swipes at the reflections of light it emitted onto Aurotos's belt and clothing.

Aurotos responded with the only words he could seem to find. "Thank you," he said as he slid the blade back into the scabbard holding it tightly in his hands. The appreciation he felt for Armatay was almost palpable yet he kept his composure. "How is it that you came to have this in your possession if my parents' bodies were never recovered?"

"One could say that the blade reveals itself only under certain conditions. None of which are evil, and one of which happens to be me. As the phoenix Ai'ner was never seen after the death of your parents, and since your parents were never found, it seemed that only I had the capability to retrieve it at the time. I wish I could have helped find your parents, but I am sad to say that was no longer possible," Armatay explained.

"Thank you for keeping it safe and for delivering it to me; it means a great deal." Aurotos knew there was something mysterious about Armatay that he had yet to recognize, but he didn't wish to press the matter as it was getting late.

"Ai'ethe will respond to your abilities in all the ways your own cinder sword does. To master the sword's gifts, you will require training to discover the secrets of the blade. I am afraid that those secrets are not known by the elder knight of your order. If you wish to learn how to attune yourself to your father's sword, I can teach you. I could teach you what I can now, but beyond tonight, I would only be able to train you if you are coming with me," Armatay said, hoping to appeal to him once more.

Aurotos was conflicted and felt the turmoil within. He was stunned by his burning desire to know how to wield the sword of his father; it pulled on his heart strings as if it were his father's lost beckoning call. He believed that going with Armatay would help him to feel closer to his parents and it was a gut-wrenching sensation he experienced as he debated with himself. There was something about holding his father's sword that nearly broke his will to tell the sage no.

"The offer is tempting Armatay, but I'm afraid I must go soon. The evening grows and I'll require rest before dawn drills in the morning. With the news we received I expect the morning announcements to be wild ones," Aurotos said, being sure not to allow his hidden turmoil to show.

"I understand. I will guide you back to our volgriff friends, and one of them can fly you back to the city."

"Alright, Armatay." Aurotos sheathed the blade and placed it upon his side.

While the two walked back down the long winding stairs, Aurotos found himself wondering how Armatay could know as much as he did. He knew he had hidden qualities that Aurotos had never seen in a seer or magi. As they entered the large chamber at the base of the tower, Kayris hopped up from a chair by the now lit fire and moved quick to meet the two by the short hall leading outside.

"Ay, leaving already?" Kayris remarked.

"Yes, Kayris, I must return to my quarters before it gets too late. Take care of yourself," Aurotos said.

"Ay, thank you. You take care of your little friends and be careful. That storm's brewing fierce. En, I will guide you to the volgriff you flew in on."

As Aurotos and Kayris walked through the short hallway toward the tower's exit, the rain turned into an unrelenting storm with thunder and lightning, which became louder as they approached the door leading outside. Just as Kayris was about to open the door, Aurotos heard the sage's voice one last time.

"Aurotos, are you sure you wouldn't rather stay here tonight? That storm sounds quite vicious, and we have several quarters upstairs where you are welcome to stay. The volgriff can always take you in the morning; the presence of darkness is especially strong on the darkest nights, and my senses tell me it will be a very gloomy night."

"There's nothing to be worried about tonight, but I appreciate the offer. I would really be more comfortable in my own bed," Aurotos replied. He found himself very tempted to stay, but he remained unwavering. "Farewell, Armatay, Kayris."

As Aurotos exited the tower and walked toward the volgriff, he felt his two cats becoming reluctant and uneasy in their pouches. He comforted and secured each of them safely before mounting the auvinot. As the volgriff charged forward and lifted off into the air, Aurotos looked back to see the two below waving at him, both still appearing concerned.

Aurotos could barely see in the storm, and he felt that maybe the sage was right about how much darker the night seemed to be. Even for a storm, this was darker than anything he was used to seeing. As he flew over the city and further away from the sage's tower, he found himself thinking more and more about what the sage had said. He enjoyed one final dive on the volgriff before landing just outside the door of his quarters. He pet the black and red volgriff a final time and thanked it for its help before watching it dart back off into the dark, stormy sky, leaving only its musky aroma behind.

As Aurotos entered his quarters and illuminated the room, he found himself grateful that he was not clawed by Siam again before he landed. He took a seat in his chair and enjoyed some time playing with his two friends, who he could tell were happy to be home. He tossed the ball of string along the floor, dangling it and bouncing it around while his pets leapt and clung to it. They enjoyed playing generally but were even more pleased to be playing with him; this brought him great joy.

As Aurotos started a fire and prepared to make himself some dinner, he reflected on how he had seen the sage start a fire of his own without using any words of magic. He knew there was something more to the sage. He felt his secret was safe with him, but what Armatay had shared troubled him—because, despite his strong will against it, he believed the sage was right. Something was lingering in the cold darkness of that night.

CHAPTER 6

BY THE STORM

The storm raged on and the low rumble of thunder tempted Aurotos to fall into a deep sleep as he laid in his bed. Both Angor and Siam were nestled up tight against his legs, and while Angor could sleep through storms easily, Siam was not so fortunate. Something from his early days as a kitten had caused him to be very overwhelmed by alarming sounds. As such, anything loud was sure to wake him, leaving him to scan his environment for some time.

Outside their home, street lamps seemed very dim, and even the ambient illumination of the plants seemed to be suppressed by the dark storm outside. Every so often when the thunder or lightning peaked, Siam was quick to raise his head and listen.

It was very early the next morning, and the storm was still raging outside when Siam was again startled by the sound of the lightning crashing. While his small head was raised up, Siam found himself staring toward the windows where the light was flashing into the room. As his breathing rate decreased and his head began to lower, he scanned the room once more until something seemed to catch his eye.

Across from the bed, in the opposite corner of the room, something drew his attention under the table. The fire in the fireplace had cooled, no longer producing flame, so it was not able to illuminate the corner of the room where the table was. Siam stared intently for several minutes and began lowering his head as his attention waned, giving way to how sleepy he was.

Moments later, Siam was startled once more, but this time, it was not by the sound of lightning. There was something under the table that he was quite alert to. Something about that corner seemed unnaturally dark in a way that differed from the rest of the room. If Aurotos had been awake, his Auron eyes would have surely been able to make out whatever was hidden there under the cloak of the unnatural darkness.

A silhouette emerged from the dark corner—a figure with two small, beady eyes glowing with a faint crimson red. It appeared to be a small silhouette of a very short person. As the figure took steps very slowly toward the bed, it stopped just beneath the chair by the table. Siam began to dig his claws into the blanket covering Aurotos, who remained fast asleep.

The more Siam became disturbed by this small figure, the more awake Angor became as he, too, had woken up sensing the unsettling feeling in the room. Had there been any noise at all, Aurotos would have awoken, but the silence was almost deafening to him. Both cats had crept to the edge of the bed, looking underneath the chair. As they both began to hiss and make noise, Aurotos started to become disturbed.

At last, the silhouette revealed itself to be a small gnome shrouded in black clothing with its head nearly against the seat of the chair. The gnome silently launched itself into a fierce jump upward toward the bed. All that could be seen clearly of the gnome were its eyes and the two daggers in its hands, which were covered in some sort of black matter.

In an instant, Aurotos awoke to the sounds of his cats, who had growled much louder before they pounced onto the gnome and brought it down to the floor where they were ferociously attacking the intruder in an effort to keep them safe. As Aurotos sat up and looked down below, he realized that there was something in the room that his two cats were trying to stop. It was just as he was hurrying to get out of bed that he heard the painful screams of his two cats. The gnome had stabbed each of them, leaving Angor and Siam falling to the ground on either side of it. The gnome withdrew its daggers and stood up, leaping toward Aurotos.

As it closed in, with its daggers raised over its head, streaming a trail of blood between the bodies of his companions and himself, Aurotos raised his hand and a ball of flame exploded toward the gnome, blasting it back into the corner of the room. Its corpse fell onto the table, bathed in flames, after crashing into the wall above. The flame burned so fast that the gnome was reduced to a pile of ash in just a matter of seconds, leaving a scent of acrid smoke in the air.

Aurotos collapsed onto the floor where both of his cats were lying in torment. As he slid his hand under each of their heads, he could see fear and suffering in their sad eyes as they looked to him for help, crying out in agony. Looking down at their broken bodies, their blood had pooled and mixed with the black substance that had infected them, he knew that in only seconds their wounds would probably take their lives. He investigated each of their eyes for hope, but their eyes grew darker. "Good boys." He leaned his head down further toward them where he could hear each of them let out a purr before their breathing stopped, leaving both Angor and Siam dead cradled in his hands.

Desperate to be wrong about what he was seeing, Aurotos picked their broken bodies up into his arms and defiantly uttered his plea, "No, please, no." His words held no power in changing the fate of his two precious companions who had fallen protecting him, and with their final moments, granted him the time he needed to survive the gnome assassin.

Aurotos stood up, holding the lifeless bodies of the two cats in his arms, and turned around toward his bed. He could smell their blood mixed with the black poison and it was all that was needed to ensure what happened next. Tears began streaming from his dimmed eyes as he lowered his arms, placing both Angor and Siam down, facing each other. He closed their eyes and placed their heads touching one another, as if they were asleep and cuddling as they had done many times before.

His tears felt like rivers flowing from his eyes down his face, dripping onto the blanket below. The sorrow nearly overtook him as he whispered from the depths of his heart, "I'm sorry, boys, it should have been me."

As he kneeled beside the two, the familiar pain of loss darted through him, as powerfully as lightning. The thoughts of the pain he experienced when he lost his parents had returned and seemed to welcome the loss of the two innocent creatures, which were his only friends. Aurotos knew that he was now truly alone and his grief grew quick to anger. The two cats were laying on their favorite blanket, and Aurotos placed a kiss on each of their heads before folding the blanket over them and wrapping them into a bundle on his bed. As he stood up, looking down at the blanket that now held his two dear friends, he tried to make sense of what had just happened.

There, in the darkness of his room, question after question presented itself to him. He thought of the gnome, now a pile of ash on his table, and worked to make sense of why he would be attacked. Was it because of his visit to Avestan? How could this have happened? What was the reason for the attack? Someone had planned to kill him in his sleep, and had it not been for his two friends, they may have succeeded. That was when he heard the city bells tolling from outside.

The bells were ringing out all around him, undoubtedly from every watchtower along the city walls. The bells meant the city gates were closing, and all citizens were to lock their doors. For the city guard and the knights, this meant it was time to report in to prepare for a threat to Valenthreas. Aurotos stood, clenching his fists, and the golden glow in his eyes almost seemed to be bursting with light. There was no time to clean himself up. He knew he needed to don his armor and cloak and make his way to the order hall of the knights with haste.

In a matter of just a few minutes, Aurotos had equipped his armor and cloak. On his face, the blood of his two pets remained. He placed his father's sword on his side, but tucked it well under his cloak, and moved to exit the room. As he opened the door, he could see that it was still some time from dawn, but clouds were beginning to clear. Exiting his home, he securely shrouded himself under his cloak and paused in sadness, for his two companions would no longer be tucked away in his pouches. He wanted justice for their murder, but justice would have to wait; his duty called him to the order hall where he was hoping to find an answer.

The dawn's light was still absent by the time the knights arrived at the order hall. As Aurotos entered the gateway of the order, he left the vacant streets of the city behind him to the audible voices of the knights ahead. He could sense the uneasiness that gathering so early evoked in his comrades. Most of the knights had already gathered ahead of him and converged into formation. Aurotos moved slow as he took his place up front. He could see that Valothas was already standing before the knights, but his stride was unchanged.

As Aurotos moved to the front of the formation, he noticed that Valothas also had blood splattered on him, although he seemed uninjured. Valothas wasted no time explaining the situation to the gathered knights. "In the early hours of this morning, a series of attacks were carried out within our city. Several guards were killed, and their bodies have been found. I will soon be off to the council chamber to speak with the stewards and leaders of our city to fully assess what has taken place. Once I return, you should be prepared. This attack will not go without punishment. There are other events unfolding that we must address, but for now, I require that you all make ready."

Valothas then looked toward Aurotos and noticed the blood on his chin. "Before I leave to speak with the council, I must ask if any of you saw anything out of the ordinary. Have any of you witnessed an attack or anything suspicious?"

Aurotos knew he would have to divulge what he experienced. There was no use hiding it, he had to share. "Yes, Valothas. There was an intruder in my quarters earlier. It was a gnome assassin but it's dead now; its ashes lie in a pile on the table in my room."

Valothas looked at him concerned and nodded. "Very well, Volir. You will accompany me. Is there anyone else?" Valothas looked over the knights, who all remained bewildered as they whispered about the facts being presented to them.

"Leavesa, I leave you in charge of everyone here until we return. You all remain vigilant in our tower and watch over the spire. The city guards are already attending to their own matters and have secured the city. Stand fast, knights. Volir, with me. Ol'nar, my friend, circle the spire above the gardens."

"We'll see it done, Valothas," Leavesa said as she looked toward Aurotos curiously. "Volir," she said as she nodded.

Aurotos knew Leavesa's nature all too well. He suspected she would secretly be working away at the puzzle, trying to figure out why he had been targeted by an assassin. He wouldn't give her any clues though and was quick to follow the elder knight. "Leavesa," he said as he moved quick to follow before Leavesa could eye him too much.

The sky above had grown a bit lighter, beckoning the dawn as Valothas made his way toward the gateway. Ol'nar flew above him, igniting into flames as it moved toward the prominent spire at the center of the gardens nearby. As Aurotos followed Valothas, he wondered what to expect before they reached the council hall. The stewards would be there, and he had not spoken to or interacted with them since before his parents had died. He also expected there would be questions as to why he was a target. He was, after all, only supposed to appear as any other knight who served the people. While the knights' order was not filled with thousands of members, most were well-known among elves, while only few remained enigmatic or known for their deeds, and he had been both.

Soon, Aurotos and Valothas had made their way through the gardens toward the great city spire. Aurotos felt that his leader was unusually quiet under the circumstances. As Aurotos inhaled the fragrant scent of the flowers and leaves of the Vaelothi Gardens he scanned the area and took notice again of the blood on the elder knight's clothes.

"Were you injured?" Aurotos asked.

"The blood on me was that of the gnome who tried to assassinate me. I was awake, so when it attacked, I was able to cut it down before it had a chance. Now is that your blood on your face and hands or that of the gnome?" Valothas asked.

"Neither," Aurotos said, lowering his shrouded head further.

"Not Angor and Siam…"

"Both died as they tried to protect me. Their attack on the gnome woke me and gave me time to stop it, but the daggers… There was nothing I could do to save them."

"Oh, I am sorry, they were happy little ones at your side."

"They were my happiness," Aurotos replied, and a silent mourning filled their steps.

As the two knights walked through the large doors of the spire, the Solguards raised their spears in front of them and dropped them to salute. Aurotos and Valothas both brought their right hands up, beating their clenched fists onto their breastplates as they passed through the doorway. Entering made Aurotos all too aware of his surroundings, even though his eyes were well hidden under his hood. He realized that his desire for justice after what he had lost had surpassed his reluctance to draw attention to himself. Nevertheless, every step he took toward the center of the spire felt like waking bittersweet memories.

The inside walls were large and reached high, meeting arches that led to the center of the spire's rooms and corridors. The white stone was trimmed with red and gold that shimmered under the light of the enchanted golden orbs floating overhead. Large curving stairs on the left and right hugged the outer walls of the spire. The design resembled that of Avestan. Far into the center of the spire lay the great hall of the king. As they entered, passing through the hall, tall pillars rose to the high, arched ceiling. Aurotos saw his parents' thrones ahead, which had not been occupied since their passing.

Not far behind the thrones was the council chamber. Two large doors with Solguards on either side of the doorway led into the chamber. As the two knights passed by, the guards saluted, the sound of aurosteel's clash echoing throughout the chamber. In the center of the chamber, there was a large round table at which the seats were never assigned. Here, all people met as equals and as servants of their realm and the gods. The ceiling stretched far above with arches meeting in the center, and hovering high above the table were two orbs of fire circling one another in perfect synergy, symbolizing the Twin Flames and their sync with one another much like the suns in the sky.

As they approached the table, Aurotos and Valothas took a seat at the two chairs before them. The stewards of the city, Evolin and Ethlain Thri'nethil, were sitting to the right and close to one another. Both stewards had light olive complexions. Ethlain, a thin elf, had much shorter, pointed ears, which was a hallmark feature of most elves, save Aurotos. Both stewards were two of the first elves to be born after their parents were made by the Twin Flames following the early days of the Auron leaders.

Ethlain had golden blonde hair, with braids starting on the side of his head and crossing over to tuck behind his ears, where they fell with the rest of his hair down below his shoulders. His bright green eyes were complemented by thin, tidy, arched eyebrows that were a bit darker compared to his golden hair.

Evolin's bouncy, bright, blonde hair flowed down in loose waves which hung over her shoulders and back. Her thin eyebrows were kept in perfect arches. She was petite, about a foot shorter than her husband Ethlain, and had very light blue eyes. While she was considered one of the most beautiful elves to have ever existed, her beauty was said to have paled in comparison to that of Eilendrei Va'Threas.

To the left of the knights was Oenthial, a captain of the city guard, who appeared to be there in place of the city watch commander. He was of medium build and had a warmer olive complexion. He had brown hair and was clean-shaven, with bushy straight eyebrows and shoulder length hair tucked behind his ears, and his eyes were a burnt orange color.

Straight ahead of the knights were Armatay and Kayris who were no strangers to visiting the council chambers. Valothas looked around the table and remarked, "Evolin, Ethlain, I am glad you both are safe." As he looked toward his left, he nodded toward the guard captain. "Where is your commander?"

"I'm sorry to say he was slain in the night," Oenthial said.

"This is sad news," Valothas said as he turned his attention across to the sage. "Armatay, Kayris, it is good to see you both are safe."

"Ay, thank you, and you too," Kayris said.

"It is good to see that you are unharmed, Valothas. I see you have brought another knight with you," Armatay said as he smiled toward Aurotos.

"Yes, I have brought Volir, one of our knights who was attacked. I thought he could tell his story when we spoke of the matter."

"One of the knights? What happened to you?" Ethlain asked, looking toward Aurotos with an inquisitive stare.

"A gnome assassin," Aurotos replied. "I suspected maybe it was because I'm one of the strongest knights of our order. I was curious if more of the knights had been attacked, but aside from Valothas, that was not so." He paused for a moment, contemplating his words as the room fell into silence.

Valothas looked at the other members of the council, gauging their reactions. It was clear that they were all deeply concerned and trying to make sense of the situation. It was also clear to Valothas that Volir had more to share. "The enemy has clearly targeted those of us in special positions." The others nodded in agreement. "Still, there is one thing we must understand," he said as he looked back to Aurotos. "Can you think of any other reason the gnome may have attacked you?"

"Yes, there is. I'm really trying to understand how they could have known," Aurotos said.

"Could have known what?" Evolin asked as she stared more curiously at him.

"Who I am," Aurotos said as he peeled back the hood of his cloak and broke its enchantment to reveal his bright golden eyes leaving no question to any that he was their destined leader.

Upon first sight, both Evolin and Ethlain stood to their feet. Oenthial also rose, while both Valothas and Armatay remained seated. Kayris leapt to his feet onto his chair in excitement and began jumping around. "Ay, finally, this has driven me to the woods," he said.

Ethlain stood there, seeming so surprised that he only uttered a single word. "Aurotos," he said. He raised both of his hands together in front of his chest and continued. "We feared the worst when you disappeared."

"This is incredible news, my lord, but for how long?" Evolin asked as she tried to understand why he would have hidden himself from his people.

"By the flames, Lord Va'Threas," Oenthial said, seeming unable to express his shock at what he was witnessing.

"Please, sit, I'll explain," Aurotos said. He soon noticed that Valothas did not appear shocked by his reveal. He had not expected a reaction from Kayris or Armatay, as they both had known who he was, but he had expected Valothas to be surprised.

"I returned to Valenthreas several hundred years ago and joined the Knights of the Phoenix as a recruit under an alias as Volir. I wished to learn the ways of my parents, but I had no desire to rule, so I concealed my identity. You all have ruled well, and I chose a life of solitude that I was very content with," he said. Aurotos looked toward Valothas with a perplexed expression and addressed him. "I expected you would be surprised to learn who I was after serving all this time with you."

"Did you really think I would not discern after all these years that I was training the son of my best friend? I knew that if you wished to remain unknown, it would be unwise of me to expose a secret you worked so hard to keep. After some time, it was clear to me that your cloak was enchanted. While others had missed it, I knew there was more to it, and I recognized your voice, even if it no longer carried the same joy and happiness it once did," Valothas said. "I would not dishonor you in such a way, and I hoped that one day, you would rise to bear the crown as our leader, just as your parents once did."

"I knew you were pushing me hard to lead, now I understand why," Aurotos said. "I appreciate that you kept my secret."

Right when Aurotos finished speaking, large bellowing laughter burst out from the sage, who was keenly directing his attention toward Aurotos. The sage appeared fuller of joy and laughter than the Auron could have even imagined. Aurotos looked to Armatay with a curious expression, his raised eyebrows seeking an explanation.

"It is a fine blessing that on such a dark day you have revealed yourself to the people of your kingdom. Many years have passed as they have wished for you to be alive," Armatay said before his eyes dimmed with concern. "Your two small friends; oh, I am sorry."

Aurotos lowered his head slightly as he took notice of Kayris's eyes swelling up with sadness. He would not allow himself to stay present with his grief so he responded. "Thank you, Armatay. Had they not intervened…"

Valothas interrupted and leaned forward, sternly explaining the status of events. "I am afraid we must develop a plan to deal with what befalls us. At least one member of our council has been killed with attempted assassinations on key leaders of this city. We can no longer ignore what Armatay has brought to our attention about the shifting presence within the world. Even Aurotos has sensed the shift in nature, and it is the belief of Armatay that Merdah may have extinguished the empyreal flame of Anieva. Her sorrow was felt before at the fall of the Dahaka and is believed to have been felt again this year as we approached the end of Duskfall. Last night the avolan Feycir delivered a message to us from the coast. Our plan this morning was to gather some of our knights to meet the Aurodites who escaped Illonel. Now there is more to consider as we plan the defense of Valenthreas and aid the people of Aurotheros." Valothas looked toward Armatay. "Please, your wisdom."

"I believe your plan to send a group of knights to the hidden coast is wise, Valothas. I wish to accompany them and hope for the assistance of Aurotos if he would join us," Armatay said. Then he looked to the stewards. "Ethlain, Evolin, what are your thoughts?"

"We can work with the guards and the knights so that the citizens are aware they will be protected within the walls of Valenthreas until we understand what is at work here. We can aid the people to become more understanding that securing the city is a precaution for the time being. If the people knew that Aurotos was with us, I believe it would ease the fear of all within the walls. Would you agree, Evolin?" Ethlain asked, looking to his lady.

"I would, darling," Evolin said. Both stewards looked toward Aurotos for an answer.

Aurotos knew he could no longer remain hidden under the false sense of secrecy that his cloak had been providing him for so long. The cost was already too great. First, he lost his parents, now his two small companions, and he found himself driven by a desire for retribution. He couldn't help but think if he had taken Armatay up on his offer the previous night, maybe Angor and Siam would still be alive. His complacency had come at too great of a cost and he felt the full weight of his decisions brewing within him. "I understand what you're asking of me," he said as he contemplated the idea of joining the party and revealing to his people that he lived.

"I believe it wise to assign the city guard under instruction of the Knights of the Phoenix until we know the threats at hand. In any war effort, the knights have always guided the city guard and our elite Solguard," Ethlain said as he looked to both Oenthial and Valothas.

Oenthial nodded in agreement. "Yes, I'd agree, the city guard will always direct their attention to the knights, I will be sure our guardians report to the order to receive regular instructions moving forward."

"We all seem to be in agreement," Valothas said. "I would like to send Aurotos to lead a group of our finest knights to the hidden coast. From there, they can identify if there is a way to work with the Aurodite magi who fled Illonel. Anaryen Valenvon is among them, and she must have valuable information if she is requesting the knights to join her there. I suggest that we also send word to all those throughout the realm of Aurotheros to seek refuge in our city. If our knights can stop Prince Drazius, or at the very least identify his plans, then we may be able to put an end to this before it begins. We will plan our defenses here in the meantime as a precaution and send word with the avolans."

The council had agreed, and Aurotos found himself as the one to whom they all had directed their attention. They were troubled by the events yet seemed very happy to know he was alive. For the first time in a very long time, Aurotos Va'Threas felt a desire to change the course of events that had been set in motion. He sought justice for his parents and for his small companions who lay dead on his bed.

After a moment held in silence, Aurotos realized he would need to give them an answer. He looked at each person around the table and then met the sage's eyes before responding with the only words that mattered to any of them. "Drazius must be stopped. It's time I let the knights know I'm alive. I'll lead them and see that we fulfill our duty."

CHAPTER 7

CHOSEN KNIGHTS

Aurotos stood silent at one of the pyre pedestals within the holy district of the city. He had just placed his two beloved pets on top of the column, unwrapping their broken bodies from their favorite blanket. Saying goodbye to them was one of the last personal obligations he had left before he would join the chosen knights at the order hall and attend to his duty of leading them to the hidden coast.

Aurotos raised his hand and cast a scorching flame onto the remains of his companions. They would no longer purr or play around him, which had once brought him joy. The thought of their suffering wounded him, reminding him of their trust. Tears rolled down his face beneath his cloak, concealing the swelling of his eyes, as the flames before him gave rise to billowing plumes of smoke that quickly ascended into the sky.

The pungent smell lingered in his nostrils as he closed his eyes to squeeze out the last of his tears before wiping them away. There, with his two small friends for the last time, he felt an overwhelming desire for justice and to bring an end to whatever Drazius was planning. He lingered there and could feel his jaws tighten as if to brace himself, passing through the moment.

As the flames diminished, Aurotos stepped forward toward the pedestal to gather the ashes of his two dear friends. He reached out and wiped their ashes into the reinforced glass bottle he had brought with him. As he pressed the dense cork into the bottle, he knew the best place to carry it was in one of the pouches on his belt, where his cats often accompanied him. Taking a deep breath, he squeezed back his tears and began making his way to join the chosen knights of his order who would soon learn that he was still alive.

Aurotos passed through the gates of his order, and he knew that things would never feel the same as they had before. Prior to today, he was known as Volir among the knights. It was very likely that the same knights who awaited him in the courtyard of his order had held preconceived notions about him as Volir. The truth remained that they did not know him, and he had not befriended any of them. Most of the mistakes he made during training came at a cost to the greater whole, and today they would learn who he was all along. What would they think of him once they realized who he was? This was something Aurotos focused on even more as he walked closer toward those who could see him approaching.

Ol'nar, perched up above on the banister railing, noticed Aurotos and searched around for his two companions, knowing they would usually have joined it up above. When Ol'nar could see they weren't there, it became noticeably sad. The phoenix knew that the pair of cats would not have been missing from his side unless something had happened to them. Realizing this, Ol'nar amplified its senses discovering the ash odor on Aurotos. As it understood what had happened, Ol'nar screeched in its sorrow before regaining its composure and focusing its attention, observing Aurotos move toward Valothas.

Aurotos heard the noise but did not allow himself to look up above, as several of the knights before him had. Ahead of Aurotos and the knights was Valothas, who he could see was well prepared. He made his way toward the elder knight, who only slightly lowered his head to acknowledge him. Aurotos responded in kind and took his place standing by his side before the ten knights.

"Knights, converge," Valothas shouted. The hooded knights formed themselves into a line before the pair. Aurotos could see a man off to his right, sitting on a bench against the wall of the courtyard, wearing black and dark green clothes with a black hood over his head. While he was not sure who the man was, he expected Valothas had a good reason for a human to be allowed within the order's sanctum.

"Knights, it is time that we discuss what has happened. As you know, early this morning, a group of gnome assassins infiltrated the city, killing several of the city's guardians. These intruders then carried out assassination attempts on key members of the city important to Valenthreas and its future."

The chosen in front of the elder knight began whispering among themselves, but before there was much opportunity for discussion, Valothas continued. "You know of the actions carried out by Drazius Khorvek, the human prince who murdered his father. Some of you may have noticed our messenger friend, Feycir Feanir, who arrived close to dusk yesterday evening. He delivered news that the Aurodite stronghold at Illonel has been destroyed, leaving only three survivors. These surviving magi made their way to the hidden coast where they now await us."

None of the knights had a response but both Valothas and Aurotos could still hear them whispering amongst themselves about Illonel. One word slipped out faintly, "Illonel."

"Yes, it is atrocious what has become of Illonel. The prince is also behind an attack being planned on this city, our city, for we have already been made aware that he is pursuing that goal. The method is not yet clear, but we will be sending aid to meet with the surviving Aurodites and pursue the dark prince ourselves. The ten of you have been selected to accompany your leader for this mission. Please remove your hoods and reveal yourselves."

One by one, the knights before Aurotos and Valothas dropped their hoods. Aurotos surveyed those who would accompany him to the hidden coast. Starting from the left side, he noticed the first, Leavesa Solendrei. Her shimmering auburn hair and vibrant blue eyes were unmistakable, and even though she was petite, her armor made it hard to tell. Most were often in awe of her beauty or capability in her use of the flame. Her presence was a most welcome sight, for Aurotos knew she was a fierce combatant and natural leader among the knights.

Moving his eyes slowly to the right, he saw Arvasiel Oranthiel, who stood shorter than Aurotos yet was quite tall for an elf. He was a strong knight with a large build and an affinity for solar shields. Of all the knights, his shields rarely weakened, and when a knight bonded their shields with his, they were sure to be stronger. He had dark brown eyes and long black hair pulled back into a tight braid that was clasped several times with aurosteel cuffs and split into two smaller braids at the middle of his back. He also had a patch of hair on his chin, which was clasped in a tight aurosteel cuff that enclosed all the hair tightly underneath. His high-arched eyebrows were quite dark, except for auburn streaks, which caused them to appear lighter.

As he continued down the row of knights, Aurotos saw Syvon Sorelion. This knight enjoyed wielding two short cinder swords, and unlike the traditional knights of the order, he was known for being incredibly fast in combat, dual-wielding with true fury in his delivery of slashes upon enemies. He was about average height for most elves, with medium olive skin and light brown hair pulled back tightly in a short bundle above his neck. He was clean-shaven, with hazel eyes and straight eyebrows. He had several scars on his face from wounds he had received in battle in the past. While his eagerness to challenge himself sometimes left him with scars, his quickness in combat was unlike anything most living beings had ever seen.

Drelion Droveva was the next knight Aurotos observed. He was a true master alchemist, and it was no doubt he would be of service to his fellow knights on any quest. He always carried a bag of herbs, bottles and vials and his skills were known far outside the walls of Valenthreas. He was notably short for an elf and very fair-skinned, but what he lacked in size compared to most elves, he made up for in dedication to others' care. He had light blonde hair that was straight with streaks of auburn spread lightly throughout. It hung over his shoulders with many braids mixed in. He had a short beard to match and light green eyes that nearly appeared grey some days.

The next knight he saw was the proud Salenval Esoleval. The knight wielded a great cinder sword and was known for delivering shattering strikes in combat. He was tall with a stocky build for an elf and was incredibly strong. When he walked, his steps could at times be felt on the ground by those near him. His head was shaved except for the large, thick, orange braid which hung far down his back from above the crown of his head. He had thick, straight eyebrows, and a thick line of hair that extended down in front of his ears as sideburns, carrying down across his jawline. He had light olive skin and dark green eyes, and nearly always appeared with a stern expression until he could be caught laughing.

Kaervo Reaova was the next knight Aurotos noticed. He was known for his very traditional elven appearance, standing taller than most humans with fair olive skin, blonde hair, and green-blue eyes. His elven braids hung over his flowing straight hair, which dropped below his shoulders. He was clean-shaven and could spin out a barrage of flames from his blade in a matter of seconds. He was very famous among the knights for his great skill in blade churning of the flame.

Further down the line stood Tarothas Rothiras, a tall yet thin elf with dark blonde hair, green eyes, and fair skin. He had short, straight hair that extended to the top of his shoulders, with braids that hung in front of his ears. He was one of the younger elves of the party, nearly one hundred years old, and had not witnessed the great war. However, knowing the devastating effects of the war, he had joined the order to help aid in detecting threats for he was an echo ear and was capable of hearing clearly at great distances. He spent nearly all his life honing his skill in the great wilds to the southwest among the nayrans before he joined the knights.

The next up was Nahul Aenthiul, who was well-attuned to the ways of nature. He stood tall with broad shoulders and light blonde hair that ran far beyond his shoulders. He was clean-shaven and had light green eyes. The braids on the sides of his head were often bound by twine of the wood. While most elves shared a much closer attunement to nature than the other races, Nahul was remarkable in that sense. He was able to relate to most animals and created near-instant bonds with those creatures who hadn't endured extreme suffering. As a result, he could call upon most animals created by the gods and sometimes ally with them, being granted their aid.

Nearing the end of the line of knights stood Kaylos Athelos. He had light brown skin and brown eyes. His hair was dark brown and pulled into a knot on the back of his head, with some loose hair draping below his neckline. He had neat arched eyebrows that often made him appear angry to others, and had a short patch of hair on his chin that matched his short sideburns. He was of average height and build for an elf and carried several smaller cinder blades and daggers to complement his stealth, known as a shade walker among his fellow knights. He could quickly blend into shadows and hide himself but his specialty was his capability to attack often from unforeseen places.

Vael Na'Viel was the final elven knight that stood before Aurotos. He had many long braids of thick black hair that hung down to the middle of his back. He had dark skin to match it with a black goatee, and two braids hung down from the corners of his mouth to the end of his facial hair. Below the center of his lower lip hung a central braid, and this one had a gold clasp at its tip in the shape of a phoenix. He was tall for an elf, with slightly longer ears. His eyes were a deep blue, and he was known for having the gift of far sight, which allowed him to see at great distances or easily during dark nights. He notably belonged to one of the eldest of the elven families.

Aurotos was not surprised why each of the knights before him had been chosen. They were the most superior knights of the order and were often selected for demonstrations. A newly trained singular Knight of the Phoenix was known to be able to vanquish up to one hundred drothkin in battle. This group alone could destroy a small army of enemies. As such, this is one of the reasons the city of Valenthreas was almost never in danger.

"Now, to meet the knight who will lead you," Valothas said. None of the knights could have prepared themselves for what they witnessed next. Aurotos took a deep breath as he pulled back his hood, revealing his glowing eyes. The illuminated fire of the Twin Flames shown as the group of great knights bore witness for the first time. Aurotos saw their expressions shift quickly from shock to reverence, and even joy.

"I am Aurotos Va'Threas, the son of Vorthelos and Eilendrei, once your king and queen," he said. In an instant, the person known to them as Volir disappeared from memory as they all lowered in honor, kneeling before their sovereign.

"Please, there's no need to kneel. I never meant to deceive any of you by hiding my identity. I had only wished to be another knight while I served the order, just as many of you have. With the events that have taken place, I can see that will no longer be possible, and such was the reason why I too was attacked. Somehow, those who orchestrated the assassination attempt knew my secret when I believed only a few could have. I'll serve with you on this mission, and together we will learn what the dark prince has planned. We must protect our people."

Leavesa appeared concerned and excited all at once. Vael wore a look of confusion mixed with respect while Tarothas seemed almost to stare in adoration. The most common sight upon all their faces was reverence but he didn't expect anyone to simply be happy after knowing what he had hidden from the elven kingdom, nay, the world. He wanted to explain more, as he could see the varied expressions upon their faces, but that would have to wait.

"Indeed, we will, Lord Va'Threas," Valothas said before raising his hand, and drawing everyone's attention to the hooded figure at the bench. "This is Corlith Koralen. He is familiar with the human prince and once aided the realm to the north when King Nailor Khorvek was still alive. He will serve as your equist and scout."

Corlith walked toward the left side of the knights and stepped ahead close enough to be visible to them. As he did so, the scent of pipe herb filled the air around them. The sweet, musky scent lingered as he bowed and then lowered his hood. He had dark features against his tanned skin with shaggy, dark hair and stubble on his face. He looked every bit a survivalist and wore his clothes over a thin physique.

"I'm honored to accompany your order. If there's anything I can do to make the journey easier, I'm at your service. I'll be standing by with the steeds at the Valenquin Stables when you're ready," Corlith said.

"Thank you, Corlith," Valothas said. "There is little time to spare; forge master Dronoc will have your full plate armor prepared for you by the cinder forge. Gather the resources you need, then meet Corlith outside the city gates. There at the stables you will find your khallion steeds. You will also find the sage, Armatay, standing by. He will accompany you and help aid your cause on this mission. Go with the Twin Flames, may the light guide you."

The knights echoed back the same as they broke formation, each bowing a final time as they stepped away. With their instructions quite clear the knights left not far behind Corlith, wasting no time to prepare themselves for the duty ahead of them.

"Aurotos, a word," Valothas said.

"Yes, elder knight," Aurotos said turning toward Valothas with an inquisitive stare.

"It's nice to see the light of the twins in your eyes so freely, and though you may not know it yet, it will bolster the morale of the knights now under your charge. We will ready the city here and prepare our defenses. The task of dealing with the prince is in your hands now."

"I understand, Valothas. I assure you we will protect the realm."

"I know you will. Drazius revealed his plan when he attempted the assassinations, yet there is something more at play here. It will be your duty to lead your knights and seek out an answer to what that is. I know leadership has not been something you have desired, but your light will guide them. You must lead and trust them; only together can you achieve success in whatever lies ahead."

"It will be done, I promise."

"In that, I have no doubt. Your parents were very dear to me. You may not realize it, but they were more than the Lights of Auro—they were family to me. That is why I have pushed you as hard as I have and respected your desire for secrecy. My final lesson as your elder knight will be this: trust your instincts, your knights, and the light within you. Now go, and walk with the Twin Flames, may they guide you always."

"May the light guide you, Valothas," Aurotos replied as he walked away.

As he departed, Aurotos began to feel a sense of leaving family behind. It was not something he expected to feel; though he had been closed off from others, the ties between Valothas and his family could not be denied. As he walked through the gateway of his order for the last time, he made no effort to cloak his eyes any longer. A part of him knew that if the elves of the city saw him revealed, it would give them hope, and the word would spread once he left the city. For now, he would make his way to the city's forge master and acquire his plate armor which could better protect him from the threats which lay ahead.

Aurotos wasted no time and arrived at the great forge of the city well before the suns rose to their peak in the sky. He had witnessed more elves bowing and filled with joy than he could have expected. Sure, he anticipated surprise, but he did not anticipate this kind of reverence. As he entered the large doorway into the forges of the city, there, behind the sacred cinder forge, was a stout dwarf giving instructions to a much taller vorelan who was polishing away at a bright breastplate.

Walking through the large building, he caught the scent of flame and molten metal heating the air around him. As Aurotos stepped up to the counter by the dwarf, he could see it was the forge master, Drolluc Dronoc himself. Drolluc was one of the eldest dwarves he had ever met, being several hundred years old. Drolluc stood quite tall for a dwarf, and as Aurotos stood across from him at the counter, the top of his head met the center of Aurotos' abdomen in height. He had reddish-brown hair and wore a heavily padded chain apron with various blacksmithing tools in a belt wrapped around his waist. He had thick gauges of metal in his ear lobes with braids and clasps throughout his long hair, which rolled down to his shoulders. His beard was long, but he kept it bound in clasps and tucked under his apron as he worked. He had a large, round nose and thick, bushy eyebrows. His green eyes were intently fixed on the vorelan who was polishing away under his instruction.

"There ye go, lad. The buff brings the light out from inside the gems. Under them suns, yer sure to see it," Drolluc said as he continued looking past the vorelan's arms. As the dwarf turned back toward the counter, he could see Aurotos standing before him and blundered as he greeted him. "Well, I'll be a peri's tit if it ain't the eyes of a Va'Threas standing before me."

"Yes, Forge Master Drolluc," Aurotos said, now staring into the dwarf's eyes.

"Hold it there, Volir? You've been the lost king all this time? Well, I'll be," he said chuckling with pleasure as he peered back behind Aurotos, taking notice of the onlookers of the city.

"Perhaps not so lost after all, Drolluc," Aurotos said sharing a smile with the dwarf. "I'm here to gather my full plate set before our party leaves the city."

"Of course, ye are, we got it right here for ye," Drolluc said as he smiled with pride.

The dwarf pulled the breastplate out of the hands of his vorelan apprentice, who was staring at Aurotos in disbelief. It was a standing rumor that vorelans had a great allegiance to the dark master, having racial ties of their origin to him, but the elves and many others knew this was not true. Still, many vorelans avoided the great elven city and other lands out of fear of persecution. Others believed they avoided the races now because the rumors were true.

The vorelan man stood very tall and was almost the same size as Aurotos. In appearance, the vorelans looked very much like their human counterparts, yet they were taller and had much broader shoulders. They also had large, round ears, and the bridge of their noses connected straight above their brow. They also naturally carried a great deal more muscle mass and could often be viewed as hulking over humans. The women among them carried the same traits, but theirs were far more subtle with just as much emphasis on their female form.

"Hello," Aurotos said as he looked toward the stunned vorelan. "I don't believe we have met."

"No, my lord. My name is Norithan. Norithan Volnorath, your majesty. It is an honor meeting you."

"Please, just call me Aurotos. It's good to meet a vorelan. We so rarely find your people here."

"The lad traveled far to learn the ways of the dwarven smiths. He's done well. I've been impressed with his skill with a hammer. Anyhow, yer sure to need your armor. The knights have all come and gone now. Yer the last."

"Well then, I thank you both," Aurotos said. "I shouldn't make them wait long then."

As Aurotos removed his plated gloves and boots, Norithan was quick to place the new breastplate and pauldrons on him. He continued to add plates over his arms and legs, which felt only a bit heavier than the armor he had been wearing. The new breastplate had the symbol of the Twin Flames at the center. It was a breastplate fit for the royal house of Va'Threas. The pauldrons now laying on his shoulders were similar but appeared as that of a phoenix on each shoulder embracing a golden sun. The armor was far more ornate than the full plate set the knights had come to pick up. Aurotos knew the stewards, the sage, or Valothas likely had a hand in this. He had not wanted to appear different, yet he felt it was nice to wear the armor of his family.

Now that Aurotos was suited up, he had only his final farewell to give. "Thank you, Drolluc, Norithan. I must go now; the knights are waiting."

Both of the smiths bowed as Aurotos left the city forge. While exiting through the doorway he could see more of the elven citizens looking to catch a glimpse of the lost Auron heir. He bowed his head to them and continued toward the main gate of Valenthreas. They seemed just as surprised as he was. He had remained unknown to most for hundreds of years. When he returned to the city from his adventure, he now knew, nothing would be as it was before.

As Aurotos arrived and made his way toward the main gates of Valenthreas, the guards snapped to attention, unsure of whether they should bow or kneel. Aurotos raised his right hand and beat it on his breastplate offering them a knight's salute. He was far more comfortable returning a salute than he was to respond to all the bowing. Even still, there had been many who had bowed to him as he walked along the main street that led him there.

As he stepped closer toward the gate, the guards opened it, allowing him to pass. For a moment, he paused, standing within the massive arched gateway. He looked behind him at the great spire climbing toward the sky and he could see that many of the people who had watched him had now gathered to see him leave the city. Many of their eyes were full of hope and comfort; this was what Valothas had meant. Aurotos leaving to confront the dangers to the elven realm was beyond comfort to the people of his homeland—it was hope.

As his eyes traveled back down from the people to where he stood, he understood what it meant to protect the people of these lands. He looked ahead of him at the towering statues along the road outside the gates with the figures of the Twin Flames on either side, each holding fire within their hands, raising them toward the heavens. He passed in between the two great gold and white statues and gazed over the beautiful elven lands, its trees bearing purple and amber blossoms. The sweet fragrance of flowers filled his nostrils, another reminder of what was at stake.

Behind him he could hear the cheers of his people. Ahead of him, just beyond the gates of the city, he caught sight of the Valenquin Stables, where he would soon meet the knights and Armatay. He could clearly see the central white tower where the stable hands and horse masters lived. The expansive stables surrounded the tower and encircled the living quarters. As he walked along the white stone road, he could see the split of the roadway that led to the stables. There, trainers rode the great khallion steeds around some of the fenced areas. The lands around the great city were perfect riding grounds for these steeds as the foothills rolled toward the south, meeting the wide-open land of the Olynthian Plains.

The knights stood around the steeds, which were much larger than traditional horses, both in height and muscle size. They had much larger manes and tails that glided in the breeze as they stood still. For even when stationary their motion unified with the air, making no noise. Everything about them flowed from form to movement.

Drawing closer, his nostrils were filled by the rooty hint of residual sweat from the horses. With the knights were Armatay and Corlith who was tending to the steeds. It seemed that only Aurotos had kept them waiting for they had already gathered the horses from the stable master and fully made preparations to leave once he arrived. As Aurotos approached the retinue, he saw Armatay shaded under his big, pointed toppled hat with his staff in hand. Aurotos had not seen the staff before. It appeared to be carved wood that began to twist toward the top into wooden claws holding two yellow crystals, one circling the other.

"Greetings, Aurotos. What a fine day that we may meet again. We await your command," Armatay said, unable to hide the great smile on his face.

"Hello, Armatay, a great day for a ride, wouldn't you say?" Aurotos replied.

"Oh yes, yes, I think it certainly will be."

Aurotos caught sound of the horses neighing, aware of the eyes upon him from the knights. "Everyone, we have a long road ahead, but our khallion steeds will help us reach the hidden coast by tomorrow, provided we only stop tonight. Corlith, I will look to you for aid with the horses when we stop. I may call upon your skills as a scout from time to time as well."

"Anything you need, my lord. I'm at your command," Corlith said.

"Please call me Aurotos."

"Aurotos, yes, my lord."

"Knights, mount up! Let's fly upon these steeds, today we'll test their namesake," Aurotos said as the knights replied with quick cheers of affirmation and moved to mount their horses.

Aurotos mounted his large steed and took the reins. He sped off along the road ahead, the knights following closely. Armatay and Corlith were at the rear, and so the party was off on their adventure. Aurotos had always wanted to get away, but under very different circumstances. He thought about the knights having few words to say as they mounted up. He thought of his two cats whose ashes were placed where they used to rest in his pouches. The thought caused him to ride faster, and the speed was exhilarating.

Riding was a good way to think things through, and he found himself curious for some time as to why the knights responded with few words. Perhaps it was his new armor, or maybe because they didn't truly know him, or his pained history. He thought that even if he had not chosen to develop relationships with others before, it might be important now that he got to know the knights better. He would need their trust, and he did not expect his golden eyes would be enough to gain it from them. Leading wasn't something he had ever felt comfortable doing, and neither was making friends. He feared it would take more than leadership to face the road ahead. If he sought the sage's counsel, he had the sneaking suspicion that he might hear the same thing in reply.

CHAPTER 8

THE AELETHRIEN ROAD

The suns had risen high into the sky as Aurotos and his retinue sprinted away from the city of Valenthreas. They had traveled several miles along the Aelethrien Road and were soon to cross the large Aelethrien Bridge, which stretched far across the river sharing the same name. They had only just begun approaching the bridge when three large stones, the size of boulders, came hurling toward their party.

Several of the knights launched themselves high above the party below, while the rest of the group dismounted their horses. Syvon rose up over the knights, drawing his two swords and preparing for a fight. Kaylos followed him up in the air, holding a dagger in each hand, ready to engage at the first sight of the threat. Salenval jumped off his horse, which had come to a stop, and raised his heavy great sword overhead.

Aurotos slowed before leaping off of his steed. "Corlith, watch the horses and stay with Armatay," he shouted.

Arvasiel rushed to the ground and raised his arm, which soon illuminated with the radiating strength of his solar shield. Nahul and Drelion moved to each side of him, growing the shield into a bastion of light that now protected Armatay, Corlith, and the steeds.

Tarothas and Vael also moved behind the light and focused their attunement with the world, seeking out anything they could see or hear with their heightened senses.

Kaervo and Leavesa stood before the shield on either side of Aurotos, who was centered before the bastion of light. As Kaervo readied his

103

cinder sword, Leavesa sought answers. "What is it? We need to know where that came from."

Kaervo feverishly listened ahead, but he was silent, unable to answer her.

Vael had made a discovery and his eyes were squinted as he looked ahead of him. "I see them on this side by the water. Ougars, three, preparing to throw stones again. They're tearing them away from the bridge right now."

'What? Tell me you're joking," Tarothas remarked.

Aurotos was just as perplexed as Tarothas had been. "Ougars, here?" he asked in disbelief.

Syvon and Kaylos had barely landed on either side of the road before Salenval came crashing down between them, his braid whipping in an expansive circle around him. As Salenval stood up, he rested his massive sword on the ground in front of him. "Just give the order, my slasher's ready," he said. It was all too clear to everyone that the threat had to be eliminated immediately and Salenval had made himself the readied voice of combat for them all.

The three ougars began to charge up the rocky bank of the river, revealing themselves to have large chunks of white stone they had stripped away from the bridge. The ougars were as ugly as Aurotos remembered them to be. Much like a deformed bulky human mixed with several other beasts, the ougars had been bred by the servants of Ohrimah before the great war. They were very big and much taller than even Aurotos, with large flat noses and red eyes hidden under the mane surrounding their heads, shoulders, and upper back. Although their legs resembled those of a muscular auroch, most of their bodies' skin was exposed, revealing their clammy, gray flesh, aside from the thick fur on their forearms and parts of their lower legs.

With the carved rocks over their heads, Aurotos witnessed the awkward ougars screaming through their horribly jagged teeth as they began to launch more rocks at their position.

"End this," Aurotos shouted.

The knights reacted in sync with Aurotos' commands, eager to eliminate the threat before them.

"Die elves, die," shouted the leading ougar who confidently stood ahead of the others, sneering with black saliva dripping from its teeth.

The ougars did not hesitate and threw their rocks toward the knights. Leavesa cast her large fireballs at the stones, scorching them into ash that exploded overhead as the knights moved forward. Kaervo had set his sword ablaze and launched a barrage of flames, destroying the final boulder trailing behind the falling ash.

Seeing that the rocks had been destroyed, the ougars began clutching at the dirt and mud at their feet, aimlessly throwing the terrain at the charging knights. At the front of the charge, Aurotos rushed toward the foul creatures, striking the first one with his cinder sword ablaze in his hands, but not before being splattered with mud. Syvon and Kaylos also delivered devastating blows upon the ougars, but they too were covered in dirt and mud.

Salenval, now laughing hysterically at the sight of the muddied knights, delivered his powerful arcing strikes, vanquishing the first ougar before him. With the last two trailing behind, both Aurotos, Syvon, and Kaylos delivered blow after blow, their flaming swords leaving the ougars lying dead before them. The elimination of these three enemies was done so precisely that it would have honored any to witness the short battle.

The flames on their weapons left the ougars ablaze on the ground. While the knights gathered themselves, the ougars continued to burn, the smoldering fire sure to leave them as no more than piles of ash where their dead bodies now lay.

The shrieking cries of the ougars were a terrifying sound, and for the elves, it was rare to feel enjoyment in the death of another creature. Yet, it felt good to know that whatever had driven these ougars to be here had been stopped.

Syvon looked down at his two swords in hand and saw the black blood dripping off the blades. "Ohrimah's filth, disgusting," he said.

Behind the four knights, Leavesa and Kaervo broke out into laughter as they looked at the four muddy knights standing over the slain ougars.

Salenval also joined in the laughter but with a plea. "Leavesa, please, this is downright disgusting," he said.

Leavesa was completely overcome with laughter at the sight of her fellow knights and their responses only caused her to laugh more, leaving her unable to speak.

Aurotos looked toward Leavesa with only a smirk as he wiped the mud off of his face. As he did so, he saw a shadow cast on the ground from whatever was flying overhead. In fear that something above could incite danger, he looked toward the sky, aimlessly peering into the brightness of the suns. The sky provided no answers nor did the landscape, and he thought only to clean the mud off of himself for he believed it may have obstructed his vision.

As Syvon wiped off his blades, he made a suggestion. "I think we should all go and clean ourselves off before we continue on. I'd really like it if I wasn't covered in all this."

Aurotos didn't respond, but he too wanted to clean the ougars' filth off. As he started walking where the ougars had come from, he signaled to Leavesa. "Just a moment, Syvon's right, we really should clean ourselves off. You all prepare yourselves and we'll be along once we've cleaned up."

"Yes, of course, my lord. We'll just wait on the other side of the bridge," Leavesa said, still unable to contain her giggling.

Aurotos scanned the other knights standing by the horses. He could see they all wore the same smile, finding the situation humorous. Even Armatay was giggling in a way that was much akin to a child's laughter. Aurotos could have been sure he saw the sage glowing under the light of the flames in the sky but he also felt his vision a bit obscured by the mud on his face and eyelashes and assumed he was seeing things.

The water of the river was very clear, and one could see everything underneath, but as beautiful as it was, it was dangerous to wade too far into the water. The swift current could cause one to be swept away quickly by its force. Aurotos walked into the water and continued further until he was nearly submerged. Then, with only his head visible, he dunked himself deep under the weight of the shimmering water before rising back up from below its surface. He felt very refreshed and invigorated under the combination of water and sunlight that he felt on his skin.

His fellow knights were not as careful as he was, for Syvon and Kaylos were almost swept away. This only caused Leavesa to begin laughing more as she and the others made their way across the bridge. Salenval and his sturdy stature kept him weighted down while he cleaned himself off, cleansed by the water that ran so surely from the mountain, Aelenrith.

Aurotos witnessed the majestic falls cascading down off the steep rocks above, delivering the river to them. The crystal water was a glorious sight to the elves, as this flowing river meant much more than simply hydrating the world or its creatures. To the elves, this river was named after Aelith, one of the Twin Flames. It carried along the eastern wall of the city of Valenthreas and ran swiftly while delivering its gift to the land far to the south and the east. On the other side of Valenthreas was the Aulonthrien river named after Aulon which stretched far to the south and the west, delivering the same nourishment to the land which spread far beyond the mountain.

It was along that particular river that the expansive Mosslands began, leading far to the west toward Aspysteros, the woodland realm of the nayran people.

"It looks like these vermin tried to destroy the bridge," Syvon said.

Aurotos had begun following his three fellow knights back toward the base of the bridge, where he could see that several of the large stone blocks had been pulled away from the bridge. The ougars hadn't caused enough damage to lead to the destruction of the bridge, although it would be something that their people would need to repair in the future. But for now, there were much more pressing matters at hand.

"Salenval, it seems there's a hole in the ground at the base of the arch of the bridge. Do you see it?" Kaylos asked, now pointing directly at what he saw.

Salenval walked toward the area that Syvon was pointing at and he too could see there was some sort of opening. It was hard to see it, but Salenval seemed aware there was something there. "What in the..." he said.

Aurotos reached the knights, and he too could see that there was a small hole in the dirt at the base of the bridge. The ougars had caused something to give way beneath the surface of the terrain by throwing the heavy rocks at them. As the four knights stood peering at the hole in the ground, Aurotos noticed that the sage and the others had already taken the horses across the bridge, where they were awaiting them. Knowing they needed to move on, Aurotos was about to instruct them all to pay no more attention to the hole. In an instant the small hole expanded quickly before the knights who had all gathered too close to it. Both he and Salenval felt their footing break away beneath them leaving them to fall into the ground that had opened below.

Kaylos and Syvon remained above after nearly falling into the hole, which had become much larger now. As Salenval and Aurotos laid in the hole looking up, they could see the alarmed faces of the knights standing above them. As they were removing debris off of themselves, they noticed a rusted chest against the wall of the small chamber they had fallen into.

Aurotos could see that it was some sort of storage cache which belonged to the Knights of the Phoenix during the great war. He remembered hearing of these hidden storage placements across the land at strategic positions which aided the knights of old. These storage locations were often full of a variety of provisions, weapons, and other useful items that helped them in their various quests. Many of these safeguarded locations had been lost in time, but it seemed that they had found one. As Aurotos pulled the chest open, he could see inside where there were old potions and reagents, most of which included cinder sword oil.

It was clear the stash was overall depleted, but as these could be useful for what lay ahead, Aurotos threw the wooden chest up toward Kaylos and Syvon. "Be sure you give these to Drelion; I know he'd make good use of them. Now, please help us up," he said.

Aurotos looked at Salenval and clasped his hands tight, offering a step to help the knight up. "After you, Salenval," he said.

Salenval looked at Aurotos a bit surprised, visibly impressed to see that even as an Auron, he hadn't let his authority cause him to behave as if others were below him. "Thank you, my lord," he said.

Salenval placed his foot into the hands of the highborn who helped lift him up, where the other two knights pulled him up from above. Once above ground, Salenval peered down curiously into the hole. He realized that because of Aurotos's height, they would only need to take his hand to aid him up.

Aurotos reached up toward the knights who raised him to the surface. He looked toward Kaylos and Syvon and made a quick command. "You two, roll that stone that the ougars weren't able to hit us with over this hole so others don't fall in," he said.

Once the knights had positioned the stone in place, Aurotos was ready. He realized that no matter what lay ahead of them, they were in it together, no turning back. "Alright, forward and onward," he said.

As Aurotos approached the rest of the knights who were already upon their steeds, he could see the concern in Leavesa's eyes. "Is everything all right?" he asked.

Leavesa scanned the land, keeping a watchful eye over their surroundings. "I know ougars are troublesome creatures; they rather enjoy their destructive ways, but this is unlike them. Something must have emboldened these three to roam so far from the wilderness, and to try to destroy the bridge so close to Valenthreas of all places."

"More mysteries present themselves to us," Aurotos said. "I don't expect this to be the last time we'll encounter trouble in Aurotheros. You're right, though; something has encouraged these ougars to think they would be safe committing such acts so close to Valenthreas. I share your concern."

Armatay looked down at Aurotos as he was preparing to mount his steed. "Are you done having fun? The flames above only burn for so long each day, and we have a great distance yet to travel," he said.

Aurotos looked at the sage with confidence. "Of course, we must stay the course. We need the answers that the Aurodites carry."

"I know you do. I see you found one of the storage vaults from the old days. Was there anything useful inside?" Armatay asked.

"Nothing much, just cinder sword oil and some other old reagents. Things that Drelion will find very useful," Aurotos said.

"Heh, and did you find the water refreshing? It is a beautiful place, the realm of your ancestors," Armatay said.

"Oh, yes. The Aelethrien river always brings me a sense of renewal with its waters. There's something about the warmth of the sun on my skin just after feeling the river water that I have enjoyed since I was young," Aurotos replied.

The sage belted out a loud laugh, finding Aurotos's response to be overly funny. "Oh, it does make one wonder why anyone would ever want to leave such a beautiful place," he said.

Aurotos looked at the sage and gave the only response he could, by pulling his hood back over his head and repeating the sage's own words back to him. "We should get going, the flames only burn for so long each day, Armatay."

Armatay chuckled on. "Of course, Aurotos, we would be wise to cover as much distance as possible before nightfall. At your command, my lord."

As the knights mounted their horses, Aurotos took another look up toward the sky, curious about what had caught his attention earlier. Had he imagined the shadow, or was something up there? There was no time to ponder that answer, but he did agree with the sage. Even though he didn't admit it, the land was beautiful, and it would be hard to believe he'd ever want to leave the realm, even though it had always been his personal goal to do so.

Leavesa noticed Aurotos was looking into the sky and it alarmed her. "Something catch your eye up there? You're fixed," she said.

"It's nothing. I'm just confusing myself," Aurotos said before moving his steed forward, passing by the rest of the knights.

He sensed a greater element of respect and reverence from them, but he couldn't imagine why. The ougars, although misplaced, were not an overwhelming force to be reckoned with. They were barely even practice for the knights. It was curious to him that they seemed to almost forget his previous identity. Still, Aurotos did think on the situation for it was one story in the many chapters they could share with others once their adventure came to an end.

Looking upon the knights, he showed his first subtle smile, which most seemed to acknowledge as he made his way past them. Still, he wondered where else there could be danger in Aurotheros and what other vermin of the dark master were now roaming the lands.

As the knights charged toward their own fate, hoping to put a stop to Drazius and whoever was pulling his strings, they knew that many creatures could be roaming free, ready to exact their dark desires upon the innocent. It was clear that someone or something had set the ougars on their path, but what else was at play?

Aurotos and his knights continued to charge forward along the road. He was dedicated to the journey they were on, wanting justice for the two innocent companions that he had lost. Feeling the wind against his skin, Aurotos felt a sense of belief he had not felt before; he would uncover the intentions of the dark prince and bring him to justice.

Night fell across the realm of Aurotheros, and the land of the elves glowed under the light and beauty of the moons, which had now risen high into the night sky. The moons radiated the light of the cosmos and were sculpted by the gods. The great crystal moon bathed the knights in the night light of the world as they rode on their steeds.

Up ahead of the retinue, Aurotos could see a large golden tree glowing under the night sky and raised his right arm to signal the knights to slow to a stop. "This would be an ideal place to stop, let's setup camp for the night," he said.

Leavesa was the first to respond. "Absolutely! I do so adore the golden trees. They've been my favorite since I was a child. I'm sure you'd know why golden trees are so sacred, my lord," she said merrily.

"Of course, golden trees were the first trees that ever took root once the saena trees were formed by the Twin Flames. They served as guides to all other trees whose roots stretched out beyond their own," Aurotos said.

"You know he knows, Leavesa. I've always been partial to the amber trees that glow at night; they're downright the best out there," Salenval said smugly. Leavesa only replied with a feisty look upon her face, squinting her eyes as she looked in his direction.

Armatay seemed to be pleased by the choice too, and it was clear to all that the sage had become quite tired. "My old bones could use a rest after the long day we have had, I cannot think of a better place."

As Aurotos and the knights dismounted their steeds, Corlith led the horses to an area by the large tree where a small stream ran. There, he setup to tend to the steeds and prepare them for the morning.

Aurotos signaled toward the ground under the golden tree. "This would be a safe place to build our fire for the night. We'll have plenty of visibility surrounding us under its aura; we can see quite far in every direction as the land glows."

Aurotos could see that Corlith had already begun tending to the horses and thought to check on him before sitting down and creating a fire for the rest of his companions.

As he approached, Corlith was digging through his pack before Aurotos stopped to check on him. "Is everything all right, Corlith? Do you need any help with the horses?" he asked.

Corlith appeared very startled by Aurotos as he hid a stone in his hand deep into his pack. "Oh, thank you, my lord. I'm all right. I was thinking about leaving for a while to scout out the territory just in case there are any other creatures roaming. With your permission, my lord," he said.

"That's wise and it's certainly your duty, just don't stay away too long tonight," Aurotos said.

"Yes, my lord. I'll be gone no more than an hour, and I won't tax this steed any more than I must," Corlith said.

"We appreciate your service to us," Aurotos said as he turned, leaving the scout to his privacy and preparations.

The night sky was dark and clear, but the heavens could be viewed all around them. The world glowed and that was never unappreciated by any of the elves. As the sage sat down against the tree, Aurotos threw a cinder stone into the ground before him. With the stone embedded in the dirt between the sage and himself, Aurotos raised his hand and spoke. Instantly, the cinder stone exploded into a brilliant white and amber light that radiated warmth for all effected by its glow.

As the knights gathered around and withdrew their provisions from their packs, the old sage sat smiling. "It is a sight to see," he said. The knights, along with Aurotos, looked toward the sage, waiting for him to share more about what he meant.

"The beloved Knights of the Phoenix and the Last Light of Auro gathered before me," he continued.

"Well, you sure do seem to be quite sentimental, Armatay," Leavesa said, smiling as if to let him know she agreed.

The old man smiled back, giving her his answer, and she glowed, knowing she was right to suspect as much. As the knights around the glowing flame began sitting down, Aurotos became aware of their gaze at his glowing, golden eyes.

He did not speak, still uncertain how to feel about building bonds with them. He closed his eyes for a moment and inhaled the brisk autumn aroma of the leaves and the scent of the hot stone of the fire before opening his eyes. He was unsure of what the future would hold and where the journey would lead them as they continued toward the hidden coast.

The knights' gazes shifted toward the sage, who had continued speaking. "While you all gather around the flame, I should tell you what is believed to be happening by the wisest among us. You elves know more than most the nature of the fade and how it influences those who give in to strife or sorrow. It is our belief that Prince Drazius has likely been corrupted by the fade and is under its control."

"It's been an age since we've seen the fade's infection among people," Drelion said. He was not alone in his worry, for among all, concern was visibly written on their faces. All of them except Aurotos, who sat gazing into the flames rising up from the cinder stones.

Armatay fixed his gaze on Drelion. "It could be by way of Ohrimah, but most likely I expect it is Lord Grindam. You all know the importance of our dedication to the noble tenets and how this strongly influences one's attunement to magic and the way of the Twin Flames. The closer one becomes to the Twin Flames, the more potent their capability with magic is," he said.

Drelion got back to grinding up his herbs as the old man's gaze caused him to appear uncomfortable. "Ha, don't be uneasy Drelion," he said. "We have always seen this potency in you knights and with the magi. Although your cinder swords and solar shields are just tools gifted by your devotion and practice of your craft. The stronger these tools become, of course, depends on the knight. The same can be said for when one is conflicted by strife and sorrow."

"The fade always diminishes the light at the core of all; I have seen it," Vael said confidently. "Too many members of my family were infected by the curse of Merdah. The fade is a wicked thing, truly."

"You would see it in ways most would not, Vael. When the fade takes hold, skills diminish, but some of the darkest forms of magic arose from the diminishing of the light within by the dark master. The gloomveil, as we know it today, exists as an unseen world, a dark world hidden beneath the light of both the day and the night. That is where the dark master holds his greatest influence and dominion. It remains an immaterial plane created by the dark master from the slaying of too many souls. If one falls to the fade, they completely break from the path of the Twin Flames, and their soul fractures—"

"They've used the darkness as a way to come and go from our world for too long," Aurotos said.

"I once saw his dark creatures when I walked in the shadows, it's why I don't linger there often as a shadewalker. It's too dangerous to stay stealthy for very long. The shadows used to be just as safe as the dark, now neither are safe in the gloomveil's presence," Kaylos said.

"Of this I have no doubt, Kaylos…and Lord Aurotos is right, the damage of the dark master's influence and the influence of his minions is beyond measure. Ohrimah, of course, twisted many beings in order to give birth to his creations. Perhaps the worst creatures he has been capable of creating are the ones that can be molded within us. I think this is what has become of Prince Drazius Khorvek. We believe this is how he has come to kill his father, and I believe it is through some form of dark power that he was able to influence so many to follow him. It is still unknown how many have perished in the dark prince's kingdom—"

"Beyond counting I'm sure, just like the countless creatures Merdah so cruelly murdered and tormented. I've heard the whispers of suffering still uttered by the animals living out in the wilds," Nahul said.

"I know of what you speak, Nahul. We must be prepared for anything because there is a balance to magic and to its potency. Something in the very nature of this world has shifted, and it is up to us to answer what that change is."

"Do you believe that Prince Khorvek can be saved?" Leavesa asked.

"That, I do not know," Armatay responded mournfully.

"If the prince has been consumed by the fade, then he is beyond simply being infected by it. That truly leaves one to wonder how he might be stopped," Vael said.

"That is the question of questions," Armatay said as he shifted his gaze back upon Aurotos, who only continued to stare into the flames before him.

"Something in the world has changed; I too have felt it," Aurotos said. With this statement, he commanded the attention of everyone present. Even Drelion, who was crushing away at his herbs in the mortar and pestle before them, stopped to look in acknowledgment, along with the other knights.

They all looked to one another, yet none knew what they could possibly say to fill the affirming silence, for it was a moment of quiet contemplation between them. Each knight present posed questions to themselves and was careful not to burden one another with their thought.

The beauty of the scene surrounding them, the beauty of their world, seemed amplified in that moment by the risk being posed against it. The dark forces encroaching upon their world, though unseen, seeded a desperation among the knights—they had to protect their realm. So, the silence persevered among them while each knight tended to themselves and to one another.

In the morning, they would travel the distance between them and the hidden coast. For now, the knights would rest, and as they talked amongst one another, there was one who spoke very little, one who continued to stare into the fire before them. He with whom they had served for many years, yet never truly known. The last Auron in whom their dedication was unwavering.

At some point during the night, each of them found themselves staring at Aurotos and his glowing eyes, which seemed to be even more illuminated in the presence of the flames before him. Aurotos would be their guiding light as they continued their journey forward, seeking answers for the prince's motives and that which the fade threatened.

CHAPTER 9

THE HIDDEN COAST

The knights had traveled far, and just before the night of the next day they had covered the remaining distance between themselves and the hidden coast. The retinue was perched upon the rocks above a vacant shoreline which their attention was directed toward. Aurotos exhaled a sigh of relief as they had all ridden hard and covered such a great distance thanks to the expedited speed of their khallion steeds.

"At last. Let's make our way down; the Aurodites are waiting," Aurotos said.

Confused by the sight of the empty shoreline, Corlith spoke up. "Where are we going? I can't see anything down there."

Aurotos found it funny that their human companion was so confused. "It wouldn't be much of a hidden coast if you could find it easily. Just this way—follow us closely," he said.

The pathway leading below was invisible to all except those who knew where to look. Aurotos continued to guide his horse forward toward the edge of the cliff, leading the way for the rest of the knights who followed.

As he reached the edge, Aurotos started going down, but he did not fall. Instead, it seemed that his horse had found footing on a rocky pathway close to the cliff face, a pathway that remained invisible to the naked eye.

The route was there, in a very specific place known only to those who had been there before. One after another, the knights continued down the cloaked pathway leading to an apparent empty shoreline beneath the cliff's edge.

Aurotos turned back to see Armatay following the knights, sending a large grin toward Corlith. "Come on, young friend," he said.

Corlith continued to follow the sage and appeared in awe that he was able to see the path before him which was not visible until he stepped onto it. "I'll be," he said. "Had I not seen you all ahead of me safe, I never would have had it in me to blindly step off the edge in such a way."

"Heh, some things in this world require faith, my young friend," Armatay said.

Corlith only sneered back, and his expression spoke volumes to Armatay in place of his absent words.

Aurotos knew that none of those present would explain to Corlith why this safe haven was able to be hidden from the eyes of those who gazed upon it. It had been one of the greatest secrets held between the Aurodites and the Knights of the Phoenix, for they had safeguarded it between themselves since the great war. It was one of several safe havens unknown to the enemies of the Twin Flames in those days.

The closer the knights got to the bottom of the shore, the more visible the elven structures below were. Further ahead of them on the coast itself were the visible elven, human, and umeran ships tied off along the docks. As they neared the shore, they caught scent of salt water and wet wood amongst the breeze blowing from the ocean.

The group continued down the pathway that was built along the wall which had expanded along their right until they found themselves entering an archway. When they made their way through it, they found the coast on their right and the shore leading to the great hidden cavern on their left. The elves attention was guided by the light of the crystals within the cavern which pulled at their very being as if a beacon calling them home.

Hidden far beneath the rocky cliffs was a deep cavern full of elven architecture illuminated by glowing amber crystals mounted against the cavern wall. If one hadn't known better, they would have believed that the inside of the cave was lit from the suns above.

The truth to the lighting within this place was that it was an illusion gifted to it by the great crystals. Even on the beach outside of this safehold, giant stone pillars stretched up toward the sky, disappearing the closer they got to the elevation of the stone cliff's edge.

"Heh, it has been so long since I visited the halls of Mai'elzin," Armatay said.

"Mai...what?" Corlith asked.

"Well, it's our word for this place. The umeran people have long protected it for us, so we named it in their honor," Leavesa said.

"It's been an age for me as well," Aurotos said. "Come on, we must continue through the gates, I'm sure the Aurodites are within the stronghold now."

To the umeran people who resided at the hidden place, the knights were welcome and expected. But what many had not expected was to see one among them wearing the armor of a Va'Threan. They watched carefully as the knights dismounted and removed their hoods. From the moment Aurotos dropped his hood and revealed his glowing eyes, the voices of shock and awe resounded against the cavern wall ahead.

Some of the umeran people bowed their heads, while others kneeled, their heads lowered in reverence. Those who were the most shocked simply stared, amazed at the sight of Aurotos.

Aurotos was unsure how to respond to this but reacted in the only way he thought to. "You honor me, please stand up."

"Well, you should get used to it, my lord. This is going to begin happening much more wherever you are seen," Leavesa said, seeing how uneasy he appeared to be. "Especially by those who honor the history of your family and the teachings of the gods."

'You know, some might even see you as royalty around here," Salenval said as he worked to control the laughter brimming from within.

Armatay let out his usual joy-filled laugh but said nothing more, for as he looked ahead, his attention was interrupted by an umeran who was approaching them.

Many of the knights had not seen an umeran in quite a long time, as they were rarely encountered away from the coasts, being that they were the aquatic people. The umerans primarily lived within the depths of the ocean, although some of them lived among coastal towns and cities. They were popularly known for navigating their swift naval fleets constructed by the kelp bark found on the trees of the sea.

The umeran now standing before them was about as tall as a human, yet his skin was light blue. His ears were similar to that of the elves, but their auricles resembled fins, and they had gills behind them, allowing them to breathe underwater when they weren't walking among the other races. He had large blue eyes with flaps of skin between his toes and hands, which were easy to see, as umerans don't wear shoes or gloves.

He wore a loose white shirt, allowing the large flap of tissue in his armpit that connected to his torso and upper arm to spread freely under his attire. He wore matching light pants, which gave him a lot of freedom to move or swim without discomfort. As far as umerans went, he looked a bit more human than other umerans, aside from the fact that his head had the distinct shape of his people.

The umeran was not expecting to see the Auron heir but that didn't stop him from delivering the perfect customary welcome for the guests who had arrived. "Hello, Lord Aurotos, and welcome, Knights of the Phoenix. I am relieved to see you arrived safely. I am Zeydi," he said. "Please follow me, the Lady Anaryen Valenvon and the other magi are waiting for you within Mai'elzin. I am sure the lady will be relieved to see you all."

"Corlith, please tend to the steeds. We must speak to the Aurodites now," Armatay said.

"Rest and make yourself comfortable. I expect we'll be leaving by morning. Your scouting services won't be required this evening," Aurotos said.

"Uh...I'll be standing by then, my lord," Corlith said. It was clear to Aurotos and the others that, even though Corlith was doing his duty, he was unhappy that he wasn't being included.

The knights followed the umeran who led them along the walkway, leading them into Mai'elzin. As they walked forward, they approached the large gateway, with its walls appearing as brightly as the white sand under their feet. The walls were engraved with one crest on the left, the symbol of the Knights of the Phoenix. Respectively, on the other side was the crest of the Aurodites. At the top of the Gateway was a symbol representing the umeran people, who had long served both of the great orders.

The knights made their way through the gateway and were honored by many of the umeran people who lived within the safety of the cavern walls. As they all moved closer to the threshold, the umeran guards at the gates saluted them, and each knight responded with a crash of metal on their chest.

"The course of time moves quicker for them. It's easy to forget that what seems like a short period for us may be several of their lifetimes. I don't know why I expected the last leader of this stronghold would be here to greet us," Aurotos said.

"Oh yes, Lord Va'Threas, there is a lesson to be taken from that realization. The umerans live the shortest of all; one could learn a great deal from their people when it comes to mindful living," Armatay said with respect.

"It's hard to think I could study a single tome on herbology for a hundred years before mastering the skills within, and in that time, one of their kind will have already lived and died. They change so fast," Drelion said.

"Don't forget about their fighters," Salenval said sternly. "The abyssal warriors are downright glorious. Some of the best our world has ever seen. The way they move in water—imagine swimming like that."

"Well, I hope you're all reflecting on how important what we're doing is. So many rely on us," Leavesa said. Her words resonated and met with grunts of agreement which came from the rest of the knights.

The knights continued through the walkway leading deeper into the cavern. At the very back, deep within the stronghold, was another set of large doors leading into the alliance hall. The protected sanctum's walls blanketed the back of the cavern, with its grand doors framed by two large glowing stones atop pillars leading halfway up the cavern.

As Aurotos and the knights stepped into the alliance hall they could see all of the dedications to the original magi and knights who saw to the creation of this place. There, high in the back of the great hall before them was a dedication in the words of his own parents. Just under the dedication on the wall stood three Aurodite magi wearing their blue mages' cloaks and battle armor.

As Zeydi entered through the doorway of the protected sanctum, he waved toward the magi and made his honorable introductions. "May I introduce Lord Aurotos Va'Threas and the Knights of the Phoenix. They have arrived accompanied by Armatay, of Avestan."

The magi looked shocked, and Aurotos was aware that they had not expected to see him accompanying the knights.

Zeydi did not linger and continued to carry out the introductions. He redirected his attention, now guiding Aurotos and his retinues attention to the magi.

"May I introduce you to Lady Anaryen Valenvon of the kingdom of Eden Throvon and her two associates, Molvalan Molandro and Elenfia Ven Louten. May they receive you. I will be outside to show you all to your quarters when you are ready," Zeydi said as he exited the large hall, shutting the doors behind him.

Aurotos found himself at a loss for words initially, for he was fixed on Anaryen whose hood lay covered by her long, flowing, golden hair. Around the crown of her head was a bright aurosteel chain that held her hair down. At the center of the chain, on her forehead, was a golden gem with a blue, round gem hanging below it. Her bright blue cloak hung down to the ground, draped over her delicate shoulders. The silver shoulder guards covering her mages' robes were bright and shimmered with a blue aura under the effect of the light in the room. Even under her robes, Anaryen's fine feminine shape was clear, drawing Aurotos in with attraction. Moreover, he found her to be the most beautiful woman he had ever seen.

It was odd to Aurotos to be so moved by a woman's beauty. While he'd objectively recognized the attractive nature of women around him, never had another's mere presence stilled him so, causing him to lose his words. Even if he had been interested in a woman in his past, he had cast out those feelings, dedicated to his solitude and secrecy. Now fully inhabiting his true identity, this attraction felt different.

There to her left was Elenfia Ven Louten, who was a thin woman with red hair, delicate features, and bright green eyes. She had freckles across her cheeks and on her nose. Standing to her right was Molvalan Molandro. The man had a thick mustache which led down to a sharp pointed goatee. He had dark brown eyes and long brown hair combed back behind his head. He had a peculiar look about him that made him seem strange to Aurotos.

Aurotos had known of Anaryen's family and was surprised to see one of human royalty serving as an Aurodite. It appeared she, like him, chose to serve her people even though she could have reigned in her kingdom. He was curious about why she was at Illonel, and her beauty continued to distract him so much that when she spoke, it would leave him speechless.

"Hold on, Va'Threas? You're the last Auron? Of course, there's no mistaking those golden eyes of yours. So, you've returned after all this time to save everyone, yet these are all the knights you brought," Anaryen said.

Aurotos stood there, unsure of what to say, while the sage, now looking at Aurotos, thought that someone should say something. "Greetings, my lady," Armatay said. "We understand you have important information regarding Prince Drazius Khorvek and those plans of his which you overheard during the fall of Illonel."

"Yes, Armatay, I fear some bad days are ahead of us. I'll tell you all everything I know," Anaryen said.

Over the course of the next hour, Anaryen would tell Aurotos and the others the story of how Illonel had fallen, how the prince was seen with a brand on his neck which many of his soldiers were also seen bearing on their own skin. She told them of how they were all wearing ohrinite armor, and how their presence darkened the night in an unnatural way. She spoke of the two commanders, Griles and Holcurt, and what she overheard them say. She told them everything, and Aurotos bore witness to her fierce and commanding spirit.

After hearing her story, Aurotos spoke in frustration hearing one particular point. "Lord Grindam lives," he said. His face grew red for only a brief moment gaining the attention of all present.

"Yes, he lives, but I think we all have bigger concerns to worry about right now," Anaryen said.

"Yes, Lady Valenvon, we do," Aurotos said.

He took a step back and looked around him at the rest of the knights, he looked to Armatay, and then he looked back toward the magi and Anaryen. "I believe in the morning we should leave and seek out the northernmost communities at risk. The nayran alchemists are responsible for teaching many at their college to the north at the saena tree there. We should begin there and then head along the northern border until we gain any indication of where they have entered our realm. In the time our Aurodite allies traveled through the tunnel, Drazius may have already trekked through the mountains to the north of our borders," Aurotos said.

"Very well, it's a good plan, we'll be leaving with you in the morning," Anaryen said. "We would be a great support to you, and we too demand justice for the lives of our friends. Drazius must answer for his crimes."

"My lady, don't you think—" Aurotos said.

"We're going with you," Anaryen said defiantly, seeming to know what Aurotos would say before he finished.

"Very well, then we will work together. I saw there were additional khallion steeds in the stables; you'll need them to join us. We'll be moving very fast, so make your preparations tonight. We ride out at dawn," Aurotos said

"Very well, not a moment after dawn," Anaryen said. She took no additional time to discuss the situation further and made her way out of the hall. Both Molvalan and Elenfia trailed behind her bowing quickly toward Aurotos as they exited the room with her. Neither one of the magi spoke outside of their greeting. Why would they need to with as fierce of a leader as they stood beside?

"That lady's got downright fire in her blood," Salenval said. "I like her."

"Well, I think she's going to be fun to have around," Leavesa said as she looked toward Aurotos with a big grin. "She'll be keeping you hawk-eyed, my lord."

"My lord, if you are ready, I will show your knights to their rooms for the evening. I hope you will find them comfortable," Zeydi said.

"Yes, Zeydi, please lead the way," Aurotos said.

As Zeydi led the knights to their rooms, Aurotos continued to think about Anaryen and her deep blue eyes. He wondered what would come from having the Aurodites join them in the days ahead. The umeran led each knight to their rooms, and the one Aurotos found himself in was small but served its purpose. It felt more like his own knights' quarters in Valenthreas than he expected. Before he was able to get settled in for the evening, he heard a knock at the door. When he opened it, he saw Armatay.

"Greetings, Aurotos. Now, if you remember, I had offered to teach you how to attune yourself to your father's sword. I was wondering if you would still like me to show you how to wield the blade. I thought we might do so before we leave in the morning," Armatay said.

"Of course. I think it would be best for me to learn what you have to teach me sooner than later," Aurotos replied.

"Great, now if you will accompany me to the docks. I believe the beach area where we arrived should have plenty of space for us to practice."

"Lead the way, Armatay."

Aurotos and the sage walked beyond the gateway of the elven safehold onto the empty beach where no one else seemed to be present. It was late and most of the people here were getting rest. But before Aurotos would sleep, he was determined to learn what the sage had to teach him. As the two walked to the edge of the beach, Armatay was ready to begin. "Okay then, first, I would like to test your skills. Yes, yes, I know I have seen you in combat already, but it is important that I get to observe you directly. I would ask you to fight as fiercely as you would any great enemy, and do not be worried, for you will not harm me. I am going to unleash an attack upon you now. Do everything you can to protect yourself," Armatay said.

"Understood, I won't hold back, so watch yourself," Aurotos said as he dug his feet firmly into the sand.

Armatay raised a white radiating bubble that completely surrounded his body, and it was clear to Aurotos that this was far superior to the solar shields that he used, for they could only protect him in one direction.

Aurotos pulled out his cinder sword and ignited it in a low flame. He wasted no time and threw flames from his sword that arched over his head toward the sage. Although hitting him with his attacks, the sage, patient behind his shield, seemed to be absorbing the magic fully.

Aurotos leapt toward the sage, bringing down his sword overhead onto the barrier with a devastating blow, only to be deflected, his cinder sword flame extinguished. Appearing perplexed, Aurotos had only one response. "Interesting."

Aurotos took several steps back once more as he thought about what he might do next to bring down the sage. But before he could think of a strategy, he was met with a barrage of arcane bolts being levied against him by the sage. Aurotos was quick to raise his arm, emblazoned and protected by his solar shield. The sage's attacks were nothing to poke fun at, as even Aurotos felt how destructive it may have been had he not been skillful enough to protect himself in time.

"Impressive, Armatay. You know if I hadn't blocked that, it could have injured me pretty greatly."

"Yes, well, I have faith in you, Aurotos. But this time, I would like for you to use only your cinder sword to deflect my attacks. Ready yourself," Armatay said once again with his usual tone of laughter, as if child's play.

Again, the sage let loose a fierce barrage of arcane bolts which flew swiftly toward Aurotos. With one swing after another, Aurotos deflected each arcane bolt back toward the sage, who absorbed it with his arcane shield. Aurotos wouldn't show it, but there was nothing he could do to help himself from being impressed by the sage's capability. He could see that he was clearly more than just a wise man. Yet, as enigmatic as his true identity was, Armatay did not reveal anything to break that façade.

"Heh, well done, Aurotos," Armatay said. "Well done indeed, I noticed you were not able to absorb any of my attacks with your sword. The blade of your father would serve you better now and it is just the thing for absorbing attacks as it bolsters itself against its enemies. It has other special attributes that you can use as well, but for now, I would like to teach you how to use it to absorb my attacks."

Armatay walked toward Aurotos with a plea, "Please put away your cinder sword and withdraw Ai'ethe. There is something I need to show you, but it will require the radiant blade. And this time, I wish for you to do this with your eyes closed. Do not worry about being injured. Trust your instincts. Feel the pull of your sword in hand, let it seek out the objects that come toward you. If you are hit this time, it will only sting a bit."

"Armatay, I can't block what I can't see," Aurotos said.

"When you attune yourself to the radiant blade, even with your eyes closed, you will be able to sense what you cannot see. And in time, even without the blade's help, you may be able to see far more. With or without the blade in hand, you will see that you have much greater visibility. The blade will help you to see more clearly, not only at close range but also at great distances."

"Alright, I'm ready," Aurotos said, closing his eyes. As he withdrew the blade of his father, he could feel the difference in both the weight of the sword and its size in comparison. Although the blade was much larger and wider, it somehow was much lighter than his cinder sword counterpart. It felt like the sword of a king.

"Now, ready yourself," Armatay said as he again released another barrage of arcane bolts toward Aurotos. These bolts were much lighter and smaller and they flew toward him quite fast.

Aurotos raised his sword in front of him and moved his blade aimlessly in an attempt to block the bolts. Only once did he feel that he had an awareness of the projectiles heading in his direction. Each of the ones that hit him impacted him hard, but he was well protected under his armor and it felt like nothing more than rocks being thrown at him.

"I couldn't sense anything different, maybe once, but I don't feel anything that could help me protect myself from what is coming. Even at first, I couldn't tell if that sense was real or just my imagination," Aurotos said in frustration.

"Use your senses, trust your instincts, and the Twin Flames. Let their light guide you. When you are attuned, it will feel almost as if the light itself shows you the true nature of things," Armatay said.

Aurotos once again closed his eyes and raised the radiant blade before him. Again, the sage launched a barrage of small arcane bolts in his direction. He deflected one bolt but felt the impact as the rest of them hit him all over his armor. Frustrated, he thrust his blade into the sand before him. "What is it that I can't seem to get right with this blade?" Aurotos said.

"Heh, you are frustrated. It will pass," Armatay said. "Your weakness with this blade is not about how skilled you are. It is your lack of faith in the Twin Flames, and your indecision to open yourself to the world and those you share it with. Heh, you must trust these things and in the noble tenets. I offer a bit of advice to you, there is great strength in being vulnerable. This lesson will aid you in working with your allies; they too can bolster your strength beyond measure. In humility and even vulnerability, lies great strength and purpose. We will have another lesson later, for now, think on what I shared, and rest yourself this evening. I will see you in the morning."

Armatay made his way back toward the quarters where the others had already been preparing to sleep. As Aurotos followed loosely behind the sage back into the stronghold, he could see that several knights had gathered. Syvon, Leavesa, and Salenval had all witnessed the lesson but did not say anything to him as he passed by.

Although it caused him to feel uncomfortable, Aurotos reflected on the sage's wisdom. He couldn't deny that Armatay spoke the truth about something that he had often pondered when left to his own thoughts. As he arrived in his room and prepared to get sleep that night, he couldn't stop wondering if he opened himself up to the sage's instructions, could it change the course of things to come? Could the possibilities the sage suggested truly be so much better for him, not only in combat but in matters beyond the blade? As Aurotos laid himself down to sleep that night he continued contemplating what Armatay had said. There was a stirring within him and a yearning for more. Not just as a leader, or as the last Auron, but as a person. As he drifted away, he found himself thinking of the golden-haired beauty who had captivated him and, in some way, seemed to pull at his heart strings unlike anything he had ever experienced before.

CHAPTER 10

THE SAENA TREE

The next morning when Aurotos awoke and made his way outside, he saw that the knights and magi had already gathered by the stables. Corlith was there leading the horses out to the different members of the groups of magi and knights. The sage was there too, waiting patiently. As Aurotos closed in on the group, he saw Molvalan leaning against the stable wall where he appeared to talk to someone even though he was alone. Aurotos already felt concerned about the dark, shady appearance of the magi, and this didn't help matters much. Although Aurodites could be trusted, this one seemed a bit suspicious, with his maniacal laugh as he continued rambling to himself.

As Aurotos approached the group, he saw that Anaryen was waiting for him. In her commanding voice she spoke up and was clearly prepared for what she had to say to him. "Aurotos, we should be off right away. I have had a dreadful feeling all morning that the saena tree may already be under attack, and if it isn't already, then it will be soon."

"What makes you think that he might already be there, my lady? If they're under siege, the watchers here would have seen something from the north to indicate an attack. By now, we'd already know," Aurotos said.

"That's just it," Anaryen said. "If they're under attack, I don't think we'd be able to see it. Drazius is surrounded by a veil of darkness wherever he and his army ride. I'm sure it would conceal any hint of an attack. If there is anything for him to destroy on his way to Valenthreas,

129

he will. He seems to be enjoying the terror he causes; if he was to attack a place that is defenseless, news could spread throughout the realm that no place is safe."

"Alright, I can agree with that, we should move," Aurotos said.

"Remember, I was at Illonel where he killed innocent students, and many of them were young. It wasn't a military location and look what happened. I'm so worried about the nayrans and anyone else who could be there."

"I know, we'll hurry. Soon we'll know if he's made it there or not."

As Anaryen walked toward her magi, Aurotos looked upon his knights and spoke. "I've talked to Lady Anaryen and we're both in agreement that we should move as fast as our steeds will allow us to the saena tree. Although we received no sign here of an attack, it would still be best for us to move swiftly," Aurotos said.

"What's going on? Does Lady Anaryen know something?" Leavesa asked.

"She doesn't know for sure but she suspects an attack may already be underway," Aurotos said. He could see Leavesa's face turn to concern as urgency set in.

Aurotos had made his commands and everyone in the company soon made their way up the hidden path, leaving only a singular order to Zeydi and those who remained protected at Mai'elzin. "Prepare your defenses and await word from us on how to proceed as we uncover what danger Drazius brings to Aurotheros," Aurotos said.

"As you command, my lord; be safe and may the light of the Twin Flames protect you all," Zeydi said bowing in respect.

As Aurotos and his retinue moved up the hidden path, he felt a sense of dread set in. Was this the same feeling that Anaryen was feeling? His concern for her distress had set his senses on fire.

The group of companions charged north along the coast of the elven lands into the afternoon. It took them less than a full day to reach the dominion at one of the world's great landmarks. This saena tree had become the center for a nayran college of alchemy and herbalism. As the companions grew closer, they could see smoke rising from under the tree just over the horizon. It did not seem that the tree itself was burning, but instead, it appeared to be the ruined structures ablaze at its base.

As Aurotos got closer to the outer borders of the now ruined school, he immediately signaled the others to stop. Ahead of them it was clear that a group of drothkin were scavenging the buildings and roaming around the outskirts of the college. Aurotos and the party could hear the screams of those who remained alive, and to them, it sounded as if the people were being attacked or, even worse, eaten alive.

"Aurotos," Anaryen said as she looked to him, a plea in her eyes. They had to act, and fast.

"Oh, not the alchemists—they're innocent" Drelion said. "By the Masters, we're too late."

Aurotos scanned the rest of the group and could see mixed expressions of shock and bewilderment among them. He knew all too well that Drelion had studied among the nayrans at the school for many years before he came to be a Knight of the Phoenix. He felt sympathy for his fellow knight and had no intention for any of them to stand by while the enemy brutalized the innocent that could still be alive. "Onward, to the tree. Save who you can. Cleanse the school of these drothkin," he commanded and the retinue darted forward.

Aurotos could hear Anaryen shouting too as she and her magi charged forward as fiercely as any of the knights. Every member of the party rode straight in and cut through the drothkin who were scavenging along the outer walls of the alchemist's school. The steeds moved so quick that the drothkin had no way to escape and any caught roaming were slain.

Each knight's sword was coated in the burnt blood of the beasts they had cut down before they made their way deeper, passing through the walls of the college. They pressed through the southern gateway into one of the squares only to realize that every building had collapsed—it was unlikely that anyone studying here survived under the burning rubble of the buildings that were desolated around them.

Neither the knights nor the magi seemed to be able to make out any survivors. Survivors would be hard to hear as many of the wooden structures were crackling and popping under the raging fires which had swept across the alchemist's school. The metallic odor of blood in the air was strong, and the thick smoke from the fires blanketing the area hindered their efforts to find anyone left alive.

Even the old sage who had struck down several of the final drothkin trying to escape had a difficult time holding out hope that anyone could be alive. He uttered, "Oh, Twin Flames, please guide your children back. May the Masters bless their souls and cleanse them of their sorrow."

All of the drothkin that had been visible were dead at the hands of the knights except for one that had been hiding and was noticed leaping over the school's outer wall, dashing away to the west. Aurotos thought to send Corlith and several of the knights to seek other escaping drothkin, but he knew their first charge must be tending to survivors. He also knew it would be unwise to split up their group until they knew what they were up against.

Anaryen dismounted, and quickly stopped the fire from spreading to the massive tree above, sending a cold mist across the roots nearby which the flames were threatening. In doing so, she found an old nayran who had barely survived the drothkin, abandoning its kill only to seek an escape when the knights and magi arrived.

Anaryen aided the nayran and was determined to extinguish all of the fires. "Elenfia, Molvalan, help me," she said. Her fellow magi cast their spells to nullify the fire that was destroying everything around them.

"Where are the bodies? All I see is blood soaked into the grass, but I can't see…" Elenfia said until she stopped where she stood in horror.

Aurotos had been watching as Anaryen displayed the power of her skills with frost and ice, blanketing all the buildings with a cool mist that grew icy, its crystalline structure consuming any fires that had been present. He could see how desperately she fought to search for survivors. In their search, Elenfia had just come to find the body of a dear friend. Elenfia's childhood friend had been murdered along with many of the nayran people, her body lying there on the ground before her.

Elenfia sat on her knees crying over the body. Molvalan stood behind her as if waiting for instructions on what he could do to help her. "At least there is still a body to mourn over," he said.

"Molvalan, please…" Elenfia said as the thought of the drothkin that could have eaten her friend caused her to appear sickly.

"I'm sorry, Elenfia, I would never wish to make things worse for you," Molvalan said.

"I know you didn't. Just stay with me."

"There's nowhere else I'd rather be," he said as he laid his hand on her shoulder. She leaned her head on his hand and Molvalan could feel her tears running onto it. "I'm here," he said as he offered to pull her in closer.

"You're sweet, that means a lot," Elenfia said as she moved closer to him, taking in his affection.

Amidst all the chaos, Aurotos was still captivated by Anaryen and her powerful display of skill with the elements. He was so impressed in fact, that he almost couldn't hear the nayran below him pleading for his help. The old nayran who Anaryen had helped earlier had come to Aurotos for his aid. "Ay, please help me, my brother is underneath the flames, en just there," he said as he pointed to the rubble behind Aurotos.

As Aurotos looked to the rubble, he had trouble believing the nayran's brother would be alive beneath the smoldering ruin of the building. Still, Aurotos thought he had to try and so he shouted for help. "Anaryen, I need you to extinguish these flames," he said.

Anaryen was quite surprised by Aurotos' request as even she didn't think it was possible for anyone to be alive under the hot flames consuming the collapsed building. She didn't expect him to heed the nayran's plea as it seemed hopeless to everyone else there. "Yes, okay," she said as she cooled the flames until the ruins were no longer on fire.

"Stand back. Just tell me where he was," Aurotos said.

"Ay, just there," the old nayran pointed.

Aurotos began lifting stone after stone following the instructions of the old nayran who seemed sure that his brother was beneath the rubble. Anaryen had been watching his desperate attempt to save the nayran's brother and her tough exterior began to crack as tears swelled in her eyes, moved by how hard Aurotos fought to find him.

"Oy, Iseni, en I'm here," said a quiet, muffled voice from under the final stones laying before Aurotos.

"Ay Neroni, I hear you, en we're almost to you," Iseni said, tears filling his big green eyes.

As Aurotos lifted the final stone, the old nayran screamed with happiness. "Ay, thank you, thank you, my brother, you saved my brother." He hugged Aurotos, poking his leg with one of his horns.

Neroni took Aurotos' hand and was lifted to his feet. Remarkably, he didn't even have a scratch. Aurotos brought both brothers together who met with their horns and closed their eyes, holding each other's hands in a brother's embrace.

Aurotos sat down on the large stone he had pulled out of the rubble. "Lord Va'Threas," the brothers said together as they kneeled. They had realized who it was that had helped them, and it made them both very excited even though they were so tired from what had just occurred.

"You're welcome, now please stand," Aurotos said. "Let us help you, Nahul, Drelion please," he said as he signaled for the two who both appeared ready to help.

As Aurotos sat down, he saw something dark move close to him out of the corner of his eye. A shadowy, snake-like creature attempted to bite his hand, but before it got close enough, Aurotos saw it and was able to slice its head off, leaving it oozing black matter on the ground before him. The strange serpent creature had two small arms with small, damaged wings.

"By the flames, what was that? I suppose I should be glad it couldn't fly," Aurotos exclaimed as he took a closer look.

The situation had caught both Armatay and Anaryen's attention causing them to move in to inspect the creature. "Oh my, what's that?" Anaryen said. "Some sort of serpent, but it's not one I've ever seen before."

"It looks like a spawn of the Merdah," Aurotos replied, looking to Armatay for reassurance.

"Oh, yes, it is. This creature was created for a single purpose, to infect others with a dark sickness. Had it struck you, it could have infected you quite horribly with the essence of the fade," Armatay said, looking at the remains of the creature shriveling into a black powder.

"I've never seen one of these. Could there be more?" Aurotos asked as he scanned the surrounding area.

"Hmm, I doubt it. The last time I heard of one of these being found it was..." Armatay's face turned pale.

"What, Armatay? Tell me," Aurotos demanded.

"Heh, all I wish to say is that it was in a situation much like the night you were attacked in Valenthreas," Armatay said.

"You were attacked?" Anaryen inquired.

Aurotos's face was drawn with sadness and he felt his guarded façade slip under Anaryen's gaze. "It was the night before we left the city. While I was asleep, a gnome assassin tried to attack me, but my two cats Angor and Siam protected me. I lost them that night."

"Oh dear, I'm so sorry," Anaryen said as her own guarded demeanor fell for a moment. "They must have loved you so very much."

For a moment, Aurotos could have sworn he saw Anaryen's hand begin to reach for his. He hastily looked toward the sage to see if he noticed and was only met with Armatay's subtle smile as if proud to see that Aurotos was making a connection with Anaryen. But the smile was fleeting, for the sage's fear seemed to be of primary concern.

"Aurotos...these are never left in places unintentionally. This was set here as a trap," Armatay said. "We must be careful, the closer we get to Drazius, the more surprises like this we may find."

"It seems that way. I don't like surprises," Aurotos said.

"Yes, well, I should help the others get ready," Anaryen said as she awkwardly began making her way back toward the knights and magi.

As she did so, Aurotos could see she was quite comfortable ordering others to gather herbs and other items so she could heal another one of the injured nayran survivors. It was clear, as she knelt over the survivor, that she possessed healing skills that Aurotos had not been aware of.

Lady Anaryen spared no discretion in directing her orders to both the Knights of the Phoenix and Aurodites. "You two could help our nayran friends here by collecting the undamaged road wagons and carriages that are still usable. You can attach them to the aurochs I saw by the building over by the gateway we came through. I think that will do just fine."

Under her instructions both Nahul and Drelion looked to Aurotos with curious expressions as if unsure about the lady's orders.

Aurotos nodded toward them in agreement, and they knew they would be expected by him to honor her commands. Seeing that Aurotos had supported her, the lady smiled for the first time although it would have been hard to tell as she continued to heal Neroni's wounds.

Aurotos gathered himself but couldn't stop watching Anaryen as she healed their broken bodies with the magic radiating out of her hands. There was something about her spirit that reminded him of his mother, and he liked how at ease she seemed to be while giving orders. Anaryen had every making of a future queen. Like his own mother, she too was commanding and fierce but also loyal and compassionate. For a moment, he had seen her compassion for him. But had he really seen her almost reach out for his hand or was it all in his head?

There was more that he found himself captivated by. It was rare to see a magi who practiced both elemental magic as well as magic of the divine. Aurotos knew that she must have had a very strong devotion to the gods, for if she did not, she couldn't possibly wield the power to heal. Even more captivating was that Anaryen must have practiced her skills for many years to be as proficient as she was. Such skill did not come from a life lived within the walls of her kingdom's castle. She was no ordinary princess, and he wished to unravel all of the things that made her who she was.

Under the orders of Anaryen, the two knights brought the nayrans some food and blankets. Drelion gave the two some salves he had on hand for he was always sure to be stocked with herbal remedies. He continued setting out several vials to prepare some potions and elixirs which both brothers seemed excited by. As alchemists themselves, the three began chatting away about all the different ways the herbs could be used; to an observer, it was hard to tell whether it was the knight or the two brothers who were more excited.

Nahul chuckled at the three who were chatting away and blanketed the two brothers who had sat down on some of the rubble. He wandered off and prepared a couple aurochs that were still alive so the survivors could use a road wagon to head somewhere safe. There was little time to prepare the survivors and themselves, so both the Aurodites and the Knights of the Phoenix made quick work of their duties.

Not long had passed and it seemed that the survivors were all prepared to leave. Aurotos instructed them to move away from the tree. "I'm counting on you two to get the others to safety. I know there aren't many of you, but you should get to Valenthreas. You will be safe there until the prince is stopped," Aurotos said.

"Ay, on our word, my lord," Iseni said. Both brothers had agreed they would guide the wagons to Valenthreas themselves along the southernmost route. As they hopped up into the wagon and led the aurochs forward out of the gate, the two took a final look back and waved at Aurotos who wore a large grin as he waved back.

Anaryen had seen the smile slip from where she stood by her horse. Aurotos had seen her looking and was compelled to check on her, so he made his way toward her. "Lady Anaryen...you have a gentle touch. I must commend you on your healing skill."

"Thank you, my lord. You should know, I think you fought admirably to save the life of Neroni's brother."

"Each person who places their trust in us is one worthy of our best efforts. I wouldn't be much of an Auron if I didn't do at least that much for them."

"Well sure, but you didn't have to. No one would have believed his brother was alive under all that."

"Maybe not, but it was important to me that I tried."

"You know, you surprise me."

"In what way, my lady?"

"Oh, it's hard to explain. You seem pretty closed off to people, yet I sense a gentle nature about you," Anaryen said as she smiled coyly.

"That's the first time I've heard anyone refer to me as gentle," Aurotos said, laughing a bit, catching himself by surprise. He wasn't used to that kind of laughter, not since his youth. Having a smile or laughter escape him in such a way hadn't occurred since he had his two small cats by his side. Even when they made him laugh it wasn't like she did. For a moment he felt the need to guard himself again but that tendency of his would be fleeting.

"I don't know what to say, you have me at a loss for words, my lady."

"Oh, do I now? I've been wondering if you're usually at a loss or if that just happens to be when you're speaking to me."

"Ever only you, my lady," Aurotos said, ensuring he gazed deeply into her eyes so she knew how important the moment was for him.

The words seemed to strike Anaryen deeply and the blush in her cheeks couldn't be hidden. As she appeared to be speechless, Aurotos had to investigate what he was also curious about in her. "You surprise me too, my lady. I wouldn't have expected the princess of Eden Throvon to be serving as an Aurodite. That seems like such an unlikely thing to be true."

"Is that so? Oh well, you're probably right. It's the normal custom of any lady to serve her king and queen within the royal court. The expectations placed upon me at such a young age really weren't any different," she said.

"Except, you're the eldest daughter and your parents are the ruling monarchs."

"It's true. If my father had his way, I would have been expected to marry another ruling family to keep the peace and tranquility within the human realms secure. It's just that…"

"It's just what?"

"You know, I always wanted to do more than that. I love my parents and I would never wish to harm our kingdom but if I marry, I want it to be only out of love for someone that will last through all of eternity. The world's suffering is a problem; as an Aurodite I could still serve the people and I thought I had to choose one or the other. I don't know, it seemed like the best thing I could do was honor the Twin Flames through my service in such trying times."

Aurotos appreciated her perspective and he felt that they might share a lot more in common than he originally believed. More importantly, her words about honoring the Twin Flames struck him deeply as a reminder of his own path and choices. "I can see why you might believe that you would have to make that choice. I don't see why you shouldn't have both, my lady."

"I know, you're right. I've always believed that too, but I've just put it aside."

"I know what that's like," Aurotos said as their eyes met and they shared a final curious smile toward one another.

For a moment the two stood side by side watching the knights and the magi gather up their own steeds to prepare themselves to pursue the attackers.

As Anaryen walked toward her fellow magi who were standing with their own horses, she could see that Elenfia was wiping tears from her eyes while being comforted by Molvalan. "Oh, dear. I'm so sorry Elenfia, I'm here for you my friend," Anaryen said.

"I know, my lady. It's just hard seeing the nayrans leaving knowing that Edetta's body is in the back of their cart," Elenfia said. "It's a shame we can't retrieve any of the other bodies, the drothkin are vile."

"I can only imagine the kind of pain you must be feeling," Anaryen said. "Listen, what do you say we go find the ones who did this and stop them before they hurt anyone else?"

"I think...yes. I'm ready, my lady" Elenfia said as she wiped away the last of her tears and leapt up on her horse with the aid of Molvalan who hadn't left her side since she found her murdered friend.

Before leaving, Aurotos was met by Armatay who he could see was prepared to deliver another lesson of sorts. "You know that is something you and your father share. He too would have been willing to help those in need even when others may have thought that hope for them was lost," he said.

Aurotos did not respond, but it did cause him to think about his father. As he stood there, the sage continued by telling him about a moment during the great war in which his father believed in aiding others, even though they were believed to be dead. His father was remembered fondly for his deeds which had inspired great devotion and admiration from the people that he led and the people he served as king.

Aurotos continued to listen to Armatay who he felt give him a pat on the shoulder, and as he prepared to mount his own horse, he contemplated this truth. He knew that this was a trait shared between he and his father, but he had not expected he would display that trait today. He had never been in a situation like the one he had just witnessed, where he could change the fate of those who found themselves in such a hopeless state. While he was a Knight of the Phoenix his time had been spent protecting the elven borders or seeking out dark creatures that needed to be vanquished across the lands.

Something he was sure of was that the snake-like creature that had attacked him was unlike anything he had seen before, and he wondered what would have happened if it had bitten him. There was no more time to think about it. The knights and their new companions, the Aurodites, would pursue the drothkin who had escaped to the west. They hoped that it could lead them to the one who had commanded them and reveal the truth behind the plans of the evil already set in motion.

CHAPTER 11

NEARING TWILIGHT

After a short time pursuing the drothkin with his retinue, Aurotos remembered what the sage had told him about the motives he had suspected Prince Khorvek was working under. Armatay had warned him that he did not believe it was solely the dark prince or the dark orc who had truly orchestrated the events unfolding before them. Sure, Lord Grindam had a hand in things, but the prince and he were only pawns under the guidance of Master Ohrimah.

Aurotos found himself fixed on the sage and his warnings about the nature of the dark master. He believed the sage was right: Ohrimah was plotting something within his realm of darkness, pulling at the strings of his minions like puppets. It was not only the drothkin who served him but also other creatures and people whose will had been broken by either strife or sorrow. Aurotos was mindful of Armatay's warning that the dark prince must have murdered his own father as part of a greater plan to set things in motion. The events were currently unfolding before them exactly how the dark master had devised.

The retinue rode faster and harder as they closed the gap between them and the enemy who had fled away from the saena tree. No matter how hard Aurotos rode, his mind remained fixed on the dark master. His instincts assured him something much larger than he could conceive was most certainly at play. Deep down there was a sense of dread that another false victory would come to the elves and the countless souls across the world.

Armatay had caution to share with the extended group of companions once more. "You all must remember this. Whatever the dark prince has planned, we know only a fraction of. We must learn what his main goal is and we must learn it soon."

"We will Armatay, we will," Aurotos said knowingly.

The knights and their magi allies had pursued the drothkin for what seemed like several moments before they spotted a group of them marching alone toward a point of interest just ahead to the west. Seeing that the drothkin had slowed down, the party stopped to take refuge underneath a large tree and its sagging branches, being careful to remain far enough behind so as not to give themselves away. Beyond the tree was a field stretching past the top of the hill not far ahead of the drothkin where the edge of the Valendreth Forest lay.

Aurotos knew he had to act fast and beckoned the scout to come closer. "Corlith, the drothkin are slowing; they may have stopped over that hill. I need you to scout ahead and report back as quickly as you can," he said.

"Yes, my lord, so it'll be," Corlith said as he dismounted his horse and dashed away.

"I think it best that we tie off our horses here, my lord," Leavesa whispered.

"Good idea, alright, let's get to it everyone," Aurotos said.

As they were dismounting and preparing themselves, Anaryen took interest in how one of the knights was able to ease the horses who appeared distressed by the nearby drothkin. "Nahul, was it? You seem to have a way with animals," Anaryen said.

"Indeed, my lady, all animals are innocent and I protect them when I'm able. It makes me ill seeing them suffer, especially to such evil," Nahul said as he glanced in the direction of the drothkin. He paused shortly and bowed slightly toward Anaryen before he moved away with urgency to continue aiding the horses who he then tied off at the tree's trunk.

"Nahul has spent a great deal of his life dedicated to the betterment of nature. He offers a great deal of care for animals created by the Twin Flames or the Masters. You should see how he marvels at an auvinot,"

Aurotos said standing just ahead of her, between his retinue and whatever laid beyond them.

"It seems each of your knights has their own talents," Anaryen said as she moved closer to him.

"As do you and your magi, my lady."

"And what of your talents?"

"Well—"

"Heh, well, I believe his have yet to be realized," Armatay said as he appeared just beside them with an amused look upon his face.

"Is that so? Oh my, that is curious," Anaryen said offering a hint of a smile for Aurotos, daring him to look as her tone was playful enough to cut through even his stoicism.

Armatay chuckled, and as Aurotos felt himself tempted to look the conversation was cut short as Corlith had returned. "My lord, I can't see any larger mass near the drothkin we found. There's maybe one hundred of them and they're not aware that we're here. They seem fixed on gathering just at the edge of the wood," Corlith said.

Elenfia had overheard the scouts report. "If there's only a hundred of them, then we should kill them now. Those vile creatures murdered my friend. I just can't stand to let them live after what they did," she said.

Anaryen was visibly becoming very concerned for her fellow Aurodite. "You must calm yourself, Elenfia. I know you grieve but you can't give in to your sorrow, you can't let it guide your actions, you know the dangers," she said.

"I know, my lady, but if we do nothing now…I just can't, I swear I'll finish them here," Elenfia replied. "I'm sorry but I can't let them continue, I'll see to it myself," she said as she started walking beyond the tree into the field ahead.

"Ah um, my lady, I must go with Elenfia, I cannot let her do this alone," Molvalan said as he looked toward her reluctantly and began moving close behind his companion.

"Aurodite or not, this is typical human carelessness," Syvon said.

"Try not to be so quick to judge, Syvon; could you remain perfectly composed if you lost someone dear to you?" Anaryen asked.

"My lady, I lost both of my parents in the great war long before you were born—" Syvon said.

"Syvon, this isn't helping," Leavesa said.

"Alright then…alright," Syvon said as he fought to remove the scowl forming upon his face.

"Aurotos, I have my reservations, but I can't let her go forward alone. My lord, please," Anaryen said as she looked toward him, her hope filling her eyes.

"He's right, she has a look of vengeance to her, but this is what we do. I say we clobber them, my lord," Salenval said.

"My senses are against this, my lord, something isn't right about this," Arvasiel said.

Aurotos looked to Vael and Tarothas and sought their recommendations. "What about you two? What do your senses tell you?"

"I can see nothing save the drothkin before us," Vael said. "If there is anything beyond them, I cannot see it."

"I am uncertain, my lord, I have a sense that there's more before us, yet nothing I can hear," Tarothas said.

"And what of the creatures?" Aurotos asked.

"I wish I could tell you something more, my lord, but they're terrified of the drothkin. Indeed, all creatures within range of my senses are silent," Nahul said.

Aurotos had to decide and he had to do it fast. Evening would soon turn into night, and the world glowing around them would be bathed in the light of Valos once more. Maybe the attack could work in their favor. He had a sense of hesitancy about pursuing the enemy so close to the tree line, yet he had trusted Corlith to scout ahead for any danger.

Aurotos leaned toward agreeing to fight, but he couldn't explain even to himself why, among the group, it was Anaryen whom he feared being hurt. He struggled to understand why he didn't want to see her in danger. Finally, Aurotos decided. "If we are to move, then we must do this stealthily," he said. "Anaryen, your Aurodites may proceed with our knights."

"Wait, they will join us," Molvalan said as he stopped Elenfia who had no longer even been paying any attention for she was consumed with her desire for retribution.

"Kaylos, Syvon, Salenval you come with me. Armatay, you'll move with us too, we'll proceed south, covering your flank as we move along the slope of the hill. The drothkin aren't far from the tree line, so if they move to escape, we should be able to intercept them through the woods. We can use the high grass of the field to provide us with cover. Leave the horses," Aurotos said.

Beyond the western slope of the hill, the drothkin were camping just on the edge of the woods. High ground was all around them, both beyond them where the trees resided and were Anaryen and Aurotos's group would be moving. The magi and knights all had the benefit of high ground.

Aurotos signaled to the knights to proceed, and he and his group advanced. The sage even removed his large hat, ensuring that it wouldn't stand out in the tall, dark grass. As Aurotos and his companions moved closer toward the forest, it became all too evident that the area around them grew darker. It seemed as though the proximity to the trees caused a dimming effect, affecting not only the moonlight above but also the ambient light of the surrounding foliage.

"Oh my, I sense the gloomveil," Armatay said. "Whatever this dimming is, it is affecting the grass; this just might help us move unseen for a time."

Aurotos sensed something different, a feeling that reminded him of the night his two cats were killed. He winced, wondering if things would be different if he'd sensed its presence in his room that night. Now, experiencing the effects of the gloomveil himself, Aurotos could only nod back in understanding.

As Anaryen and her group neared the ridge of the hill, it was all she could do to not light the way in the darkening terrain ahead of them. "I don't like this," she said. "It reminds me of Illonel."

"Nor do I, my lady, but Elenfia is set," Molvalan said.

"Just about there," Elenfia said, her focus unaffected.

Salenval stayed low by Aurotos as he peered ahead toward the drothkin and then back at the tree line and uttered his only care. "The woods are extra dark, maybe we could attack from there," he said.

"Agreed, the wood should aid us. Kaylos, be ready to blend through the shadows once we reach them," Aurotos said.

"You know I will, my lord, just give the word and I'm gone," Kaylos said as he lightly placed his closed fist over his chest.

Over the hill below, the drothkin fought amongst themselves and wandered aimlessly, almost as if they were waiting for something or someone to command them. Aurotos looked to the sage, who was looking back at him and holding his hand up, signaling to pause. Soon after, all of those with Aurotos shared the same look. It was almost immediate, as each got a sense that something wasn't right, but it was too late to communicate this with the rest of the knights, for they and the Aurodites had already begun charging toward the drothkin from over the hill.

Aurotos and his companions could only watch in awe as Anaryen fearlessly led the charge, accompanied by her Aurodites. The scene unfolding before them was nothing short of spectacular. The Aurodites unleashed a relentless onslaught of spells upon the drothkin. Anaryen, with her mastery over ice, froze many of the creatures in place, while Elenfia conjured a tempest of lightning that struck down numerous foes, leaving them stunned or lifeless. The Aurodites' magical prowess was truly remarkable, once again earning the admiration of their knight comrades. Molvalan displayed extraordinary control over the earth and raised the very ground around the fleeing drothkin, trapping them in a makeshift prison of dirt and stone. The skill and precision with which they manipulated the elements was breathtaking. Inspired by their display, Leavesa followed suit, casting fireballs that ignited the drothkin, leaving them screaming in misery, left to die bathed in flames.

The magi displayed an equal measure of precision and skill in harnessing the elements, much like the knights who wielded their flaming cinder swords with expertise. The use of fire became almost unnecessary, as the charging knights swiftly dispatched the few drothkin who managed to remain standing. It was evident that the beasts stood no chance against the combined might of the knights and magi. Even Corlith, appearing more annoyed than jubilant, proved himself by eliminating several drothkin, showing just how deadly he could be with his short bow.

Just as the Aurodites approached the tree line, they were taken by surprise as Commander Griles emerged with a platoon of branded human soldiers. Anaryen and her two magi found themselves suddenly entangled by bolas that came flying from the depths of the forest. Rope darts swiftly followed suit, tightly binding their feet and hands, pulling the captured Aurodites toward the edge of the trees. Commander Griles stepped forward, his laughter tinged with madness.

"That's it, any sudden movements, and see that these magi meet their end," he commanded, relishing in the unexpected gift before him. "Lady Anaryen Valenvon and her escaped magi, accompanied by the Knights of the Phoenix, all under my control. Now, the question remains: what to do with you?"

Griles looked toward the knights with disgust as he spoke. "Drop your weapons, elves, or they die," he said.

"Very well. Knights, stand down; we won't be responsible for the death of the Aurodites," Leavesa said.

"That's right elves, do as the she elf commands. Now where is the rest of your group? We know there are more of you," Griles demanded.

Salenval was ready to rush the enemy; Aurotos could see it in his eyes. "Steady," he said as he glanced toward Salenval. "Let them talk, we'll intercept them through the forest," Aurotos said.

Swiftly, Aurotos and his party ventured into the woods, moving with utmost care to avoid making any noise. Fear gripped their hearts, aware that the darkness could betray their presence. They stilled their movements, pressing deeper into the woods. In the distance, outside the tree line, they could hear Griles Grentin's voice echoing.

"Come now, there were others with you. Have them reveal themselves and surrender, or tell us where they hide. Either way, you will all be captured and brought before my prince."

Griles was met with silence, as none of them dared to respond. His gaze scanned over the group of companions before him until his eyes locked with Corlith, who reacted with a peculiar gesture. Filled with rage, Griles shouted and forcefully brought Anaryen forward, holding her captive on her knees, with his black dagger pressed close to her skin.

"Tell me where they are," he said as he gripped the blade more firmly against her throat.

"Tell this traitor nothing," Anaryen said as her eyes locked with Leavesa's.

"Oh please, how heroic. If they won't speak, perhaps your blood will reveal the secrets you hide and loosen their tongues," Griles said.

As Griles stiffened his grip further, preparing to cut Anaryen, he heard a shout behind him that commanded his attention in a way that not even his prince could.

"You have your answer," Aurotos shouted.

Shocked and taken aback, Griles sensed sudden explosions of fire erupting from behind him. Startled, he turned around to see only a handful of knights decimating his platoon of soldiers. Salenval charged one soldier after the next delivering powerful strikes which cut down the enemy in a single blow. Darting around him was Syvon who moved so fast he could barely be tracked visually. Every so often he caught a glimpse of Kaylos fading in and out of the shadows leaving a soldier passing in his wake.

That was when the commanders shock seemed to change. In that moment, Griles caught a glimpse of Aurotos leading the charge, his eyes glowing with sunlight. Aurotos could see his disgust and hatred intensifying, realizing that the voice he had heard came from the last surviving Va'Threan.

As the branded soldiers became engulfed in flames, Griles felt Anaryen slip from his grasp, causing him to stumble backwards in shock. Suddenly, his survival instinct kicked in, and he thought only of saving himself. Without uttering a word or offering any resistance, he turned and fled deeper into the trees, seeking his own selfish escape. However, his escape came at the cost of every branded soldier who had been assigned to serve under his orders.

While Griles faded into the darkness of the trees, Aurotos and his knights thought only of attending to their companions. With the final arcing swings of their blades, Aurotos and his knights cut down the branded humans who remained.

Armatay moved fast and attended to Anaryen, comforting her. "Are you all right, my lady," Armatay asked, appearing worried.

"Yes, I'm fine, Armatay. Don't worry yourself, all is well," Anaryen replied.

"I'm sorry, my lord. I was certain there wasn't anyone else here," Corlith said.

"Release your burden, Corlith. There is a certain darkness to this place and it seems to be fading," Aurotos said now shifting his attention to Griles and his escape.

Elenfia rushed toward Anaryen offering her aid. "Please forgive me, my lady," Elenfia said. "I should have listened."

Aurotos also moved to Anaryen's side with his own worries. "Anaryen, did they hurt you?" he asked as he took her hand and helped her to her feet.

As Anaryen looked at him, Aurotos could see the hardness fade from her eyes replaced with a glowing warmth which stilled the world around him. If only for a moment, time seemed to stop as he made sure she was safe.

"I'm alright, thank you," Anaryen responded, turning her attention to her fellow magi. "Are you two okay?"

"Yes but, my lady, I'm so—" Elenfia replied and her eyes filled with tears under realizing the weight of her mistake. Molvalan moved behind her and placed both of his hands on her shoulders providing what comfort he could.

"Calm yourself, Elenfia. It's alright, let's put it behind us," Anaryen said.

"Their commander is getting away, he can't be allowed to escape after how he threatened you," Aurotos said.

"Don't go after him," Anaryen urged. "It could be a trap; the woods are too dark."

"Don't worry, he's alone," Aurotos said.

Wasting no time, Aurotos was off, charging after the commander. His desire for justice was brimming beyond measure. He would not let this commander get away after placing a knife to Anaryen's throat. Griles had betrayed the world by serving the dark master but that crime paled in comparison to the threat he had placed on Anaryen who he was growing increasingly fond of.

Seeing Aurotos was set on seeing his will done, the sage commanded everyone to remain where they were as he trailed behind him. "Aurotos, you must stop, you cannot chase him alone in the gloomveil's presence."

Aurotos was closing in on the commander, and as he did so, the commander let out a maniacal laugh as he spoke. "So unwise, sacred one."

Suddenly from out of the ground arose a dark entity. Aurotos knew all too well what this was and realized he had played right into a trap. It was a daevos from the realm of the dark master. In shock, Aurotos slipped, falling backward onto the ground to see the demon rising before him. The demon was absolute blackness with red eyes and horns. Large black streams of energy reached out from behind it as if seeking something to connect to. It was barely a solid form before him. Had it not been for his Auron eyes, he may not have seen it at all at first. As it now stood over him, he could hear the commander trailing further away, continuing to laugh in his escape.

Before Aurotos could withdraw his blade or cast any flames, he saw the demon raising its arm, and with a screech, it struck down upon him with its claws. Aurotos immediately raised his arms in an attempt to block the demon. He felt the impact seem to penetrate his plate armor before hearing the welcome sound of Armatay just behind him.

As the sage reached him, he raised his staff, pointing it straight toward the demon and let out a command. "Back to the darkness demon," he shouted. "Back to your dark master, you shall not survive in the presence of pure light."

Armatay, now standing over Aurotos with his staff raised high, illuminated the woods, bathing it in a purifying light that pulsed forward, pushing the demon back. His staff created a bubble of light that extended over both himself and Aurotos.

"I see you daevos, back to the darkness," Armatay said, his radiating light penetrating the demon's body like flame across parchment.

Before the demon could attack further, the light pierced through it, dispersing the entity into nothing. As it disappeared, it let out a terrifying screech that echoed through the woods. Its form vanished with only the foul odor of sulfur and smoke being left behind. To the magi and the knights who remained at the tree line, the terrifying sound was one they wouldn't soon forget.

As Aurotos lay there looking up at the sage, he could sense a certain frustration for the very first time from Armatay. "How reckless of you to leave behind your companions, charging into the woods like that. There is no place in our charge for anyone to go off on their own and carry out their will as they see fit. This is especially true for you Aurotos. Such recklessness will not keep anyone here safe, nor will it help deal with the threat at hand. There are much deadlier creatures created by the dark master, and they can harm you in far worse ways than the daevos I just sent away. You have to learn to work together with others if your quest is to be a success."

"So, it would seem," Aurotos said as he looked up at the sage, still towering over him.

Armatay let out a sight and then offered a smile. "It would be wise for us to return to the group."

Aurotos nodded at Armatay almost as if to offer an apology. "Alright, Armatay," he said. The sage extended a hand down toward Aurotos, who took it, welcoming help up off the ground. As he rose, he looked at his left arm where the daevos had struck him. He could feel an ache, but his armor appeared undamaged.

"Did the demon injure you?" Armatay asked.

"No, I'm fine," Aurotos replied.

"Oh, very well, let us get back then. I know of a place we can rest for the night, not too far away from here, just to the south by Lake Endreth. We can check and see that the people there are also safe," Armatay said.

"Let's get to it then," Aurotos said, steeling himself once more.

Aurotos and the sage regrouped with their companions, who they could see had already burned the drothkin corpses down to ash. Upon exiting the tree line, the knights and the magi looked toward the two with concerned expressions.

"Is everything alright? We heard a horrible sound from the woods," Anaryen said.

"Yes, it's true, we nearly came to help you, but the lady said we should respect the sage's instructions," Leavesa said.

"Oh, well then. Lady Anaryen, you honor me," Armatay said, looking to Aurotos as if to indicate he should take her previous warning to him as a lesson.

Aurotos spoke up: "We encountered a daevos. It appears you were right, my lady. It was a trap, but I'm glad you listened, Leavesa. It's time we grab the horses and make our way to the south toward Lake Endreth. There is a small community that we should check in on, and we can stay there until morning."

The company made their way toward the tree where the steeds and Corlith were waiting. The companions all mounted their steeds, following Aurotos who had begun leading them away. It wasn't long before Armatay became aware that Aurotos was no longer ahead of the group and had begun trailing toward the back behind them.

"Oh, go forth everyone, it is just that way," Armatay said as he pointed south with his staff. "There, you can see the lights. You go on now. I must speak to Aurotos for a moment, and we will be along shortly."

As the sage slowed to the rear, he could see that Aurotos appeared unwell. In fact, he appeared to be struggling. Aurotos was holding his left arm, and as soon as the sage met him, he could see that Aurotos was in pain, close to an oblivious state.

It was at that very moment that Aurotos came under a psychic attack. He could hear voices in his head, which caused him pain. He heard a voice clearly telling him to join them as it spoke. "Why must you fight me? If you do not join me, it will only get worse for you and worse for those who follow you. Your choice will determine how many are meant to die. You must submit yourself to me. You will submit."

Before Aurotos could respond, his trance was partially broken by the sage who caught him as he began falling off his horse. Armatay guided his falling body and tended to him as he lay on the ground below the horses. He was quick to pull off the glove and gauntlet from Aurotos's left arm to reveal a black set of marks on his forearm.

"I asked you if you had been injured or not. I had to know if it had struck you," Armatay said.

Aurotos did not respond. He felt delirious and sick between the pain in his arm that pulsed through his body and the voice in his head demanding that he submit. He was nearly unaware of the fact that the sage was kneeled over him tending to the wound on his arm.

Seeing the black marks, Armatay placed his hand over Aurotos and then hovered his hand upon his forearm and closed his eyes. From the palm of his hand, a glowing white light radiated across his arm. After a moment of focus, the black marks on his forearm disappeared, fading into black smoke which rose from his skin. As it did, Aurotos opened his eyes.

"You were infected with the fade; the demon's blight created a bridge between you and the dark master's realm. What did you experience?" Armatay asked.

"I heard a voice telling me to give in and surrender to it. It said that if I didn't submit, the lives of those who follow me would be at risk," Aurotos replied.

"Was it a voice you've heard before?" Armatay asked.

"I've never heard the voice before, and it didn't give me a name."

"Oh, I see…it was likely the dark master. It could have been Lord Grindam, but without a communion stone, it seems unlikely."

"The voice did seem otherworldly. What does Merdah want with me?"

"What he always wants—control and allegiance."

"I know, you're right…I didn't know you had the power to heal, Armatay."

"Oh, I have the power to do a great many things, my young friend, but for now, I'm hoping to get a good night's sleep in a nice warm bed. A tavern is just there by the lake, the Starlight Inn is what they call it. Best we be on our way now, don't you think?"

"Yes, of course," Aurotos said as he accepted the sage's hand, helping him up off the ground for the second time that day.

Aurotos leapt onto his horse and began riding toward the lodging. As he and the sage continued to ride forward, it became very clear to Aurotos that under the clear skies of that night, the world was illuminated and alive once more. The light of Valos shined bright over the land, and although he and his companions were now safe, he knew that the commander had gotten away and would return to the dark prince with news of their pursuit.

As Aurotos and Armatay approached the outskirts of the glimmering crystal lake, they could see the knights gathered outside of the inn where Corlith was guiding their steeds toward a nearby stable. The knights were entering a wide, two-story, stone building with a large, vaulted, wooden roof; it's back was up against the forest, and it had a number of chimneys where smoke could be seen rising into the cool night.

In front of the inn was a dock with a number of small boats that could be used for fishing on the lake. There was a quaint waterfall at the edge of the wood line just off to the left of the inn, which was flowing into the lake to the east. As they neared, they could see the crystal windows and the motion of people gathering inside.

"The Starlight Inn, an establishment of Dezren and his wife Avigail who have run this lodging for a great number of years. It has been in their family for quite a long time. Here you will find a cheerful bunch who are always happy to hear the stories of those who visit," Armatay said.

"It certainly appears cozy," Aurotos said as the two drew nearer to Corlith.

"Eh, sorry about earlier, my lord," Corlith said. "I feel horrible about it, and um, I promise I'll do better. Can I tend to your horse?"

"Not to worry, and yes, thank you, Corlith," Aurotos said as he and Armatay handed off the reigns to their steeds.

The two walked up several steps leading to the front door. As Aurotos opened the door, he could see the knights had already gotten comfortable at tables spread out in the open area toward his left. To his right, there was a set of stairs and directly next to that, in the center of the right side of the room, was a bar. Behind the bar was a door to a large kitchen where food was being prepared, and a man and woman sharing the duties of serving the patrons. Above some of the beverages, a number of keys to a number of different rooms were hanging on the wall.

Aurotos had only stepped a foot into the tavern before it fell silent. Aside from the knights and the magi who had been sitting at several of the tables, there were humans and elves who appeared to be gossiping. Some were happy to see the knights and the magi and were greeting them, while others minded their own business as they drank at their tables. Everything changed once Aurotos stepped into the tavern. Before him, everyone fell silent as he pulled back his hood, revealing his glowing, golden eyes.

He could hear them, the whispers, the secret hopes carried by all the people he'd never met, who had seen he was real. Nearly everyone in the tavern stood with their eyes set on him. He who had now come to the full realization that he was no longer hidden from the world. He was no longer a mystery and would be realized as real to everyone who would see him.

"Oh, there's no mistaking you, my lord. I wouldn't have believed it myself if I hadn't seen it with my own two eyes. The Last Light of Auro lives after all, praise be to the Twin Flames! Whatever that prince has in store for everyone he's sure going to be surprised when he sees you," the man behind the counter said. "We already heard about that nasty news of the drothkin. Can't thank you enough for ridding us of them. Who knows what would have happened if they had made their way down here. We heard from the avolan messenger that you had been alive this whole time. Now here you are, standing in front of us. Oh, but I forget my manners, my lord. I'm Dezren and this is my wife Avigail."

Dezren was a hefty man of average height for humans with a thick brown beard as dark as his eyes, wearing a green vest and pants with black boots and a black flat hat. He had an olive complexion with hairy arms, shown as his sleeves were rolled up to his elbows. There was an opening above his vest and his shirt, revealing more of the same bushy hair. Around his neck was a black leather cord with two golden suns overlapping, representing the Twin Flames.

His wife, Avigail, was a voluptuous woman wearing a large purple dress, and a black corset, with her brown hair pulled back in a ponytail. Her eyes were blue but almost seemed purple to match her dress. She was pale which made her freckles stand out much more, and she clearly ran the business side of things at the inn.

"Oh, your majesty," she said as she knelt gracefully in her dress. "Anything you need, whether it be food, drink, or help with your rooms, don't hesitate to ask. Once you're ready to turn in for the night, I'll be happy to lead you to your room. Just say the word. If there's anything we can get you, please don't hesitate," she said with a warm glowing smile. "Welcome to the Starlight Inn."

"Thank you, kind lady. I'll be sure to," Aurotos replied.

Seeming to blush, Avigail headed back behind the bar where she was writing on a pad, away from the drinks or food which could dirty her dress. Before her husband could join her, a voice blurted out down to the right of Aurotos. "Oy, the last descendant of the Twin Flames here before us. A sign of prophecy, yes," the voice said.

Down below, Aurotos could see a small nayran wearing a brown shirt and pants, with brown boots and gloves. He had brown, fluffy hair all over him and an orange nose, with yellow eyes and streaks of burnt orange throughout the mane covering his head. His ears flopped very low to the sides, and he had mini antlers like a great stag. He also smelled like fish.

"Oh, don't mind Poyro, my lord, he's a bit of an odd one, but he's a great help to us. He gathers mushrooms, fish, and game from the woods nearby, and in return, we offer him regular lodging," Dezren said.

Aurotos looked down at the small Poyro and offered a smile, which seemed to bring happiness to the little nayran. It was clear to Aurotos that he was simply trying to be a part of the moment, and while others may have shunned or ridiculed him for being odd, Aurotos offered only kindness.

Aurotos watched as the sage acquired his key and was about to head up the stairs. As he scanned the room, he could see that Anaryen was sitting with her two magi at a table, looking in his direction with a hinted smile. He believed she was much more than just her great beauty and he really wanted to understand the lady who had captivated his attention so fiercely.

"Always glad to have you here, Armatay," Dezren said.

"Oh, it is always my pleasure. Thank you, Dezren," Armatay said as he gave a slight bow back to Dezren before turning toward Aurotos. "I will look for you outside at dawn, Aurotos. I think I will take Avigail up on her offer for a room and see about finding something to eat before I rest. I would suggest you and your knights do the same. I hope that you will reflect on what I said today. Good night, my young friend," Armatay said as he offered a slight bow before he turned to the stairs.

"Good night, Armatay, I will," Aurotos replied, feeling somehow a bit sentimental toward the sage and his wisdom, though he wouldn't dare let him know that.

"Heh, and may the light guide you," Armatay said as he chuckled, then trailed toward the stairs which led to the rooms above.

CHAPTER 12

THE DARK PRINCE

Not far to the southwest of the Starlight Inn was the elven town of Veri Elath. It was just to the north of the town on that same evening that Commander Griles Grentin made his way back to the dark prince. Drazius and his branded troops had just begun preparations to siege the large town below. There they perched themselves out of sight on the far side of a high-rising hill. The prince and his branded waited there in the darkness peering down toward their next conquest.

The prince noticed Griles had returned and that he was not accompanied by any soldiers or drothkin. Suspecting failure, he lashed out in a rage. "How dare you return alone. You reek of failure," he said. "Where are the drothkin? Where are my soldiers? That nayran school had better be in ruins."

"Yes, my prince, please forgive me. We destroyed the alchemist's school but soon after, we were intercepted. Your trap almost worked but...um."

"But what Griles, speak," he demanded as his very presence darkened. He couldn't imagine what could have stopped the daevos that had been covertly stationed within the woods as a safety measure for his troops.

"But...the last Va'Threan was there with the Knights of the Phoenix and three Aurodites," the commander said angrily.

"You presume to blame me for your failure," the prince replied, his stare gazing into the depths of the man. He wanted Griles to be terrified of what he might do to him, it was working.

"Never, my prince. I would never," Griles said, his voice nearly trembling.

"How could they have known we were in their territory already? You said there were Aurodites with them, explain how that could be."

"I don't know, but one of them was the lady of Eden Throvon."

"Anaryen Valenvon, of course," Drazius said as his memories resurfaced only briefly. The Valenvon family was from a different kingdom within the collective of human realms but were close allies of his father, King Nailor. He thought about how he had once fancied the lady in his childhood, however, she had not returned his interest. He could still feel the wounds of that rejection. "There's no way the Aurodites could have warned the knights of Valenthreas unless she was there, she must have escaped somehow."

"I don't know, my prince, but I suspected the same when I saw them there."

Drazius raised his hands as if he sought to tear into the very air itself, clenching both fists as he looked toward Griles and screamed in fury. "How could you have allowed them to escape? Holcurt, get over here."

Drazius relished in their obedience as Holcurt and Griles fell to their knees before him, his rage-filled state placing them both into a status of absolute fear. He dropped both of his clenched fists to his side and pointed to each of them, infuriated. "Tell me who was responsible for allowing them to escape from Illonel. How could they have gotten away?"

"My prince, we cleared all the spell flingers from the quarters we were assigned. They must have escaped from somewhere within the spire, there had to be a hidden exit," Griles said.

"Do you presume to say it is I who am at fault? You know it was I who rose to the top of that spire. I am the one who saw that every Aurodite lay dead at my feet before I killed Etrius. You presume to blame me for your failings?" He didn't need an excuse to punish them but he wanted a way to shame them and someone would be made an example in the cold dark of that night.

"No, my prince. I only meant to say I'm sure they couldn't have escaped beyond the outer walls. They couldn't have been hidden where we were tasked to search; Holcurt and I checked everywhere. There must be a hidden way they escaped, somewhere within the stronghold. I'm sure the archmagus found a way—"

"Silence, commander, lest I end you here. I will suffer your insolence no longer." Drazius was practically snarling at them and the feeling was almost all consuming. He felt almost drunk with power in their state of conflict.

Griles fell even lower to his feet, saying nothing outside his plea for forgiveness before the dark prince, who was living up to that title. For in his eyes, only a blackness shone from his helmet, only a shadow, and from his strong, deep voice, only a sickening of strife and rage. He could almost feel the darkened soul he now carried and it pulsed like a faint heartbeat throughout his body.

It was in that moment that the prince felt the lingering essence of his humanity stir. Rousing memories of the voyage he had undertaken for his kingdom. A journey which led him far from the human realms into the west and eventually beyond, into the frozen northern wastes that were filled with unspeakable danger.

He remembered it well for the journey began much like the bowing of the commanders before him, yet in his past it was he who was bowing before his father. For a moment this flicker of humanity whisked him away into the memory of the day he last honored his father.

With his head hung low, Drazius begged the king for his permission. "Please, your majesty...father. Let me do this for you. I've never been given a charge outside of these castle walls. I beg you, let me answer this call for our people," he said.

King Nailor Khorvek was a wide shouldered, towering man. He had a strong physique and a very gentle nature to the look in his eye and the tone of his deep voice. He had a thick black beard with streaks of white hair that had formed over his many years as king. He had neatly trimmed long hair which was combed back and hung down almost to his shoulders. He had neat eyebrows which were arched and gave him a daunting appearance. His crown was gold with a large red gem at the center which glowed between two golden gems representing the Twin Flames. The crown banded the king's hair loosely and glowed under the daylight that shone into the throne room.

He placed a hand on Drazius's shoulder and squeezed it with care. "I know you're eager to lead, my son, but this is a dangerous quest and you are my only heir. If something were to happen to you…" he said, the care in his heart reverberating through the deep vibrations of his vocal cords.

"But father, something could happen to me every day. To live is to die—you taught me this. As your only heir I know it would mean so much to the orcs if I were to go in your stead. I need to show you and our kingdom that I am worthy of that crown I shall one day inherit," he said, now looking up toward his father with devotion in his eyes.

Drazius listened carefully. The throne room was so silent one could hear the sound of a nail drop upon the red and white marble tiles only to reverberate throughout the vast halls. The white stone pillars which reached up toward the high, white coffered ceilings only ensured the sound would echo more loudly for there were only a handful of guards present aside from the two.

King Nailor contemplated the request. Drazius could see through his expression that his father was aware he made an argument that was difficult to disagree with. "Perhaps, my son. If only your mother were still here, she always advised me best on such matters where you were concerned."

Drazius was touched by the sentiment his father shared for he knew bringing up his mother was difficult for the king. Still, he pressed on. "I've trained for years with our best warriors and you've guided me with your great wisdom. I'm ready, father. Please trust I can do this."

Drazius's father was known for his wisdom and humility. He knew the king understood through his many years of ruling that one day he would have to choose to let him prove himself. The prince only hoped that his moment to lead had come.

Nailor let out a sigh which Drazius thought sounded both fretful and relieved. "I know you're right. I can't protect you from the evils of this world forever…maybe it is time. If I grant you leave to answer their call then it will be with a battalion of our finest warriors."

Drazius's heart sank as he remembered the words he spoke next. "Anything you command, this I swear." He lingered in his sadness only long enough for the darkness to grip onto his very soul more strongly through his sorrow.

King Nailor pulled a dark stone from his pocket and extended his hand with it facing up in his palm. "Take this communion stone so that I can use it to speak with you. Once you learn what is happening you must contact me first and I will advise you in how to proceed."

"Yes, father. I'll keep it safe at all times." Drazius was smiling and took the stone into his hand eagerly. The approval from his father filled him with overwhelming joy and confidence that it took everything in him not to leap to his feet and hug the king.

"Now rise, my son, and hear my decree."

As the prince rose, he caught the scent of rose water and honey vines blowing through the throne room and they reminded him of his mother. With absolute determination Drazius looked into his fathers' eyes and listened intently.

"Prince Drazius, I am ordering you to lead a battalion of our warriors to the dwarven kingdom of Klindroin. Once you arrive there, High King Gilron Gundrav will supply you with access to ships so you may cross the sea to reach the northernmost orcish realm of Vorlanok. Once you arrive, Overlord Noldam Nainok will update you on what has been happening along the northern border of his kingdom. Assess the situation and report whatever you learn back to me using the stone I gave you. This must be handled very carefully, Drazius. Any questions?"

"I don't understand, father. Why hasn't Overlord Nainok sent word to Valenthreas. Surely the elves will—"

"No, Drazius, we mustn't tell the stewards yet. To put it plainly, Noldam is afraid of what problems this could cause and he says he will only trust our house to share this with before he notifies the elves. He knows how the other orc leaders will react to floods of ships entering their lands and if the elves are notified, he suspects a war could erupt on two fronts. One which attacks this malignant intrusion along their northern borders and one from other orcs who would see armies entering their lands as intruders seeking to conquest their kingdoms."

"What do I tell High King Gundrav if he asks what we're doing?"

"Tell him nothing. He cannot know what this is about. Tell him only that this is your first command and that it is nothing more than training exercises. You're there to learn from the orcs in the ways of their finest warriors, the Ivoru Guard. This is all you can tell them for now. Once you contact me with news, I will instruct you on what to do next."

Drazius was concerned but understood his father's wisdom in treating their alliance with the orcs so carefully. The Khorvek family was renowned for their efforts in fostering peace and prosperity throughout the human realms and beyond. They had sent their troops to train with all of the races at one period of time or another.

"I understand, your majesty...and father, I won't let you down."

"Of that I have no doubt, my boy." Nailor gave him a long hug and ushered him off.

He remembered leaving that day duty bound, with a rising sense of ambition to perform his task for the king flawlessly. While Drazius was entranced, captive by his memories, he had forgotten about the commanders kneeling at his feet. It was almost as if what glimmer of humanity still left was fighting to remind him of what had happened to him. What had ushered him along the dark path he was now on. He hated the memory and as much as he wanted to stop the thoughts right then and there, he couldn't stop revisiting the moment he lost his soul to the darkness. The memory was almost intoxicating—he both loved it and hated it—but what part of him felt what? Not even he knew anymore.

In his short remembrance he darted through the memories of marching his battalion west beyond the human realms and into the dwarven lands at the western reaches of the continent. He had been relieved when High King Gundrav didn't press him on the details of his mission and instead had prepared a regal feast when he and his army stopped at the kingdom of Klindroin. Then he sailed with the dwarven ships across the bitter cold seas into the orcish realm of Vorlanok.

Drazius's memory jumped again, this time to the moment he met the honorable overlord. He remembered the encounter all too well for it was when everything changed for him. He recalled how Overlord Noldam Nainok had shared the troubling news about the incursions that were taking place along their borders to the frozen wastelands of the north. Every so often they would come across dark entities the likes of which had never been seen.

He reflected on the moment when he thought to contact his father, but instead chose to venture north of the orcish borders with his men. The overlord warned the prince that when these beings became hostile, they could not be killed unless they were consumed with fire. The prince had to see firsthand what was at play before he would contact his father. He was unable to deny the truth of that moment and so the suffering remnant of his humanity weakened under the flood of memories which came next.

Drazius was so very cold but had just finished marching his men toward a large, inverted, dark vortex. He couldn't see anything inside for all visibility was obscured by the tall rising point leading to darkness which seemed to blot out all hope for the light to endure.

Surrounding the base of the vortex he could see several people roaming around aimlessly. They stumbled around as if dazed or injured and that's when he saw what really made no sense. These people were far too underdressed to be walking in such bitter cold and should have been frozen outside in such a state. The temperatures were well below freezing, and as they walked, they emitted some dark matter which couldn't be made out.

"It seems we found the source of what plagues these lands but I need to inspect what state these people are in before I speak with our king," Drazius said to the captains who rode nearby.

Captain Loren fought loudly to produce enough sound to break through the noise of the howling winds. "Prince Drazius, what would you have us do?" he asked.

Drazius dismounted his horse and handed the reigns to a squire. He then looked to the other three captains. "You three stand by with the rest of the battalion," he said as he pulled up at the white fur mantle around his neck and shoulders. "Captain Loren, I want you to take one platoon from your company and follow me on foot. We'll investigate these people and find out what foul magic has gripped them."

"Yes, my lord," Captain Loren said as he dismounted his horse and took command of one of the platoons from his company of soldiers.

As Drazius and his troops approached the people he could see that these dark rovers were walking corpses. A blackness oozed from their mouths, eyes, and wounds which seemed to be the cause of their deaths. That's when he realized that they had become aware of he and his men. In an instant the nearly twenty dark rovers began to herd in their direction.

"Don't attack them unless they become hostile. You mustn't let them touch you, use fire if you must," Drazius said and he looked intently upon his troops who all carried their swords in one hand and steel torches enclosing flames in the other.

In unison Captain Loren and the rest of his platoon shouted "whoa!" and the troops began moving forward behind the prince.

Emboldened by the loyalty of his men Drazius steeled himself as the adrenaline coursed through his body. He was suddenly feeling very warm and as they drew closer to the rovers, one by one, the dark beings attacked.

Drazius took the first swing at one of them, cutting its head clean from its body. The head fell to the ground by its corpse, with the head's teeth chattering in the cold. The troops followed the lead of their prince and severed the heads off the rovers which all attempted to lunge toward them and bite them. They set the bodies aflame where they lied and the fires consumed them fast, their bodies almost acting as an accelerant.

"Now to see what magic is causing the sky to be so dark," Drazius said. He gazed deep into the vortex and walked closer. He could see something at the center. "There's something inside; I'm having a closer look."

"My lord, maybe you should use the stone to talk to the king. He might—"

"Not yet, Captain Loren, I have to learn what this is before I contact his majesty. I must have an answer for this."

"Yes, my lord, but what if this vortex is what turned these people into monsters."

"I don't believe that, captain; these people were dead long before they became infected with whatever animated their corpses. Stand by, I'm just getting a little closer."

"My lord—"

"It's alright, don't worry, Loren."

Drazius turned back toward the spiraling vortex before him and stepped forward. As he pressed ahead into the vortex he sighed with relief as he felt no change aside from the darkening of the space around him. With just a hint of visibility he looked toward Captain Loren and shouted. "I'm alright, it's just darker."

Although the captain couldn't be heard, Drazius continued ahead deeper into the gloom of the vortex. He grew closer to the object which he had seen and then the darkness around him seemed to fade away into a clearing within the spiraling shadow which reached high into the sky above.

There before him was a black polearm embedded into a large block of ice. He continued drudging his way through the snow that blanketed the land underneath him until he reached it. The blade was so far into the ice that it took all of his strength to break the blade free from it. But there was a problem. As soon as he grabbed it the prince couldn't unclench his hand from the handle of the weapon. All he could do was pull and hope that his hands would break away.

As soon as the weapon gripped him, he heard an ominous voice speak, grinding its way into the depths of his mind. "Prince Drazius, how lucky for us that it is you who reached for this weapon."

"Who are you? What have you done to me?" Drazius asked. He couldn't break free and he felt himself slipping away, consumed by the power of the weapon which gripped his very soul.

"I am Grindam, the necrolord of this weapon. I call it Nolcrolesh. It is the bringer of the dark rovers you no doubt encountered. I expected this would have baited one of my fellow orc leaders but you are a much greater prize to serve this weapon and my master, Ohrimah."

Drazius didn't know what to do and terror set in as he realized he was experiencing the fade's influence as it spread through his veins. "I'll never serve Merdah!"

"Oh shahaha, silly boy, you can't fight this. The fade has taken you— surely you feel it. I'm afraid you don't have a choice."

As Grindam's voice faded away in laughter, Drazius felt himself stand up with the weapon in hand. He felt powerful, intoxicated. He surged with a feeling of great strife for everything he had once held dear. As his humanity slipped further away he was filled with an overwhelming sorrow as his suffering consumed him. His entire being filled with a rage to break the order of the world made manifest through suffering.

As he succumbed to the control of the fade which coursed through his body, he heard a voice that was calm and controlling. "By my purpose and desire, so you shall be." The prince felt the last of his self-control fade away only sure that the voice he heard could be none other than Master Ohrimah. It was the last moment he experienced control of himself. The dark master had full use of him and immediately forced him to commit unspeakable acts. For as he felt himself move and speak the actions were not his own. He could feel that he was nothing more than a passenger in his body, all because of the weapon Lord Grindam had crafted to imprison him.

With access to all of Drazius's memories, the dark master took on a new persona as the dark prince everyone came to fear. First, Ohrimah made Drazius kill all of his men. Then he used Nolcrolesh to raise them from the dead as an army of dark rovers which he left to roam the frozen north. The dark prince left the north soon after and returned home across the frozen sea, bypassing everything until he made his way back home.

Drazius Khorvek was now a shadow of the man he once was. There was little evidence of the man who had once ventured so far with the hopes of accomplishing so much good in order to return home and prove himself to his father. What he brought back instead was the pole-arm he carried and a black in his eyes which signaled only that he had been almost entirely consumed by the fade.

Once he plunged his dark weapon into his father and revealed his new power to others, there was nothing his kingdom could do except give in to their fears and at worst, their sorrows. The pain of that moment gave way to his sorrow and immediately his darkened shroud consumed what little humanity was left to salvage.

As the prince snapped back into the present moment, he heard his commander's desperate reply. "Akrell, my prince. It must have been Akrell. I commanded him to lead a squad into the spire to clear the Aurodites out before you left to kill Etrius," Griles said.

"Bring me Akrell now," Drazius said.

"Yes, my prince," Holcurt yelled. "Akrell, bring me Captain Akrell immediately!"

Captain Akrell was ushered through the crowd of soldiers, confused as to what was happening. The branded captain pressed through the crowd, nearly as fast as he was shoved forward.

"Yes, Prince Drazius," Akrell said as he fell to his knees between the two commanders.

"You were in charge of clearing the spire of Illonel, were you not?" Drazius said.

"Yes, my lord," Akrell answered, fear blanketing the whole of his eyes.

"You have been chosen by your commanders to serve as an example of how failure is to be punished." As Akrell began to shake before the prince, Drazius shouted one final warning to every soldier who stood before him. "Three Aurodites made it out of Illonel, and your commanders have laid the blame on Captain Akrell for letting them escape the spire. It is he who carries this shame. May this be a lesson to all who choose to do anything less than what you are commanded."

"Please, my lord," Akrell pleaded.

Prince Drazius let out a horrifying roar that terrified not only the branded who served him but also the drothkin who followed them. Under the sound of his scream, all who bore witness trembled in terror as Drazius pulled back his polearm and thrust it forward into the captain, whose plea was met by an impale that lifted him above the commanders, his blood and life draining out onto the ground between the two.

As the corpse of Akrell remained impaled, raised above the prince, the captain slowly became engulfed in a black flame that burned through his corpse, leaving only ash to fall over those near his remains. Drazius's authority and power could not be underscored by anyone who witnessed the event. It was not only the drothkin or the branded soldiers, but the world itself that seemed suppressed under his might. In the presence of the gloomveil surrounding him, nature was dimmed and darkened for the prince and his army, who seemed bolstered further in their dedication to the darkness and their leader. The prince uttered in determination, "Veri Elath will fall, and I will show you all what it means to conquer."

Before him were thousands of his loyalists who stood upon the green grass of the field, preparing to move at the first order from the prince, who sat before them upon his black horse. Drazius commanded his soldiers and the drothkin in a furious rallying cry, signaling them to set their sights on the town. "Below us lies Veri Elath, one of the many places that opposes our great master. Remember your brand and the price of your failure. Not a single soul may be allowed to escape; leave none alive. I don't care if they are old or young, leave none who may be allowed to praise the Twin Flames. If you fall remember that you will be reborn in the world of our dark master. Now forward, for the glory of Ohrimah," Drazius screamed.

The nightfall had lit the world in beautiful glowing colors everywhere else but here. The town below had no way of knowing the enemy had been perched above them that night. The solace of their night would soon be disturbed by the shouting voice of Drazius, who was rallying his soldiers to decimate their homes and their very existence.

Drazius and his dreadful army, enraged and chanting, marched toward the elven town that had no idea of the savagery soon to be visited upon them. A horror that had been commanded through the guise of a once beloved prince, now only a remnant of the man he once was.

CHAPTER 13

THE STARLIGHT INN

Back at the Starlight Inn, Aurotos approached Elenfia and Anaryen, who were sitting at a table enjoying a warm brew with Molvalan. As he neared the table, he knew he must explore more of what he had been feeling toward the princess. "Would you mind if I had a seat with you?" Aurotos asked, the whole of his intention focused on Anaryen who had locked eyes with him.

Elenfia looked toward Anaryen and gave her a reassuring smile as she stood. "It's about time I get some rest myself. You're welcome to my seat if you wish, my lord," she said.

"Thank you, Elenfia," Aurotos said as he nodded his head in thanks. Secretly he was glad he might have the chance alone to talk to the lady of Eden Throvon.

"But...um, Lord Aurotos," Elenfia said as she lowered her head in respect.

"What is it, Elenfia?" Aurotos was a bit unsure of what to expect next. He wasn't used to such awkward interactions and it had him feeling a bit bewildered.

"I just wanted to say, I hate that I acted the way I did. It was careless of me to give in to my sorrow. I won't jeopardize any of you like that again. I promise," she said as she lowered her head even still.

"Don't worry about it. I can understand you must have felt very torn after losing your friend. Everything turned out alright in the end. Now please, rest well."

Elenfia looked back up and gave him a hopeful smile, before bowing toward the two. "If you need anything, my lady, please don't hesitate," she said as she gave a subtle glance to Molvalan.

"Sleep in solace, Elenfia, goodnight," Anaryen said.

Molvalan watched Elenfia attentively and seemed eager to follow her as she was walking away. "So...um, the drink was delicious, but I too should get settled in," he said as he stood and bowed to the lord and lady before rushing away, trailing behind Elenfia.

As Aurotos sat next to Anaryen he laughed a bit. "He sure seemed eager to catch up to her."

"Oh yes, he did. I believe something blossoms between the two," Anaryen said as she laughed a bit before she continued. "Why did you take off into the woods like that earlier? I told you it was too dangerous, you shouldn't have—"

"I know," he said, and he could have sworn he caught her by surprise in saying so.

"Oh, you know...well alright," she said now with a pause. "It's just that I was worried that..."

"You were worried?"

"Well, you know, we were worried," she said as she began to blush. Anaryen paused again, this time hardening herself with the fierceness akin to when they first met. "Listen, you should have known that the commander was leading you into a trap," she said before her demeanor softened again. "Anyway, after seeing you might have been injured, I thought you could use this." She pulled out a small medicine bottle from her small waist bag which held a salve. "This will help you with any pain you have, just be sure to place it wherever it hurts and the pain should be gone by morning."

"Thank you, my lady," he said, revealing a subtle smile. "You seem to mend all things you are near. I will remember both your wisdom and kindness."

Anaryen smiled back and then stood up and bowed. "See that you do, my lord," she said playfully.

Aurotos thought he might have even heard a giggle from her as she spoke. He moved quick to stand and meet her, bowing back while he felt warmth fill his cheeks. She affected him so, and while he wasn't well versed in the art of flirting, he was sure that was exactly what had just happened. She had flirted with him, and he found himself at a loss.

"I should get some rest too; the dawn comes soon and we'll all need our rest for what's ahead. Sleep in solace, Aurotos," she said.

"Goodnight, my lady. May your dreams bring you the peace your kind heart deserves," he replied. As soon as the words left his lips, he knew he had done it too. It happened so effortlessly.

Anaryen's cheeks became red before she finally walked away toward the stairs. As she did, Aurotos could only look on in amazement at the beauty he felt himself witness to. He found the red in her cheeks to be almost as beautiful as the look in her eyes and it brought happiness into his heart knowing he could make her smile.

It wasn't long before he realized everyone present was also witness to the moment. As Anaryen made her way up the stairs, he could hear the muffled laughter of several of the knights who could see that he was enamored by her. Now aware that the knights were watching, Aurotos caught himself smiling and straightened his mouth out.

Before he could say anything, he heard Leavesa speak. "Never mind them, my lord, they have little appreciation for romance. Anaryen is a great leader and a very strong woman; she would make a great queen."

"Little mind? Hold on...did you just call us small minded?" Salenval asked.

"Oh, hush," Leavesa said as she giggled through her authoritative vocal tone.

"But she's a human, don't you think it would be better for Lord Aurotos to choose an elf?" Syvon questioned, his bias toward humans blatantly clear once again.

"Well, I think it best to check your prejudice for humans, Syvon. That kind of disdain will get in your way one day," Leavesa argued as a bit of silence fell amongst the knights.

Aurotos could appreciate the authority she commanded over the others and the support she gave toward him. "Thank you, Leavesa," he said. "Syvon, she's not wrong."

"I meant no disrespect, my lord, I just think our kingdom could benefit from an elven queen," Syvon said.

"While I cannot argue with what Syvon says, truly, one should remember that Lord Aurotos answers a higher calling. It is notable for it transcends the desires one may seek for their own kingdom," Vael said, expressing the classical viewpoint an elder elf would have coming from such a notable lineage as he.

Tarothas awkwardly spoke, his youthful admiration for Aurotos and his heritage very obvious. "I can't believe that Lord Aurotos should have to marry anyone other than his destined spark. We all know that too is part of the path to ascendency."

"It's hard to argue that point," Drelion said in a proud tone. His scholarly nature was difficult for most to dispute.

"Our lord should always trust his instincts, far be it for us to debate that our opinions should dictate much of anything," Arvasiel said in a defensive tone.

Aurotos grew very uncomfortable with each passing comment, and was eager to make his escape. He was still trying to understand his own emotions for Anaryen and having the whole situation debated by his fellow knights who he was just growing to trust only made his head spin more. Not only that but he was so used to keeping such things to himself. Having his emotions exposed by those whom he had known for so long under a certain level of anonymity now was more than he could handle.

"It's plain to see you're all making Lord Aurotos pretty uncomfortable," Kaervo said.

"Indeed…so," Nahul said as he nodded along in agreement.

"It's alright. I don't take any of your feedback lightly," Aurotos said as he offered an awkward smile. "I think I'll just go enjoy some of the moonlight, get a bit of fresh air. We have a big day ahead of us so I suggest you all get some rest as soon as you can. I'll see you all at dawn. Goodnight."

As Aurotos made his way back toward the front door, their chatter diminished, and the knights stood showing respect for him as he made his way outside. As he passed through the door, he continued straight toward the dock which reached out over the crystal water of the lake. There was a dock ahead with scattered boats used for fishing and recreation.

On either side of the dock was a short stone wall that seamlessly blended the dock with the land surrounding it. Scattered around either side of the dock's entry point were several tall, weeping velotheon trees, their hanging branches all leading to singular glowing lights like tears flowing toward their tips. The foliage that hung toward the ground moved like waves through the cool chill of the breeze that evening. The most notable noise that night, aside from the light splashing sound of the water, was the rustling of the trees' leaves—a sound that had always been very pleasant and relaxing to him.

The beauty of that evening could not be underscored as he took in the view across the water and beyond. The lake itself seemed to serve as a deep mirror reflecting the auras and the landscape around him. He felt entranced by the calm of this place and felt a peace wash over him as if the waters themselves reached up to greet him to this private corner of the world.

Aurotos leaned upon the right wall, resting his elbows along its top border, then he took in a deep breath of fresh air that filled his nostrils with the distinct scent of the peaty leaves all around him. Relaxed, he looked toward Valos and its radiating azure light, which grew closer to the aureate moon Ailos on that cool night. The blue moon's influence here was nothing short of magical. The world not only glowed enchantingly under its illumination, but even the water seemed to sparkle in a manner that welcomed one to be nurtured by the healing capability of the imbued waters.

Aurotos could see that the ecosystem surrounding the lake was no doubt vital to the inn. With the magical features surrounding the lake, Dezren and Avigail had everything they needed for a thriving business. What was even more true was that the provisions gathered here could be used in countless ways for medicine or luxurious products. Still, it was a rarity that he enjoyed such a sight unbound by the reach of greater civilization and under the light of the uninhibited night sky. His bright glowing eyes sought answers from the night sky. *Are you up there somewhere, my little friends? I hope wherever you are, you're happy and at peace.* He couldn't help but miss them and wonder about where their spirits were at that very moment.

Aurotos also felt untrusting of the darkness that cloaked the wooded areas beyond the lake. As he peered off in that direction, he reminded himself that he was outside to get a chance to unwind from the day. After all, the knights would be rotating watch duty throughout the night once everyone was sleeping, and he needed to heed his own guidance about getting rest soon.

Time under the moonlight seemed to pass by quickly until he began to feel uneasy, getting a sense that he was no longer alone. He turned and looked to his right to see a woman walking along the lakeside and heading his way. Her black hair flowed like water and she had blue eyes that seemed very bright as she approached. Her bright blue flowing dress clung to her thin, curvy body, and she seemed to shimmer almost in a light blue hue which made him think she must have been pretty pale. As she made her way close to him, he became curious where she had come from, as he had not seen anyone around when he walked outside.

"Tis a beautiful night," she said.

"Yes, it is," he responded as he continued to question her origin internally. He had not remembered seeing her inside the inn earlier and something about her demeanor seemed odd.

"Tis one of my favorite things, the stars shining over the water. I so love how it silently offers its own pale reflection back. Water here is pure and clear and deep…there is no better place to behold," she said.

"I see why you enjoy it so," Aurotos said. He looked to meet the woman's eyes, then as he looked back toward the water, he could tell her gaze remained still, set only on him. He also found it strange that she had not mentioned anything about his eyes or who he was. Since he first revealed his secret, it seemed to be one of the first things people noticed or reacted to. That was not the case for the woman beside him, and he found it very strange and out of place.

It wasn't very long before the woman spoke again. "What is your name?" she asked.

"Aurotos, what's yours? Do you work at the Starlight Inn?"

"Riella," she said. "And no, I do not work at the inn. I live not too far from here, just on the other side of the lake. Would you like to accompany me home? I think we could both find ways to enjoy this night even greater still."

"I'm afraid I can't do that," he said, feeling very uneasy by such a proposition.

The woman laughed and leaned further toward him, intending to continue her pursuit. As he looked into her eyes, he noticed they were growing a brighter shade of blue and it caused him to feel strange. Her remarks were interrupted as she became aware of someone standing behind Aurotos underneath one of the bright willow trees. As she caught the attention of the figure, her demeanor shifted, causing her to seem threatened or afraid.

This concerned Aurotos as well, and seeing that the woman had begun backing away from him, he too looked only to see that Molvalan was lurking suspiciously under the tree.

"What are you doing there?" Aurotos said.

"It would seem I am looking out for you, my lord," Molvalan chuckled. As he did so, the woman moved further away.

"Looking out for me? How is that?"

"Um…I am surprised you didn't realize it, my lord. You were in the presence of a maie, an el'ani to be exact. You must know how dangerous Anieva's dark creatures are."

Aurotos did remember how dangerous the el'ani were. As Anieva was paired to Ohrimah, she had created many dark creatures under his influence. Many believed that she created the various maie as a result of her own deep sorrow while becoming more and more sullied through her own union with him. "A love fiend? How could you tell?"

"Well, um…you should always be suspicious if a woman approaches you dressed like that on a night like this. They are notorious for seeking out males who are alone by waters. I must admit I am surprised to see that one here instead of the seaside. I thought you might be glad though. I would never have let you go with her, my lord," he said as he became filled with a harrowing laughter.

"I would never have, wait…" Aurotos said, realizing the woman who was beside him moments ago had vanished. "I just expected you would have turned in for the night."

"Oh yes, well I was tending to Elenfia; she's finally resting now, my lord."

Aurotos's attention was drawn away to the front of the Starlight Inn where he could see Avigail opening the door and looking toward them. "Just preparing to close up the inn if you two feel you're about ready. With all the dangers out, we thought we'd lock things up for tonight," she said.

"Oh yes, Avigail, quite prudent," Molvalan said as he rushed to make his way through the door.

"Of course, that's a wise decision," Aurotos said as he moved toward the door, which Avigail locked behind him. She handed him a key, pointing toward the stairs. "You'll be in room 11 just up there. It has the best view overlooking the lake. I just wanted to say that my husband and I are both so happy that you are out here looking after your people. It sure does make us all feel a whole lot safer, if there's anything at all you need, please don't hesitate. Just ring that bell in your room, and one of us will be up as fast as we can. I hope you have a great sleep tonight, my lord," she said, as she bowed.

"Thank you for your hospitality," Aurotos replied.

As he made his way up the steps that led to his room, he reflected on how Avigail's presence reminded him of how nurturing his mother used to be. Whether she knew it or not, her compassion helped him feel very comfortable at the Starlight Inn. Arriving outside of his room, he opened the door to see a clean, tidy space with a small fireplace and a window overlooking the lake. Through the window, he could see the two moons, the trees, and the water shimmering under the moonlight. As he took off his armor and cleaned himself off, he knew he wouldn't sleep deeply. Even though the Starlight Inn was comforting and the knights would be taking guard shifts throughout the night, he knew that somewhere not far away, the prince's army may already be on the move.

The following morning came quick and Aurotos, sensing the dawn, planned to be one of the first outside awaiting his companions. He made his way down the stairs and was greeted by Avigail and Dezren who gave him refreshments and breakfast. Finishing breakfast, he made his way toward the door leading outside, although it seemed he was not alone. For as he opened the door, he could see that Armatay was already there waiting for him.

"Somehow, I'm not surprised to see you outside so early," Aurotos said.

"Heh, well, I would say there is no better time to learn how to use the radiant blade than at dawn," Armatay said.

"Very well, lead the way, Armatay."

Armatay led Aurotos toward the dock, and before the two reached the stone wall, he veered to the right, following closely along the water's edge, stopping on the green grass just near the waterway that led from the forest to the lake.

"Once more you must try to deflect my attacks just as you were instructed to last time. Close your eyes and let the blade serve you. Now ready yourself and may the light guide you," Armatay said.

Aurotos drew the radiant blade out over his shoulder and held the blade upright with both hands in front of him. He closed his eyes and tried his best to believe that the light of dawn that was shining upon his face may indeed guide his blade.

He could hear Armatay once again launching a barrage of arcane attacks. As he felt them nearing, he could also sense that the blade sought to guide his movement. With nothing more than complete instinct, Aurotos swung the blade and deflected every attack the sage had launched at him.

"Well done, Aurotos. Now tell me, what was different?"

"This time I felt the blade guide me to react. It was as if it wanted to move me, so I let it. I swung my blade where it directed me, but there was something more. Even with my eyes closed, I felt like I could see where each of the bolts were."

"Good, that is because you could. That sense of sight you experienced, even when your eyes were closed, can become much more for you. In time, the blade will serve as a tool only second to the sight that it has taught you to develop. Now, let us continue, and I want you to try to see more clearly what you experienced as your eyes were closed."

Aurotos felt a growing confidence and was eager to try again. "I understand. I'm ready."

Aurotos and Armatay continued practicing, and as they did, Aurotos continued succeeding. His eyes remained closed as he proceeded to deflect one attack after another. Armatay pressed on by increasing the strength of his attacks, and as he did, Aurotos still deflected them. Even with his eyes closed, he could nearly see everything he defended himself from almost as clearly as if his eyes were open.

In the time the two were training, Anaryen and her magi, as well as all of his fellow knights, had begun gathering. His companions watched him in astonishment as he wielded the legendary blade of his father, deflecting every attack from the sage with shut eyes. Even as Corlith had gathered their steeds, he looked on to watch the spectacle; it would not end until every one of the patrons of the inn and the innkeepers themselves had gathered to watch a spectacle unlike any other. For the first time, all were beginning to see the making of a true king.

Sensing the silence, Aurotos opened his eyes and looked toward the inn where he could see an audience had grown. He was uneasy with that kind of attention. He spent so many years working to avoid the stares that could expose him in some way. Now he felt completely laid bare in a situation he already felt vulnerable to. But as he scanned the faces of those with whom he served he felt confidence in seeing their expressions, especially the smile Anaryen wore upon her face. In that moment he felt some sort of nudge within, and he knew he must leave some aspects of his old self behind.

"Gather closer, knights. You too, magi. I think it wise that I teach you all how to use your magic to create more than your magic shields, something you Knights of the Phoenix have long been known to use. You all must understand how to create a powerful shell to protect you from greater threats than you have yet known."

Aurotos felt like the sage had a bit of a different demeanor to him now. One that almost seemed to challenge them all on a fundamental level. He could respect the sage's wisdom but to be asked to break the very rules they had been taught was unexpected and quite concerning.

"Armatay, to create a magic shell is to cross a threshold we have been taught never to go beyond. To do so could cause us to pull too much from our own spark, leading to a certain death," Aurotos said.

"Listen, with respect, Armatay, you must understand. We have learned to use shielding techniques, much like the knights, and we've been warned against syphoning magic in excess for the same reason," Anaryen said.

"It is true, such magic can come at a cost, but you all will face unknown dangers ahead. We know Drazius has drothkin, and that he has many soldiers in his army, so it is important that all of you have the tools to defend yourselves no matter what may lie ahead. This may be the only thing that will protect you in a moment of life or death. This ability does not defy the tenets of the Twin Flames. My friends, the calling that you all answer to has a far greater purpose than the orders you belong to. You must trust me when I say that the Twin Flames and the Masters will understand."

Both Anaryen and Aurotos looked to one another, and although they knew they would be breaking rules set by their orders, it seemed clear to them both that they all must be prepared for whatever lied ahead, no matter what the cost. In the end, their orders' mission was the same: protect the innocent and safeguard life, even if it meant sacrificing themselves.

It took no time for the Knights of the Phoenix and the Aurodites to learn to harness a protective barrier of energy using methods they already knew. Where the knights were accustomed to using their fist and forearm as the source of projecting their shields, the Aurodites used the center ahead of their body, raising a hand forward as a place to focus their power for the shields they cast before them.

Armatay taught the knights to focus their shield as if they were creating a bubble of flame which arced around their body, connecting behind them. Each Aurodite was taught to pull their hand closer and hover it over their chest, imagining the energy flowing from their hand, through their chest, and extending to the same distance behind them.

The onlookers of the inn witnessed hope and a pledge of safety for their futures as every knight and magi stood next to one another learning to enclose themselves in protective bubbles. The magi had surrounded themselves in blue arcane energy, whereas the knights had surrounded themselves in bubbles of light akin to flame. The companions all looked at each other, seemingly proud of how easily they could master the skill.

As the sage concluded his instruction, he left them with a final remark. "These shells can be formed from all elements of magic. For one among us, it can be formed from the very light of creation itself," he said as he looked toward Aurotos.

As the magi and knights lowered their hands and dropped their protective barriers, each of them reacted to what the sage had said by looking to Aurotos, who became uncomfortable under their gazes once more. "Thank you, Armatay," Aurotos said. "We should all prepare ourselves to head to Veri Elath. It's not far away, and the people there will be the next we should warn. Leavesa, please instruct our hosts to send word by way of the avolans. Have them head to every stronghold and tower, and warn them to prepare their defenses. If they can't do so, have them seek refuge in Valenthreas. We should also warn our city so they can prepare to receive refugees," Aurotos said as he continued instructing his knights to prepare, signaling Corlith for their steeds.

"Molvalan, Elenfia, mount up," Anaryen said as she prepared her magi and nodded to Aurotos, a sign of her support.

Aurotos thanked Dezren and Avigail for everything, humbling them both and causing them to bow with as much adoration and loyalty as possible. All of the companions were quick to make themselves ready and say their goodbyes to the two hosts who had been so generous. The knights and magi had now set their sights to Veri Elath, a seat of knowledge, art, and wisdom long known for its peace and safety.

CHAPTER 14

A NOBLE SACRIFICE

The goal for Aurotos and his companions was clear as they set off to Veri Elath. Within its borders, the town only had a small mobilized group that were battle-ready to defend it.

It was uncertain to him whether or not the dark prince would seek to siege the town, but as Drazius had sought to destroy the school under the saena tree, it was prudent to warn the citizens there. Aurotos wondered if he and his companions would arrive before the prince might. And, if they found the town to be safe, where else could the prince be?

Having just departed from the inn, Aurotos called Corlith to his side with a request. "Corlith, do you think that you could travel ahead toward the borders of Veri Elath? I'd like you to scout out the town. It's not clear to me whether or not Drazius seeks to destroy it. You should learn what you can and return back to us before we arrive," Aurotos said.

"Yes, my lord, but how can I do that and still reach you before you make it there yourself?" Corlith said as he was clearly confused by the request.

"Drelion, do you have any haste potions on hand?" Aurotos asked as he looked to Drelion with confidence. "Corlith will be needing one."

"As you wish, my lord. Here you go," Drelion said as he pulled the potion bottle from his saddlebag and launched it into the air toward Corlith.

Aurotos could see the scout appeared confused on what to do once he caught the potion. With a chuckle in his voice Drelion continued,

"You'll feed it to your steed. It will hasten your travel time so you are able to get there and back much faster. Now, pay close attention to your horse; mounts tend to experience a period of exhaustion after the effects of the potion wear off. Just give it some water and a few minutes and you'll be right as radiance."

The scout nodded and looked to Aurotos again, this time with an awkward expression. "I mean no disrespect but do you really think when we find Prince Drazius that those bubbles the old man taught you all to use will really be any good? It doesn't seem smart to break the rules of your order," Corlith said smugly.

"The sage has been watching over this realm for many years, and we're fortunate to have him at our side. Whether we break the rules of our order or not is for each of us to decide. Now, prepare yourself," Aurotos said.

"I meant no disrespect. It just seemed like the wrong thing to do, don't mind me. I'll return as soon as I can and meet you back along the way."

"Very well, Corlith, see you then."

As the scout fed his horse the potion and charged ahead, Aurotos found it odd for him to bring up such a thing. Still, his only hope was that his outrider would return with good news. He knew time was precious, and he wanted more than anything to spare the innocent from suffering throughout the reaches of his realm. Realizing that they wouldn't be moving as fast, Aurotos thought to follow up with the magi, his knights, and Armatay as they made their approach to the town.

Aurotos enjoyed light conversation with several of the knights, Anaryen, the magi, and the sage. Many of the conversations had gravitated between their theories of what type of attack or assault Drazius may have in store for Valenthreas. Armatay took special care to remind Aurotos to continue to focus on the skills he had taught him and encouraged him to place his trust in his devoted allies. But as Aurotos and his retinue rode onward to Veri Elath, he couldn't kick the sense he had that something felt wrong.

Time seemed to move slowly in the hour or so that had passed since Corlith darted ahead of the group. Aurotos and the sage began to question the scout's delay when Vael and Tarothas interrupted them.

"Lord Aurotos, I'm picking up on a sound that I'm unable to place; it nears us fast yet it remains concealed somehow. I just, I'm sorry, I can't determine its nature," Tarothas said, maintaining tension as he tracked the unknown sound that was alarming him.

"I would agree with Tarothas. I am unable detect a silhouette or any movement in the land surrounding us, yet the very terrain which guides us appears unsettled with vibration...as if there were galloping horses nearby," Vael said as he remained fixed on the land below him.

Aurotos looked toward the sage, and saw that he shared his own growing concern. "Everyone, be on alert. Nahul, do you sense anything from the creatures that surround us? Vael and Tarothas are picking up an unsettling presence, yet they don't know what it is," Aurotos said, sharing a look of concern with Anaryen through a quick glance. Desperately he hoped that maybe her magi could sense something via the elements.

Nahul, now paying close attention to the world around him, also became alarmed and spoke up. "My lord, the animals are silent. They seem to be distancing themselves from us, from the creatures on the ground to those which fly in the air. Something approaches and they are very afraid."

Aurotos could sense the growing alarm of all his companions. Unknown danger was imminent. That was when it struck. He could see the sage looking backward, and as Aurotos looked to see what caught his attention, it appeared.

Behind the party, a crack splintered its way through the terrain in their direction. From the crack rose a blackness that looked like ash instead of dust from the dirt below. This rift, now tearing its way to them, was accompanied by a strange echoing cry as if the planet itself was weeping in anguish from the scar it would soon carry.

The howling cries coming from the crevice forming behind them swallowed anything that fell into it from the land above. It was then that Aurotos heard the sage shout. "Ride forward as fast as your steeds can carry you. We must get to the ridgeline up ahead. Move now," Armatay said.

The sage cried out to Aurotos. "Move, Aurotos. We will be safe ahead, hurry to high ground," he said as he fell back toward the rear of the charging horses.

He knew there was no time to waste. "To the ridgeline, hurry everyone," Aurotos shouted as he led the charge ahead as fast as he could.

Both the knights and magi desperately advanced toward the ridgeline where they could see vast stones entrenched deep into the terrain. With every second, they sped forward, while the rift swallowing everything behind them seemed to accelerate at unnatural speeds. At last, they had all reached the ridge nearly seconds before the dark rift reached them. There Armatay turned around atop the hills divide, pointing his staff down below as he spoke. "By the light of the Twin Flames, Au'rua," he said.

From the sage's staff, a brilliant prismatic beam of light shot downward, penetrating the land in front of him. A radiating wave of light followed like a shield rising in defense of the party. As the wave of light blasted forward and passed through the dark crevice below, the horrifying screams of a great terror erupted before them, leaving only smoke to rise throughout the tear in the terrain. Armatay had cleansed the land of whatever dark trap had been set upon them.

"We're blessed to have you with us, Armatay, but what in the gods…" Leavesa said. Her big blue eyes widened and her shocked expression solidified.

"It was another of the daevos that was beset upon us. Had it reached us, it would have risen from the crack itself to pull us below into its darkness. I fear it would have been a dreadful fate," Armatay said.

"Yes, but how could it have known where we were? This doesn't make sense; it's like something is tracking us and our own eyes and ears fail us in broad daylight," Aurotos said.

"That it does, my lord. I am afraid there is something more at play and we must discover what that is. There is no time for us to wait, we must get to Veri Elath now," Armatay said.

"Hold on, another trap? Aurotos…" Anaryen said as dread spread across her face.

He remembered the last time Anaryen's instincts had been right. As the dreadful reality of what had just happened sunk in, he found he felt more unified with his companions than he ever believed he could be. He trusted everyone's instincts, and he couldn't afford to ignore his own. "Make haste to Veri Elath," Aurotos commanded. "I fear we may be too late."

Prince Drazius watched on with pleasure as his army was breaking down the last of Veri Elath's defenses. His assault which started overnight was soon to deliver him another victory and it was an intoxicating feeling for him. The town's defenses would soon fall for the siege engines had been steadily sending crashing stones upon the large gateway, barely holding itself shut. Under the rising sun, the massive army pressed feverishly upon its walls.

The drothkin had completely surrounded every avenue of escape and were attempting to climb up the walls, one standing on top of the other. The sight filled the prince with a kind of high that was deepened by the roars coming from the drothkin alpha that dominated the group of creatures' every movement.

At the rear of his army Drazius stood tall before his steed with a platoon of his best branded along with his two commanders at his side. There he caught sight of a human scout quickly approaching and, seeing the reaction of some of his men who were prepared to defend him, he uttered a simple instruction. "Leave him be."

The prince could see that the scout moved with purpose as he galloped toward him, eagerly preparing to meet him. The closer the scout came to the prince, the dimmer the light of the suns were. In fact, wherever the army seemed to dwell, a shadow was present even though there wasn't a cloud in the sky.

As Corlith neared, the prince could see a grimacing smile upon his face, speaking only one word. "Finally."

Corlith approached the prince and dismounted his steed dropping to his knees to report. "The trap has been set, my lord. The Auron elf and his followers should be paying the ultimate price as the daevos swallows them from below. I followed your command precisely. Now it's my pleasure to join you and see this realm destroyed," he said, clutching his communion stone in hand as if he safeguarded a sacred relic.

"Yes, and you might be pleased to know that the elf who scorned you will lie dead in that town before us once we raze it to the ground," Drazius said.

"Yes, my lord, all sacrifices for our great master," Corlith replied.

"Speaking of sacrifices…would it trouble you to learn that the trap failed," Drazius shouted, as he aimed his polearm overhead, taking aim at Corlith.

Corlith collapsed lower on his knees. "It would, my lord. I did exactly as you instructed. I swear, I don't know why it didn't work," Corlith said as he begged for forgiveness.

Drazius relished in the fear taking hold of the man before him; it was so strong he could almost smell it, and so he lowered his polearm. "You may relax, you will have your chance to atone. Why don't you start by helping us slay every elf in this city," he said.

The prince raised his polearm overhead, from which darkness seemed to deepen over himself, his commanders, and the elite branded by his side. He looked on either side at each of his commanders and then toward the front gate, which had just been broken. Seeing that the way in was open, he let out a bellowing command. "Charge! The time has come that they accept our master's judgement, and the drothkin hunger. Leave none alive who do not serve Master Ohrimah."

Drazius charged forward, blazing a path with darkness emanating from his polearm overhead. A bolt of dark energy shot from the prince's weapon crashing through the front gateway of the city, delivering a clear entry paved by destruction into the doomed town. Whatever defenders were present within would surely pay with their very spark, as would the people therein, under the unbearable weight of destruction which swarmed throughout the town. The place once known for its beauty and safety now felt the crushing weight under its falling towers and the swarm of drothkin about to feast.

It seemed like a mere blink in time as Aurotos and his companions raced toward Veri Elath. Even with their khallion steeds it had taken longer than they'd hoped to get there, more time than was comfortable for them. Their dutiful charge only drew them closer to pillars of smoke which rose into the dimming sky. They were too late, and Veri Elath had succumb to tragedy that morning under a great siege. Seeing this, the companions all instinctively rode harder and faster, feeling a sense of desperation to stop whatever horror they might soon find.

As they rode over the top of a final hill, Aurotos was granted visibility to see that the great place of beauty had already been brought to ruin. It was clear the siege had run throughout the night and that the people within the walls had no chance to escape. What was more alarming to him was how the vast army of drothkin and branded soldiers were beyond counting. They could see that every tower had fallen onto the protective walls, crushing most of the homes or buildings.

Aurotos raised his right arm, commanding all of them to come to a quick halt. As they stopped, he looked to Tarothas and Vael, who looked back at him, giving only disappointing acknowledgments that they could neither hear nor see anyone alive down below. Even Nahul wore a sorrowful expression, pronouncing that the animals in the surrounding wilds were grieving the horrific event.

"There must be someone left alive," Aurotos said, looking expectantly at both Anaryen and Armatay.

Anaryen looked at Aurotos without speaking, only showing him her sad eyes, which swelled with tears. She was joined by Elenfia and Leavesa who also seemed overtaken with sadness, having a sense that life down below had been completely extinguished.

Armatay looked to Aurotos unfavorably and shook his head, signaling his answer as he spoke. "None, I am sorry my friend," he said.

"Aurotos, it's the same darkness…the same presence we felt at Illo-nel. It shrouds everything where his army stands," Anaryen said.

"Oh yes, my lady, it is the same oppressive darkness we felt around us that night," Molvalan said slowly as his eyes widened, scanning the sky and the darkness before him.

"It's the same evil; he's here…" Elenfia said as her expression scaled beyond worry.

"Prince Drazius," Aurotos said. "He must be there at the center of the darkness."

"Well, that's not good. He's got far more soldiers than we expected. We can handle the drothkin, my lord, but that army is too large for us to take on by ourselves," Leavesa said.

Aurotos hated hearing it but he knew Leavesa was right. Maybe if Drazius's army was half of what it was now, they'd have a chance to repel the invaders; even then it would take careful coordination and skill. Looking over the army he could see that the prince easily had upward of ten thousand soldiers and drothkin. They would have to run or fight, but Aurotos knew if they played this right, they could eliminate some of the army before getting overpowered.

The party would not be allowed a moment's reprieve, for they had now become visible to the dark prince, who was mounted above the rubble of the eastern outer wall which was nothing more than a ruin. With bloodlust in his eyes, Drazius lifted his polearm, which was drip-ping with blood, pointed it at Aurotos and let out a cry. "Kill them all," he screamed.

The drothkin alpha let out a screeching howl and the great horde pack reacted. The drothkin stopped consuming the elves they were feed-ing on and looked to the east, where they could see Aurotos and his com-panions, and they began to charge. Drazius's soldiers let out their own war cries and joined in. The difference between the drothkin and the branded was dramatic. As the drothkin charged forward relentlessly unorganized toward the companions atop the hill, the branded soldiers exited the town, creating organized formations outside of what had been the walls.

Every branded soldier knew the drothkin were expendable, and they treated them as such. They, on the other hand, followed only the instructions of their commanders and captains. Both Holcurt and Griles moved up to the front of their formations. Drazius also made his way to the front lines of his army, and as the drothkin poured forward for Aurotos and his knights, Drazius sat atop his steed, filling any silence with his ominous laughter.

In his desire to dispel the beasts and send a message to their master, Aurotos shouted, "Dispatch the drothkin, on me." He charged forward and withdrew the radiant blade, setting it aflame.

"We must cover the knights and guard their flank. We can't let the enemy surprise us," Anaryen shouted as she led a charge behind them. Both Molvalan and Elenfia raised their illuminated hands, focusing the power they wielded as they prepared themselves to cast their magic.

It was a glorious sight to see the Knights of the Phoenix living up to their name with their emblazoned blades in hand charging down the slope of the hill to meet the enemy before them. It was only a fleeting moment, but Armatay remained on his steed, watching the coordinated group of magi and knights pressing forward in their unified cause and in defense of one another. As he swelled with pride and smiled, he too, charged forward to aid the small alliance of elves and humans.

The knights met the drothkin, and their blades cut through the creatures, leaving a trail of blazed corpses behind them. For any of the drothkin that somehow remained unscathed, the magi quickly finished them off with bolts of the arcane or the elements. Elenfia rained lightning down, destroying many drothkin scattered behind the knights. Then, Molvalan cast his spell unto nature, which caused the ground to reach up and rooted hundreds of drothkin at a time.

The knights were organized and rode in a circle formation before the magi, creating a steady loop of destruction as the drothkin continued to charge forward, falling into corpse piles. The sage was just at the rear of the circle formation but still ahead of the magi, hurling his own arcane bolts toward the drothkin before most could reach the knights. His arcane bolts exploded like mines, hurling tens of drothkin into the air at a time, before crashing into the ground and leading them to a certain death.

Aurotos saw the prince gloating in amusement before his army of branded soldiers, but that amusement soon shifted into rage when their eyes met.

Drazius abruptly shouted to his commanders, "Send a battalion of our soldiers to put an end to this Auron." His violent voice echoed off the crumbled town walls.

Armatay looked on as the vast army rode fast toward the knights. The magi followed, but before they reached the sage, he dismounted off of his horse and pointed his staff skyward. As he did this, a beam of radiating light seemed to break the spell of the surrounding gloomveil. It reached high and then arced down all around him, creating a dome of light that completely enclosed the knights and magi nearby.

None were more surprised than Drazius to see this kind of magic at work. Those drothkin who continued to charge and reached the dome first exploded into ash as they collided into the light-forged barrier which had halted them. Seeing this, the rest of the drothkin came to a stop and began beating against the light in an attempt to break through. Some of them caught fire which sent them running away, screeching in agony.

The branded soldiers who had been sent forward continued, but as they got closer, it became harder for them to see, and their approach seemed to slow them into a daze. Drazius signaled to his commanders, who both screamed out commands for the branded soldiers to come to a halt.

Aurotos looked toward Armatay, alarmed, as were the rest of his companions. Armatay looked back with a hearty smile and spoke. "My friends, it would seem our destinies now divide us."

"No, Armatay, whatever you're thinking—" Aurotos argued.

"Ha oh, my friend. Surely you know his army is too large and I can sense the power he wields now is too great. I know of a way to weaken him but I need you all safe away from this place. I must say farewell. Accept this act of service as my parting gift."

"Armatay, you don't have to do this. We can—" Anaryen said.

"This is why I am here. Retrieve my message when the danger is gone. Until next we meet, may the light guide you, now and forever," he said.

In a blinding flash of light Aurotos, his companions, and their mounts were teleported to the safety of an overlooking cliff to the north of the fallen city, leaving them helpless to intervene as the sage remained far down below, left to confront the dark prince himself.

Aurotos shouted as he knelt down at the cliffs edge. "No," he said as he stared down at the white bubble surrounding the sage which had begun to drop. Behind him, both the magi and knights shared the same sense of helplessness they could see in Aurotos. Anaryen rushed to his side, kneeling beside him and placed her arm across his shoulders, providing comfort and support he had not felt in a very long time. Together, the two looked on desperately, trying to see what was happening so far down below.

The series of events that occurred below were barely visible, but as Aurotos watched, he could see a pulse of light followed by an explosion from the sage's dome that spread outward as it vanished. In what seemed like seconds, Aurotos and his companions witnessed explosions of light and darkness. There, they were helpless to watch as the sage stood alone against the dark power being wielded by the dark prince. It wasn't long until there was a final explosion of light which seemed to briefly pierce the veil of darkness surrounding the prince and his army until there was no hint of the sage's light left.

Aurotos took Ai'ethe in hand and honed his vision, desperately seeking any hope of the sage's presence down below. There was nothing left, and he was pained to realize that the sage was no longer alive. In the deafening silence that was his passing, Aurotos remained still for a moment. He reflected on all he had lost, all that he had gained because of Armatay, and he swallowed his sorrow.

There, high above upon the ledge, Aurotos and his companions could see the enemy army beginning to move away. As Aurotos looked on in dismay, comforted by Anaryen, he arose and turned toward his companions, knowing he had to say something.

"I can see Armatay's light with my eyes no longer. We must return down below and find what may be left of his remains. We owe him that much."

Anaryen, standing by his side, looked to him, her brilliant blue eyes shining in acknowledgment. "We are with you, Aurotos." She gazed upon her two magi companions for support, and they both nodded in agreement.

Aurotos looked up to see that both the magi and his knights all seemed to share his sadness for the sage. Still, they all shared the familiar look of dedication he had come to appreciate, and he knew they were all with him. To reaffirm this, Leavesa spoke up. "Well, you know we stand with you, my lord."

"Ah, that's right, we're with you Lord Aurotos. I say let's go," Salenval said.

"There should be no doubt they will be moving to Valenthreas from here," Vael said.

"Then let us make haste down below and honor Armatay's wishes," Aurotos said.

The sage had placed them in a well-hidden spot on the edge of the mountains just north of the city. It was just out of sight but close enough that it only took them a short time to get down a pass leading to a hill on the north side of the town. It was clear to everyone that Armatay knew exactly where to put them so as to remain unseen and still be able to make their way back down without losing too much time. It was even more clear to Aurotos that the sage must have thought this plan out well in advance to know so specifically where to place them all. It took some time, but the party made their way back down to the ruined town.

Nearing the battleground, Aurotos and his companions surveyed the outskirts. There would be no survivors within Veri Elath, as there was not a place without flame inside the crumbled ruins of the town. As they neared the side where they last saw the sage, it was clear that Armatay had killed thousands of the drothkin and the prince's branded soldiers. He had somehow single handedly cut nearly half of the prince's army down, maybe even more. The bodies were all ash but the armor and weapons could be seen spread all over the field. It appeared to be the majority of the front half of the prince's army. The odor across the land was horrible, a wretched scent of burnt corruption mixed with ash.

As Aurotos scrambled to find the sage, he came upon a crater in the dirt not far from where he had previously been standing, but closer to the town's ruins. At the crater's center, he could see something shimmering and it caught his attention. With the shine drawing him closer, he turned to Anaryen and the knights with a query. "Do you all see a light there?" he asked as he pointed.

"A light?" Anaryen asked. "I can't see anything."

None of them could see what Aurotos was able to see. As he drew closer to the shining object at the center of the crater, its light grew brighter and brighter, drawing him closer to pick it up. As he did so he heard a voice speak. "Dedicate," the voice said.

Instantly, Aurotos found himself observing Armatay and his confrontation with Drazius as if he was right there with him. He observed and watched as the sage lowered his staff and pounded it onto the ground. The staff let out a pulse of light, knocking back all those surrounding him as the bright dome fell. Grasping his staff firmly, he looked toward Drazius in defiance before pulling out a communion stone from the pouch secured on his belt. While grasping it firmly in his right hand, the sage uttered a single word. "Dedicate," he said as he held it tight.

Seeing that Armatay was now alone, the prince shouted. "Halt, do not intervene. This fight is between us," he said.

As Drazius walked toward the sage, both of his commanders smiled like children receiving toys on their birthday. His army's morale was exploding and they cheered as they watched their leader move forward with the power of the fade in hand.

Armatay could see that the prince was pleased he was alone, but that did not stop him from carrying hope that Drazius could be saved. "It is not too late to turn back from this path you have been walking, Prince Drazius. It is not too late to make amends for the murder of your father and the betrayal of your people. You can still redeem yourself in the eyes of the Twin Flames," he said.

"The Twin Flames are helpless here, they have not stopped me so far, and they cannot stop me now. You won't stop me either, old man," Drazius said laughing. "Valenthreas will fall and the elves will know their place, just as you are to learn yours." Drazius lunged forward, arcing his polearm over his head and slamming it down onto the sage.

Armatay reacted quickly, raising an arcane shell around himself, leaving only a burst of light over his head where the polearm would have struck him. With his staff and hand raised, maintaining the shell, Armatay continued his plea. "I know your actions are guided by another. Yes, your dark master rejected his aspect of good purpose long before you were born. You must understand his agenda will only end in the further ruin of this world. That your soul will only be left to wither and fade into nothing if you continue. You are only fuel to Ohrimah; he does not care for your loyalty; he only cares to destroy you and everything your family stood for."

Drazius brought down another fierce blow onto the shell the sage had maintained as he shouted back. "You think me a mere puppet? You don't know the power I wield, sage. Tell me, how is it you can teleport this elf and his followers away and delay them from their end? For this, you will suffer alone."

"I walk in the light of the Twin Flames and their good Masters. I serve the people of this world. Their empyreal flames protect me, but they will not protect you. This path will only condemn you to darkness forever."

"The fade is freedom," Drazius shouted as he began beating upon the arcane shell, which now began to show its cracks. "I will show you the power and the freedom my master has granted me."

Each blow the dark prince delivered to the sage's magic shell was radiant and blinded most of the drothkin and soldiers nearby, though the sage's gaze upon the dark prince was unwavering. "The power you wield is not freedom, Drazius. It is enslavement, and your soul's very spark is the price that will be paid for the power you wield," Armatay said.

Drazius delivered blow after blow onto the arcane shell until it at last shattered, leaving the two fighting, polearm against staff. With every blow Drazius dealt, a burst of darkness erupted as the sage blocked the attacks with his staff.

"You will not destroy the city of Valenthreas with your dark army, dark prince. The light will not allow it, and neither will Aurotos Va'Threas."

"I saw that Auron. You saved a weakling who's done nothing but hide in the shadows for these hundreds of years. My master knew where he hid. Now shall I tell you the destiny of your precious city before I end you?"

"Taunt me if you must," Armatay said as he pointed his staff forward, erupting a bright light and knocking Drazius backwards to the ground on his back.

The dark prince laughed once more as he stood back up with the aid of his blood-soaked polearm. In defiance, he shouted again. "Don't you know my master has slain Anieva and used her very essence to turn Valos into a weapon? He embedded The Master's Core that holds her essence into the very moon itself. In doing so, we now have control over it."

Armatay looked back at Drazius with absolute shock, to utter such a sin was to invite annihilation to the world. "No, that cannot be," he said, as if he was trying to convince himself that his own worst fear had not come true.

"I speak the truth. I was chosen to crash the very moon itself into your sacred city. I'll bring it down onto this realm, and once that city of light is gone, all of these fools will know freedom from the tyranny of the elves and their false gods."

"The murder of countless innocents is not freedom. It is evil and it is darkness, and you will be lost forever," Armatay continued as he began radiating a light toward the prince from the tip of his staff.

Drazius, laughing, pointed his polearm forward and began blasting darkness toward Armatay. The two beams of dark and light connected, and the harder the sage empowered the light, the more overwhelming the darkness from the prince became.

"You cannot win, Drazius," Armatay said.

"I have already won, heh. A pity you won't be alive to witness it," Drazius said as he pressed forward upon Armatay, overpowering him. The darkness raced toward him so fast that it began to cover his staff in black tendrils before shattering it. Then the darkness enveloped the sage, causing him to scream in anguish as the corrupt energy slowly began to shred away at his very being.

With his left arm up in an attempt to provide some cover from the blast, Armatay held the communion stone with his right hand close to his chest. His left hand quickly met his right as he held the stone tight within his grasp. The darkness completely enveloped him, and as he died, cracks of light began to show through the black matter that had completely covered and was consuming him.

Drazius, staring down pleased in his victory, was shocked to see the cracks of light. In alarm, he began to back up, but it was too late. The sage exploded into a burst of light which, for a moment, seemed to lift the veil of darkness that had dimmed the daylight. It was a devastating shock and awe to both the prince and his forces. The explosion sent Drazius flying backward, killing thousands of drothkin and branded soldiers in the process.

Armatay was gone, leaving only a crater where he once stood and delivering wounds that had burned Drazius's face and any areas of his skin which were exposed under his armor. Many of the front battalions of his branded soldiers were reduced to piles of ash, aside from their armor. The same could be said for the majority of the drothkin which had surrounded the sage's dome of light.

Every member of the prince's army that wasn't destroyed or wounded had been knocked down to the ground. Griles and Holcurt stood up to see Drazius lying ahead of them and scurried over to his aid, in shock that over half of their dark army had just been reduced to nothing.

The prince had not walked away from the fight unscathed, and as he stood up, the rage within him seemed only to grow as he felt embarrassed for appearing weak before his army, an army which had now been partially decimated.

"Gather the men and what's left of the drothkin, and leave any dead. We still have our army, more than enough to carry out what we have yet to do," Drazius said.

The vision gifted to him by the communion stone began to fade and Aurotos had seen everything. Now he knew what the prince was planning, but he still didn't know exactly how. Much worse, he learned the dreadful news that the dark master had killed his counterpart. That he had embedded the core which holds Anieva's essence, into the blue moon Valos. The very moon he was planning to pull down and crash onto the great city of light. He also witnessed that Corlith remained alive as the prince's subject, having clearly betrayed them.

Suddenly, everything Aurotos had wondered about regarding the sage made perfect sense. He now understood the reason he was so much stronger than everyone else in the party, the reason he knew how to create magic shells, and the reason he was able to protect them all in the way that he did. Armatay must have been one of the auros, beings of light who walked among the people of the planet while guided by the Masters they were individually in service of.

It was clear to Aurotos that Armatay had used the communion stone to warn him, revealing all of the dark plans Drazius had shared during their conflict. The sage had committed himself to one last act of service before he left them, and sacrificed his physical form to reduce the prince's army to an enervated state.

Aurotos had become surrounded by all of his companions who had seen him go into a trance as he held the stone in his hand. When he came to, he placed the stone into his own pouch next to the ashes of his cats and then, looking toward all of them, knew it was time to develop a plan around everything he had just learned.

"I have just borne witness to the events gifted to me by Armatay. The dark master has planned a great apocalypse for Valenthreas. He killed Anieva and placed the last of her essence into Valos. He plans to use the moon as a weapon to collide into our city and snuff out the light of the Twin Flames there forever. If we are to stop him then we must disrupt their plans and send news to all people across our realm. They must prepare to seek safety from the fall of Valos."

"Oh my…then so be it," Anaryen said.

Aurotos looked toward his companions and though they all appeared to remain speechless, taking in all they had learned, he could see dedication in their eyes. Between the knights and the magi, he knew what must be done, for the elven realm itself was in danger of being annihilated by the dark master and those who served him.

He knew the prince would want Valenthreas to be defenseless, and he could not allow that to occur. For now, he would send word to every corner of the realm and instruct them to prepare to defend themselves. Aurotos would have Valenthreas know that he and his allies would intercept and stop the dark prince. Still, it would take every person trained to wield magic to deflect the cataclysm sure to be caused by the magical moon itself. The danger Drazius posed now felt so much worse to Aurotos. Even though his army had been cut down in size, what could stop the moon from crashing into their planet?

CHAPTER 15

THE ENIGMA ELIXIR

The countdown had begun, and the fate of Valenthreas, and the realm of Aurotheros, was now at stake. The people needed to be warned, from every tower to every town, city, harbor, farmstead, and beyond. It was the duty of Aurotos and his companions to ensure the message was spread.

Aurotos and his party formed a circle, mounted on their steeds, and he surveyed his companions noticing the absence of two members: Armatay had fallen, and Corlith who was with the enemy. Aurotos had seen how the prince's army had suffered significant losses due to the sage's final act, and he was determined to pursue Drazius in order to gather as much information as possible about the state of his forces. He also recognized that this was their chance to ensure that every safe haven was prepared to defend itself against the impending fall of Valos.

Keeping these considerations in mind, Aurotos was set to present his plan, fully aware that it would require dividing his group for the first time. He understood that not everyone would immediately grasp the reasoning behind his decision, but he hoped they would respect it nonetheless.

Addressing his companions, he felt ready. "Friends, nightfall approaches swiftly. There's no doubt that Drazius will make his way directly to Valenthreas, but I believe he will avoid passing through the Dragonstrike Woods, and the machines they carry will be too difficult to transport through there. Furthermore, there are no other towers or outposts along his path. Our mission is clear: we must warn everyone about the imminent dangers and summon all available magi and knights to defend the people we are sworn to protect. We need to gather intelligence on Drazius's whereabouts and assess his capabilities."

Pausing briefly, Aurotos scanned the faces of Anaryen and the rest of his companions who watched him intently. "I would appreciate hearing your suggestions as we prepare for what's ahead today."

"Very well, my lord. With our magi friends, we have the capability to destroy a significant portion of the army we expect to still be alive," Leavesa began, her voice filled with concern. "However, I fear that we may not be able to stop them all. Even with our best efforts, if the siege on Valenthreas is successful, the city could be left unshielded and have no chance against a calamity as immense as we expect this to be."

He understood her position, and she wasn't wrong—they had to find an edge. So, he looked to the lady of Edin Throvon whose leadership and clarity he had come to rely on. "Lady Anaryen, I'd value your insight," Aurotos said.

"We still don't know how he will do it. How will the moon be collided into our world?" She seemed to ponder the question herself before she continued. "I agree with Leavesa, I think we need to disrupt their attack. I wonder if the changes in the world that some of us have been experiencing already indicates that the moon itself has shifted out of place. By nightfall, if my suspicions are correct, many others will notice it too."

Aurotos understood the wisdom in their words. However, from their vantage point on the cliff above, it had been challenging to determine the precise capabilities and remaining forces of the prince. The battlefield was enveloped in smoke and debris for the gloomveil had permeated the area, obscuring the details of the full conflict.

"It's true, and I share your concerns regarding the moon," Aurotos acknowledged, casting his gaze toward the others. "However, I believe it is crucial for us to assess his army. That's why I'll be asking several of the knights to accompany me on a reconnaissance mission. Meanwhile, under the assistance of Nahul, the rest of you can prepare to dispatch as many capable creatures in the realm as we can find. They will carry messages on behalf of both our knights and magi companions, warning the people and preparing them for what lies ahead."

"Hold on, you want us to split?" Anaryen asked in a tone of authority he had not heard since she scolded him at the Starlight Inn. "I don't know how I feel about that, especially when considering the danger posed by his forces. He wields an unnaturally dark power and he's so consumed by rage, it's evident to me that the fade has consumed him. He is no longer the person I once knew. There is nothing familiar about him, making him totally unpredictable and more dangerous."

"I understand your concerns, Lady Anaryen, I truly do," Aurotos reassured her. "But I ask you to trust me on this. I believe it's crucial that you and your magi help carry out the task of assisting Nahul to warn the people. Our watchtower to the southwest should now be vacant as those knights have been recalled back to Valenthreas. That tower would provide an ideal location for you all to prepare to send out the messages."

"I can't argue that warning the people is equally as important as interrupting the prince's plans. How will Nahul be able to help us accomplish this?" she asked.

"Nahul's skills are unmatched among those in our order. He has the ability to call upon many creatures and should be able to gather animals to carry messages abroad."

"Indeed, my lord speaks the truth, my lady. You can count on me," Nahul said as he bowed his head slightly.

"Then there's no time to waste, who's going with you, and who's going with the magi?" Syvon asked, making it clear he was eager to move on from this place as he bore a look of disgust from the smell of the burnt drothkin whose corpses stunk up the air.

"Syvon, you will accompany me along with Leavesa, Salenval, Kaylos, Kaervo, and Vael. I will need all of your expertise to accomplish my plan."

"Listen here, if we have to fight, they won't know what hit them," Salenval said, nudging Syvon and Kaylos who were near each side of him. He chuckled in a playful tone seeing the two react in surprise at how hard he bumped them as he carried on. "Ah yeah, you can count on us, my lord."

"Of this I have no doubt," Aurotos said with a smile he couldn't hold in. "Drelion, Tarothas, Arvasiel, I'll be asking you to accompany Nahul and the magi to the knight's tower. That will be our rallying point for when we return. Nahul, seek out as many twin-tailed birds as you can find, but any beast will suffice. Tarothas, I need you to keep watch there to warn the others of danger early if it approaches. Arvasiel, you can help shield the tower entry if it needs defending before we meet you there. Drelion, I need you to conceal the words in the message so the contents remain hidden if intercepted. The tools available there will aid you in your preparation."

"As you wish, my lord. Great idea, people will know what the twin-tailed birds symbolize. Those receiving the messages will know it comes from ones dedicated to the Twin Flames," Drelion said.

"Oh yes, yes, that makes perfect sense," Molvalan said, his voice carrying hope for the plan.

Elenfia supported him in agreement reaching to place a hand on his arm as she spoke. "Molvalan is one of the wisest among our order; I know I'd defer to his judgement."

Anaryen's commanding aura seemed to wane as she supported her allies. "We'll be ready, but don't take too long. Nightfall will be on its way, and I expect Drazius to move quick."

"Don't worry, our khallion steeds are faster. If he's where I believe he is, then we shouldn't take long and will make it to you just after you've sent out most of the messages," Aurotos said, trying his best to ease her concerns.

"Then we'll leave as soon as your knights are prepared, assuming you don't have any other instructions for them," she said, as she looked to him with a reassuring smile.

It brought Aurotos a sense of ease to see she was supporting him even though she had been questioning the idea at first. He felt a smile creep up but it was snuffed out as his next idea crept in. "Just one, it's for you Drelion."

"As you wish, my lord," Drelion said as he focused intently.

"I'm going to ask you to make some enigma elixirs. Don't worry yourselves with why now, it will become much clearer when we return."

"I'll see it done," Drelion replied with curiosity painted through his demeanor.

"Let's be off then. We'll meet you as soon as we can. If all goes well, you shouldn't be waiting long," Aurotos said, looking toward his knights, who appeared ready for their tasks.

Aurotos exchanged an elusive smile with Anaryen, and with those final instructions, the group split and made their way toward their objectives. The two groups were working under the cover of approaching dusk, and if successful, they would meet at the knight's watchtower before nightfall. Aurotos had great confidence in Anaryen; in his eyes, she was a remarkable leader and it was her capability that had inspired him to rise to the role that lay before him.

As he rode swiftly south with his party, he found himself reflecting on the kind of leaders his parents were. They cared about people and gave everything to ensure the well-being of others. As leaders, they were loved deeply by all nations, not only because of their divine origins, but because of their great humility and compassion. This was something he found he now wished to embody himself. He wondered if some of what Armatay had said to him was actually true. Perhaps deep down he was always more like his parents than he would allow himself to see.

It was easy to love his parents because of their role in the world, but Aurotos loved them so much more because of the kind of love they showed him. He remembered the lessons they presented to him about the Twin Flames and the noble tenets. He could never erase the ways they left their mark on his very being, nor would he want to. In his eyes there were no better parents a child could ever hope to have. There was never a better set of leaders that a kingdom could wish for. No matter how hard he had tried to suppress who he really was over the past several centuries, he was only left with the truth. He was more like his parents than he cared to admit and maybe it was time to honor them in the way that he knew they deserved. He only hoped that when this was all over, he would be able to honor them by living up to their legacy.

Dusk was approaching rapidly, and in no time, Aurotos and his knights had located the prince's army. The knights slowed their pace, seeking guidance from Vael. Aurotos' hope was realized as Vael not only identified the prince's position but also recognized the companions riding alongside him. Vael's attention was drawn to a person of interest—Corlith, their own scout, who rode near Griles at the rear of the army. The prince himself was positioned closer to the middle, while Holcurt was situated toward the front of the army.

"My lord, the army is maybe half the size it was before, truly far smaller. I noticed a much larger drothkin, no doubt an alpha, leading what is left of the drothkin horde. I see Corlith rides at the rear with one of the commanders. It appears to be the same commander that escaped us," Vael said.

"This will make our goal very easy then. We need to retrieve Corlith and take out any soldiers or drothkin who oppose us, it must be done fast. Vael, I'll rely on you to keep an eye on the greater army as I don't expect they will notice the assault right away, but once you see that they do, you must let us know," Aurotos ordered.

"It will be done," Vael said.

"Wait, what's going on? Are we here for a rescue or…" Leavesa asked as her tone filled with curiosity seeing that he was riding freely, unbound by the enemy.

"Leavesa, Corlith has been a spy, I was able to see that he was working with them through the memories of Armatay in the communion stone that was left behind," Aurotos explained.

"Yes, of course," Leavesa said as the full reality of the betrayal set in. "This explains so much, every place he attacked before we could make it in time. Corlith must have kept him apprised of our movements."

"It would seem one human is as corrupt as the next. Just as bad as the filthy beasts they have tagging along," Syvon said, his revulsion made all too clear through his scrunched facial expression.

"Relax, Syvon, you can't say that about every human you meet. They're not all that bad," Kaervo said, sounding a bit defensive as he did so.

"There's no time for this. Lord Aurotos brought us here for a reason and we can't squander the time we have while we're here," Leavesa said, her tone shifting to one which reaffirmed her respect from the knights.

Aurotos was very appreciative of her continued support and he felt at some point he needed to let her know that it meant a lot to him. He also had growing concern about Syvon's contempt for humans and how it might interfere with his ability to carry out his duties effectively, but there was no time for that now.

"She's right. You three will assist me as we move to the rear of the army," Aurotos said as he looked toward Salenval, Kaylos, and Syvon. "We'll suppress the enemy forces while Leavesa and Kaervo use their ranged expertise to dismount Corlith and Commander Griles. Leavesa, Vael, the two of you will capture Corlith and secure him, then move to the rear of the army and provide us with ranged support. I need everyone to be ready to move to the watchtower once I give the command."

"A quick snatch and grab, I like it," Salenval said. "Come on now, who's ready to smash more of these fools?"

"Ready, huh? Kind of like those ougars you smashed before they covered you in filth," Leavesa said as Salenval's playfulness seemed to ease her sternness for a moment. She giggled for a bit before she became more serious again. "Well, we'll need to ready our horses for a quick sprint, so make sure you protect your steeds from injury."

"Oh, these khallion steeds are the best, they'll pull us through," Kaervo said as he moved to join Leavesa, who was readying herself and her horse for takeoff.

"Knights, prepare yourself for battle," Aurotos ordered. Soon after he and his knights sprinted their way toward the tail end of the army. Aurotos, wielding the radiant blade, prepared himself to cut down as many enemies as he could, sure to devastate any opposition. Leavesa and Kaervo moved methodically as they spun flames toward Griles and Corlith, knocking them off their steeds.

Corlith had barely gotten to his feet before Leavesa bound him in twin quill cord and covered his mouth, throwing him on the back of her horse, while Kaervo continued bombarding Griles who was still on the ground. Kaervo was slinging so many flames toward him that all the commander could do was hide behind his now burning horse, using it to protect himself from certain death.

Griles desperately screamed. "Drothkin, soldiers, attack, the enemy is here," he said.

The rear battalion of drothkin and branded quickly charged for his location, readying themselves as they moved to attack the knights. Several horns were sounded, and the battalions ahead of them leading up toward the prince became aware as well, but by the time they heard the horn sounding, Aurotos and his knights had already begun laying waste to the army's rear battalion.

Bursting one flame after the next, the knights dealt destructive blows to the approaching beasts, leaving their charred corpses on the ground just moments before they could reach them. Their steeds moved swiftly, allowing the knights to leave a blazing trail in their wake as they cut through the charging army.

The destruction of the army was effortless, and although the branded soldiers were much stronger than the drothkin, they were still standing on the ground, and the knights had a horseback advantage. The army's own cavalry was far toward the front, and those steeds were not capable of the speed that theirs were.

"Down go the drothkin," Salenval exclaimed, offering a hearty laugh as his weapon shrieked while he cut through the drothkin.

"They're lucky I'm not using the shadows. I could do this all day," Kaylos responded, laughing in return. "I'll bet I get more than you do," he said as he looked to Salenval who appeared to be focused on the next beast he could count.

"Better watch, then; I'll definitely get the most," Syvon replied as he sliced the enemy nearly as fast as his horse was moving.

Aurotos could see that Leavesa and Vael had safely extracted Corlith, taking him to the rear of the army. However, he couldn't restrain himself; he yearned for justice for Armatay and those who charged him would pay the price. As he pressed forward, deeper into the enemy forces, he became surrounded and inadvertently separated from his knights. He felt the burning rage of retribution heating the light in his eyes, as his brow furrowed and he clenched his jaw tight. Every purposeful strike was a sentence he delivered to the soldier or drothkin who opposed him, and he would let nothing stop him from delivering his verdict.

He soon realized that he was being overwhelmed, and amidst his relentless assault on the drothkin, a voice spoke to him. "You must depart now. This is not a battle you are prepared to win, young Aurotos," the voice said. "Your duty lies with those you lead. Hurry back to your companions." The voice he heard was unmistakable—it belonged to Armatay.

There was no time to think; he knew he had to get back to the watchtower, and protect the lives of those under his charge. It was then that he kicked on the sides of his steed, charging back through the ruined battalion and toward his knights as he shouted. "Fall back knights, to the rally point," he said.

The knights promptly regrouped around Corlith, and made their way back northward, evading the army of Prince Drazius. As Aurotos as his companions raced away, he looked back once more to see the drothkin alpha towering above, screeching as it held fast at the rear of the army.

He could see Griles standing over his fallen horse, a sight that paled in comparison to the numerous bodies left in the wake of the escaping knights, whom the prince and the army would not be able to catch. The mission had been a success and Aurotos was filled with vigor as he and his knights rode away. Still, he wondered how he came to hear Armatay. Had it been his imagination or did the sage really speak to him? He wasn't sure if he had just imagined it, or if it was really just his own instincts telling him to act fast. Either way, it was comforting to think Armatay might still be watching even though he could no longer be riding by their side.

Nightfall was approaching as Aurotos and his party made it to the watchtower where the rest of his companions were awaiting him. The tower was made of the same white stone found in their capital city, with red and gold paint surrounding the doorway. Below, at the base of the tower was Arvasiel, who was standing guard. The two braziers which stood in front of the door were unlit, and at the top, where the usual fire would burn, he could see the magi standing next to Tarothas.

As Aurotos dismounted next to Leavesa and Kaervo, he rushed toward the door. "Please take him inside, it's time to find out what the traitor knows. Leavesa, you know what to do; have Drelion help you."

"Yes, of course, my lord. We'll see it done," Leavesa said as she signaled Kaervo who had him under guard by her horse.

As Aurotos entered through the doorway, he spotted Anaryen standing alongside Drelion and Nahul. Anaryen had noticed his return and her expression lit up with joy.

He could also see that the two knights appeared quite satisfied with their achievements. "I take it you were successful," Aurotos said.

"Indeed, my lord. We have sent twin tails far and wide carrying our warnings. By morning, most of those we have sent the messages to should be preparing their defenses," Nahul said.

"And the enigma elixirs, Drelion?"

"Ready, just as you commanded, my lord. Will you now share why we need these?" Drelion asked.

"We have retrieved Corlith. I'm afraid he was a spy, an agent for the dark prince. I'll need you to gather every bit of information you can from him. We must learn everything he knows about the prince's plans. Leavesa and Kaervo should be in shortly with him."

"Oh, Masters no...Corlith betrayed us?" Drelion asked as disbelief filled his eyes, widening them.

"I'm afraid so. I had seen it in a vision by way of the communion stone that Armatay left for us," Aurotos replied.

"Such a shame. As you wish, my lord," Drelion said.

Aurotos took a step to the side, where he could see Anaryen smiling and he found it to be the most welcome sight he could have hoped for. As he walked toward her, he couldn't help smiling back as their eyes locked.

"I'm happy to see you've returned safe, you know, that you're all safe," Anaryen said.

"I'm glad to see you as well, my lady," Aurotos said hoping she may get the hidden meaning of his message, that he longed for her.

Anaryen's cheeks blushed, and her blue eyes shimmered under the pale light that filled the watchtower. Aurotos had not yet expressed to her how she made him feel, and he thought that there might be time for him to try to tell her. There never seemed to be a good time while they pursued justice, and he knew that both of their duties compelled them to lead. But things were still so fresh and they had only met recently. A part of him was reluctant and perhaps too guarded to be so vulnerable, yet he had never felt anything like her presence and the effect it had on him.

How he felt for her was something he had never felt before, and he couldn't explain it, although he knew it was powerful. He didn't know yet if it was love as he'd never actually been in love before. He also knew they probably wouldn't get many other chances before they clashed with the dark prince and he felt a sense of urgency to discover whether or not she was feeling the same.

"Would you walk with me, my lady?" Aurotos asked, gesturing toward the door that led outside.

"Of course, Aurotos," Anaryen replied, following him to the tower's exit.

As the two approached the door, they could both see that Leavesa and Kaervo had bound Corlith to a chair against the wall, and that Drelion had already administered the enigma elixir. The elves were questioning the spy, and they appeared to be getting a lot of information.

As the two walked through the doorway toward the horses before them, Aurotos moved up behind Anaryen and looked over her shoulder. "It seems Valos has already begun to move closer to our world," he said.

"Yes, but it's still very beautiful," Anaryen said and he could tell she was trying hard to hide the fact she was blushing. He hoped she would feel safe with him and if she did, then maybe she could understand his feelings for her.

"Your eyes remind me so much of that moon," Aurotos said. "So beautiful." Again, he was flirting effortlessly. He was starting to feel as if her presence almost commanded that his feelings be revealed.

Anaryen stood unwavering, yet her cheeks grew a stronger shade of red, and Aurotos could see it as he looked over her shoulder. As she stood silently, he wondered what she was thinking. He thought her silence was telling, for she was rarely speechless, something very uncommon for the valiant magi leader.

Feeling himself vulnerable, Aurotos thought of what else he could share to change that. "It's as I feared. I knew something was upsetting the balance of our world; I felt it long before leaving Valenthreas," he said.

Then came the question he thought Anaryen was bound to ask eventually. "You must tell me, why did you choose to remain absent from the world all this time?" she asked, turning around and locking her eyes with his once again.

He thought she wanted to ask that day they met at Mai'elzin but had chosen not to. As the cool breeze blew across his skin, he felt soothed, but it also reminded him of how silent he was as he explored how to answer her. "I thought about staying at first, but I just felt lost and consumed with grief. My parents were...they were everything to me. I left the city and lost my way for a time, but then I chose to return. Once I did and saw that the stewards had taken on a leadership role, it seemed there was no need to reclaim what I had walked away from. So, I chose to serve the Knights of the Phoenix as my father once had. I was there among them nearly the whole time. I used an enchantment to hide my true identity until that night when..."

"Oh dear, when you lost your cats. I'm sorry that happened, it seems like they were all you had," she said and she took his hand into hers and squeezed it for a moment.

He had been looking away as he spoke to her, but then his gaze met hers once more as she continued. "I can understand turning away from your duty. It's something my father impressed upon me more times than I care to admit. He wasn't understanding of me joining the Aurodites. At first, I believed it was because he didn't think I could do it. That only made me work harder to be the best there was, and I proved that when I became the understudy of Archmagus Evenon," she said, a hint of sadness revealing itself through her eyes.

"I'm sorry, my lady. I knew him to be an honorable man and leader. His loss was felt among our people as well."

"The last time I saw Etrius, he told me I was one of the most skilled magi he had ever seen. He told me he wanted me to take over as leader of the Aurodites once he stepped down. I just never imagined his time as our leader would end so soon."

"I could see you leading the Aurodites."

"You know, the funny thing is I never wanted to lead after I joined. But I came to realize just how much I'm my father's daughter. Of course, Etrius knew my father quite well," she said as she pondered her own path. "I've wondered whether or not he knew that the archmagus was planning that. I'm still curious how he'd feel if I took on that role instead of the role of princess in my own kingdom."

"It would seem we have more in common than we both knew. Valothas had been pushing me to lead the knights. Of course I came to learn that he knew my identity most of the time anyway," Aurotos said as he laughed.

"You know, it sounds like he was encouraging you to reclaim your kingdom," Anaryen said as she giggled back at him playfully.

For a moment, the two laughed together, their eyes locked intently. Aurotos knew he had to share something more. She brought him a sense of happiness he had never felt, and in the moment of shared laughter, he thought about a world where she stood at his side. The thought was exhilarating but he knew better than to be whisked away by something like infatuation. With her, there was something more, something deeper at play. He wondered—what if?

"Anaryen, you should know that I'm growing quite fond of you. What I mean to say is that you're becoming very important to me."

"Well then, you should know I feel the same way," she said as her grin widened, her sincerity telling him all he needed to know, that he wasn't alone.

Silence filled the moment once more, allowing him to take in what he was feeling for her. That he was falling for her. Just as he contemplated how to explore their connection more, the two were interrupted as Leavesa stepped out of the doorway of the tower eagerly seeking Aurotos.

"My lord, we've extracted everything there is to know from Corlith," Leavesa said looking very concerned.

"Tell me everything, Leavesa," Aurotos said, now turning away from Anaryen who moved up by his side.

"Well, the prince destroyed Veri Elath for his own pleasure, but Armatay inflicted devastation upon his army. As a result, the prince has decided to besiege Valenthreas tomorrow. His army will gather at the south side of the Dragonstrike Woods, where they will establish a position to initiate the siege from a safe distance. Their objective is to weaken or completely obliterate any remaining defenses before Valos crashes into the city. And, with The Master's Core embedded deep within it, the prince will be able to create a tether to it. It seems Merdah's aim, through the prince, is to bring about the destruction of the majority of Aurotheros, the city being the focal point," Leavesa explained.

"Well, they aren't close enough yet to begin a siege. How can he tether to the moon?" Aurotos questioned.

"Well, there's some beacon they're hauling that they'll use to bring it down into Auro. It will only take a couple hours once they start it up. Turns out the dark orc may have helped him build it. Corlith didn't know much about that though," Leavesa said.

Aurotos paced back and forth, deep in contemplation. "So that's his plan. Drazius intends to use the woods as a shield for when the moon falls. The trees that sprouted from the Dahaka's remains possess unnaturally strong bark and branches. Those trees might provide protection along with whatever magic he wields. That's why no one has been able to clear those woods out."

"The way that man acts, he seems mad enough to sacrifice himself or his army just to see it done," Salenval said as he approached with a honey vine sticking out of his mouth as he chewed away on it.

"I expect he'll have patrols around that area to warn him of our approach. That leaves us with only one reliable option to offer us the element of surprise. I know some of you aren't going to like it," Aurotos said as he looked back at Anaryen. She returned his gaze with concern, almost as if she knew what he was about to suggest.

Far to the southwest of the knight's watchtower, the dark prince pressed forward, marching into nightfall, making his way toward Valenthreas. To his side, mounted on his own steed, was Griles, shamed after having been punished for his failures. As they rode along, Drazius could tell that the commander seemed alarmed upon hearing the prince speaking to someone who was not there.

The prince clutched the communion stone tight in his hand, and listened to the stone as the dark orc himself had begun speaking. He knew that only he could hear the voice, for the stones only worked for those attuned to them. The prince knew Griles wouldn't dare mention anything after how he had lashed out on him, threatening to kill him earlier.

"Foolish boy," Grindam said. "I have not granted you this power for so long only to see you fail to stop that elf and his knights. By tomorrow, Valos will fall, and you will hasten its course with the beacon I prepared for you."

Clutching the stone harder, Drazius responded in frustration. "Yes, Lord Grindam. The auros was unexpected; had it not teleported them away I assure you, they would have died at Veri Elath. I already took matters into my own hands and killed him."

"Oh yes, you killed the body but its spirit will endure. That thing killed most of the drothkin I sent you, and those loyalists of yours too."

"I won't fail our master. We will be in position tomorrow, and before the night comes, Valos will lay waste to this land."

"It must, or your fate will be worse than your father's. We will not suffer your failure any further. You will see it done. I'm watching you, and so is Master Ohrimah."

"I will not fail my master and I will see the light of the elves destroyed forever."

"See that you do boy. You have no reason for meaningless detours. Get there now, my patience is wearing thin."

"My lord, we're nearly there. Lord Grindam, are you there?"

The dark orc may have been done talking but he had always tuned in to watch since that fateful day the prince was made to serve him. It wasn't long after the fade took the prince that he began to take actions without being aware he had done them. Even though he acted on most things out of pure intoxication from his sorrow or strife, his choices seemed little like his own even though he knew he made them. He was a loyal pup to his master's call and never questioned what he was expected to do.

He followed his orders like an automaton and the part of him that was aware this was the case was so scarcely present from one moment to the next that he had a hard time knowing what was real. Deep down in his soul, the spark of his existence was entombed inside a dark entity he was merely a passenger in.

As the blue crystal moon drew closer toward the planet, the dark prince stood atop a beacon that was well guarded by his soldiers. There, at the center of his army, the lights of the distant city of Valenthreas could be seen just on the horizon. With both of his commanders by his side, he looked upon his branded soldiers. "Tomorrow will be the first step in freeing this world from the oppression of these false gods," he shouted, and his army roared in response.

The prince knew that it would be the first step in bringing the world of the dark master closer to theirs and beckoning the dark convergence sought by his masters. Drazius spoke of the days ahead in which they would live freely in a blessed union with their dark master, Ohrimah, after their liberation. Drazius boasted about how they had defeated one of the sacred auros and that although they had lost many troops in vanquishing it, that it was proof of their destiny and proof of the freedom they were promised when they set their dark crusade on a path to destroy the kingdom of the elves.

With his final words he ushered in his truth. "We will no longer be subjugated under the tenets of these false gods. You know that Auron elf is revered by most people of the world, but he is nothing more than a false idol. Aurotos and all those who aid him will lay dead as we destroy his city and the whole realm. Remember that if you fall you will be reborn through the glory of our master when we bring about the beginning of our new world," Drazius shouted. "We will suffer them no longer. Now, ready yourselves, men, and claim the glory we have always been denied."

The men were clearly bolstered in morale under the praise of their prince. Drazius ordered his commanders to send their roaming assault parties throughout the surrounding land as they prepared to move forward to the staging area where they would deliver their assault on the city of the elves. By morning, the dark prince would be gathering his army, and the time would soon run short for Aurotos and his allies to stop him. One thing was sure, if the moon fell, the world at night would surely be a darker place for all.

Back at the watchtower, Aurotos, the knights, and the magi had gathered. They had decided to leave Corlith bound tightly to a stone pillar atop the watchtower facing the southwest, where he would be left to witness whatever fate was to befall their land. If, through his betrayal, he had indeed aided in the destruction of these lands, then the group of companions saw that he would share in their fate. If the elves would succeed, then he would have to witness the failure of his dark prince. One way or another, he would be left to answer for his betrayal, as the knights had every intention to deliver him to Valenthreas in the aftermath of whatever was to come.

As Aurotos spoke, a fiery determination blazed in his bright, glowing eyes. He addressed his companions with unwavering resolve. "My friends, we are well aware that Drazius intends to launch an assault on Valenthreas, right at the southern fringes of the Dragonstrike Woods. I know that none of you have forgotten that those woods serve as a tomb for the Dahaka and countless others. It is a place seething of darkness, concealed beneath the shroud of those dark trees. I have just as much reluctance as any of you to venture through that treacherous place, for its where I believe my parents lay at rest," he said, seeing Anaryen cast him a sorrowful gaze, and Elenfia wearing a similar expression, while the others listened intently, maintaining a high level of respect.

He paused momentarily to regain his composure before continuing. "I propose that we approach the woods from the northern side, making our way through it early tomorrow morning, reaching the other side before their attack. I'm aware of the potential dangers that lie within, but with our combined skills, I'm confident that we can overcome them. I believe this is our best course of action, and I have faith in our ability to succeed."

"Must we travel through there? The dark woods have always seemed…evil," Elenfia remarked, her voice filled with concern. "That place, I don't know."

Molvalan drew closer to her, offering solace. "Perhaps it would be perilous for individuals embarking alone, but I have faith in us and our shared mission," he reassured.

"You should know I share your reservations, Elenfia, but I agree with Aurotos. Time is precious, but more importantly, we need an element of surprise," Anaryen concurred.

"I'm ready to tear up anything in those woods," Salenval said. "Some dark trees won't stop us from seeing this done."

Leavesa giggled at the always brutish nature of Salenval before she managed to steel herself with the authority everyone had been accustomed to. "I'm sure I speak for the rest of us when I tell you we're with you, my lord," she said confidently.

There wasn't a disagreement among them, something that brought Aurotos a rising explosion of joy and gratitude. He wouldn't let them see just how happy he was but he was sure Anaryen could see it in his eyes based on her expression which matched his sentiments.

With that, Aurotos and his companions were off to make their way west, en route to the dark woods, the tomb of the great Dahaka and countless souls who perished in the great war. The large trees within would now provide Aurotos and his companions an opportunity to surprise Drazius and his army and put an end to his dark plans, but first, they needed to get there. The path would be illuminated under the beauty of the night sky. Tonight could very well be the last night that they'd be blessed by the light of the glowing blue moon.

CHAPTER 16

HAVEN OF DARKNESS

Aurotos and his allies arrived at the dark woods just at the peak of twilight. High into the sky, the moon was approaching on a collision course with their planet. It no longer maintained its dominion, and it was dreadfully clear that no new auvinot would be born at the end of the year. The moon seemed to hover closer in the sky on a steady course toward the world. The night grew brighter the nearer the moon came, and while the dark woods did not glow under the moonlight like the rest of the plants and trees across the world, it did seem to shimmer now as its trees' shiny bark and leaves almost acted as mirrors for the light of the approaching moon in the sky.

As the companions sat upon their steeds and peered into the darkness of the woods, they could make out the scale-like bark covering the trunks and branches of the trees. The thick red leaves also held a scale-like shape, and the trees almost seemed metallic. Although they did sway to the breeze like any other tree, these particular ones were dark and ominous, and approaching them created a sense of unease for all who stood before them, for they towered high toward the sky, an unnatural height compared to most trees of their age.

"Well, here we are," Leavesa said as she looked to Aurotos for guidance.

"I just can't help but think there's something evil living in there," Elenfia said nervously.

As Aurotos jumped down off his horse, he looked to the rest of his allies. "I'm afraid our steeds won't be taking us the rest of the way, their size could give us away, even though they're quiet."

"I think you're right. We'll have to stay alert in here. I fear anything evil lurking will have an advantage over us," Anaryen said.

"Tarothas, Vael, do you sense anything? What do you make of this place?" Aurotos asked.

"One could see no further than I, my lord, and my eyes cannot penetrate the dark before us. Truly, something seems to block my far sight," Vael said as he squinted his eyes, trying even harder to see but appearing even less confident in his ability to do so.

"I hear nothing within the wood, my lord. I can't even hear the rustle of the leaves on these trees. Something about this place is suppressing my ability to hear what I usually should. I'm sorry, I wish I wasn't so useless right now," Tarothas said.

"It's alright, Tarothas, I would never expect you to do the impossible and neither should you," Aurotos said as he could tell how upset Tarothas appeared in being unable to provide him with an answer.

"Have the elves not traveled these woods? It surprises me that you wouldn't have after all this time," Elenfia said, appearing bewildered by the situation.

"So, to the elves, this is a corrupt place. The darkness lingers here and being present near the Dahaka's corpse, well, not something they would choose. The fear of infection from the fade makes traveling here an endeavor no sane being would contemplate. Not even I, in my great curiosity, would have ventured here, were it not for our quest," Molvalan said supportively as he looked up at the sky, his tone shifting to a more woeful one. "Valos...I would not wish to be here for any other reason."

The rest of the companions shifted their gaze skyward to see the moon set on a collision course for their world. There was a stillness to their silence as each contemplated how things might go, at least that was the impression Aurotos had as they all stared on in their stilled states.

"Well, Molvalan is right," Leavesa said to the group. "It turns out this is the one place most sane people fear, because that creature lies under the trees. Its remains are what we will be walking over. Don't let the rolling mounds deceive you, for it only covers its broken body, and that won't be soil you feel beneath your feet."

"I think I can see a cave up ahead," Nahul said. "It doesn't seem too far away. It could, indeed, serve as a refuge for us to set up camp overnight. It makes me ill to think of us laying out in the open, exposed in this dark place. That would be safer for us to use. We could make our way through the rest in the morning."

Syvon spoke up, seeming disgusted as the inflection of his voice made it quite apparent. "You want us to lay inside some of this creature's filth? You must be—"

"Listen here, I don't like it any more than you do, Syvon, but I'd like to get this night over with. I'd rather be fighting a thousand drothkin than staying here any longer than we have to. Downright silly to worry about this if you ask me," Salenval said.

"Agreed, we'd best make our way there. Let's move," Aurotos said confidently as he slapped his steeds rear and sent it running back to the stables. He made his way forward on foot, guiding his allies into the woods. Suddenly, Aurotos felt a sharp pain in his ears and a dimming in his eyes, causing him to fall to his knees just within the tree line.

Anaryen rushed to his side, wrapping her arms around him. "Aurotos, are you alright," she said. Her voice fell on deaf ears as she desperately attempted to get his acknowledgement.

Aurotos had become entranced and saw the cursed moment when his parents were sacrificed to Ohrimah. He witnessed the dark orc upon the back of the Dahaka claim the lives and the light within his parents. He witnessed the moment that the monster consumed them, causing it to die from an eruption of light from within its massive body. The explosion of light threw the dark orc far off the black dragon's back as it fell, leaving him wounded before he escaped later that day in the hour of twilight.

In his vision, his worst fears were actualized and it left him wondering who or what caused him to see it. The area where the Dahaka fell was indeed the resting place of his parents, whose bodies were somewhere deep within the creature itself. The dark orc had completed a horrible ritual using his parents' own souls to bridge a gap between the material plane and the realm where the dark master reigned. Aurotos could see that souls remained trapped in this desecrated place and that many of those souls fueled the dark master's plans, along with the souls of his parents who were, in death, enslaved to Ohrimah in the hidden realm within the shadows of their world.

It was a wicked place which had sprung up on the outskirts of the great elven city and had, in fact, become another focal point where the dark master had the strongest influence over his creations that roamed the material world. This was a true haven of darkness, and yet Aurotos could also sense that something deep within it labored to undermine the dark powers toiling away.

As he awoke from his trance, he found himself being comforted by Anaryen and his heart was full. It was then that he chose to whisper to her what he'd seen. As this happened, the knights and the magi seemed to watch helplessly, bearing witness to him and his return from torment.

He wouldn't dare speak it for fear of discouraging his companions, but in his mind, it was set: if it took his own death to stop the dark prince, to put an end to the dark master's hold on the world, he would gladly perish. It was justified. The purpose of his life would have been to end a cycle of darkness that had persevered for far too long. "I'm alright," Aurotos said as he stood up, thanking Anaryen for her comfort. "I had a vision which revealed the truth of these woods, but it changes nothing where our mission is concerned. Let's get to the cave and get some rest."

The cave that they had seen wasn't far inside the woods. In fact, up ahead, it appeared as no more than a mound under the roots of one of the large trees. Aurotos and his allies moved cautiously, knowing this would determine whether or not they would be able to surprise the dark prince.

Walking toward the cave, they could see that it wasn't just a cave; it appeared to be one of the large collapsed claws of the Dahaka. Its palm served to create a canopy of what was likely one of the only safe havens within the dark wooded wasteland.

As he moved up to the vacant area, he could smell the musky, damp odor that permeated the woods. The woods didn't smell pleasant like one would expect; instead they were malodorous in a way that couldn't be described. Where one would usually expect to see lush lichen and moss in a wooded area, here mold covered the ground and the base of some of the trees. It was an uninviting place with a murky fog that concealed most things and prevented them from seeing very far into the wooded area around them.

The entrance was draped with black and red vines, and the inside of the cave was dark, cold, and almost foggy, but Aurotos thought it seemed safe enough for them to setup a camp. They stacked their provisions and their packs and began to relax, taking advantage of what few comforts they actually had. There would be no fire that night, as they would lay spread around the wall of the dark hovel to get rest that evening.

Aurotos had just gathered his things into a pile and was about to turn around when he heard someone walk up, apparently waiting behind him. Curious, he did an about face to find Leavesa standing there. She seemed to be pondering something as her eyes met his with a spirit of inquiry about her.

"Leavesa, is everything alright?" he asked as he could see that she appeared very intent on discussing something with him.

"Well, I hope you won't be offended but I have to ask…what did you see, my lord?" she inquired and went silent, her normal light-hearted nature replaced by her strong will to know the truth.

He pondered whether he should tell her or not. She had constantly supported him. She too had always been such a valued leader among the Knights of the Phoenix. He wasn't sure if he should tell her everything but he felt like he could trust her. After all, she had never questioned any of his orders and had always been loyal throughout their quest together.

"My visions, I have them sometimes. I've never fully understood how I get them or why I had the one at the threshold of this dark place," he said as he felt himself vulnerable and embraced the moment. "I'm afraid this place is a prison, a focal point that Merdah has used since his Dahaka fell here. Somehow, he was able to trap the souls of the dead and use their energy to empower himself in the gloomveil in a similar way to his strength in the frozen north. His creatures seem to be safe here; I just don't understand why we haven't seen them dwell here over the years. I can't understand the full depth of this place's secrets—it's troubling."

"Well, could you see who's trapped here or..." Leavesa said, appearing mournful and for the first time since he had known her, she looked scared.

"I'm sorry, I couldn't tell for sure. I know that my parents were sacrificed here. I..." he felt a burst of emotion at the thought of his parents being used to fuel the dark master's agenda. An eruption of emotion he had to swallow.

"I thought they...but they saved us all," she said as her eyes swelled, and her own vulnerability shook him.

"In a way, they did," he said. He could see there was something more she wasn't saying. "What is it?"

"Well, my parents died here too. I joined the knights not long after."

He remembered she had been in the knight's order well before he joined but he had never thought to ask or question her about her past. He always assumed they were likely close in age but he didn't know they also shared this painful history in common.

"I'm sorry, I didn't know."

"The idea that they aren't in peace..." she said as her eyes dimmed and her head hung low.

"I know, it pains me too," he said as he placed his hand on her shoulder, trying his best to show her she wasn't alone in her feelings of grief. He knew that pain of loss just as she did and he realized for the first time what he had missed out on in friendship. If only he'd given such things a chance over all those years serving together, they could have shared in this.

"You know, I always wondered if you lost your parents too. Back when you joined as Volir...I had a feeling you were going through the same kind of sadness I was. In reflection, I never could have imagined you were our king returned to us." Her voice was now filled with admiration. "I'm glad you came home, even if you waited so long to share the truth with us. I just hope you know you'd have found yourself among friends, my lord."

Aurotos realized for the first time why she had always seemed to challenge him. He understood why she had always appeared to place herself in his way over all the years they served together as knights. She had been trying to offer him friendship, something he now regretted not having accepted from her. He felt appreciative of her friendship now and he knew he could never make that mistake again.

"I do. It's something I realize now thanks to you all," he said as he removed his hand from her shoulder, feeling awkward about how to continue navigating what felt like such a foreign situation for him to be in.

"Alright then, good. Well, I hope when this is all over, we can figure out a way to free them, my lord."

"Trust me, my friend, we will."

With those simple words, he watched as hope and a growing trust seemed to fill her very being. He could appreciate the true value in leading her and the others in a way he hadn't quite fully understood before. His confidence grew in a new way and he thought he was beginning to understand some of what Armatay had been trying to teach him. He now believed it was much better to have friends than it was to just have allies.

As his companions prepared to rest, he parted from Leavesa and made his way to the outer fringes of that hollow place. There he looked back in admiration as Leavesa prepared the watch order and instructed the rest of the knights on their duties for the night. As he turned around, he scanned the woods for any threats and found none, something which was comforting even though the dark woods kept him profoundly on alert.

Aurotos remained outside the cave, staring up at the moon growing ever closer. As he continued to gaze toward the sky, Anaryen walked up behind him. As she approached, he was reminded, yet again, of the beauty of her blue eyes and how brightly they seemed to glow under the moonlight, something which brought him a sense of peace amidst all the chaos unfolding around them. She was the calm to his storm, his light in the darkness.

As she stepped up by his side, he smiled and he could sense her smile back. There were no words to communicate what the moments between them meant to him, but as they looked at one another, he could feel his care and desire for her growing and he was excited for what the future might hold between them. A future he had every intention of securing once they ended the threat awaiting them on the other side of the woods.

Aurotos and his companions had been lying in the dark cave for several hours into the night. Many of them were having difficulty sleeping, though they tried to get what rest they could, and Aurotos was no exception. Across from him in the dark hollow, Anaryen and her two magi lay restlessly as the night carried on. To his left, it seemed that Salenval didn't have their problem as he was fast asleep, grumbling in his dreams.

Just at the edge of the entrance, Leavesa and Drelion stood guard in the late night. As Aurotos listened, he overheard Drelion talking about how strange it felt for him to no longer be able to sense the creatures in the world around them. Leavesa had noticed his deep concern and comforted him in the best way she knew how. She had spoken to him about how dreadful it was to her to see the moon growing closer, this sentiment was one Aurotos could relate to.

The sense of doom that many of the companions felt only seemed to compel them all to further dedicate themselves to their cause, and this unified their bonds even more intensely. It had been hundreds of years since elves and humans had traveled or worked together in the way that their group was, and Aurotos could not deny the sense of camaraderie and unity that he too had grown to know. It had been so long since he had seen this unity firsthand, and it reminded him of his parents who had led not only the elves but all of the races with whom they shared the world of Auro.

The uncomfortable silence of that night was interrupted by the sound of Leavesa shouting. "Get up, Knights of the Phoenix. Wake up now, we are under attack."

"By the Masters, hurry, we need your aid," Drelion shouted as he lit his sword aflame, preparing himself for an attack.

Leavesa had already begun throwing fireballs forward as arrows rained down at the entrance of the cave. She took special care to burn what arrows she could but still their supplies were hit and exploded behind them. The magi were quick to react and spared no time as they moved to the exterior, accompanied by their counterparts, the knights, who along with Aurotos, rushed toward the entrance of the cave.

With haste, the knights shielded their fellow magi behind their illuminated shield walls, as Anaryen cast frost onto the provisions and put out the fires. Molvalan rooted the group of drothkin that had just reached the entrance while Elenfia sent a surge of lightning from her hands, the current connecting between all of the drothkin, causing them all to burst into ash.

"If I could only see further. Truly, I cannot tell you if there are others," Vael said as his disappointed tone was confirmed by who spoke next.

"I can't believe it; I can't hear anything beyond our space. This is madness," Tarothas said as he desperately tried to make out any sound. "I hate that I can't hear them coming, I'm sorry, Lord Aurotos."

"Tarothas, it's alright," Aurotos said as he scanned the woods for more drothkin. As he realized there were none left, he became aware of the light which was being produced by their spells. "Drop the shields, the light," he commanded softly.

"I hope my spell didn't cause too much, I just..." Elenfia said as she looked to the knights, cringing. "I just reacted, I'm sorry, I didn't think about it."

"Ah, come on now. I'd prefer your lightning any day over those beasts calling others to join them," Salenval said.

"As do I, Elenfia. You helped us stop them fast, we cannot linger in combat," Molvalan said.

"It's fine," Aurotos said. "Is everyone alright?"

"Oh, dear. Our food was burned with most of the provisions we had in our packs. It was probably by accident, but they set our supplies on fire with their arrows. I did my best to put the flames out, but..." Anaryen trailed off, a hint of disappointment in her tone.

"We're safe, that's what matters, Anaryen. It may not serve as a blessing under the circumstances, but we'll either be in the city tomorrow night, or meet our fates in battle. I don't know about you all, but I have no intention of letting Drazius succeed. We aren't far from Valenthreas. What we do tomorrow is what counts most," Aurotos said.

"My lord, I think I speak for all of us when I say there's no way we'll allow him to win while we still draw breath," Kaylos said as he and the rest of the knights all drew their fists over their chests one by one in a silent salute.

"Yes, of course, but there's one thing that puzzles me," Leavesa said as she looked back upon the rest of the group. "Why would the drothkin travel alone without any of the soldiers? Why patrol the woods so carelessly?"

"You know, Leavesa's right. I find it strange too. Maybe he didn't want to risk his men in here," Anaryen said as she seemed to be pondering the pointlessness of the encounter. "Anyway, we should consider all possibilities. We have to be mindful that they may have set traps."

"You're right, my lady. We'd be wise to consider your wisdom," Aurotos said as he looked into the black shadows within the woods. "We'll continue our watch shifts as we had planned. Get what rest you can, and by dawn, we'll spread out through the woods and clear any patrols on our way to the other side. If we deal with them fast enough, there should be no way for them to signal our presence."

"It's hard to think they'd attack first instead of alarming the army," Drelion said.

"Those beasts are downright witless; all they do is slaughter. Don't expect them to make sense," Salenval said as he laughed bitterly for the enemy.

Aurotos knew that although the night was treacherous and they were at risk of another attack, there was only so much they could do to prepare themselves for the unknowns of the dark woods. Drothkin were the least of their concerns, for there were far more ominous things lurking in the darkness. For the rest of the night, he would have them continue their watch and rest their eyes.

As the morning hours drew closer on that dark night, Aurotos found himself still unable to sleep. His thoughts were consumed with the idea that if he could intercept and kill the dark prince before his army had a chance to begin their siege, then he might be able to end this before the prince's army had a chance. Aurotos knew that his allies were more than strong enough to decimate the majority of the prince's forces. Still, without Drazius alive, the morale of his forces could be laid to waste under the combined strength of the knights and the magi.

He had a plan and he believed if his plan worked, then no siege would happen. Even if the moon was to fall and some of the realm was destroyed, the people would survive and the great city would be safeguarded under the magical protection of its defenders. The idea that the city could be placed under another assault was unfathomable, and his desire to end the prince's threat was all-consuming.

As he stood up, he could see that most of the knights were able to rest, and as they likely wouldn't be awake for another hour, he thought to appeal to Anaryen and Leavesa, who were standing guard at the entrance. He felt confident his wishes would be respected, and as he made his way toward the two, he felt joy seeing how well they got along. He had a great deal of respect for both of them, and in all of his years as a knight, they were two of the best leaders he had fought beside.

With grins on their faces, both of them turned toward him, and sensing his approach, they tried to hide their smiles. "I can't help but wonder what you two might be laughing about that would cause your expressions to change so quickly as I approach," Aurotos said. "Care to share?"

"Oh, don't worry, it's nothing," Anaryen said as she looked to him with a shy smile before inquiring about what the growing seriousness on his face might be about. "Aurotos, you have a look about you, and it tells me you're going to say something that I wouldn't want to hear."

"I think the lady said it as well as I could, my lord. What's going on?" Leavesa asked.

"You're both probably right, and it isn't my intention to worry you. What I require from you now may be difficult to understand, but I ask that you honor my request," Aurotos said as he looked to both of them hopefully.

"Listen, saying it like that does worry me. Alright, go on then, let's have it," Anaryen said.

"In one hour, I'd like you to divide our group into two parties. Anaryen, you and your magi will travel with some of our knights through the western part of the woods. Leavesa, you and the rest of the knights will travel through the eastern part of the woods. Your two groups should clear any roaming drothkin and eliminate them before we reach the other side where we'll intervene and stop the prince. I think that the south side of the woods will be the perfect location for us to regroup, it seems he will set up there and siege from the east side of the river. That location will provide him with a natural barrier from any any-one who would approach from the west. The only way for troops to cross is by bridge and the nearest bridge is far to the south. I plan to leave soon and head through the center of the woods. I'll meet you all on the other side at the central edge of the tree line and that will be our rally point."

"Very well, my lord, but I'd rather you take some of the knights with you. I would just feel better if we all left at the same time," Leavesa said.

"I know that my request to leave ahead of you is troubling, but I need you to honor this request," Aurotos said.

"Yes, of course, my lord. I'll see it done," Leavesa said as she bowed her head slightly and backed away. She could see Anaryen wasn't happy with this plan and didn't appear to want to be a part of what was coming.

Anaryen's fierce and dominating presence asserted itself fully as she spoke, commanding Aurotos's attention with what she had to say. "I let you run off into the woods before and look how that worked out. No, just because you're the last Auron doesn't mean you should expect me to—"

"Anaryen, I give you my word—I won't be moving through the woods carelessly. I'm not disregarding your concerns either. I'm just ask-ing you to trust me to scout ahead and clear a safe area for us all to meet. I have no desire to command you, I'm just asking you for your support, please."

Anaryen looked at him suspiciously, seeming to contemplate his sin-cerity. "I don't like the idea, but if it's that important to you that you have my support, then you have it. And of course, I'd be honored to lead my magi with some of your knights," she said reluctantly as she stared into his eyes, seeking the truth from his very soul.

"Thank you, my lady...and thank you, Leavesa. I appreciate you both, and I'll meet you there. Just remember to move cautiously and eliminate any potential threats before they can raise an alarm and warn his army. We'll decide on a plan once we all reach the edge of the woods."

Aurotos thought for a moment to share more of his feelings for Anaryen, but in the presence of Leavesa, he wasn't prepared to declare them. Instead, he took Anaryen's hand, bowed his head, and honored her. Then he turned to Leavesa only to see her smiling, perhaps one of the largest smiles he'd ever seen from her. She seemed very pleased by the display of respect and affection he had shown to Anaryen. Still, he hardened himself and placed his clenched fist over the left side of his chest. "May the light guide you, Leavesa," he said, as his tone softened compared to his rigid posture.

Leavesa bowed her head and responded in kind. "And with you, my lord. We will not fail you."

"Of that I have no doubt," Aurotos said as he offered a smile as his assurance.

As Aurotos ventured through the heart of the woods, he couldn't help but feel a sense of pride in his allies. Where he once had felt reluctant to bond with others, he had found companions whose safety mattered a great deal to him. They were people he had grown to care for and felt a need to protect. What's more, he was feeling something he knew was real. He was in love. He loved Anaryen, and he cared so much for those who had ventured at his side, showing him such steadfast loyalty.

Along his trek through the woods, he cast occasional glances upwards, keeping a watchful eye on Valos. Normally, it appeared smaller in the sky compared to Ailos, but things were different now. It seemed much closer, growing larger and overshadowing its counterpart. Its close proximity revealed the intricate details of its crystalline surface and a pulsating light at its center, a feature that had previously gone unnoticed when they looked upon the nearing moon. Aurotos couldn't help but speculate that this luminous core, possibly The Master's Core under the control of the dark master, had set Valos on its perilous course toward them.

Aurotos had spent over an hour moving carefully through the dark woods until he came upon another large group of drothkin. With his radiant blade in hand, he surprised them, killing them all and leaving nothing but piles of ash to further blanket the already blackened terrain. He had hoped that as he moved through the forest, both his knights and the magi would make their way safely along, clearing out any of the enemy that would be present.

His goal was much different than what he had told Leavesa and Anaryen before he left. His intention was to see if he alone could kill the dark prince, and he wouldn't know what possibilities lay before him until he could see Drazius and his army for himself. He knew that while he hadn't actually lied to them, it would probably infuriate Anaryen later. Incurring her wrath was a risk he was willing to take if it meant seeing her and the rest of his companions safe.

The truth of the matter was, he didn't want to lose them like he lost his cats, like he lost his parents. Now he had loved ones he would risk his life for and he had no doubt he could use his great power to defeat the prince. He would not let them be assaulted by the prince's dark power the way Armatay had been. He had no intention of being careless though—quite the opposite—he would be calculated in his plan, and if there was a way to stop the prince before the siege started, then that victory would make protecting his friends almost guaranteed, or such was his belief. He had only one thought now: he wouldn't stop until the prince was vanquished; somehow, he would find a way.

CHAPTER 17

HUMBLED HEARTS

At the southern side of the Dragonstrike Woods, the dark prince gathered his army, setting his sights on the city of light. He had already commanded that the beacon be locked in place, and the siege engines set up at the river's edge, directed toward Valenthreas. Before him was his great army, and to his back rose the light of dawn.

Surrounding his army were the great armaments that had been developed by the vorelan people of the southwestern-most continent. His army had set up their barricades and defenses long before the morning came. Drazius stood upon a rising foothill with the beacon's sights set upon the moon's surface which was expanding further across the sky the nearer it came, soon to blot out the suns that would rise behind it.

So it was that the dark orc's beacon would serve to anchor the great moon which had begun to blanket much of the sky above. Although Drazius never said it, he felt as if Lord Grindam was a coward, hiding far to the northwest in his frozen, dark kingdom. There he was easily guarded by the dark rovers and the various dark incarnates which remained hidden by means of the gloomveil there.

"If Lord Grindam was really as true of a servant as I, then he would be here leading the army with me, with those dark incarnates beside him," Drazius said under his breath where only he could hear himself speak.

To the prince there was nothing more important than this moment, as it would usher in a new era for all people across the planet. It was strange to him that most of the dark creatures across this land would be withdrawn far away, yet to the dark prince, this was only viewed as weakness and betrayal. To him, he served the noblest of causes: freedom and rebirth of life across these lands.

Still, Drazius had been eager to put this beacon to use, and as the dawn rose, that thought only seemed to bolster his resolve and belief in Ohrimah and his promise of a new world where he would reign alongside the Master. Secretly, he held a firm desire that Lord Grindam's weakness would come at a cost, and that he would pay that cost with his very life—a life that had already been blessed by his dark lord to continue living far longer than any orc ever had.

Even though Lord Grindam had been the maker of the great weapon he held, a small part of Drazius hated him for the control and power he held over him. A hate which was no doubt a symptom of the strife he carried within. He hoped that when this was all over, he would receive an even greater blessing from Ohrimah than Grindam had. This thought continued its reinforcement within him as he prepared the beacon, aiming it directly at the moon which would soon become tethered, guiding its fate, and the certain destruction of Valenthreas.

Not far from Drazius's location, Aurotos approached the edge of the wood line. There he was able to witness the dark prince fire the beacon into the sky, its dark beam connecting to the moon, which now seemed firmly grasped as if the very hand of the dark master himself rose out from the planet to secure it, hastening it closer toward the land.

This was his moment to obliterate the beacon and defeat Drazius. Aurotos felt sure that even if it cost him his life, he could save all of Aurotheros and the people who lived freely within his homeland. Perhaps he could save the knights and the magi; perhaps he could save the city and be worthy of people's devotion to him.

He was beginning to realize that in his desire to stop the prince, he would be completely overwhelmed by the odds. Watching the beam securely anchored on the moon above, he felt himself giving in to his fear of losing others. In doing so, he recognized he had once again placed all the responsibility of success on himself.

Nearing the wood line, Aurotos withdrew Ai'ethe. He planned to charge swiftly for the dark prince, ending him before this farce could continue any longer. Just as he was about to set foot beyond the last few trees, Aurotos was stopped by the sound of a voice springing up behind him.

"Lord Aurotos, please wait, not like this," a voice said. Aurotos turned to see a figure with their right hand reaching out, beckoning him to return back into the shroud of the woods.

"You, what are you doing here, and why aren't you with the magi? Why are you following me? This isn't the first time I've caught you lurking around me. Explain yourself," Aurotos insisted.

"Ah, um, it was Lady Anaryen, my lord. She asked me to come ahead and see to your safety. Now I know her instincts were right. You were about to do something very foolish," Molvalan replied, urging him to step away.

"It's not foolish that I seek to end this myself and protect all of you, all of my people from his madness," Aurotos argued.

"Perhaps not, my lord, but to do so alone? Please let us help you," Molvalan urged.

Aurotos hesitated for a moment, considering the magi's words. Perhaps he was right, maybe he shouldn't be attempting to do this alone. "Very well," Aurotos said. "But time is running out; you can see it's already begun."

"I know, my lord, but we still have time," Molvalan said. "The Twin Flames are with you; everyone wishes to face this with you. We made it this far together. Please, just wait; let us help you."

Aurotos considered his words for a moment, and stepped away from the wood line. He thought about the trouble he'd be in with Anaryen if he moved forward without her and the others. She knew him better than he realized. Once more, she surprised him in ways he didn't think she would. He had to stop underestimating her. He had to stop imagining himself doing anything without her.

"Now, I know that you see me as strange," Molvalan continued. "It is not the first time someone has thought badly of me. As a youth, I was disliked by people because they found it odd when I spoke to the gods. I have long praised the Masters and the Twin Flames. Through their will, they have gifted me with foresight. I cannot see all, but I do know that if you are to succeed, you can only do so if we all stand together. If you will only believe in me the way I do in you, if you would believe in us, we will not fail you, my lord. Every one of us would lay our lives down because we trust you."

Aurotos couldn't deny that he spoke the truth. He had found Molvalan odd, and he had been untrusting of many long before the knights or the magi, yet he never had good cause to be. This was something he had often done and it had kept him alone for so long without friends or those he could rely on. He thought of his companions who, if he waited, would soon join him. How even in the city ahead of him, he had no home except the one he had started to feel in the presence of Anaryen and the rest of his allies.

Aurotos knew he had to trust them. The sage had always told him that he hadn't been trusting his instincts, and if he was really honest with himself, Armatay was right. He knew he was only giving in to fear and doubt. He hated the thought of what it might do to him if he were to lose Anaryen and the others he had grown to care for.

"You're right," Aurotos said. "I've been untrusting of you and many others; such has been true for longer than I care to admit. And no, I have no good reason to mistrust you as you've given me no cause; it's clear Anaryen sent you."

Aurotos knew he was right about this, and the truth was, he had come to feel that he could trust the people he traveled with. The Aurodites shared a close alignment to the Knights of the Phoenix, and their devotion to the cause of protecting others was as solid as any of the knights he knew. He also knew what he felt for Anaryen, and didn't want to disrespect her trust in him either. Seeing this mission successful was the greatest feat he believed he could accomplish in his life, and he couldn't risk failing his charge or the woman he had grown to care so deeply for.

"Very well, Molvalan, we'll wait for our friends," Aurotos said.

Molvalan dropped to his knee, bowing before Aurotos. "Thank you, my lord, I cannot thank you enough for trusting us to help you see this through."

"Please, there's no reason to kneel, Molvalan," Aurotos said. He still wasn't comfortable with that.

"Pardon me, my lord, but there is," Molvalan replied, his head hung low, happiness radiating about him.

No sooner had Molvalan dropped to a knee, than they heard the pulsing sound of the beacon and the crackling noise in the sky, as if the moon itself were fracturing under the strain of the beam, which was now pulling it even closer, faster than before. It was hard to tell how long they had before the moon would reach the point of ensuring devastation. It was clear to both Aurotos and Molvalan that if this moon were to fall at the speed it was gaining, it would not only destroy the elven realm, but maybe even the lands beyond. There would be nothing left where the moon's impact would reach.

As Molvalan stood up, he saw the strain of the beam on the moon. "Ah, um…my lord, it moves quicker now," he said.

"It does. Do you see the beacon? It appears to be made of the same material as these trees. If it was harvested here, I just don't know how they could have moved throughout our territory undetected," Aurotos said, confused by the prospect.

"Ah…I cannot say, my lord, that truly is worrisome."

It was dreadfully clear that Valos would impact their world well before midday, and by the time it drew close enough, it would appear as if the night itself would be upon them for the last time. Valos had, in fact, already begun to darken the sky. The fact that the bark of the dark trees in the woods may have been harvested and tempered down into the very material that made up the beacon was shocking to them, but any further thought on the matter was interrupted by what they saw occurring in the city.

As the sky darkened, Aurotos could see the great city of Valenthreas raise a large dome barrier of light that spread far outside of its walls, extending to the mountain in the north and nearing both rivers on the east and the west, extending just as far out to the south. Magic could be seen streaming from a multitude of points around the city's walls, and even from the great spire at its center. Anyone who could cast magic was working at reinforcing the great barrier, maintaining its strength and empowering it.

Far off in the surrounding land, at the different towns and cities, similar domes of light could be seen. The city of Valenthreas had been successful in spreading the word, and they had gathered and coordinated a valiant defense for every inhabited place across the elven lands. The great magi and countless defenders of the realm had arrived to protect the greatest beacon of hope the world had ever had, but the siege of the great city had not begun yet, and if it succeeded, Valos' destruction of the city was ensured.

Aurotos knew that he and his allies had to succeed, for as every second passed, the blue crystal moon grew closer at an expedited rate. The very city which, just days ago, he'd longed to escape was now the only placed he longed to return to. Much like his father, he too felt the importance of safeguarding all life across the land for which the city maintained its dominion.

Soon after Aurotos had made his reflections, he could hear the approaching of Anaryen who led Elenfia and the knights who had supported them. Molvalan rushed toward Elenfia, happy to see she had arrived safely. As Anaryen approached, Aurotos smiled and moved to meet her. "Glad you made it safely, my lady. How was your route?" he asked.

"You know, we ran into a pack of drothkin, but your knights killed them pretty fast. Nothing much aside from those beasts," Anaryen replied, returning his smile before sharing what concerned her most. "Although…there was something very strange we experienced the further we traveled. We felt as though we were being watched."

"I felt the same. I thought it had been the drothkin, but I now believe it was something more. So, you sent Molvalan ahead."

"I hope you aren't upset. It wasn't out of mistrust—I was just worried. I had a strong feeling that I needed to send him ahead."

Anaryen gasped as she looked up at the sky and saw how close the moon had moved. "Oh my, it's so close now. That machine, is it…"

"Somehow the prince was able to harvest the scaled bark off these trees right from under our noses to make that infernal contraption."

"Hold on, how?"

"I wish I knew. I fear it's unlikely we'll ever know. One thing I'm certain of is that my blade can destroy it. What I need is help from everyone here to cover me as I do so."

"I'm with you, we should share this with the others, oh, my...Valenthreas," she said, staring at the glowing aura of the magical shield protecting the city.

"It appears that our messages were delivered. I just hope that our efforts will be enough. One thing I'm sure of is that we have to be methodical in our attack. We have to consider that the moon will devastate these lands, but we can't allow it to take the people behind these barriers."

As he spoke, he could see Leavesa and the rest of the knights making their way toward him and was pleased. He could see that everyone appeared unharmed. As the group of knights approached, Leavesa was the first to make her way to him, moving quicker than the others.

"It's good to see you all made it safe, Leavesa. I take it everything went alright," Aurotos said.

"Well, no drothkin my lord, but Syvon was under attack from the fade. It happened after we started to sense we were being watched, but there was no trace of who or what was there," Leavesa said.

"We all had a similar experience on our way here, but what happened with Syvon?"

"He said he heard voices, then fell to his knees, it was hard to watch but I shook him out of it."

Aurotos felt saddened hearing what had happened, although he had already been concerned with Syvon's blatant aggression toward the drothkin and frustration with the magi. He knew that the fade could easily prey upon one's feelings of strife or sorrow in a place so close to the dark master's realm. Still, he needed to know what his fellow knight heard when the voices spoke.

Aurotos looked toward Syvon and motioned for him to come over. "Syvon, a word please," he said. As Syvon neared, he could see the troubled look on his face and inquired. "What did the voices share with you?"

"It was a blur but they kept telling me that the magi were working with the prince and that I needed to kill them. At first it was intoxicating and I felt angry. Leavesa grabbed me and kept telling me to remember my oath, then I knew what was happening. I would never let him take me, my lord," Syvon said as he looked into his eyes, with a look of shame about him.

"I'm glad you fought it off. You have to remember not to let your prejudice drive you; it's too easy for the fade to undermine us here."

"I know, my lord, I apologize for my weakness. I assure you, nothing will get in my way again. I swear it," Syvon said, sincerity saturating his tone and expression.

"Good, because I'm counting on you," Aurotos said as he placed his hand upon his shoulder, jerking his pauldron playfully.

With that one motion, Syvon straightened himself up further, appearing more invigorated in a way Aurotos never noticed before. He felt happy to know he could have such an impact on his fellow knight.

"Oh, well alright, it's really happening," Leavesa said, as she looked up at the sky and then the city.

"By the Masters," Drelion said, as he approached not far behind, along with the rest of the knights and the magi who all stood gazing skyward with the realization that the world was soon to change, regardless of their actions.

"My friends, I know we've all sensed we're being watched, so we need to remain cautious as we make our preparations here. The siege has not yet begun…though I expect we'll need to allow it to start before we move against Drazius's army. Take a moment to get ready, and we'll discuss our plans soon."

As the magi and knights stood gathered, Aurotos was unable to hold back the sense of pride he was feeling. He saw the unity of their two groups working together in a way that would make the world proud. He knew that regardless of what the future held, he'd always want this group of companions at his side.

It wasn't long after Aurotos had started contemplating plans for attack before his thoughts were interrupted by Anaryen. "Lord Aurotos," she said. "If you could spare a moment, I'd like a word in private."

"Of course, my lady," Aurotos said, curious about what was on her mind.

Anaryen led Aurotos away from the group behind a tree where she stopped and looked up into his golden eyes. As she stood before him, he couldn't help but realize how strong his feelings for her had grown. He knew unquestioningly how real they were and how he desired nothing more than for her to be at his side for all time. With her, he found a sense of security unlike ever before.

His yearning for her was teased by the soothing sound of her voice. "You know, I feel I owe you an apology for when we first met. I assumed things about you I shouldn't have. Now that I've come to know you, I understand why it's probably been so hard for you to let anyone close," she said.

"Anaryen, there is no need—"

"No, Aurotos, I need to say this. I behaved horribly when we first met. The truth is that I was shocked to see you were alive and I was carrying a lot of sadness for the magi who died. I wanted to see Drazius pay for his crimes and I lashed out on you because it was easy to be mad at you. I just wish you knew how much we all needed you through these dark times."

There was nothing that could have stopped him. She was everything he could have desired in someone he might give himself to. Her humbling heart and honesty with him was more beautiful than the blue sparkle of her eyes or the way she smiled. All he wanted her to know was how she made him feel, so as she continued to speak, he drew closer to her, placing his hands around her waist.

As he moved in, she lost her words and stood helpless in his embrace. He knew it was time to fully let her in on his feelings for her—this could very well be his last chance. As she stared expectantly, her curious gaze was met by the gentle clutch of his intentions as he moved his right hand up to the side of her face. As he did so, she appeared lost in the moment, and held on to him tightly.

As she gave in to him, the words flowed out of his mouth as easily as water down a mountain. "I'm yours, Anaryen, and I need you to know I love you," Aurotos said.

His glowing eyes pierced into her every being, and she surrendered her heart to him. "I love you too, Aurotos. I'm yours forever," she said as her lips curved into the sweetest smile.

They connected passionately as Aurotos took her lips into his filling all her heart with his love for her. As they kissed, it was as if even their lips made love, and the two lost themselves in one another, connecting in a way neither had ever experienced. The kiss meant far more than any kiss ever could for it was a symbol of their undeniable fates, and their souls intertwining as one.

"I haven't been myself around anyone in so long, but with you, I can't hide who I am. I knew it would be impossible to resist you from the moment we met," he said seriously as he looked to her in the sincerest way, a way he had never looked at another person.

"Oh, I feel the same way. Promise me that no matter what happens, we'll stand together," she said, looking to him with absolute adoration.

"I promise you, together forever," he said.

As the two held one another, they looked for their companions who had all witnessed the moment from a distance. Each of them appeared joyful to see what transpired. Kaylos and Syvon were laughing quietly as Salenval seemed to be egging them on. Leavesa stared on glowing, captivated by the moment. Aurotos and Anaryen were unified and even under the very falling of Valos, they were strengthened in their resolve, knowing that soon they would face their fates together.

In that moment, Aurotos was overwhelmed by a wave of unexpected emotions. He realized that the path ahead would be uncharted territory for him, but he drew strength from the sacrifices his parents had made and the unwavering dedication they had shown for their cause and the well-being of their people. As he held his beloved close, he reflected on the profound significance of that moment. With the knights and the magi standing united together, he believed that, for the first time, they had a genuine chance at success. Their unity would be their greatest strength—something every one of them seemed sure of.

CHAPTER 18

PROMISE TO THE PERI

High up in the sky, dark clouds formed at an alarming rate, as if the approaching moon's fall caused the whole world to mourn its anticipated devastation. As Aurotos stood before his allies with Anaryen by his side, he could sense the planet's pain, and he knew that he would stop at nothing to bring the prince's plans to an end. For the first time, he knew he was capable of self-sacrifice, and looking upon his allies, he had never felt more trust in others than he had in them.

He looked upon the beauty of Anaryen one last time before turning to face his allies who had gathered, for they too were ready to stop the dark prince and the siege of Valenthreas. Looking upon them all proudly, he began to share his thoughts. "My friends, I know what I must do," he said, but before he could continue, he sensed the same presence once again observing him and his allies among the dark woods.

His abrupt stop drew closer attention from Anaryen and his allies, who now wondered what had caused him to pause. They all sensed that he was distracted by something—a presence that soon became apparent to them as well.

"My lord, something is watching us again, I can feel it," Leavesa said as she drew her sword.

"I know, I sense it too," Aurotos said before challenging whatever was hiding in the dark woods. "Show yourself. We won't overlook your presence any longer."

As soon as he sent his command into the darkness, he and his allies became prepared for anything that might reveal itself. Elenfia and Molvalan moved their backs against the center, against Anaryen and Aurotos who were preparing themselves for a possible attack. The knights formed a circle around the four at the center and readied themselves for whatever was watching.

It was at that moment of preparedness that a haunting voice spoke from the darkness and reverberated quietly around them. "Do not fear us for we will not harm you. Please do not attack and we shall reveal ourselves," the voice said.

Aurotos and his allies were steadfast as they began to make out the shape of women whose breasts were covered by thin golden vines wrapped across their body as clothing. The same vines clothed their hips and hung at their front and rear draping their loins. Most of their bodies were exposed outside of the vines, revealing their golden olive complexion. Their hair was golden blonde and flowed behind them as if lifted by a breeze. Their wings were shadowy but appeared more like the dark blue one might see in the night sky. Within their wings were scattered speckles that sparkled like stars but as their wings fluttered, they gave off a mournful sound which was reminiscent of quiet shrieks instead of the pleasing harmony they should have made. Their eyes glowed like the suns in the sky now hidden behind the approaching moon.

"Peri, here? Why would you dwell in this place instead of in the forests created by the Masters? Your place is to support nature, not to hide in a place of death and darkness," Aurotos said.

"My lord, look at them. They don't glow like the peri should—their light has faded. They could be some of those who turned to Merdah before the great war. It makes me ill to look upon them; this is wrong," Nahul said.

"He's right. You look as if you're influenced by the fade. Explain yourselves and why you stalk us," Aurotos said.

"I am Ieva, Queen of the Peri. Our duty is to observe nature, and though we remain neutral to conflict, we know of those who aided Ohrimah. We are not the dark peri; we are true to our purpose, but we have become bound to the presence of the gloomveil here. We came to these woods not for the great evil that fell or the darkness that lingers. We came here because we wished to purify the trees that grew over the land tainted by the Dahaka."

Aurotos and Anaryen both signaled to their companions to lower their weapons and ease their guard. As they did so, they formed a new line facing the peri, who now hovered closer to the ground before them, revealing themselves much more clearly.

"You must tell us how long you've been lost here. What makes you appear this way when you should be as bright as the heavens themselves?" Anaryen questioned.

"I do not know how long it has been. Time for us flows differently than it does for you. Yet, from the moment you entered into these woods, we knew who you were—the last light of the Twin Flames. We were only curious because you arrived here and we wanted to understand why."

"If you have been observing this place for so long then maybe you can tell me how the dark prince came to harvest the scales off the trees here. Somehow, he did so while remaining unseen to those of us who dwell in the city. If you've been here and bore witness to it, then you should tell us what happened. Why aren't there any dark creatures in the woods aside from the drothkin we have already slain?" Aurotos asked.

"We do not take sides with the races of Auro or become involved in their affairs," Ieva said.

"Come now, Queen Ieva, it's hard to believe a peri could be stuck here," Kaervo said.

"To allow yourselves to dimmish this way," Nahul said awkwardly.

"You don't wish to be involved, yet you followed us and chose to reveal yourself now. All along you stood by and watched as evil was at work here. Where is your devotion to this world and the gods responsible for your existence?" Aurotos asked, his patience being tested as the crackling sound from the moon above made itself noticed.

"I assure you all that dwelling here so long was not our choice, nor was losing our radiance. As you wish for our help, I shall make a request. If you are willing to honor that request, then I shall give you any answer you seek," Ieva said mournfully as she too was aware of the moon above.

"Name your request, Ieva. If it's reasonable, I'll see that it's honored," Aurotos said

"We know you shall fight those who linger outside these woods, and while we cannot be a part of that conflict, we also cannot leave even though we have tried. For whatever reason, we are bound here. I believe you can do what we cannot. If you would promise to help cleanse these woods when the danger has passed, we shall finally be free, and our radiance shall return once more," Ieva said, staring intently at Aurotos.

"I don't know about this," Syvon said. "There's no way to know that they aren't the dark peri. For all we know, they could serve Merdah."

"Oh, come on. I'm sure nothing bad could come from cleansing a forest growing off the Dahaka," Salenval said as he and Kaylos snickered silently amongst themselves.

"I understand your doubt, my friends, but this might be the only opportunity we have to learn the truth before we face the prince and his forces. Right now, what's most important is stopping that army," Aurotos said.

Although some of them did not feel comfortable with the decision, it was also clear to many of them that he was right, and it was their duty to seek the truth. After no more than a moment of reflection, more crackling in the sky could be heard as a storm high above them was beginning to form. Dark clouds spread across the sky as far as the eye could see, and the only visible light came from Valos or the bright barriers protecting the towns and cities.

"Very well, Queen Ieva. I give you my word that once the danger here is gone, we'll find a way to purify the land and heal these trees. Now, please tell us all you know about how Drazius could have come to harvest the bark from these woods," Aurotos said.

"It was the jinn. They moved back and forth for months, scouring through the deepest parts of these woods, pulling the bark off of the trees. Although they remain invisible to most, we were able to detect their movements," Ieva said.

"Where have the dark creatures that remained here gone? Surely beasts of the dark master dwelled here," Aurotos said.

"The dark entities disappeared many days ago. We were only able to observe some of the ougars leave and most did so under the cover of the darkest nights. The dark incarnates do not dwell in the illuminated world, and they were able to come and go in the darkness here as they pleased," Ieva said.

"To imagine one would stand idly by and watch such evil, truly," Vael said.

"Makes me ill to think," Nahul said, shaking his head.

"We do not interfere. It is not our purpose. We serve as watchers, and tend to nature, mending its wounds and nurturing growth," she replied.

"If only all the peri still believed that," Aurotos said, remembering how the dark peri had aided Ohrimah in perverting nature and countless creatures during the War of Strife and Sorrow.

A great sorrow became evident within the queen, knowing that some of those under her charge had once chosen to serve the dark master. As she gazed upon the knights and the magi, several tears bloomed from her eyes, the sparkles of twilight quickly dimming as they rolled down her face.

"I know what they have done, and I am sad to say that those few who did help are truly lost. I do not know what came of them. I can only speak now for those who remain true to their purpose," Ieva said.

"Queen Ieva, are there any other dangers lurking in these woods that you know of? We must know that we will be safe from danger once we leave," Anaryen asked.

"Only we peri remain, and you are the only other living creatures within these woods. Once you leave, only we shall remain, imprisoned here until this land is cleansed. It is a horrible scar upon this world, much like the saena tree of the dwarven lands which fell long ago to the dark witches. We could not save the tree or heal it then, but we believe this place can be spared. Still, it is beyond our skill. I trust it can only be healed by one who carries the light of the Twin Flames," Ieva said.

Once again, Aurotos found himself the center of attention. This time not only by his knights and their magi companions, but also by all of the peri who now looked upon him hopefully, as if he himself was the remedy to the darkness which persevered. Although he showed little to no reaction at their gazes, he did find himself hopeful and sanctified in the renewed trust he had in the Twin Flames, that somewhere within him lay the power to help. Perhaps somehow, he could cleanse this darkness just like that evil which Drazius himself carried beyond the tree line.

"Very well, Queen Ieva, thank you," Aurotos said.

"Please remember your promise. We shall ever watch over the wood," Ieva said

Each of the peri placed their hands together over their hearts and closed their eyes, slowly beginning to fade from sight. For Aurotos and his companions, it was a strange sight to see them fade away into darkness when they were known for their beauty and their light across the Aeth'Quelinth Forest to the west. Here within the Dragonstrike Woods they were only prisoners.

Aurotos somehow felt as if he received a final gift from the queen as they faded away into the realm of the peri. He felt the truth behind his existence and he believed that with the help of Ai'ethe, he might be able to perceive an even greater sense of the world around him. He knew that the blade itself was not the true gift he wielded, but it served him just as it served his father before him. He believed it could provide him with a way to better perceive the truth of the dark woods.

Standing before the knights and the magi, Aurotos pulled the radiant blade from the scabbard on his back and brought it down before him, piercing it into the roots and mold beneath his feet. He closed his eyes and tried to sense not that which could attack him, but instead the very life of the world itself.

He opened himself up to his inheritance, the light that created the world. Immediately, he felt it, and with his eyes closed, he could see all the Essa flowing beneath him. The energy of life that coalesced there was not only in the remains of the Dahaka but within the very network of life beneath the trees. He could sense the balance of nature working around him and the corruption below that pushed back against the will of the planet.

The space around him radiated, and even in that dark place, he could see life pulsing through the roots as if they were the veins of the world itself. He could see the life in his companions, in the plants, and far beyond them in the surrounding lands. It was as if Auro was under his command, revealing all of its secrets. As he looked to the sky and Valos, he could see that the moon wept, and at its very center was the dark seed that was The Master's Core weaponized by Ohrimah himself, tethered to the planet by the beacon under the control of Drazius Khorvek.

Aurotos made the decision to open his eyes, and as he did, his perception of the world blossomed further, allowing him to see the very life flowing in all things. He realized the blade had provided him a sort of communion with the world itself. He knew that the gods were present, for he sensed it. He realized he was being gifted with the sight of creation, and that the blade had served as a key, unlocking his ability to see things in a way previously unimagined.

Beyond the forest, Aurotos was able to see the life that coursed through the prince's branded soldiers and in the land around him. The prince himself was but a black cavity among the light of the world, and the drothkin only shades of life barely visible to him. The blade served as a bridge between creation itself and he, allowing him to see so much more beyond the bodies which held life.

Aurotos released his hands from the blade, and to his surprise, he continued to see all of life's energy and all of the great darkness that worked against it. It shocked him that while his eyes were not shut, and he no longer held the sword, he continued to see the world in such a way. He looked upon Anaryen, and his sight showed him he was right—he had found his soulmate.

"I can see everything, the light and the darkness, even here under this veil," Aurotos said.

With his Auron eyes now truly opened, he could see through the dark woods and witness the presence of the dark prince in a way that was impossible before. The prince was at his strongest, bound by his duty, tending to the beacon. With his polearm in hand, he wielded something very wicked, an evil weaponized through the dark power gifted to him by his master. Aurotos knew that it was time to stop Drazius before he could desecrate the world any further.

To his companions who surrounded him, there were no words. They only stood in awe of what they were witnessing through Aurotos. He seemed as if he was in a trance and observing a whole world they could not.

"Yeah, so, I wonder if we should try to get his attention," Salenval said.

"Hold on, Salenval, not yet," Anaryen said.

"He finally sees with the sight of the Twin Flames. He has awoken," Molvalan said.

It was just after Anaryen spoke that his focus was broken. "I think that I was…" Aurotos said. "I can see everything in a way that I never could before. The blade gifted me the sight of creation. I saw the Essa flowing around us. I could see the veins of the world and the light present within all life, everything except where the darkness lies. It's as if the world itself is telling me everything we need to know so we can end this."

"Oh my, that sounds wonderful, Aurotos," Anaryen said.

"It truly is, Anaryen. It's a beautiful world, and that's what we're here to protect," Aurotos said.

Aurotos stood closer to the knights and the magi with Anaryen close at his side, and as his eyes dimmed slightly from the bright golden aura that had been present, Aurotos smiled. He was proud they were all with him, and he knew that only with their help could his goals of putting an end to the prince be achieved, for the enemy was many, and they were few.

"The dark master once again plans to harm our world, and Drazius seeks to bring about a dark convergence between his master's realm and ours. We can't allow this. I'll need your help to protect me and hold back the enemy as I destroy these engines of destruction with Ai'ethe."

"Alright then, what will you have us do, my lord?" Leavesa asked as she readied herself, followed up by the grunts of her fellow knights, a resounding tone of acknowledgement.

"Let's have it, Aurotos. Whatever we Aurodites can do to assist you, we're at your command," Anaryen said, as Molvalan and Elenfia stepped up together, nodding in agreement.

As he looked before him, Aurotos could see the unwavering dedication of his allies, humans and elves alike. He explained his plan to destroy the engines first with his blade, and then the beacon. His companions would need to hold the prince and his army back while he carved a devastating path across their front lines, first to destroy the engines and then to make his assault upon the beacon itself. He knew that the prince would not allow the beacon to fall without defending it himself and that he also wielded his own dangerous weapon, but if his allies were with him, Aurotos knew they could accomplish it.

They all knew that the trees could provide sanctuary after the battle if they were successful, yet there were so many branded and droth-kin that it was uncertain what their fate would be if their goals were achieved. This was something that Aurotos spoke to. "I can't say what will come after. I can only say that I trust all of you as you have trusted me. We can't know what fate may have in store for us today, but we must stay true to each other. The Twin Flames are with us, my friends. It's an honor to fight with you by my side."

As his companions bowed their heads Aurotos pulled his sword from the ground and, with it in hand, raised it over his head. His knights wanted to beat their chest with their gloves in salute of their leader, the Last Light of Auro. Even the magi wanted to shout, but instead, each of the allies raised their weapon silently in a show of unity that would inspire anyone who might bear witness. As he walked forward to the edge of the dark woods with his companions close behind and his lady by his side, Aurotos thought of the Twin Flames and his parents. *Today the light will be unwavering.* On this day, he knew that he would do whatever it took to protect his people, his friends, and stop the evil plan which directed a dark crusade to their homeland.

CHAPTER 19

END OF A BLOODLINE

The land surrounding the dark prince was cloaked in darkness, shrouded by the gloomveil and its blackening aura. High into the sky, the moon drew closer still, hastening the fall that would inevitably devastate the land. He surveyed the landscape and could see all the glowing butterflies around him flutter aimlessly, clearly confused with nature's guidance. Seeing them in disarray, Drazius was pleased and threw his helmet to the ground, pointing his blackened polearm forward, pointing first toward his army and then at the city which stood shielded on the other side of the river.

Raising the polearm gave him power and ensured a dominion that made even his commanders and subjects drunk with a desire to destroy anything that stood in their way. With one hand on the beacon and the other pointing toward that which he wished to conquer, the prince steadied the rage coursing through his veins and prepared to bolster his army.

He felt his confidence swell and relished in it for a moment before commanding his subjects. "Today is the day this city falls. The moon that once blanketed our world with enchantment at night will now be brought down by the might of Master Ohrimah. Here, today, we're the ones who will bring about the end of the false gods and their subjects who hide here. Look beyond the river before us, brothers, think of those brands you carry and who you owe your allegiance to. Allow it to guide your efforts to see that shield around their city crumble away. Death to the elves. There will be no mercy. Those who serve the false gods will pay with their lives," he said as his rallying cry was met with a roar so loud it could penetrate the shielded city ahead.

As his army stared at him, the dark prince shifted his gaze to his commanders and ordered them to carry out the assault. "Holcurt, Griles, it's time," Drazius said, his authority piercing the air around him.

"For your glory, my liege," Holcurt said, with a dark stare upon his face that shifted to a grim smile.

Griles sounded out in maniacal laughter as be bowed facing his dark monarch. "Finally, my prince, the end of Valenthreas."

The drothkin alpha not far off to the prince's side pointed its snout skyward as it let out a howling screech that echoed across the field. As it did so, the packs of drothkin scattered amongst the army reacted, bolstering the army who cheered further, their dark alliance's commitments affirmed.

The commanders squandered no time issuing their orders to the captains, and the assault upon Valenthreas began. Across the front line of the prince's army, the siege engines began hurling dark munitions toward the city's shield. Each time the munitions hit it, a burst of cracks could be seen. Soon after hitting, streams of light would reach out from inside to mend the cracks as the magicians behind the shield repaired the dome.

Drazius began laughing a most ominous laugh, pleased with his dark crusade and the dark energy of the world in their presence. He reveled in the darkness reaching out for the city of light and he desired nothing more than to carry that darkness into the cities ruins and consume everything the light ahead was sworn to protect.

His treasured moment was, however, short-lived. No sooner than the first volley had been launched did he hear a shout from the far northern side of his army. The war cry he heard sent a chill down his spine and rage moved to consume every cell of his body. The rage beckoned him to fulfill his purpose and he knew he had to prove nothing would stand in his way.

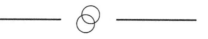

Aurotos pierced through the tree line of the dark forest, leading the charge with his allies close behind him. As he broke through the dark shroud of the Dragonstrike Woods, he let out a resonating cry of authority. "Forward, friends, the Twin Flames and the Masters are with us; may the light guide us," he shouted.

Behind him came the war cries of his allies that sent hope out across the land, ushering in their truest purpose. The Aurodites let loose their magic as the knights' swords lit up the darkness. Together the companions roared, "May the light guide us."

Aurotos knew that from where the prince stood, he likely couldn't see more than their glowing swords and the explosions of their great magic as they began to tear through the army between them and the engines that were stationed alongside the river.

Aurotos and his group made their way toward the first siege engine. He wasted no time and sliced through the engine causing flames to burst across it, which then caused an explosion that completely destroyed it.

Aurotos could see Drazius leaning forward, keeping one arm on the beacon while pointing the other at them as he sounded out with a bellowing order that could be heard reverberating across the land. "Kill them, or suffer my fury."

The prince's soldiers and the drothkin obeyed him, knowing that failure would mean their end. Aurotos felt that Drazius's certainty in his master and the power he wielded had completely clouded his judgment. To him, there was nothing else that mattered except seeing the city destroyed, and Aurotos believed that with each engine obliterated, the army's morale would wither away, making the battle against them much easier.

Aurotos continued to execute his charge across the front line from one siege engine to the next. To his left side, the knights covered his charge, cutting down the soldiers or drothkin that opposed them. The magi unleashed fierce magic which spread across the soldiers and drothkin ranks.

Each time Aurotos laid a strike across an engine, Anaryen would raise a wall of frost just behind them, covering their rear as they laid waste to the front lines of the enemy. As she did so, Molvalan would pull stones and rocks from the ground behind them, hurling great boulders into the army, rolling the stones along their left flank as they progressed. Elenfia brought lightning down from the clouds and electrocuted the soldiers who dared move toward them. The further they moved, the more the clouds above released rain down upon them. While the wet, earthy aroma was cooling, it served another purpose, making it more difficult for the army to make sense of their exact location. The drothkin screeched with fear and retreated as countless among them were being annihilated.

From the hilltop, they could hear the dark prince cry out again, this time directing his words toward Aurotos, who had just made his way to the center of the army, having laid waste to the siege engines behind him. "Aurotos, lay down your arms now, and no harm will come to you or the fools who follow you. But I warn you, if you continue your attack, there will be none left alive—none in the city, and none who stand with you."

Aurotos had only one response for the dark prince as he shouted back through the storm. "The light's justice reigns," he said as he continued carving a devastating path across the front lines, destroying more of the siege engines, left as no more than piles of burning scrap.

In his wake followed the remarkable spells of the magi providing cover to the knights whose cinder swords caused many soldiers to weep while meeting their end. No matter how hard Drazius's branded tried to make their way to Aurotos they only fell, vanquished by his companions. The knights' defense was destructive and the frost wall left behind them by Anaryen was insurmountable by the enemies blocked behind it.

Aurotos' war cry had only bolstered his allies who continued to slay more of the enemy. No matter the class of enemy, those who stood before Aurotos and his allies were falling, vanquished in utter defeat as their stormed assault raged on.

Aurotos could tell that Prince Drazius was enraged as he let out another desperate order. "I want these fools kneeling before me now. I want them to watch as Valos crushes their city. Unleash it all. They must not proceed further. Fail and die by my hand," he screamed, as he looked upon the drothkin alpha who howled and screeched as if given its own order to attack.

The prince's rage only seemed to darken and chill the world around them further. As Aurotos and his companions pressed forward, their cold breath and the steam from their bodies became visible, the only warmth present within the gloom surrounding them.

Now, the entire horde of the army charged the front of their ranks in a desperate attempt to stop Aurotos from progressing any further. High in the sky, lightning crackled while the moon cracked further, entering borders of the upper atmosphere. The sputters of the moon caused all living things around them to flicker in pain. Where once the world glowed in the ambient light of the moon, now there seemed only to be a sense of loss as that same moon threatened to break itself upon the world.

Griles and Holcurt led the charge of what remained at the center, screaming their commands in a desperate attempt to suppress Aurotos and his allies. Where the knights and magi were at first experiencing success, they were now beginning to feel the weight of the forces of darkness and their prince, who was shouting his demands.

"Bring them to me, I want them bowing before me," Drazius screamed as his bloodlust intensified.

Aurotos could hear Drazius from behind him but knew that he had to keep pushing forward to finish off the remaining machines. He could hear the prince screaming for his submission and for him to watch his friends die. Still, he pressed forward and fought with courage, wielding the radiant blade in a way that would make his kingdom proud. He was methodical in his attacks, and each strike upon the siege engines was an artistic expression of his skill. The well-oiled blade which was ablaze glowed bright under the darkening sky, his legacy lighting the way forward. He could see all life around him pulsing through his radiant eyes, and his attunement to the noble tenets had never been more aligned than it was there. But Aurotos had begun to stray from his allies, who were fighting more desperately than ever to cover his trail.

That's when he heard the loudest howl he had ever observed come from a drothkin. The sound seemed to be coming from somewhere near the beacon. As he looked behind him, he could see the massive alpha leap high into the sky and crash onto the ground behind Anaryen and the magi. The colossal beast swiped at the frost walls, and completely shattered them as it charged toward the woman he loved.

Aurotos hesitated as he watched the alpha racing for Anaryen. Before it could get far, she raised a large frost wall, but that didn't stop the beast as it crashed through once again and continued making its way at her. Before it could get too close, Molvalan brought plant roots up to grab the alphas feet while Anaryen blanketed the fiend in ice from the waist down.

The creature screeched so loud it pierced the ears of everyone on the battlefield. Aurotos stared on as the alpha became enraged and smashed itself to break off the ice. The shattering fragments knocked Anaryen back as the beast continued to tear the roots off its legs. Elenfia brought down a lightning bolt and electrified the alpha who appeared stunned for only a moment as it started to char from the electrical current.

As Aurotos looked on helplessly he witnessed Syvon take notice of the encounter and turn around, moving faster than he had ever seen him move before. He seemed to almost vanish before he appeared again, launching into the air over the magi as he intercepted the enraged beast. As his feet landed on the back of the alpha's shoulders, he drove both of his swords into its neck before jumping back and cutting deeper with his blades, removing the beasts head before it could make a sound.

"Sorry I took so long, my lady," Syvon shouted as he landed next to the magi. "No time to waste," he said, before rushing back to rejoin the knights who were keeping the enemy horde at bay.

Those seconds while Anaryen was at risk felt like an eternity, but Aurotos found his faith in Syvon had been rewarded as the knight placed his prejudice aside and supported the Aurodites without hesitation. It gave him a renewed sense of hope as he became aware of the enemies nearing him.

He observed each of his friends continue fighting their own battle, and the many frost walls that had shielded their rear were all gone. He knew that he either had to join them or continue forward and destroy the last of the siege machines.

As the crackling in the sky grew louder, Aurotos made eye contact with Anaryen who gave him the assurance he needed as she shouted at him. "Aurotos, you must keep going. We'll be fine. Rejoin us when you're finished."

He knew that she was right, and although he was worried about her and his allies, the engines had to fall, for once they did, only the beacon would remain. The knights were being led by Leavesa who sought to cut off the army approaching the magi. Elenfia's lightning continued to strike down and spread across all of the branded soldiers who served as lightning rods for her spells. Molvalan was quick to support the others and raised the terrain to help shield their wake.

Arvasiel shielded the knights in a glorious display of light as Leavesa hurled the largest fireballs Aurotos had ever seen. Behind her came barrage after barrage of flames from Kaervo. What didn't burn from their spectacular magic would fall to the cinder swords of Kaylos, Salenval, and Syvon, whose clean strikes obliterated the enemy. Tarothas and Vael could be heard shouting to the allies about what they could see and hear around them as they defended the magi along with Drelion. Even Nahul had brought nature itself to his aid as birds of prey dove from the sky attacking the eyes of the drothkin that charged toward them, leaving them easy prey to finish off with his sword.

Aurotos knew his allies could hold off most of the army at the center, but what soldiers remained ahead of him, along with the last siege engines, would be for him to handle alone. He knew all of their fates were uncertain, but he also knew they all had a duty to fulfill.

Seeing his allies fight so valiantly only bolstered his resolve as he continued his way forward. He noticed that most of the dark machines were destroyed, and as he neared the last of the machines which propelled their dark assault on the city, he knew he would achieve his goal soon.

He could hear Drazius screaming again as he had clearly witnessed the Aurodites who survived Illonel on the battlefield. His rage fell onto the ears of everyone as he yelled. "Show them the strength of our master. Bring the Aurodites to me, brothers," he commanded.

Aurotos glanced back to see the prince step forward atop the hill with his polearm in hand. He delivered sweeping strikes before him, first to his left, then to his right, and each swipe of his weapon unleashed a wave of dark magic that completely destroyed the solar shield Arvasiel had used to protect his allies. The dark barrages from Drazius seemed to create a foggy black mass above his companions.

After destroying the next engine, Aurotos unleashed a devastating twirl of his sword around him, laying waste to the soldiers that approached before shooting a blast of light from his sword at the dark cloud forming over his allies. He realized as he obliterated the dark spell that it might be the last favor he could offer his friends until he could return to them.

Aurotos sensed inspiration in his allies, who he could hear cheering as they fought the branded soldiers that were surrounding them. Knowing he had helped them, he pressed forward once more to destroy the next engine. There were only two left, and he knew he would be able to rejoin his companions soon, but he had to make haste, for the crackling of the moon above reminded him of his final objective, the beacon.

As he continued to carve a path forward, he would look back periodically to check on his allies. He could see them fighting desperately against the might of Drazius, who had stepped away from the beacon, delivering one concussive attack after another. Aurotos saw multiple blasts of darkness from the prince's polearm, one of which had hit Vael and broken his solar shell, leaving him to be bound by the prince's soldiers.

Aurotos knew he was too far away from his friends to help them. As his sense of urgency grew, he pressed forward faster, cutting down more soldiers before looking back to see Drazius disable Tarothas and Arvasiel, who were unable to protect themselves from the dark blasts and the mighty strikes from the prince's polearm. Their magic shells had also broken and they were bound by the prince's soldiers before they could regain their composure.

Aurotos pressed further ahead dispatching any drothkin or soldiers in his path before glancing back at his companions one last time. Though it was hard to see, he watched them attempt to protect themselves with every defensive measure they had in their arsenal, but not even the magic shells taught to them by Armatay made a difference against the dark magic of the prince. One by one, they were disabled by Drazius and bound by his soldiers.

The last thing Aurotos could hear clearly was the prince threatening the magi. "Stop or you will die like the archmagus did. Submit now or watch these knights die," he said.

Moving further away, he could barely make out Anaryen's command. "We must stop…can't cause their death," she said. Then he heard the prince laughing maniacally, and then silence.

He moved as fast as he could, and with his expedited speed, everything seemed like a blur. He knew he had to get back as fast as possible before something bad happened to the woman he loved, to his friends.

As Aurotos destroyed the final siege engine he thought he could hear all of his companion's cheer at the moment he put a stop to the assault on Valenthreas. Yet one final objective remained, the beacon tethered to the moon at the edge of the cosmos above.

Aurotos immediately began making his way back toward the place he last saw his companions. Between him and the beacon, he could only see a dark fog and the gloomveil from which the enemy poured. As the army bore down upon him, he dodged one attack after another and rushed his way back across the front lines. Yet, the harder he pressed forward, the harder it was for him to see beyond the horde of enemies he was fighting.

One sweeping swing after another, he paved a path forward while releasing blasts of light forged in flame from his radiant blade as he crossed back and forth through the field seeking his friends. He was unstoppable, and the enemy fell at his feet effortlessly on his path.

He scanned ahead as best he could, but his gift of sight couldn't penetrate the void of darkness. Still, he thought he was starting to see his companions bound on the hill just at the base of the beacon. He had his objective and set his course for them, unsure of the state they would be in. His eyes now assured him they were alive, but whether or not they were injured was something he couldn't know. Desperately, Aurotos rushed ahead until he could see a large black shadow that launched toward him from where the beacon was positioned.

It was Prince Drazius with his polearm over his head, preparing to deliver a crushing blow with the weight of the dark power he wielded. Aurotos raised his blade overhead, connecting with the forceful polearm and the weight of the prince who had leaped unnaturally high above to deliver the fierce blow.

Their weapons connected in an explosion of light and shadow. Aurotos had now felt the full force of the prince's dark power and was unexpectedly overwhelmed by it. Drazius did not hesitate as his eyes met those of Aurotos. In a rage, the dark prince sent a black force of energy before him, knocking Aurotos backwards.

Aurotos had barely gained his footing as Drazius continued to deliver the next powerful strike from his weapon. First, Drazius hit him from the right, then the left, then overhead. With each strike from the dark prince, light erupted, knocking back the prince's branded soldiers, along with any of the drothkin who were still alive.

The army was shouting as if victory was already assured at the sight of Aurotos battered under the force of the prince's attacks. High in the sky, another crackle and burst of blue light came from the moon that was drawing closer still and resounding more as the beacon's tether continued guiding it toward the planet.

Back on the ground, Aurotos had raised his solar shell as the dark prince, now pointing his polearm forward like a staff, unleashed dark eruptions of black matter onto Aurotos. The more fiercely the prince attacked, the brighter Aurotos's eyes glowed until finally, his shield was about to fall.

As Aurotos scanned the terrain beyond Prince Drazius once more, he could see that Anaryen and his allies were alive on their knees just below the hilltop before the beacon. He could see the two commanders and several branded soldiers standing guard, fully entertained as they watched the spectacle.

Aurotos felt his radiant barrier beginning to give way and his only thought was his desire to help his companions, thinking only to save them. In a swift act, he struck upward with his sword, grazing the prince across his face where the sage had previously wounded him. With haste, Aurotos continued to deliver one arcing strike over another against Drazius, who raised his polearm, sending an eruption of darkness that once again knocked Aurotos back, staggering him on his feet. He was given no time to prepare himself, for immediately after, the prince struck down with his polearm over and over, beating upon Aurotos, who was desperately working to maintain the solar shell he had barely raised in time to defend himself against the prince's attack.

Aurotos was weakening and becoming fatigued at the overwhelming strength of the attacks until he could no longer maintain the magical barrier that protected him. As he dropped his shield, he moved to dodge the polearm which crashed into the ground next to him. The prince's weapon came sweeping back up by his side and Aurotos raised Ai'ethe, allowing it to protect him against the prince's attacks.

One attack after the next weakened Aurotos until he heard Drazius speak to him, now whispering through grinding teeth. "Can you sense it, Auron? This dark moment before rebirth, a world already mourning the fall of magic."

Aurotos pressed back with his blade and looked beyond the prince to see Anaryen, then back at the prince who continued to taunt him. "Is the lady special to you? Soon she will watch you die," Drazius said smiling, then shouting for all to hear. "So, this is the last descendant of your gods. How pathetic." He whispered his last taunt, "The end comes for you, Va'Threas."

Aurotos looked him in the eyes and saw only darkness as he pressed his sword against the prince's weapon, which was bearing down on him harder and harder. He could see the pleasure the prince took in physically overpowering him, seemingly crushing him under his will. Above the prince, the broken moon only appeared to signal the end for him, his friends, and the countless lives of those across his homeland.

Aurotos pressed back with all his might, his will fixed upon a singular desire, that he would give his life to protect all of them, all his friends, the woman he loved, and all the people now endangered by Drazius and the approaching moon. He prayed to the Twin Flames and the Masters for the first time since losing his parents. In his silent prayer he offered his life to protect Anaryen and his allies and he begged for the chance to protect those whom he had been destined to safeguard.

With his strength weakening under the weight of the dark prince's weapon and the growing darkness being emitted over him, he felt a reprieve, but only for a moment, as Drazius stepped back, pulling his polearm up high. Then the prince pointed his fist forward and emitted a grueling black flame upon Aurotos, whose weapon fell, piercing the ground before him.

The blast of dark flames completely covered Aurotos, who gripped the hilt of his sword and leaned against it as he wailed, burning to death helplessly. His blade sank further into the scorched soil beneath him. Drazius eased the release of his power for a moment, staring into Aurotos's golden eyes which revealed his suffering as the rest of him was engulfed by dark flames.

Drazius smiled a sinister smile and laughed at the misery of Aurotos dying before him. As the prince stared at him with assurance, he felt as if Drazius reveled in seeing him kneeling before him, leaning against his weapon with his head down low. Not even the armor of his family had protected him from the dark assault. Everything burned, and he felt himself slipping in agony.

As Aurotos's eyes dimmed, he could hear the screams of his companions by the beacon. He looked to his allies as he heard Drazius speaking to them. "This is the fate of all who oppose us. You placed your faith in this Auron, now look where it led you."

As his eyes dimmed further, he could see Anaryen give in to her sorrow. "No, Aurotos, you must...I love you," she cried.

Aurotos could sense Drazius peering back at Anaryen and his fellow knights who were blurting out their own pleas of "no" or "my lord" while others were praying along with Molvalan. His allies were the last thing he saw, the last voices heard before he felt himself die. As he passed away from the light and the suffering of his dying body, his last thoughts were of his prayer and Anaryen.

But in that final moment, an unknown voice spoke to him. "I am Ai'ner, the first phoenix. I have awaited the moment when you would be ready. It is time. I choose you, Aurotos, and I will serve with you now into eternity."

Every being present soon bore witness to the bright flame falling from high in the sky. It pierced through the dark clouds, unaffected by the storm that raged. It was falling fast, with its sights fixed upon where Drazius and Aurotos remained. In an instant, it crashed into Aurotos, and the explosion knocked the dark prince back off his feet onto the ground.

Just before the moment of impact, the prince stared at Ai'ner who looked directly into his eyes in defiance. Ai'ner was nearly as large as a human, and its wings were twice the size of an avolans. The prince gathered himself and stood back up. As the flames subsided, Aurotos arose before Drazius, renewed and glowing in a flaming aura of light. His eyes burned brighter than ever before, and the heat from his radiance grew outward.

"The light will always endure. Drazius Khorvek, your dark conquest ends here," Aurotos said. His voice sounded half his own and half something else, as if he spoke with the voice of the Twin Flames themselves. As he uttered those words, his eyes burst with bright fire, and a radiating shell surrounded him. In the darkness that was the prince and his army, Aurotos became a beacon of light, like a sun in the cosmos.

The prince was in shock as he witnessed Aurotos lifting off the ground in his fiery aura and wings of flame as large as the phoenix that had crashed into him. It was as if he and the first phoenix had become one. Nothing like this had ever been known to exist before. Phoenixes chose certain knights, but it had never been known that one could merge with them.

To the Knights of the Phoenix, bound by the beacon, it appeared to be a most glorious sight. As the aura of light encased Aurotos, he saw that his allies' bindings were burned away. They stood free, enclosed in shells of radiance. Magi and knight alike were mesmerized, and while they were noticeably thankful he was alive, they proved unable to contain themselves. As he heard them cheering him on, he flew into the air, high above Prince Drazius.

The surviving drothkin cowered in fear at the sight of Aurotos, while the branded soldiers stared in disbelief, completely stunned at the sight they were witnessing. Drazius no longer seemed shocked and desperately sought to end him. The prince moved to stop him, and clenching his polearm in hand, he prepared to launch it as Aurotos was rising higher into the air.

Then Aurotos heard Molvalan's voice ring out. "Protect Lord Aurotos," he shouted before launching a barrage of stones he had pulled from the ground around him, shooting them fast toward the dark prince.

Aurotos watched as Drazius barely reacted in time to block the stones, seeming unsure of which person to attack. The prince stood blatantly confused as he bore witness to the knights and magi's eyes which had also become illuminated with a golden glow similar to their leader.

Aurotos hovered above the battlefield and spoke from within his lady's mind. "Together, Anaryen," he said.

Aurotos could sense Anaryen's spirit overcome with joy and inspiration as she led an assault on Drazius. "To Aurotos, let's finish this," she commanded as she and the rest of his allies charged the dark prince.

As the knights and magi made their way, they found little resistance, for the soldiers and drothkin were overcome with fear. Stones were launched, lightning was cast, and flames were unleashed upon the prince. The assault was unimaginable to withstand, but the prince still remained strong.

Drazius desperately worked to defend himself against the Aurodites destructive attacks of stone, lightning, and then frost. By the time the magi had delivered their blows, it was the knights who charged him with great strikes from their cinder swords as he raised a dark barrier around himself. His commanders, in disbelief, only stared on as they remained alone by the beacon.

"We're with you, Aurotos," Anaryen shouted, her voice filled with love and adoration, and it strengthened him.

"My lord, it's time we settled this," Leavesa said as she looked to him venerably.

In an instant, the rest of the knights and magi cried out together, and the camaraderie between the allies of Aurotos brought him to an even greater state of illumination, shining his light upon the land below. Even high up above the dark prince, a smile could be seen upon his face as he felt a sense of pride in his friends.

Aurotos looked up at the moon crackling in the sky nearby and closed his eyes. He sensed life pulsing around him, and as his solar shell dropped, he could feel the rain on his face. In a fleeting moment of communion with the energy of the planet, he knew what needed to be done to neutralize the great threat the moon posed. He knew it was time he ended the prince's reign of terror.

It was in that fateful moment that Aurotos felt himself one with the planet, and he raised his fist to the sky. He spoke in a language unknown to those around him, unknown to himself. He spoke to the falling raindrops, and offered a communion to each droplet which fell from the sky. He whispered to every particle and uttered words of power, sparking the Essa in every drop as he set fire to the rain.

The drops of flame that fell burned the drothkin to ash, and erased their corrupt corpses from existence. The unprotected parts of every soldier caught fire, and with that the army was decimated. For his allies, the rain healed both them and the land around them, renewing everything it touched. The darkness was lifting, and the gloomveil's influence was quickly being purified from the land.

Drazius, looking around him, was noticeably enraged and desperate unlike ever before as he bore witness to the end of his army. In an act of defiance, he unleashed a dark explosion that burst around him, knocking all of Aurotos's companions back.

At the same time, Aurotos pointed his blade at the beacon and sent a beam of light from Ai'ethe that connected to the machine causing a light to swell from within. The beacon glowed brightly, before cracking and breaking, and as it exploded, a blast of light shot skyward, shattering the moon into pieces.

Aurotos had noticed his allies who were knocked down, and acted fast, shifting his attention to Drazius, launching a massive barrage of flames upon him. The prince struggled, shielding himself as he fought to see beyond the flames. But Aurotos was blinding the prince, and the barrage of light and flame hitting him penetrated his dark barrier and began burning him, much like it had done to the soldiers which had fallen on the battlefield.

Aurotos watched as Drazius continued to fight through the blinding light, and that was when he chose to put an end to the prince's struggle. In an instant he flew down through the flames toward Drazius, plunging Ai'ethe into his chest, driving it into his heart.

Drazius didn't scream in agony, but instead, he let out a sigh of relief and spoke his last words. "Finally, his hold on me has ended. Thank you, Aurotos," he said, exhaling slowly as the darkness in his eyes began to fade.

As the rainfall came to an end, Drazius took another deep breath and struggled to remain standing as the blackness filled his eyes once more. Aurotos twisted the radiant blade, and from the wound, light began to shine, sending cracks across the prince's body until the light burned him from within. In his final exhale, his body turned to ash and was carried away by the cool breeze.

As a pile of ash formed below from where the prince's remains fell, a dark shade stood up and was blown away by the cold air, ushering away the last of the darkness. Whatever branded soldiers managed to survive the battle fled along with the commanders who had made their escape as soon as Aurotos set fire to the rain. They had managed to run far away, but no matter where they went, their scars would only serve to identify them as the traitors they were. For the branded and servants of the dark master, living would only be a worse punishment than death.

CHAPTER 20

THE FALL OF MAGIC

Aurotos stood before his friends, bathed in a radiant aura, an embodiment of the phoenix within. Far above them, Valos's shattered pieces crackled with the ferocity of a cosmic storm, and they all gazed skyward to witness the remnants of the moon for one last time. The world would never be the same, and the moment at hand hastened the reality that they themselves would need to seek safety.

As his companions approached him, they could see the fiery wings that had lifted him up were now draped around him like an illuminated cloak, bathing him and everything surrounding him in light. His eyes glowed brighter than they had ever seen before, as if the suns themselves were captured in his eyes, spilling energy out.

They had no words for what they had witnessed, as their own gleaming eyes faded and their shells disappeared. Aurotos smiled, a sign of hope in their desperate hour. As his smiles were returned, Anaryen wept, her tears streaming down her face, glistening as if drops of starlight.

As she approached him, he could tell she hesitated and didn't seem sure whether she could hug him or not. "It's alright, my love, you won't be hurt," Aurotos said.

"I thought I'd lost you," Anaryen said, as she gave him the biggest hug he'd felt in an age, her lips reaching up desperately seeking his affection.

Aurotos leaned down to her and gave her a kiss, which was interrupted by the laughter coming from Kaylos, Syvon, and Salenval.

"Never in my life would I have thought to bear witness to something as spectacular as that," Molvalan said, as he held Elenfia's hand, who closed herself nearer to him.

The ferocity of the moon above seemed to give her cause for concern, and she looked up, her affection interrupted. "It's going to start falling soon—what should we do?" Anaryen asked.

"Even though the moon falls, the city and most of the realm will survive, but these lands will be changed forever," Aurotos said.

"My lord, seeing you like this," Leavesa said, her eyes open widely as if still unwilling to believe the sight of Aurotos with the phoenix, still residing within him.

"Indeed, it became one with you. I've never heard of a phoenix that large...except...it must be..." Nahul said, as he gazed in amazement upon the flames of the phoenix which enveloped him.

"I'll have to take your word for it. I didn't see Ai'ner as it made its way to me," Aurotos said.

"Ai'ner? The first phoenix?" Vael inquired, looking at him in amazement.

"Of course, Ai'ner, that indeed tracks," Nahul admitted.

"I watched it falling from the sky and I could hear both flame and song. It's the most beautiful sound I've ever heard," Tarothas said joyfully.

"All phoenixes descend from Ai'ner, but it disappeared after the great war. To return now," Molvalan said as he pondered. "It must have chosen you."

"In reflection," Leavesa seemed lost in thought. "Never has a phoenix been capable of merging with one of us. Not even your father did that before when Ai'ner served with him. What in the gods?"

Suddenly alarmed, Anaryen stepped away from Aurotos's body and looked at him in shock. To her amazement, along with the rest of the companions, who were now speechless, they watched as Ai'ner began to separate from Aurotos. The fiery wings that were draping him opened up, stretched out widely behind him, and the phoenix separated from Aurotos before resting its feet on the ground and lowering.

Ai'ner stepped back and to the side of Aurotos near Anaryen, dropping its wings around itself. It stood upright, facing them, with its legs nearly as long as a human's. The flame subsided, although the phoenix was still surrounded in a glowing aura similar to that found around Aurotos before. Its wings were gold and red, with a blackened undertone toward the quills of its feathers which were bathed in small flames on their tips.

The phoenix's eyes were bright like the stars. Its head was much like any avolan across the world, and it was clear that, in many ways, it resembled all of them, or perhaps they resembled Ai'ner. Its chest was blanketed with scales of ember resembling those of a dragon, and they spread down across its chest toward its legs, yet they too were bathed in the same aura and with glowing fur covering its legs. That part of the phoenix's body was more golden and presented itself like the color of the flames that persisted at the tips of its feathers.

It was clear to everyone that, as the phoenix stood next to Aurotos, it was just larger than the avolan people. It looked at them with eyes which carried great wisdom. They all had seen it when it flew down, its tail streaming far behind it. Its claws on its feet had seemed close to its body, unlike now when they were more proportional and like an avolans feet.

It spoke out loud to them, unlike the other phoenixes which had been born after, which were only able to speak telepathically to the knights. "Your father would be proud of you for your courage, Aurotos. You honored his memory today, as did the allies who stood by your side, yet one resolution remains," Ai'ner said as it looked back upon Aurotos for further clarification.

"My friends, we could use our powers and survive in the woods, of that I have no doubt," Aurotos said, as he looked toward them solemnly. "Yet there's still one matter I must attend to and I wonder if you'll help me fulfill that commitment."

"Alright then, my lord, what is it?" Leavesa asked, looking to him as if she was ready for anything.

"Hold on, that look, I can tell you have something dire to share with us," Anaryen said as she scanned him for an answer.

"Ah, come on my lord, just give it to us straight," Salenval said.

"Ai'ner shared many things with me when our minds were one… and, you all know I made a promise to aid the peri. It turns out we can help countless souls trapped in those dark woods and honor my commitment to the peri at the same time. For that task, we must take refuge in the trees. We'll be safe there. Ai'ner has gifted me with the foresight of how we're to be protected while carrying out this task, but it comes at a cost," Aurotos said, scanning the faces of his friends as he continued. "We could slumber for many years. In the realm of the peri, time passes much slower than it does here, but using their realm is our only hope to succeed."

"That loss of time may not be much to ask of us, but for our Aurodite friends—" Leavesa insisted.

"There's more: once we join Ai'ner it will be by its magic that we are protected and safe throughout our journey. Aside from the time we lose, our bodies will change because it requires magic that bonds us to the trees. I can't know for sure exactly how much, but we should all expect that we could awaken from this changed forever, taking on some aspects of the trees themselves. I'll do it alone if I must, but I'd feel a lot better knowing I have each of you at my side," Aurotos said, and with that he had shared the worst of it, or so he believed.

He looked upon the faces of his friends and could see the emotions settling in to each of them. One after another, reluctance and dread seemed to wash away, replaced by the kind of dedication he had known them to embody. Aurotos wanted them to join him but he knew what he was asking was no small thing; it felt like he was expecting them to sacrifice their very existence, and perhaps he was.

"I know this is not what you all had planned but this is important to the fate of Auro. This must be fulfilled by Aurotos and I know that he will need all of your help if he is to succeed. I hope you will all join me soon. I will await you at the tree line," Ai'ner said as he nodded to Aurotos.

Ai'ner lifted into the air and flew for the edge of the woods, close to the river facing Valenthreas. Behind the phoenix was a large stream of light illuminating the path that would guide the companions to their safety. As the knights all watched the phoenix fly, it became clear to several that the edge of the woods did not seem to be the best place to take refuge.

As Ai'ner stopped at the tree line, Leavesa voiced her feelings passionately. "Very well, my lord, you know where I stand. If we can free the souls of our parents then we have to try. The thought of them trapped here, being used by him...No, I won't stand for it," she said, as she clenched her fists tight.

"Trapped in there, no way. I'm with you, my lord," Tarothas said, as the group collectively drew in the essence of shock shared between them.

Leavesa, unaffected like the others looked again to Ai'ner, evaluating the prospect. "Alright then, if we're to do this shouldn't we head to the center of the woods?" she inquired, ready to see to a proper plan.

"That's just it. There's no time. Besides, it's going to be easier for our allies to learn our whereabouts once they visit this place," Anaryen said.

"Exactly, they'll know where we are and Ai'ner's presence will help them understand that we aren't dead," Aurotos said confidently.

"You know I'm with you. I won't stand by, allowing this evil to continue," Anaryen said as she took Aurotos's hand and drew closer to him. "I just can't ask the same of Elenfia or Molvalan."

"My lady, we'll follow you wherever you go," Elenfia said, beginning to smile as she continued. "Besides, we've rather come to like this group of elves."

"It's hard to think those who once knew us will regard us as some form of woodkin?" Drelion asked, quite rhetorically. "By the Masters."

"We could have worse news, although I cannot say I am fond of waking to look like one of those trees either," Molvalan said as he held on to Elenfia, who appeared to be holding him even tighter.

"Agreed, the magi are right," Syvon said.

"So, how long will we be stuck like that? I pretty much hate the idea of being confined in such a way," Kaervo said.

"Ah, come on. We've faced worse," Salenval said as he slapped Kaervo on the back, causing Kaylos to chuckle unexpectedly at the force with which he hit him.

"Lord Aurotos, you are the light of the Twin Flames. I think I speak for us all when I say this. Where you lead, one should follow. Truly, this is a call we should all answer," Vael said, as a silence swept across the party who seemed to share in that sentiment.

"Thank you, my friends. I sense there's a greater plan for us once we slumber, yet Ai'ner assures me that we'll understand everything much better once we sleep. I trust its foresight as I would trust in the Twin Flames," Aurotos said, his confidence bolstering his allies, something he could sense as he scanned their expressions.

They all knew it as well as he did. The first phoenix rose from the ashes of the Twin Flames themselves. In a way, it was a part of the gods as much as Aurotos or his parents were. If the phoenix believed they all needed to do this, there was little chance any of them would argue. They would serve the gods in whatever way was needed of them and the call of service had arrived once more.

"I wish we could discuss this more, but we're out of time. For now, we should find solace in knowing that we have prevailed in our duty. Please make your way toward Ai'ner, and we'll share in our final moments before we slumber," Aurotos said.

It was a solemn moment, but they all realized that they would live on in service and one day awaken. For the elves, living endlessly was a birthright, unless a natural event or ascension was to take them from the world. For the humans, however, potentially extending their life was unheard of. While humans lived hundreds of years naturally, the chance of living beyond that was inconceivable, and for them, this made the idea difficult to cope with. Still they seemed to accept it as best as they could.

As Aurotos and Anaryen's allies made their way toward the first phoenix, the couple slowly paced behind them, and Aurotos could see that Anaryen appeared frightened, in a way he had never seen before.

"Please share your thoughts with me. I know this must be hard," Aurotos said gently, breathing in the crisp air which blew as swift as their stride.

As they continued walking, she broke her thoughts down to him. "To be like the trees when we wake, some sort of woodkin. It seems like we could be gone a long time, that means my family could pass away before…you know, it calls so many things into question," Anaryen said.

"I know, we enter a tumultuous chapter of our lives. I wish I could comfort you more. All I know is if we don't slumber, we can't achieve what we must," Aurotos replied.

"I accept it and I understand it. It's just hard to cope with when there are so many unknowns."

"I realize that, and I wish I knew more myself but I trust Ai'ner."

"So do I. I know we'll get through this," she said confidently as she smiled up at him. "All of us, together."

The two had made their way closer to the tree line just behind their companions who were laughing and talking. They were enjoying their final moments, often looking upon the city or up at the sky as they watched the falling moon's pieces breaking further apart.

As Aurotos stood on the edge of the river, he looked toward Valenthreas where the barrier remained strong. "I wish I could have shown you the city. I wish I knew what comes next for them," he said and he felt a sense of sorrow in knowing he couldn't tend to his people.

"You know what you need to, for now. They're safe because of us, because of you," Anaryen replied.

As the two stood together in their final moments, Aurotos looked upon the city and around the world he knew one last time, and as he did so, he thought of the sage and felt reluctant for a moment. He didn't wish to turn his back on the world any longer, and where this once was a notion he welcomed, on this day, he felt, for the first time, it was his duty to support and guide the lives of those who he would now leave behind.

"I am afraid that our time has run out. Aurotos, Anaryen, come. It is time," Ai'ner said as it opened its wide wings, beckoning the two to join their allies.

As Anaryen stepped away from Aurotos, she raised out her arm, beckoning him to join her. "Come here, you've done what you were meant to do. It's time for us to rest," she said.

Aurotos placed his hand in hers and followed her toward his allies and Ai'ner, who now had its wings spread wider across the front of the woods. The two joined their friends under the guidance of Ai'ner, drawing closer to it, side by side.

"What will take place now will be a divergence for you all, but I will be there to guide you. While your bodies slumber, your souls will continue your work. For there is another path we must take as we remain entombed in these dark woods. The world will change, and time will pass, but for you, that time will seem much shorter. When you wake, the world will be very different, yet you will find many will be grateful for your return," Ai'ner said.

"That doesn't sound so bad," Elenfia said, her hand still in Molvalan's.

"Not at all, Elenfia. We cannot falter as long as we stay true to one another," Molvalan said.

"I'm up for another adventure," Tarothas said, smiling.

"Indeed, that tracks, and we'll have some fun stories to tell the other knights too," Nahul said.

"My friends, it's been an honor serving with you. We must trust in one another, no matter what comes next," Aurotos said.

"Well, the honor was ours, my lord," Leavesa said as she bowed.

Before Aurotos, all of the knights and the magi bent their knees in honor of him. He was speechless to see even Anaryen bow before him, and even Ai'ner lowered its head as if reinforcing its vow to him. He was touched with an overwhelming sense of humility; he knew he had to honor them in return.

Aurotos knew there was only one thing he felt right to do in the time they had left and that was to kneel before his knights, as their equal. "My friends, we must honor each other as equals," he said as he kneeled down, humbling himself amongst them.

All of his allies were blanketed in a sense of calm and security. Whatever worries they had, whatever fears they carried about being entombed in the trees, and whatever changes they were going to go through no longer mattered. Any sense of dread was replaced by peace, and worry was replaced with assurance. As they all rose, they were ready to meet their future together.

"It's time. Let us find guidance in Ai'ner," Aurotos said.

"Each of you, find a tree just behind me and stand next to it. Quickly now, our time is almost at an end," Ai'ner said. As it turned facing the tree line, it saw each of the magi and the knights had gathered by a tree. Before Ai'ner was a singular tree unclaimed by any, and as Aurotos and Anaryen walked toward it, Aurotos pulled her close to him. They stood face-to-face together before a large tree trunk, facing the city.

"What about my tree?" Anaryen asked.

"Together, forever by your side," Aurotos said as he pulled her close in an embrace and a final passionate kiss.

Ai'ner spared no more time, for as the two remained in their embrace, it moved fast toward them, and with its wings spread out, crashed into the trees, its wings exploding across the forest, encasing every knight and magi into a stasis within the very trees themselves. Now, on the edge of the woods, the trunks of the trees appeared in the form of the knights and magi that now rested within.

The tree where Aurotos and Anaryen had been took the shape of two lovers kissing, with the phoenix's head above, and its wings raised high over them spreading through the branches of the tree which reached skyward. For now, the woodkin would slumber, and the world would change under the fall of Valos.

Not long after, the world around the entombed heroes flickered once more. Up in the sky, the moon's pieces spread further apart as it pierced through the clouds in the sky, sending the shards of Valos down into the planet. A large piece of the moon still fell toward Valenthreas while many of the other pieces continued to fall, throughout the sky, all across the elven landscape.

The bastions of light surrounding all of the towns and cities remained strong, but wherever the shards were to fall, the land would be changed. The large core fragment of Valos collided onto the golden barrier safe-guarding the great elven city. Had the moon not been slowed and broken apart, the force would have annihilated the land, but safety had indeed been secured, for as all of life under the shell worked to strengthen it, their magic endured and kept them safe.

The large core of the moon broke into pieces as it hit the shell, explod-ing outward and down around it. Where the shards hit the land below and around the magic barrier, explosions occurred. Even to the south, a great many pieces of the splintered moon erupted as they impacted the landscape leading all the way down to the southern coastal areas, causing the sea to flood into the northern land, leaving Valenthreas now an island surrounded by the sea and the protruding shards embedded in the terrain.

For the shards of the moon that broke and were sent skyward, a halo formed surrounding the city crafted from the hovering pieces. Some locations in which the shards of Valos landed, explosions took place, while in others, the shards remained embedded into the land, glowing as the evening approached.

The task of surveying where the different shards landed across the elven realm would take many years. However, every barrier that was raised did not fall that day, and any place that had served as a safe haven had mostly been spared the cataclysm that befell the elven lands. The realm had truly been changed forever.

One of the large shards of Valos had landed at the center of the Dragonstrike Woods. The trees at the center had been completely destroyed, but the shards that did land upon the trees where Aurotos and his companions slept were unable to harm the heroes under the protection of the first phoenix.

The minions of the dark master had been stopped, and Valenthreas remained unscathed by the wicked plans of the enemy. The dark prince had fallen, and soon the world would know of his defeat at the hands of Aurotos Va'Threas and the companions who stood by his side. Elves and humans had allied once more to stop a great evil, and they were forever loved by the people of the world that they protected. The unity of the Knights of the Phoenix and the Aurodites remained unbroken in spite of the dark master's failed attempt to once again unleash his wrath upon the city of light.

Aurotos and his allies now slumbered, left to safeguard their own precious questions. What of Lord Grindam and the shade that rose from Drazius when he perished? How would they honor their commitment to the peri? How could they free the countless souls trapped in the dark forest? What of their slumber and the journey Ai'ner explained they would now be on as they slept encased in the trees of the dark woods? Their answers would be revealed in due time.

Yet, those within the city of light had witnessed the battle from a distance. No doubt many saw the fire that fell from the sky and exploded on the ground only to hover above the army before its decimation. Behind the great city walls where all were safe, a great question blossomed: what happened to the heroes who'd fought for and protected them? Soon, they would have an answer.

EPILOGUE

I n the weeks following the battle, a ceremony had been held at the edge of the Dragonstrike Woods. There a shrine was erected in honor of Aurotos and the allies who fought beside him, defending the realm against the dark servants of Ohrimah. A commemoration had been made just before the tree line where the heroes remained in their slumber. Every leader across the world who guided the greater races attended the ceremony, honoring the heroes who had protected the elven realm and beyond.

It was several days after that ceremony when the renown elder knight, Valothas Ear'thol, returned to the Shrine of the Woodkin. Standing tall, he looked upon the tree where Aurotos stood embracing his love, Anaryen Valenvon. As he gazed upon the two who were entombed there with Ai'ner, he felt a swelling of joy for the child of his best friend. He had watched Aurotos grow into an honorable knight, and then, into a champion of the light. What made him the happiest though was the fact that he knew Aurotos had finally made a choice. He chose to lead, to love, and ultimately, he rose to honor his family and kingdom. What he knew for certain was the pride he felt for his comrade and he knew Aurotos's parents would have felt the same.

He took in a deep breath as his phoenix Ol'nar flew off of his shoulder and into the air. He moved past the shrine and then looked back upon it observing the carved stone. He could see Ai'ner with its wings around Aurotos and his companions atop a round pedestal with a plate commemorating their names and the date of their sacrifice. Valothas paid special attention to Armatay who was there etched onto the base of the pedestal as if he was lifting the entire group up. It served as a reminder that he needed to go soon and meet with Kayris at the tower of Avestan. The young nayran had wished to speak with him before he left for a council meeting within the spire of Valenthreas.

Valothas leapt onto his new mount, a volgriff which he had only recently acquired as a part of the newly formed Order of the Empyreal Blade. The organization which he now led had taken charge of protecting the shards of the fallen moon from any who might wish to weaponize them against those strongholds which stood against the dark master and his wicked creations. As he had decided to take on the role as leader of the paladin order, it had been his decision to choose Einthora along with her phoenix, Es'nith, to take charge of the Knights of the Phoenix moving forward.

Valothas darted off the ground and rose high into the air only as fast as his phoenix could keep up. The cold air sweeping past his face served as a bitter reminder that the time of the auvinots had come to an end. Valos, which should have been coming into alignment at that time, instead, was left embedded in the land below. As he flew skyward, he passed through the glowing blue halo which hovered high in the sky above, circling far beyond the borders of the city walls. He could see the tower of Avestan just ahead to the north and he moved with speed to meet Kayris there.

As he neared the tower of the sage, he wondered what it was that the young nayran druid had to share with him. Kayris had remained to serve in an advisory role to the council, taking over for Armatay with whom he had a long history of service. But Valothas wondered what Kayris found important enough to tell him outside of the councils' meetings, one of which they'd just been summoned to join in only an hour's time.

In moments, he had closed the great distance thanks to his volgriff. It was one of the reasons the newly formed paladin order would be using them as means to travel around the world. It was exhilarating to ride upon the auvinot beneath him, a joy soon swept away as he had arrived at the doorway of the tower. Time was precious and he was eager to hear what Kayris had to share, so he dismounted with urgency and made his way to the entrance. As soon as he could, he crashed his plated gauntlets upon the door to announce his arrival.

He didn't have to wait long before he heard a voice from behind the door. "Ay, Valothas, is that you? Eh, so it is," Kayris said, as he tugged the door open to reveal his big eyes staring upward.

"It is good to see you, my young friend," Valothas said as he walked slowly forward next to Kayris. While the door creaked to a close behind them, he looked back at Ol'nar making it clear through his thoughts that he wished for it to keep watch outside. The phoenix flew fast, rising high, and circled the tower as it awaited Valothas's return.

As the two walked forward, he made note of the neat and tidy bookshelves. There was no doubt in Valothas's mind that the young nayran took his role as caretaker very seriously. There wasn't any part of the chamber which hadn't been cleaned or tended to. Up ahead, the fireplace roared and candles were glowing all around them. There wasn't a table or chair which hadn't been cleaned, as if it was prepared for the arrival of royalty.

"Ay, please have a seat, elder knight," Kayris said as he waved his hand toward the chair, in front of the fireplace and opposite of himself.

"I see you have been keeping up with the place quite well," Valothas said, offering a smile to the little nayran as the two sat down in front of the warm hearth. The chamber smelled of wood and honey vines, and Valothas quickly felt right at home.

"Ay, I am happy to. En, I can only hope to honor my friend Armatay as he did me," Kayris said, smiling with his short fangs poking through his lips.

"So, what is it you wish to speak with me about? Why the secrecy?" Valothas questioned as curiosity beamed through his dutiful glare.

"Ay, forgive me that. Eh, did Aurotos tell you of Armatay's prophecy?" Kayris inquired, his eyes squinting.

"Of what? A prophecy?" Valothas questioned with a confused expression. "No, how have I not heard of this?"

"Ay, I cannot say. En, I…that was for Aurotos to learn more of, but now I think I should tell you too. En, I should share the part he must have learned before they melded with the trees."

Valothas hated being left out, not having all the facts. Yet, he knew it wasn't for him to question the secrets of the Auron family. "Go on then, tell me what you know."

"Ay, so Armatay knew the details of Aurotos's destiny. En, I was told about it too. Aurotos will bring an end to the dark master's plans, but not yet. Armatay knew that when Ai'ner returned, Aurotos would sleep, that he has work to do while he sleeps. Yes, so when he is done, he will awaken. En, that is when we can welcome the return of our Auron king. En, that will be when the darkness fades forever," Kayris said intently, gazing at Valothas.

"Does this prophecy say when he will awaken?" Valothas questioned, his mind focusing readily upon every word that Kayris would share.

"Ay, only Ai'ner can know when that will be. En, I..."

"What is it, Kayris? Tell me," Valothas said, his eyes giving way to the burden of the information he was settling in to accept.

"En, I fear Armatay's worries may have come true. Ohrimah must have killed Anieva and somehow set the core of her essence into the moon. En, I think it is the only way he could have influenced events such as this," Kayris said, shaking his head mournfully.

"How could Armatay know of something such as that? I know he was a wise man, but how would he know that?" Valothas asked, still trying to make sense of all he was hearing.

"Ay, Valothas, Armatay was one of the auros," Kayris said grinning in a way that even Valothas couldn't help but feel happy observing.

"An auros, here with us...this whole time?"

"Ay, how else do you think he was able to serve at Avestan for so long," Kayris said giggling uncontrollably.

"Then this is just the beginning. Merdah is still out there, and his servants will be looking for The Master's Core. Kayris, if they find it before we do..." Valothas said, the realization of all that could soon come to pass setting in.

"Ay, I worry too. En, I fear a dark age has begun."

The elder knight knew what could happen if the shards of Valos fell into the wrong hands. He was not the only one who had thought that the shards could be weaponized. For as the dark master had sought destruction by using its great power, it was clear to many that the shards filled with potent magical energy could be used to empower good or dark intentions alike. And so, the growing fear among the elves and many who sought to protect the people was that if the shards of Valos were acquired by forces with dark desires, it could wreak devastating effects across the world.

"We should carry this news to the council at once. We are already short on time. Would you like to join me? I'm heading that way now," Valothas asked, his whole focus shifting to his duty.

"Ay, yes, I would. En, I just need to find my hat," Kayris said as he rummaged through a bag next to the chair he was sitting in. As he shuffled the various pouches and supplies around, his ears perked up as he pulled a brown hat from his bag. "Ay, there it is," he said as he smashed the hat over his head, folding his big floppy ears to the sides of his face.

They made their way toward the exit of the tower while Valothas reflected on the fears he had heard rising among the citizens of the city. The people were fearful that the commanders of the dark prince were still out there, and while some trusted that they had died from their wounds, others believed they sought refuge with the Sentinels of Strife. The sentinels were known to serve the darkness and many were convinced they remained hidden in the frozen north where the dark orc was rumored to endure in his solitude, forever plotting against all the world in honor of his dark master. These were worries to address later, for in that moment, there were more pressing matters at hand.

As Valothas exited the tower of the sage he gazed upon the Dragonstrike Woods and a sense of dread coursed through his very being. Only time would reveal what would become of Aurotos and his companions, and only through time, too, could the Twin Flames' will be understood. He could feel something stirring in the shadows below, yet amidst the darkness, there was hope—a fragile thing, either rewarded or punished by fate.

ABOUT THE AUTHOR

P hoenix Rokni has been captivated by stories all his life. As a child, he often explored the woods with his brothers, wielding a cardboard shield in one hand and a wooden sword in the other. Later, he served in the U.S. Army and, following an honorable discharge, earned a master's degree in counseling psychology. After years of dedicating himself to helping others, he chose to close his private practice to pursue his true passion—storytelling. For over twenty years, he had been crafting a vast world filled with heroes, villains, magic, and wonder. Realizing the time had come to share these stories, he embarked on his journey as an author.

Milton Keynes UK
Ingram Content Group UK Ltd.
UKHW041111061224
452240UK00006B/480